SCARLETT

Volume Two

ALEXANDRA RIPLEY

SCARLETT

Volume Two

Complete and Unabridged

CHARNWOOD
Leicester

First published in Great Britain in 1991 by
Macmillan London Limited
London

First Charnwood Edition
published December 1992
by arrangement with
Macmillan London Limited
London

The right of Alexandra Ripley to be identified as
the author of this work has been asserted by her
in accordance with the
Copyright, Designs and Patents Act, 1988

British Library CIP Data

Ripley, Alexandra
    Scarlett: Sequel to Margaret Mitchell's
    'Gone with the Wind'.–Part 2.–Large print ed.–
    Charnwood library series
    I. Title II. Series
    813.54 [F]

    ISBN 0–7089–8682–X

Published by
F. A. Thorpe (Publishing) Ltd.
Anstey, Leicestershire

Set by Words & Graphics Ltd.
Anstey, Leicestershire
Printed and bound in Great Britain by
T. J. Press (Padstow) Ltd., Padstow, Cornwall

SCARLETT

Volume Two

THE TOWER

47

The *Brian Boru* moved ponderously between the banks of the Savannah River, pulled by steam-driven tugboats. When at last it reached the Atlantic, its deep whistle saluted the departing tugs and its great sails were loosed. The passengers cheered as the ship's prow dipped into the gray-green waves at the river's mouth and the tremendous paddle wheels began to churn.

Scarlett and Kathleen stood side by side watching the flat shoreline recede quickly into a soft blur of green, then disappear.

What have I done? Scarlett thought, and she grabbed the deck rail in momentary panic. Then she looked ahead at the limitless expanse of sun-flecked ocean, and her heart beat faster with the thrill of adventure.

"Oh!" Kathleen cried out. Then, "Oooh," she moaned.

"What's wrong, Kathleen?"

"Oooh. I'd forgot the seasickness," the girl gasped.

Scarlett held back her laughter. She put her arm around Kathleen's waist and led her to their cabin. That evening, Kathleen's chair at the captain's table was empty. Scarlett and Colum did full justice to the gargantuan meal that was served. Afterwards, Scarlett took a bowl of broth to her unfortunate cousin and spoon-fed her.

"I'll be all right in a day or two," Kathleen promised in a weak voice. "You won't need to be tending me forever."

"Hush up and take another sip," said Scarlett. Thank heavens I haven't got a puny stomach, she thought. Even the food poisoning from Saint Patrick's Day is over now, or I couldn't have enjoyed my dinner so much.

She woke abruptly when the first red streaks of dawn were on the horizon and ran with frantic clumsiness into the small convenience room that adjoined the cabin. There she fell to her knees and vomited into the flower-decorated china receptacle of the mahogany chaise privée.

She couldn't be seasick, not her. Not when she loved sailing so much. Why, in Charleston, when the tiny sailboat was climbing the waves in the storm, she hadn't even felt queasy, nor when it slid down into the trough of the wave. The *Brian Boru* was steady as a rock compared to that. She couldn't imagine what was wrong with her . . .

. . . Slowly, slowly Scarlett's bent head rose from its drooping weakness. Her mouth and eyes opened wide with discovery. Excitement raced through her, hot and strengthening, and she laughed deep in her throat.

I'm pregnant. I'm pregnant! I remember; this is how it feels.

Scarlett leaned back against the wall and threw her arms wide in a luxurious stretch. Oh, I feel wonderful. I don't care how awful my stomach feels, I feel wonderful. I've got Rhett now. He is mine. I can't wait to tell him.

Sudden tears of happiness poured down her cheeks, and her hands flew down to cover her middle in a protective cradling of the new life growing within. Oh, how she wanted this baby. Rhett's baby. Their baby. It would be strong, she knew it, she could feel its tiny strength already. A bold, fearless little thing, like Bonnie.

Scarlett's mind flooded with memories. Bonnie's little head had fit into her palm, hardly bigger than a kitten's. She'd fit into Rhett's big hands like a doll. How he had loved her. His wide back bent over the cradle, his deep voice making silly baby-talk sounds—never in all the world was there a man so besotted with a baby. He was going to be so happy when she told him. She could see his dark eyes flashing with the joy of it, his white smile gleaming in his pirate's face.

Scarlett smiled, too, thinking of it. I'm happy, too, she thought. This is the way it's supposed to be when you have a baby, Melly always said so.

"Oh, my God," she whispered aloud. Melly died trying to have one, and my insides are all messed up, Dr. Meade said, after I had the miscarriage. That's why I didn't know I was pregnant, I didn't even notice I missed my time of month, because it's been so undependable for so long. Suppose having this baby kills me? Oh, God, please, please, God, don't let me die just when I finally get what I need to be happy. She crossed herself again and again in confused entreaty, propitiation, superstition.

Then she shook her head angrily. What was she doing? Just being silly. She was strong and healthy. Not like Melly at all. Why, Mammy always said it was downright shameful the way she dropped a baby with hardly more fuss than an alley cat. She was going to do just fine, and her baby would be fine, too. And her life would be fine, with Rhett loving her, loving their baby. They'd be the happiest, lovingest family in the whole world. Gracious, she hadn't even thought of Miss Eleanor. Talk about baby-loving! Miss Eleanor was going to pop her buttons with pride. I can see her now, at the Market, telling everybody, even the bent-up old man who sweeps out the trash. This baby's going to be the talk of Charleston before it even draws its first breath.

. . . Charleston . . . That's where I should be going. Not to Ireland. I want to see Rhett, to tell him.

Maybe the *Brian Boru* could put in there. The captain's a friend of Colum's; Colum could persuade him to do it. Scarlett's eyes sparkled. She got to her feet and washed her face, then rinsed the sour taste out of her mouth. It was too early to talk to Colum, so she went back to bed and sat up against the pillows making plans.

When Kathleen got up, Scarlett was sleeping, a contented smile on her lips. There was no need to hurry, she had decided. No need to talk to the captain. She could meet her grandmother and her Irish kin. She could have her adventure of crossing the ocean. Rhett had kept her waiting for him in Savannah. Well, he could wait awhile to learn about the baby. There were months and months to go before it was born. She was entitled to have some fun before she went back to

Charleston. Sure as fate, she wouldn't be allowed to do so much as stick her nose out of the door there. Ladies in a delicate condition weren't supposed to stir a stump.

No, she'd have Ireland first. She'd never have another chance.

She'd enjoy the *Brian Boru* too. Her morning sickness had never lasted much more than a week with the other babies. It must be almost over now. Like Kathleen, in a day or two she'd be just fine.

Crossing the Atlantic on the *Brian Boru* was like a continuous Saturday night at the O'Haras' in Savannah—only more so. At first Scarlett loved it.

The ship soon had a full complement of passengers who boarded at Boston and New York, but they didn't seem like Yankees at all, Scarlett thought. They were Irish and proud of it. They had the vitality that was so appealing in the O'Haras, and they took advantage of everything the ship had to offer. All day there was something to do: checkers tournaments, heated competitions at quoits on deck, excited participation in games of chance, such as wagering on the number of miles the ship would cover the following day. In the evening they sang along with the professional musicians and danced energetically to all the Irish reels and Viennese waltzes.

Even when the dancing was done, the amusement continued. There was always a game of whist in the Ladies' Card Saloon, and Scarlett was always in demand as a partner. Except for

Charleston's rationed coffee, the stakes were higher than any she'd known, and every turn of a card was exciting. So were her winnings. The *Brian Boru*'s passengers were living proof that America was the Land of Opportunity, and they didn't mind spending their lately gained wealth.

Colum, too, benefitted from their opened pockets. While the women played cards, the men generally retired to the ship's bar for whiskey and cigars. There, Colum brought tears of pity and pride to eyes that were normally shrewd and dry. He talked about Ireland's oppression under English rule, called the roll of martyrs to the cause of Irish freedom, and accepted lavish donations for the Fenian Brotherhood.

A crossing on the *Brian Boru* was always a profitable enterprise, and Colum made the trip at least twice a year, even though the excessive luxury of the staterooms and the gargantuan meals secretly sickened him when he thought of the poverty and need of the Irish in Ireland.

By the end of the first week, Scarlett, too, was looking at their fellow passengers with a disapproving eye. Both men and women changed clothes four times a day, the better to show off the extent of their costly wardrobes. Scarlett had never seen so many jewels in her life. She told herself she was glad that she'd left hers in the vault of the Savannah bank; they'd pale next to the array in the dining saloon every night. But in truth she wasn't glad at all. She had grown accustomed to having more of everything than anyone she knew—a bigger house, more servants, more luxury, more things, more money. It put her nose decidedly out of joint to see display more conspicuous than hers had ever been. In Savannah, Kathleen, Mary Kate, and Helen had been ingenuously blatant in their envy, and all the O'Haras had fed her need for admiration. These people on the ship didn't envy her, or even admire her all that much. Scarlett wasn't at all pleased with them. She couldn't bear a whole country full of Irish if this was what they were like. If she heard "Wearing o' the Green" one more time she'd scream.

"You're just not taken with the American New-Rich, Scarlett darling," Colum soothed. "You're a grand lady, that's why." It was exactly the right thing for him to say.

A grand lady was what she had to be after this vacation was over. She'd have this final fling of freedom and then she'd go to Charleston, put on her drab clothes and company manners, and be a lady for the rest of her life.

At least now when Miss Eleanor and everybody else in Charleston talked about their trips to Europe before the War, she'd not feel so left out. She wouldn't say she'd disliked it, either. Ladies didn't say things like that. Unconsciously, Scarlett sighed.

"Ach, Scarlett darling, it can't be as bad as all that," Colum said. "Look at the bright side. You're cleaning out their deep pockets at the card table."

She laughed. It was true. She was winning a fortune—some evenings as much as thirty dollars. Wait till she told Rhett! How he'd laugh. He'd been a gambler on Mississippi riverboats for a while, after all. Come to think of it, it was a good thing, really, that there was still a week at sea. She wouldn't have to touch a penny of Rhett's money.

Scarlett's attitude toward money was a complex mixture of miserliness and generosity. It had been her measure of safety for so many years that she guarded every penny of her hard-earned fortune with angry suspicion of anyone who made any real or imagined demands for a dollar of it. And yet she accepted the responsibility to support her aunts and Melanie's family without question. She had taken care of them even when she didn't know where she'd find the means to take care of herself. If some unforeseen calamity befell, she would continue to take care of them, even if it meant that she had to go hungry. She didn't think about it; it was simply the way things were.

Her feelings about Rhett's money were equally inconsistent. As his wife she spent profligately on the Peachtree Street house, with its prodigious expenses, and on her wardrobe and luxuries. But the half million he had given her was different. Inviolable. She intended to give it back to him intact when they were once again truly man and wife. He had offered it as payment for separation, and she could not accept it because she would not accept separation.

It bothered her that she'd had to take some of it out of the bank vaults to bring on the trip. Everything had happened so fast, there'd been no time to get any of her own money from Atlanta. But she'd put an IOU in the box with the remaining gold in Savannah, and she was determined to spend as little as possible of the gold coins that were now keeping her back straight and her waist small, filling the channels in her corset where steel strips had once been. It was much better to win at whist and have her own money to spend. Why, in another week, with any luck, she'd add at least another $150 to her purse.

But still, she'd be glad when the voyage was over. Even with all the sails bellied taut with wind, the *Brian Boru* was too big for her to feel the thrill she remembered from racing ahead of the storm in Charleston Harbor. And she hadn't seen even one dolphin, despite Colum's poetic promises.

"There they are, Scarlett darling!" Colum's usually calm, melodious voice rose in excitement; he took Scarlett's arm and drew her to the ship's rail. "Our escorts are here. We'll be seeing land soon."

Overhead the first gulls circled the *Brian Boru*. Scarlett hugged Colum impulsively. Then again when he pointed to the sleek silvery forms on the nearby sea. There were dolphins after all.

Much later, she stood between Colum and Kathleen trying to hold her hat on her head against the attack of the strong wind. They were entering harbor under steam. Scarlett stared in astonishment at the island of rock to starboard. It seemed impossible that anything, even the towering wall of craggy stone, could withstand the crashing waves that beat against it and threw white foam high against its face. She was accustomed to the low rolling hills of Clayton County.

This soaring stark cliff was the most exotic sight she'd ever seen.

"Nobody tries to live there, do they?" she asked Colum.

"No bit of earth is wasted in Ireland," he replied. "But it takes a hardy breed to call Inishmore home."

"Inishmore." Scarlett repeated the beautiful strange name. It sounded like music. And like no name she'd ever heard before.

Then she was silent; so were Colum and Kathleen; each of them looked at the broad blue sparkling waters of Galway Bay with private thoughts.

Colum saw Ireland ahead and his heart swelled with love for her and pain for her sufferings. As he did many times every day, he renewed his vow to destroy the oppressors of his country and to restore her to her own people. He felt no anxiety about the weapons concealed in Scarlett's trunks. Customs officials in Galway concentrated mainly on ships' cargoes, making sure that duty owed to the British government was paid. They'd look at the *Brian Boru* with sneers. They always did. Successful Irish-Americans gratified their sense of superiority over both—the Irish and the Americans. Even so, it was very good fortune, Colum thought, that he'd managed to convince Scarlett to come. Her petticoats were much better for hiding guns than the dozens of American boots and calicoes he'd bought. And she might even loosen her purse strings a bit when she saw the poverty of her own people. He didn't have high hopes; Colum was a realist, and he'd gotten Scarlett's measure from the first. He did not like her less because she was so unthinkingly self-centered. He was a priest, and human frailty was forgivable—so long as the humans were not English. In fact, even when he was manipulating Scarlett, he was fond of her, just as he was fond of all the O'Hara children.

Kathleen held tight to the ship's rail. I'd jump over and swim did I not anchor myself, she thought, I'm that happy to be nearing Ireland, I know I'd be faster than the ship. Home. Home. Home . . .

Scarlett drew in her breath with a tiny squeaking noise. There was a castle on that little low island. A castle! It couldn't be anything else, it had tooth-like things on top. What matter that it was half-fallen-down. It was really, truly a castle, just like pictures in a child's book. She could hardly wait to discover what this Ireland was like.

When Colum escorted her down the gangplank she realized that she had entered a completely different world. The docks were busy, like the docks in Savannah, noisy, crowded, perilous with hurrying wagons and laden men loading or unloading barrels and crates and bales. But the men were all white, and they shouted to one another in a tongue that had no meaning for her.

"It's the Gaelic, the old Irish language," Colum explained, "but you needn't fret, Scarlett darling. The Gaelic's hardly known anyplace in Ireland any more save here in the west. Everyone speaks English; you'll have no trouble."

As if to prove him wrong, a man spoke to him

with an accent so pronounced that Scarlett didn't realize at first that he was speaking English.

Colum laughed when she told him. "It's a queer sound, and that's the truth of it," he agreed, "but it's English for sure. English the way the English speak it, all up in their noses like they're strangling from it. That was a sergeant of Her Majesty's Army."

Scarlett giggled. "I thought he was a button salesman." The sergeant's elaborately decorated short, tight uniform jacket was fronted with more than a dozen bars of thick gold braid between pairs of brightly polished brass buttons. It looked like fancy dress to her.

She tucked her hand in Colum's elbow. "I'm awfully glad I came," she said. And she was. Everything was so different, so new. No wonder people liked to travel so much.

"Our baggages will be brought to the hotel," Colum said when he returned to the bench where he'd left Scarlett and Kathleen. "It's all arranged. Then tomorrow we'll be on our way to Mullingar and home."

"I wish we could go right now," Scarlett said hopefully. "It's early yet, barely noon.

"But the train left at eight, Scarlett darling. The hotel's a fine one, with a good kitchen, too."

"I remember," Kathleen said. "This time I'll do all those fancy sweets justice." She was radiant with happiness, hardly recognizable as the girl Scarlett had known in Savannah. "Coming the other way I was too sorrowful to put food in my mouth. Oh, Scarlett, you can't know what it is to me to have the Irish ground under my feet. I feel like getting on my knees to kiss it."

"Come along, the two of you," Colum said. "We'll have competition getting a hackney, today being Saturday and Market Day."

"'Market Day?'" Scarlett echoed.

Kathleen clapped her hands. "Market Day in a big city like Galway! Oh, Colum, it should be something grand."

It was beyond imagination, "grand" and exciting and foreign to Scarlett. The entire grass-covered square in front of the Railway Hotel was teeming with life, alive with color. When the hackney set them down on the hotel steps, she begged Colum to join in at once, never mind seeing their rooms or eating dinner. Kathleen echoed her. "There's food aplenty at the stalls, Colum, and I want to take some stockings home to gift the girls. There's none like them in America, or I would have them bought already. Brigid's fair pining away for want of some, I know it."

Colum grinned. "And Kathleen O'Hara's pining a bit herself, I wouldn't be amazed. All right, then. I'll see to the rooms. You see to Cousin Scarlett so she doesn't get lost. Have you any money?"

"A fistful, Colum. Jamie gave it me."

"That's American money, Kathleen. You can't spend it here."

Scarlett grabbed Colum's arm in panic. What did he mean? Wasn't her money any good over here?

"It's not the same kind, is all, Scarlett darling. You'll find English money much more diverting.

651

I'll do the exchanging for all of us. What would you like?"

"I have all my winnings from whist. In greenbacks." She said the word with contempt and anger. Everybody knew that greenbacks weren't worth the numbers written on them. She should have made the losers pay her in silver or gold. She opened her purse and took out the folded wad of five and ten and one dollar bills. "Change these if you can," she said, handing the money to Colum. His eyebrows rose.

"So much? I'm glad you never asked me to play cards with you, Scarlett darling. You must have almost two hundred dollars here.

"Two forty-seven."

"Look at this, Kathleen mavourneen. You'll never see such a fortune in one place again. Would you like to hold it?"

"Oh, no, I wouldn't dare." She backed away, her hands behind her back, her wide eyes fixed on Scarlett.

You'd think I was green instead of the money, Scarlett thought uncomfortably. Two hundred wasn't all that much. She'd paid practically that for her furs. Surely Jamie must clear at least two hundred a month in the store. There was no need for Kathleen to carry on so.

"Here." Colum was holding out his hand. "Here's a few shillings for each of you. You can shop a bit while I do the banking, then meet me at that pie stall for a bite." He pointed toward a fluttering yellow flag in the center of the busy square.

Scarlett's eyes followed the direction of his finger and her heart sank. The street between the hotel steps and the square was filling with slowly moving cattle. She couldn't get across it!

"I'll manage for the both of us," Kathleen said. "Here's my dollars, Colum. Come on, Scarlett, take my hand."

The shy girl Scarlett had known in Savannah was gone. Kathleen was home. Her cheeks were glowing, and her eyes. And her smile was as bright as the sun overhead.

Scarlett tried to make an excuse, to protest, but Kathleen was having none of it. She pushed through the herd of cows pulling Scarlett behind her. In seconds they were on the grass of the square. Scarlett had no time to scream with fear in the midst of the cows or to scream out her anger at Kathleen. And once in the square, she was too fascinated to remember either fear or anger. She'd loved the markets in Charleston and Savannah for their busyness and color and array of produce. But they were nothing in comparison with Market Day in Galway.

There was something going on everywhere she looked. Men and women were bargaining, buying, selling, arguing, laughing, praising, criticizing, conferring—over sheep, chickens, roosters, eggs, cows, pigs, butter, cream, goats, donkeys. "How darling," Scarlett said when she saw the baskets of squealing pink piglets . . . the tiny furry donkeys with their long, pink-lined ears . . . and— over and over again—the colorful clothes worn by the dozens of young women and girls. When she saw the first one, she thought the girl must be in costume; then she saw another, and another, and yet another, until she realized they were almost all dressed the same. No wonder Kathleen had been talking about stockings! Everywhere Scarlett looked she saw ankles and legs in bright stripes of blue and yellow, red and white, yellow and red, white and blue. The Galway girls wore low-cut, low-heeled black leather shoes, not boots, and their skirts were four to six inches above their ankles. What skirts, too! Full, swinging, bright as the stockings in solid reds or blues or greens or yellows. Their shirtwaists were darker shades, but still colorful, with long buttoned sleeves and crisp white linen fichus folded and pinned over the front.

"I want some stockings, too, Kathleen! And one of the skirts. And a shirtwaist and kerchief. I've got to have them. They're lovely!"

Kathleen smiled with pleasure. "You like Irish clothes, then, Scarlett? I'm so glad. Your things are so elegant I thought you'd laugh at ours."

"I wish I could dress like that every day. Is that what you wear when you're home? You lucky girl, no wonder you wanted to come back."

"These are best dressing, for Market Day and to catch the eyes of the lads. I'll show you everyday things, too. Come." Kathleen caught Scarlett by the wrist again and led her through the masses of people just as she'd led her through the cows. Near the square's center there were tables—boards across trestles—piled with finery for women. Scarlett goggled. She wanted to buy everything she saw. Look at all the stockings . . . and wonderful shawls, so soft to the touch . . . goodness gracious, what lace! Why, my dressmaker in Atlanta would practically sell her soul to get her hands on rich heavy lace like that. There they were, the skirts! Oh, the darlings, how wonderful she'd look in that shade of red—and the blue, too. But wait—there was another blue on that next table, a darker one. Which was best? Oh, and lighter reds over there—

She felt giddy from the lavishness of choice. She had to touch them all—the wool was so soft, thick, alive with warmth and color under her gloved hand. Quickly, carelessly, she stripped off a glove so she could feel the woven wools. It was like no fabric she'd ever touched.

"I've been waiting by the pies, with water filling my mouth from hunger," said Colum. He put his hand on her arm. "Don't fret, now, you can come back, Scarlett darling." He lifted his hat and nodded to the black-clad women behind the tables. "May the sun shine forever on your fine work," he said. "I ask your pardon for my American cousin here. She lost her tongue in admiration. I'm going to feed her now and, please Saint Brigid, she'll be able to talk to you when she returns." The women grinned at Colum, stole another sideways glance at Scarlett, said "Thank you, Father," as Colum hauled her away.

"Kathleen told me you'd gone completely daft," he said with a chuckle. "She plucked at your sleeve a dozen times, poor girl, but devil a look you'd give her."

"I forgot all about her," Scarlett admitted. "I've never seen so many wonderful things all at once. I figured I'd buy a costume for a party. But I don't know if I can wait to wear it. Tell me the truth, Colum, do you think it would be all right if I dressed like the Irish girls while I'm here?"

"I don't believe you should do other, Scarlett darling."

"What fun! What a lovely vacation, Colum. I'm so glad I came."

"So are we all, Cousin Scarlett."

She didn't understand the English money at all. The pound was paper and weighed less than an ounce. The penny was huge, big as a silver dollar, and the thing called a tuppence, which meant two pennies, was smaller than the one penny. Then there were coins called half pennies and others called shillings . . . It was all too confusing. Besides, it didn't really matter, it was all free, from whist winnings. The only thing that counted was that the skirts cost two of the shilling things, the shoes were one. The stockings were only pennies. Scarlett gave the drawstring bag of coins to Kathleen. "Make me stop before I run out," she said, and she began to shop.

All three of them were loaded down when they went to the hotel. Scarlett had bought skirts in every color and every weight—the thinner ones were also worn for petticoats, Kathleen told her—and dozens of stockings—for herself, for Kathleen, for Brigid, for all the other cousins she was going to meet. She had shirts, too, and yards and yards of lace, wide and narrow and made into collars and fichus and cunning little caps. There was a long blue cape with a hood, plus a red one because she couldn't make up her mind, plus a black one because Kathleen said most people wore black for every day, and a black skirt for the same reason, which could have colored petticoats underneath. Linen fichus and linen shirtwaists and linen petticoats—all like no linen she'd ever seen—and six dozen linen handkerchiefs. Stacks of shawls; she'd lost count.

"I'm worn out," Scarlett groaned happily when she dropped down onto the plush settee in the living room of their suite. Kathleen dropped the money bag into her lap. It was still more than half full. "My grief," said Scarlett, "I'm really going to love Ireland!"

48

Scarlett was entranced with her bright "costumes." She tried to wheedle Kathleen into "dressing up" with her and returning to the square, but the girl was politely adamant in her refusal. "We'll be eating dinner late, Scarlett, according to the English custom of the hotel, and we've an early start to make tomorrow. There are lots of market days; we have one every week in the town near our village."

"But not like Galway's, judging from what you said," Scarlett noted suspiciously. Kathleen admitted that the town of Trim was much, much smaller. Nonetheless, she didn't want to go back to the square. Scarlett grudgingly stopped nagging.

The dining room of the Railway Hotel was known for its fine food and service. Two liveried waiters seated Kathleen and Scarlett at a large table beside a tall, much-curtained window, then stood behind their chairs to serve them. Colum had to make do with the tail-coated waiter in charge of the table. The O'Haras ordered a dinner of six courses, and Scarlett was thoroughly enjoying a delicately sauced cutlet of Galway's famous salmon when she heard music from the square. She pulled back the heavily fringed draperies, the silk curtain beneath them, and the thick lace panel beneath that. "I knew it!" she announced. "I knew we should have gone back. They're dancing in the square. Let's go right this minute."

"Scarlett, darling, we've only begun to have dinner," Colum argued.

"Fiddle-dee-dee! We all ate ourselves practically sick on the ship; the last thing we need is another endless dinner. I want to put on my costume and dance."

Nothing would dissuade her.

"I'm not understanding you at all, Colum," Kathleen said. The two of them were on one of the square's benches near the dancing, in case Scarlett got into any trouble. Wearing a blue skirt over red and yellow petticoats, she was dancing the reel as if she'd been born to it.

"What is it you don't understand, then?"

"Why are we staying at this fine English hotel, like kings and queens, at all? And if we're doing it, why could we not eat our fancy dinner? It's the last we'll have, I know that. Couldn't you say to Scarlett, 'No, we'll not go,' as I did?"

Colum took her hand in his. "The way of it

is this, my little sister, Scarlett is not yet ready for the truth of Ireland, or the O'Haras in it. I hope to make it easier for her. Better she should see wearing Irish garb as a merry adventure than weeping when she learns that her fancy silk trains will get covered with muck. She's meeting Irish people out there in the reel and finding them pleasing, for all their rough garments and dirty hands. It's a grand event, though I'd rather be sleeping."

"But we go home tomorrow, do we not?" Kathleen's longing throbbed in the question.

Colum squeezed her hand. "We go home tomorrow, that I promise you. We'll be in a first class carriage on the train, though, and you mustn't remark it. Also, I'm putting Scarlett to stay with Molly and Robert, and you're not to say a word."

Kathleen spit on the ground. "That for Molly and her Robert. But so long as it's Scarlett with them and not me, I'm willing to keep my tongue."

Colum frowned, but not at his sister. Scarlett's current dancing partner was trying to embrace her. Colum had no way of knowing that Scarlett had been an expert since she was fifteen at inciting men's attentions and escaping them. He stood up quickly and moved toward the dancing. Before he got there, Scarlett had slipped away from her admirer. She ran to Colum. "Have you come to dance with me at last?"

He took her outstretched hands. "I've come to take you away. It's past time to be sleeping."

Scarlett sighed. Her flushed face looked bright

red under the pink paper lantern hanging over her head. Throughout the square brightly colored lights swung from the branches of tall, wide-crowned trees. With the fiddles playing and the thick crowd laughing and calling as they danced, she hadn't heard exactly what Colum said, but his meaning was clear.

She knew he was right, too, but she hated to stop dancing. She had never known such intoxicating freedom before, not even on Saint Patrick's Day. Her Irish costume was not made to wear with stays, and Kathleen had laced her only enough to keep her corset from falling down to her knees. She could dance forever and never get short of breath. It felt like she wasn't held in at all, not in any way.

Colum looked tired, in spite of the pink glow of the lamp. Scarlett smiled and nodded. There would be plenty more dancing. She'd be in Ireland for two weeks, until after her grandmother celebrated her hundredth birthday. The original Katie Scarlett. I wouldn't miss that party for all the world!

This makes much more sense than our trains at home, Scarlett thought when she saw all the open doors to the individual compartments. How nice to have your own little room instead of sitting in a car with a bunch of strangers. No walking forever in the aisle, either, getting on and off, or people half-falling in your lap when they walked past your seat. She smiled happily at Colum and Kathleen. "I love your Irish trains. I love everything about Ireland." She settled comfortably in the deep seat, eager to pull out of the station so she could look at the countryside. It was bound to be different from America.

Ireland didn't disappoint her. "My stars, Colum," she said after they'd been travelling for an hour, "this country's positively peppered with castles! There's one on practically every hill, and more in the flat country, too. Why are they all falling down? Why don't people live in them?"

"They're very old, for the most part, Scarlett darling, four hundred years or more. People found more comfortable ways to live."

She nodded. That made sense. There must have been a lot of running up and down stairs in the towers. Still, they were awfully romantic. She pressed her nose to the window again. "Oh," she said, "what a shame. My castle watching's over. It's starting to rain."

"It will stop," Colum promised.

As it did, before they reached the next station.

"Ballinasloe," Scarlett read the name aloud. "What beautiful names your towns have. What's the name of the place the O'Haras live?"

"Adamstown," Colum replied. He laughed at the expression on Scarlett's face. "No, it's not very Irish. I'd change it for you if I could, I'd change it for all of us if I could. But the owner's English, and he'd not like it."

"Somebody owns the whole town?"

"It's not a town, that's just the English bragging. It's hardly even a village. It was named for the son of the Englishman who first built it, a small gift for Adam, the estate was. It's been inherited since then by his son and grandson and

661

so on. The one that has it now never sees it. He lives mostly in London. It's his agent who manages things."

There was a bite of bitterness in Colum's words. Scarlett decided she'd better not ask questions. She contented herself with looking for castles.

Just as the train began to slow for the next station she saw an enormous one that hadn't crumbled at all. Surely somebody lived there! A knight? A prince? Far from it, said Colum; it was a military barracks for a regiment of the British Army.

Oh, I've put my foot in it this time for sure, thought Scarlett. Kathleen's cheeks were flaming. "I'll get us some tea," Colum said when the train stopped. He pulled the window down from the top and leaned out. Kathleen stared at the floor. Scarlett stood next to Colum. It felt good to straighten her knees. "Sit down, Scarlett," he said firmly. She sat. But she could still see the groups of smartly uniformed men on the platform, and the shake of Colum's head when he was asked if any seats were vacant in the compartment. What a cool customer he was. No one could see past him because his shoulders filled the window, and there were three large empty seats going begging. She'd have to remember that next time she rode an Irish train, just in case Colum wasn't with her.

He handed in mugs of tea and a lumpy folded cloth just as the train began to move. "Try an Irish specialty," he said, smiling now, "it's called barm brack." The rough linen cloth held great slabs of delicious, fruit-filled light bread. Scarlett ate Kathleen's, too, and asked Colum if he could get some more for her when they stopped at the next station.

"Can you stay hungry another half hour or so? We'll be getting off the train then and we can have a proper meal." Scarlett was delighted to agree. The novelty of the train and the castle-peppered views had begun to wear off. She was ready to get wherever it was they were going.

But the station sign said "Mullingar," not "Adamstown." Poor lamb, Colum said, hadn't he told her? They could only go part way on the train. After they ate their dinner, they'd make the rest of the journey by road. It was only twenty miles or so; they'd be home before dark.

Twenty miles! Why, that was as far as from Atlanta to Jonesboro. It would take ages, and they'd already been on the train for practically six hours. It took all her will to smile pleasantly when Colum introduced his friend Jim Daly. Daly wasn't even good-looking. His wagon was, however. It had tall wheels painted bright red and glossy blue sides with J. DALY on them in bold gilt. Whatever business he's in, thought Scarlett, he's doing well at it.

Jim Daly's business was a bar and brewery. Even though she was landlord to a saloon, Scarlett had never been in it; it made her feel pleasantly wicked to be entering the malty-smelling large room. She looked curiously at the long, polished oak bar, but she had no time to take in the details before Daly opened another door and ushered her through it into a hallway. The O'Haras were having dinner with him and his family in their private quarters above the public house.

It was a good dinner, but she might just as well have been in Savannah. There was nothing strange or foreign about leg of lamb with mint sauce and mashed potatoes. And all the talk was about the Savannah O'Haras, their health and their doings. Jim Daly's mother, it turned out, was another O'Hara cousin. Scarlett couldn't tell that she was in Ireland at all, much less right upstairs over a saloon. No one of the Dalys seemed very interested in her opinion about anything, either. They were all too busy talking among themselves.

Things improved after dinner. Jim Daly insisted on taking her on his arm for a walk to see the sights of Mullingar. Colum and Kathleen followed them. Not that there's all that much to see, Scarlett thought. It's a pokey little town, just one street and five times as many bars as shops, but it does feel good to stretch my legs. The town square wasn't half the size of Galway's, and nothing was happening in it at all. A young woman with a black shawl over her head and breast came up to them with one cupped hand held forward. "God bless you, sir and lady," she whined. Jim dropped a few coins into her hand, and she repeated the blessing while she curtseyed. Scarlett was appalled. Why, that girl was begging, bold as brass! She certainly wouldn't have given her anything; there wasn't any reason the girl couldn't go out and work for a living, she looked healthy enough.

There was an outburst of laughter, and Scarlett

664

turned to see what caused it. A group of soldiers had entered the square from a side street. One of them was teasing the begging woman by holding a coin out to her, higher than she could reach. Brute! But what can she expect, if she's going to make a spectacle of herself, begging on a public street. And from soldiers, too. Anybody would know that they'd be coarse and rude . . . Although, she had to admit, you could hardly credit that bunch as soldiers. They looked more like big toys for a little boy in those silly fancy uniforms. Obviously they did no more soldiering than marching in parades on holidays. Thank heavens there weren't any real soldiers in Ireland, like the Yankees. No snakes and no Yankees.

The soldier threw the coin into a filthy, scum-coated puddle and laughed again with his friends. Scarlett saw Kathleen's two hands grab Colum's arm. He pulled away and walked over to the soldiers and the beggar. Oh, Lord, what if he started lecturing them about being good Christians? Colum pushed up his sleeve, and she caught her breath. He looks so much like Pa! Is he going to wade in fighting?

Colum knelt on the cobbled square and fished the coin out of the noisome puddle. Scarlett let her breath out in a slow, relieved hiss. She wouldn't for a minute worry about Colum holding his own against one of those sissy-britches soldiers, but five might just be too much even for an O'Hara. What did he have to make such a fuss over a beggarwoman's problems for, anyhow?

Colum stood, his back turned to the soldiers. They were visibly uncomfortable at the turn their joke had taken. When Colum took the woman's arm and led her away, they turned in the opposite direction and walked quickly to the next corner.

Well, that's that and no harm done, thought Scarlett. Except to the knees of Colum's breeches. I suppose they get plenty of wear and tear anyhow, him being a priest and all. Funny, I forget that most of the time. If Kathleen hadn't dragged me out of bed at dawn I wouldn't have remembered we had to go to Mass before we took the train.

The balance of the town tour was very brief. There were no boats to be seen on the Royal Canal, and Scarlett wasn't interested in the slightest by Jim Daly's enthusiasm for travelling to Dublin that way instead of by train. Why should she care about getting to Dublin? She wanted to be on the way to Adamstown.

Before long she got her wish. There was a small, shabby carriage outside Jim Daly's bar when they got back. An aproned man in shirtsleeves was loading their trunks on the top of it; the valises were already strapped on the back. If Scarlett's trunk weighed much less now than it had at the depot when Jim Daly and Colum put it in Daly's wagon, no one mentioned it. When the trunks were secure, the shirtsleeved man disappeared into the bar. He returned wearing a coachman's caped coat and top hat. "Name's Jim, too," he said briefly. "Let's be going." Scarlett stepped up and took a seat on the far side. Kathleen sat beside her, Colum opposite. "May God travel your road with you," called the Dalys. Scarlett and Kathleen waved their handkerchiefs out the window. Colum unbuttoned his coat and took off his hat.

"I cannot speak for anyone else here, but I'm going to try to sleep a bit," he said. "I hope you ladies will excuse my feet." He removed his boots and stretched out, his stockinged feet on the seat between Scarlett and Kathleen.

They looked at each other, then bent to unlace their boots. Within minutes they, too, were settled with their hatless heads resting against the corners of the carriage and their feet flanking Colum. Oh, if only I had on my Galway costume, I'd be as snug as a bug, Scarlett thought. One gold-filled corset stay was stabbing her in the ribs no matter how she arranged herself. Nevertheless she drifted quickly and easily into sleep.

She woke once when rain began to spatter on the window, but soon the soft sound of it lulled her back to sleep. The next time she woke the sun was shining. "Are we there?" she asked sleepily.

"No, we've a way to go yet," Colum replied. Scarlett looked out and clapped her hands at what she saw. "Oh, look at all the flowers! I could reach out and pick one. Colum, open the window, do. I'll get a bouquet."

"We'll open it when we stop. The wheels stir up too much dust."

"But I want some of those flowers."

" 'Tis only a hedgerow, Scarlett darling. You'll have the same all the way home."

"This side, too, you see," Kathleen said. It was true, Scarlett saw. The unknown vine and its bright pink flowers were barely an arm's length away from Kathleen, too. What a wonderful way to travel with walls of flowers on both sides of you. When Colum's eyes closed, she slowly let the window down.

49

"We'll be reaching Ratharney soon," Colum said, "then a few more miles and we're in County Meath."

Kathleen sighed happily. Scarlett's eyes sparkled. County Meath. Pa talked like it was paradise, and I guess I can see why. She sniffed the sweet afternoon through the open window, a blend of faint perfume from the pink flowers, a rich country smell of sun-warmed grass from the invisible fields beyond the thick hedgerows, and a pungent herbal tang from within the hedgerows themselves. If only he could be here with me, it would be perfect. I'll just have to enjoy it twice as much, for him as well as me. She inhaled deeply and caught a hint of the freshness of water in the air. "I think it's going to rain again," she said.

"It won't last," Colum promised, "and everything will smell the sweeter when it's past."

Ratharney came and went so quickly that Scarlett hardly saw anything. One minute there was the hedgerow, then it was gone and solid wall was in its place and she was looking through the carriage window and another open window the same size with a face in it looking out at her. She was still trying to get over the shock of the stranger's eyes appearing from nowhere when the carriage rattled past the last of the row of buildings and the hedgerow was back again. They had not even slowed their pace.

It slowed very soon. The road had begun to wind in sharp short bends. Scarlett had her head halfway through the window, trying to look at the road ahead. "Are we in County Meath yet, Colum?"

"Very soon."

They passed a tiny cottage, moving at hardly more than a walk, so Scarlett had a good look. She smiled and waved at the red-haired little girl who was standing inside the door. The child smiled in return. Her front milk teeth were gone, and the gap gave her smile a special charm. Everything about the cottage charmed Scarlett. It was made of stone and the walls were bright white with small square windows, their frames painted red. The door was red also and divided in half, with the top half open into the house. The child's head reached barely above the half door; beyond it Scarlett could see a brightly burning fire in a shadowy room. Best of all the cottage was topped by a straw roof, and the roof made scallops where it met the house. It was like a picture from a fairy tale. She turned to smile at Colum. "If that little girl had blond hair, I'd expect to see the three bears any minute."

She could tell from Colum's expression that

he didn't know what she was talking about. "Goldilocks, silly!" He shook his head. "My grief, Colum, it's a fairy tale. Don't you have fairy tales in Ireland?"

Kathleen began to laugh.

Colum grinned. "Scarlett darling," he said, "I don't know about your fairy tales or your bears, but if it's fairies you're wanting, sure you've come to the right place. Ireland is teeming with fairies."

"Colum, be serious."

"But I am serious. And you'll have to learn about the fairies or you might get in fearful trouble. Most of them, mind you, are no more than a small nuisance, and there are those, like the shoemaker leprechaun that every man would like to have a meeting with—"

The carriage had stopped suddenly. Colum put his head out the window. When he was back inside, he was no longer smiling. He reached across Scarlett and seized the leather strap that moved the window. With a rapid pull, he raised the glass. "Sit very still and don't speak to anyone," he said in a harsh undertone. "Keep her still, Kathleen." He thrust his feet into his boots and his fingers were quick with the lacing.

"What is it?" Scarlett asked.

"Hush," said Kathleen.

Colum opened the door, grabbed his hat, stepped down into the road and closed the door. His face was like gray stone as he walked away.

"Kathleen?"

"Hush. It's important, Scarlett. Be quiet."

There was a dull reverberating thudding sound, and the leather walls of the carriage vibrated.

Even through the closed windows Scarlett and Kathleen could hear the loud clipped words shouted by a man somewhere in front of them. "You! Driver! Move along. This is no entertainment for you to gawp at. And you! Priest! Get back in your box and out of here." Kathleen's hand closed around Scarlett's.

The carriage rocked on its springs and moved slowly toward the right side of the narrow road. The stiff branches and thorns of the hedgerow tore at the thick leather. Kathleen moved away from the rasp on the window and closer to Scarlett. There was another thud, and both of them jerked. Scarlett's hand tightened on Kathleen's. What was going on?

As the carriage edged along, they came upon another cottage, identical to the one Scarlett had thought idyllic for Goldilocks. Standing in the fully open door was a black-uniformed, gold-braid-trimmed soldier who was placing two small, three-legged stools atop a table outside the door. To the left of the door there was a uniformed officer on a skittish bay horse, and to the right of it was Colum. He was talking quietly to a small weeping woman. Her black shawl had slipped from her head, and her red hair was straggling over her shoulders and cheeks. She held a baby in her arms; Scarlett could see its blue eyes and the russet down on its round head. A little girl who might have been the twin of the smiling child at the half-door was sobbing into the mother's apron. Both mother and child were bare-footed. A straggle of soldiers stood in the center of the road near a huge tripod of tree trunks. A fourth trunk hung, swaying, from ropes attached to the tripod's apex.

"Move on, Paddy," the officer shouted. The carriage creaked and tore along the hedgerow. Scarlett could feel Kathleen trembling. Something terrible was happening here. That poor woman, she looks like she's about to faint . . . or go stark crazy. I hope Colum can help her.

The woman dropped to her knees. My Lord, she's fainting, she'll drop the baby! Scarlett reached for the door-latch, and Kathleen grabbed her arm. "Kathleen, let me—"

"Quiet. For the love of God, quiet." The desperate urgency in Kathleen's whisper made Scarlett stop.

What on earth? Scarlett watched, disbelieving her own eyes. The weeping mother was clutching Colum's hand, kissing it. Above her head he made the sign of the cross. Then he raised her to her feet. He touched the head of the baby, and of the little girl, and with his two hands on her shoulders he turned the mother to face away from her cottage.

The carriage moved on, slowly, and the dull, heavy thudding began again, behind them. They began to move away from the hedgerow, into the road, then into the center of it. "Driver, stop!" Scarlett shouted before Kathleen could stop her. They were leaving Colum behind, and she couldn't allow that to happen.

"Don't, Scarlett, don't," Kathleen begged, but Scarlett had the door open even before the carriage ceased moving. She scrambled down to the road and ran back toward the noise, oblivious of her fashionable trailing skirts dragging through the thin mud.

The sight and sound that met her eyes and ears halted her, and she cried out in shocked protest. The swinging tree trunk battered the cottage walls again, and its front collapsed inward, shattering windows, showering bright bits of clean, polished glass. Red window frames fell into the dust raised by the tumbling white stones, and the two-part red door folded upon itself. The noise was horrendous—grinding . . . crashing . . . shrieking like a live thing.

For a moment, then, silence followed, and then another sound—a crackling that became a roar —and the thick, smothering smell of smoke. Scarlett saw the torches in the hands of three soldiers, the flames that were eating hungrily into the straw thatch of the roof. She thought of Sherman's Army, of the scorched walls and chimneys of Twelve Oaks, of Dunmore Landing, and she moaned with grief and with terror. Where was Colum? Oh, dear heaven, what had happened to him?

His dark-suited form stepped hurriedly from the dark smoke that was billowing across the road. "Move on," he shouted to Scarlett. "Back to the carriage."

Before she could break the trance of horror that held her fixed in place, Colum was beside her, his hand clasping her arm. "Come along, Scarlett darling, don't tarry," he said with controlled urgency. "We must be going home now."

The carriage lurched off with all the speed the horses could manage on the winding road. Scarlett was tossed from side to side between the closed window and Kathleen, but she barely noticed. She was still shaking from the strange and terrible experience. It was only when the carriage slowed to a quietly creaking movement that her heart stopped pounding and she could catch her breath.

"What was going on back there?" she asked. Her voice sounded odd to her.

"The poor woman was being evicted," said Kathleen sharply, "and Colum was comforting her. You shouldn't have interfered like that, Scarlett. You might have caused trouble for us all."

"Softly, now, Kathleen, you mustn't be scolding so," Colum said. "There was no way for Scarlett to know, being from America."

Scarlett wanted to protest that she knew worse, much worse, but she stopped herself. She wanted more urgently to understand. "Why was she being evicted?" she asked instead.

"They didn't have the rent money," Colum explained. "And the worst of it is, her husband tried to stop the process when the militia came the first time. He hit a soldier, and they took him off to jail, leaving her with the little ones and afraid for him besides."

"That's sad. She looked so pitiful. What will she do, Colum?"

"She's a sister in a cottage along the road, not too far. I sent her there."

Scarlett relaxed somewhat. It was pitiful. The poor woman was so distraught. Still, she'd be all right. Her sister must be in the Goldilocks cottage, and that wasn't far. And, after all, people really did have an obligation to pay their rent. She'd find a new saloonkeeper in nothing flat if her tenant tried to hold out on her. As for the husband hitting the soldier, that was just unforgivable. He must have known he'd go to jail for it. He should have given some mind to his wife before he did such a stupid thing.

"But why did they destroy the house?"

"To keep the tenants from going back to live in it."

Scarlett said the first thing that came into her head. "How silly! The owner could have rented it to somebody else."

Colum looked tired. "He doesn't want to rent it at all. There's a little piece of land goes with it, and he's doing the thing they call 'organizing' his property. He'll put it all in grazing and send the fattened cattle to market. That's why he raised all the rents past paying. He's no longer interested in farming the land. The husband knew it was coming; they all know once it starts. They've got months of waiting before they've got nothing left to sell to raise the rent money. It's those months that build up the anger in a man and make him try to win with his fists . . . For the women, it's despair that tears at them, seeing their man's defeat. That poor creature with her babe on her breast was trying to put her little body and bones between the ram and her man's cottage. It was all he had to make him feel like a man."

Scarlett couldn't think of anything to say. She'd had no idea things like that could happen. It was so mean. The Yankees were worse, but that had been war. Not destruction so that a bunch of cows could have more grass. The poor woman. Why, that could have been Maureen holding Jacky when he was a baby. "Are you sure she'll go to her sister's?"

"She agreed to it, and she's not the kind to lie to a priest."

"She'll be all right, then, won't she?"

Colum smiled. "Don't worry, Scarlett darling. She'll be all right."

"Until the sister's farm is organized." Kathleen's voice was hoarse. Rain spattered, then poured down the windows. Water sheeted the inside of the carriage near Kathleen's head, gushing through a rip torn by the hedgerow. "Will you give me your big handkerchief, then, Colum, to stuff this peephole with?" Kathleen said with a laugh. "And will you say a priestly prayer for the sun to return?"

How could she be so cheerful after all that and with that huge leak on top of everything else? And, for goodness sake, Colum was actually laughing with her.

The carriage was going faster, much faster. The driver must be crazy. Nobody could possibly see through a downpour like this, and the road was so narrow, too, and full of curves. They'd tear ten thousand leaks open.

"Do you not feel the eagerness coming over Jim Daly's grand horses, Scarlett darling? They think they're on a race course. But I know a racing stretch like this could only be found in County Meath. We're nearing home for sure. I'd better tell you about the little people before you meet a leprechaun and don't know who you're talking to."

Suddenly there was sunlight slanting low through the rain-wet windows, turning drops of water into shards of rainbow. There's something unnatural about rain one minute and sun the next and then rain again, Scarlett thought. She looked away from the rainbows, toward Colum.

"You saw the mockery of them in Savannah's parade," Colum began, "and I tell you it's a good thing for all who saw it that there are no leprechauns in America, because their wrath would have been terrible and would have called in all their fairy kinfolk a for taking the revenge. In Ireland, however, where they're given proper respect, they bother no one if no one bothers them. They find a pleasant spot and settle themselves there to ply their trade of cobbler. Not as a group, mind you, for the leprechaun is a solitary, but one in one place, and another in another, and so on until—if you listen to enough tales—you could come to count on finding one by every stream and stone in the country. You know he's there by the tap-tap-tap of his hammer tacking on the sole and heel of the shoe. Then, if you creep as quiet as a caterpillar, you may catch him unaware. Some say you must hold him in your grip by an arm or an ankle, but for the most part there's general agreement that fixing your gaze on him is sufficient for the capture.

"He'll beg you to let him go, but you must refuse. He'll promise you your heart's desire, but he's notorious for lying, and you must not believe him. He'll threaten some great woe, but he cannot harm you, so you disdain his blustering. And in the end he'll be forced to buy his freedom with the treasure he has concealed in a safe hidden spot nearby.

"Such a treasure it is, too. A crock of gold, not looking like much, perhaps, to the uneducated eye, but the crock is made with great and deceptive leprechaun cunning, and there's no bottom to it, so you may take out and take out gold to the end of your days, and there'll always be more.

"All this he'll give, just to be set free; he likes not company so much. Solitary is his nature, at any cost. But fearful cunning is his nature, too, so much so that he outwits almost all who capture him by distracting the attention. And if your grip eases, or your eye looks away, he's gone in an instant, and you're none the richer save for a story to tell of your adventure."

"It doesn't sound hard to me for a person to hold on or keep staring if it means getting the treasure," Scarlett said. "That story doesn't make sense."

Colum laughed. "Practical and businesslike Scarlett darling, you're just the sort the little people delight in tricking. They can count on doing what they like because you'd never credit them as the cause. If you were strolling through a lane and heard a tapping, you'd never bother to stop and look."

"I would so, if I believed that kind of nonsense."

"There you are, then. You don't believe and you wouldn't stop."

"Fiddle-dee-dee, Colum! I see what you're doing. You're putting the fault on me for not catching something that's not there in the first place." She was beginning to get angry. Word games and mind games were too slippery, and they served no purpose.

She didn't notice that Colum had turned her attention away from the eviction.

"Have you told Scarlett about Molly, yet, Colum?" Kathleen asked. "She has a right to a warning, I would say."

Scarlett forgot all about leprechauns. She understood gossip, and relished it. "Who's Molly?"

"She's the first of the Adamstown O'Haras you'll meet," said Colum, "and a sister to Kathleen and me."

"Half sister," Kathleen corrected, "and that's a half too much, by my thinking."

"Tell," Scarlett encouraged.

The telling took so long that the trip was almost over when it was done, but Scarlett wasn't conscious of the time or the miles going by. She was hearing about her own family.

Colum and Kathleen were also half brother and sister, she learned. Their father, Patrick— who was one of Gerald O'Hara's older brothers—had married three times. The children by his first wife included Jamie, who'd gone to Savannah, and Molly, who was, said Colum, a great beauty.

When she was young, maybe, according to Kathleen.

After his first wife died, Patrick married his second wife, Colum's mother; and, after her death, he married Kathleen's mother, who was also the mother of Stephen.

The silent one, Scarlett commented silently.

There were ten O'Hara cousins for her to meet in Adamstown, some with children and even grandchildren of their own. Patrick, God rest his soul, was dead these fifteen years, come November 11.

In addition there was her uncle Daniel, who was still living, and his children and grandchildren. Of them, Matt and Gerald were in Savannah, but six had stayed in Ireland.

"I'll never get them all straight," Scarlett said with apprehension. She still got some of the O'Hara children in Savannah confused.

"Colum's starting you out easy," Kathleen said. "Molly's house has no O'Haras in it at all, save her, and she'd just as soon deny her own name."

Colum, with Kathleen's acid commentary, explained about Molly. She was married to a man named Robert Donahue, a "warm" man in material terms, with a prosperous big farm of a hundred and some acres. He was what the Irish called a "strong farmer." Molly had first worked in the Donahue kitchen as a cook. When Donahue's wife died, Molly became, after a suitable time of mourning, his second wife, and stepmother to his four children. There were five children of this second marriage—the eldest of them very big and healthy for all that he was nearly three months early—but they were all grown now and gone to homes of their own.

Molly was not devoted to her O'Hara kinfolk,

Colum said neutrally, and Kathleen snorted, but that was perhaps because her husband was their landlord. Robert Donahue rented acreage in addition to his own farm; he sublet a smaller farm to the O'Haras.

Colum began to enumerate and name Robert's children and grandchildren, but by this time Scarlett had already started dismissing the overwhelming onslaught of names and ages as "the begats." She paid no close attention until he spoke about her own grandmother.

"Old Katie Scarlett still lives in the cottage her husband built for her when they married in 1789. Nothing will persuade her to move. My father, and Kathleen's, married first in 1815 and took his bride to live in the crowded cottage. When the children started coming, he built nearby a grand big place with room to grow in, and with a warm bed by the fire especially for his mother in her old age. But the Old One will have none of it. So Sean, he lives in the cottage with our grandmother, and the girls—like Kathleen here —do for them."

"When there's no escaping it," Kathleen added. "Grandmother needs no doing for really, except a pass with the broom and the dust cloth, but Sean goes out of his way to find mud to track in on a clean floor. And the mending that man creates! He can go through a new shirt before the buttons are hardly sewed on. Sean's the brother to Molly and only a half to us. He's a poor model of a man, nearly as nothing as Timothy, though he's a full twenty years older and more."

Scarlett's brain was reeling. She didn't dare ask

who Timothy was, for fear of having another dozen names thrown at her.

In any case, there wasn't time. Colum opened the window and shouted up to the driver. "Haul up, Jim, if you please, and I'll get out and join you on the box. We'll be turning into a lane just ahead; I'll need to show you the way."

Kathleen caught his sleeve. "Oh, Colum darling, say I can get down with you and make my own way home. I can't wait longer. Scarlett won't mind riding along to Molly's, will you, Scarlett?" She smiled at Scarlett with such shining hope that Scarlett would have agreed even if she hadn't wanted a few minutes by herself.

She wasn't about to go to the house of the O'Hara family beauty—no matter how faded—without spitting on a handkerchief and wiping the dust off her face and her boots. Then some toilet water from the silver vial in her purse and some powder and maybe just a very, very small touch of rouge.

50

The lane to Molly's house ran through the center of a small apple orchard; twilight tinted the airy blossoms mauve against the dark blue low sky. Strict ribbon beds of primroses edged the angularity of the square house. Everything was very tidy.

Inside, as well. The rigid horsehair suite of furniture in the parlor wore antimacassars, each table was covered with a starched white lace-edged cloth, the coal fire was ashless in the brightly polished brass grate.

Molly herself was impeccable in dress and in manner. Her burgundy gown was trimmed with dozens of silver buttons, all gleaming; her dark hair was shining and neatly coiled beneath a delicate white cap of drawn work with lace lappets. She offered her right cheek and then her left for Colum's kiss and expressed "a thousand welcomes" to another O'Hara when Scarlett was presented.

And she didn't even know I was coming. Scarlett was favorably impressed, in spite of Molly's undeniable beauty. She had the most velvety clear skin Scarlett had ever seen, and her bright blue eyes were free of shadows or pouches. Hardly any crows' feet, either, and not a line worth mentioning except from her nose to her mouth, and even girls can have those, Scarlett summed up in her rapid appraisal. Colum must have been mistaken, Molly couldn't possibly be in her fifties. "I'm so happy to meet you, Molly, and just too grateful for words that you're going to put me up in your lovely house," Scarlett gushed. Not that the house was all that much. Clean as fresh paint, granted, but the parlor wasn't any bigger than the smallest bedroom in her Peachtree Street house.

"My grief, Colum! How could you have gone off and left me there all by myself!" she complained the next day. "That awful Robert is the most boring man in the world, talking about his cows—for pity's sake!—and how much milk every one of them gives. I felt like I was going to start mooing before we finished eating. Dinner, as they told me about fifty-eight times, not supper. What on earth difference does it make?"

"In Ireland the English have dinner in the evening, the Irish have supper."

"But they're not English."

"They have aspirations. Robert had a glass of whiskey once in the Big House with the Earl's agent when he was paying the rents."

"Colum! You're joking."

"I'm laughing, Scarlett darling, but I'm not joking. Don't worry yourself about it; what matters is, was your bed comfortable?"

"I suppose so. I could have slept on corncobs I was so tired. It feels good to be walking, I must say. That was a long ride yesterday. Is it far to Grandmother's place?"

"A quarter mile, no more, by this boreen."

" 'Boreen.' What pretty words you've got for things. We'd say 'track' for a skinny little path like this. It wouldn't have these hedgerows either. I think I'll try them at Tara instead of some of the fences. How long does it take to get them this thick?"

"It depends on what kind of planting you use for the foundation. What kind of shrubs grow in Clayton County? Or do you have a tree you can prune low?"

Colum was surprisingly well informed about growing things, for a priest, Scarlett thought as he explained and demonstrated the art of creating a hedgerow. But he had a lot to learn about measurements. The narrow twisting path was much longer than a quarter mile.

They emerged suddenly into a clearing. Ahead of them was a thatched cottage, its white walls and small blue-framed windows fresh and bright. A thick stream of smoke painted a pale line across the sunny blue sky from the low chimney in the roof, and a calico cat was sleeping on the blue sill of one of the open windows. "It's adorable, Colum! How do people keep their cottages so white? Is it all the rain?" It had showered three times during the night, Scarlett knew, and that was only in the hours before she went to sleep. The muddiness of the boreen made her think there might have been more.

"The wet helps a bit," Colum said with a smile. He was pleased with her for not complaining about what the walk was doing to her hems and her boots. "But really it's that you're visiting at a good time. We do our buildings twice a year without fail, for Christmas and for Easter, inside and out, whitewash and paint. Will we go see if Grandmother's not dozing?"

"I'm nervous," Scarlett confessed. She didn't say why. In fact she was afraid of what a person looked like who was almost a hundred years old. Suppose it turned her stomach to look at her own grandmother? What would she do?

"We'll not stay long," said Colum, as if he read her mind, "Kathleen's expecting us for a cup of tea." Scarlett followed him around the cottage to the front. The top half of the blue door was open, but she couldn't see anything inside except shadows. And there was a strange smell, earthy and sort of sour. It made her nose wrinkle. Was that what very old age smelled like?

"Are you sniffing the peat fire, then, Scarlett darling? You're smelling the true warm heart of Ireland. Molly's coal fire is naught but more Englishness. It's the turf burning that means home. Maureen told me she dreams of it some nights and wakes with a heart full of longing. I mean to take her a few bricks when we go back to Savannah."

Scarlett inhaled curiously. It was a funny smell, like smoke, but not really. She followed Colum through the low doorway into the cottage, blinking to adjust her eyes to the dark interior.

"And is that you at last, Colum O'Hara? Why, I want to know, have you brought Molly to see me when Bridie promised me the gift of my own Gerald's girl?" Her voice was thin and cantankerous, but not cracked or weak. Relief and a kind of wonder filled Scarlett's being. This was Pa's mother that he told about so many times.

She pushed past Colum and went to kneel beside the old woman, who was sitting in a wooden armchair next to the chimney. "I am Gerald's girl, Grandmother. He named me after you, Katie Scarlett."

The original Katie Scarlett was small and brown, her skin darkened by nearly a century of open air and sun and rain. Her face was round, like an apple, and withered, like an apple kept too long. But the faded blue eyes were unclouded and penetrating. A thick wool shawl of bright blue lay across her shoulders, across her breast, the fringed ends in her lap. Her thin white hair was covered by a knitted red cap. "Let me look at you, girl," she said. Her leathery fingers lifted Scarlett's chin.

"By all the saints, he told the truth! You've got eyes green as a cat's." She crossed herself rapidly. "Where did they come from, I'd like to know. I thought Gerald must be drink-taken when he wrote me such a tale. Tell me, Young Katie Scarlett, was your dear mother a witch?"

Scarlett laughed. "She was more like a saint, Grandmother."

"Is that so? And married to my Gerald? The wonder of it all. Or maybe it's that being married to him made a saint of her with all the tribulation of it. Tell me, did he stay quarrelsome to the end of his days, God rest his soul?"

"I'm afraid so, Grandmother." The fingers pushed her away.

" 'Afraid,' is it? It's grateful I am. I prayed America wouldn't ruin him. Colum, you'll light a candle of thanksgiving for me in the church."

"That I will."

The old eyes scrutinized Scarlett again. "You meant no ill, Katie Scarlett. I'll forgive you." She smiled suddenly, eyes first. The small pursed lips spread into a smile of heartbreaking tenderness. There was not a tooth in the rose-petal-pink gums. "I'll order another candle for the blessing granted me of seeing you with me own eyes before I go to my grave."

Scarlett's eyes filled with tears. "Thank you, Grandmother."

"Not at all, not at all," said Old Katie Scarlett. "Take her away, Colum, I'm ready for my rest now." She closed her eyes and her chin dropped onto her warm, shawled chest.

Colum touched Scarlett's shoulder. "We'll go."

Kathleen ran out through the open red door of the cottage nearby, sending the hens in the yards scattering and complaining. "Welcome to the house, Scarlett," she cried joyfully. "Tea's in the pot stewing, and there's a fresh loaf of barm brack for your pleasure."

Scarlett was amazed again at the change in Kathleen. She looked so happy. And so strong. She was wearing what Scarlett still thought of as a costume, an ankle-high brown skirt over blue and yellow petticoats. Her skirt was pulled up on one side and tucked into the top of the home-spun apron that was tied around her waist, show-ing the bright petticoats. Scarlett owned no gown as becoming. But why, she wondered, was Kath-leen bare-legged and barefooted when striped stockings would have finished off the outfit?

She had thought about asking Kathleen to come over to Molly's to stay. Even if Kathleen made no bones about her dislike for her half sis-ter, she should be able to put up with her for ten days, and Scarlett really needed her. Molly had a parlor maid, who acted as lady's maid as well, but the girl was hopeless at arranging hair. But this Kathleen, happy at home and sure of herself, was not someone who'd jump to do her bidding, Scarlett could tell. There was no point in even hinting at the move, she'd just have to make do with a clumsy chignon, or wear a snood. She swallowed a sigh and went into the house.

It was so small. Bigger than Grandmother's cottage, but still too small for a family. Where did they all sleep? The outside door led directly to the kitchen, a room twice the size of the kitchen in the small cottage but only half the size of Scarlett's bedroom in Atlanta. The most noticeable thing in the room was the big stone fireplace in the center of the right-hand wall. Perilously steep stairs rose up to an opening high in the wall to the left of the chimney; a door to its right led to another room.

"Take a chair by the fire," Kathleen urged. There was a low turf fire directly on the stone floor inside the chimney. The same worked stone extended outward, flooring the kitchen. It gleamed pale from scrubbing, and the smell of soap mingled with the sharp aroma of the burning peat.

My soul, Scarlett thought, my family's really very poor. Why on earth did Kathleen cry her eyes out to come back to this? She forced a smile and sat down in the Windsor chair Kathleen had pushed forward to the hearth.

In the hours that followed Scarlett saw for herself why Kathleen had found the space and relative luxury of life in Savannah an inadequate replacement for life in the small whitewashed thatched cottage in County Meath. The O'Haras in Savannah had created a sort of island of happiness, populated by themselves, reproducing the life they'd known in Ireland. Here was the original.

A steady succession of heads and voices appeared in the open top half of the door, calling out, "God bless all here," followed by the invitation to "come in and sit by the fire," and then by the entrance of the owners of the voices. Women, girls, children, boys, men, babies came and went in overlapping ones, twos, threes. The musical Irish voices greeted Scarlett and welcomed her, greeted Kathleen and welcomed her home again, all with a warmth so heartfelt that Scarlett could all but hold it in her hand. It was as different from the formal world of paying and receiving calls as day differs from night. People told her they were related, and how. Men and women told her stories about her father—reminiscences from older ones, events told them by their parents or grandparents repeated by younger ones. She could see Gerald O'Hara's face in so many of the faces around the hearth, hear his voice in their voices. It's like Pa was here himself, she thought; I can see how he must have been when he was young, when he was here.

There was the gossip of the village and town to catch Kathleen up on, told and retold as people came and went so that before long Scarlett felt that she knew the blacksmith and the priest and the man who kept the bar and the woman whose hen was laying a double-yolk egg almost every day. When Father Danaher's bald head appeared in the doorway, it seemed the most natural thing in the world, and when he came in she looked automatically, with everyone else, to see if his cassock had been mended yet where the rough corner on the gate to the churchyard had torn it.

It's like the County used to be, she thought; everybody knows everybody, and knows everybody's business. But smaller, closer, more comfortable somehow. What she was hearing and sensing, without recognizing it, was that the tiny world she was seeing was kinder than any she had ever known. She knew only that she was enjoying being in it very much.

This is the best vacation a person could possibly have. I'll have so much to tell Rhett. Maybe we'll come back together sometime; he's always thought nothing of going off to Paris or London at the drop of a hat. Of course we couldn't live like this, it's too . . . too . . . peasanty. But it's so quaint and charming and fun. Tomorrow I'm going to wear my Galway clothes when I come over to see everybody, and no corset at all. Shall I put on the yellow petticoat with the blue skirt, or would the red . . . ?

In the distance a bell tolled, and the young girl in the red skirt who was showing her baby's first teeth to Kathleen jumped up from her seat on a low three-legged stool. "The Angelus! Who'd have believed I could let my Kevin come home and no dinner on the fire?"

"Take some of the stew, then, Mary Helen, we've got too much. Didn't Thomas greet me when I came home with four fat rabbits he'd snared?" In less than a minute, Mary Helen was on her way with her baby on her hip and a napkin-covered bowl in her arm.

"You'll help me pull out the table, Colum? The men will be coming to dinner. I don't know where Bridie's got to."

One by one, close on the heels of the one before, the men of the cottage came in from their work in the fields. Scarlett met her father's brother Daniel, a tall, vigorous, spare angular man of eighty, and his sons. There were four of them, aged twenty to forty-four, plus, she remembered, Matt and Gerald in Savannah. The house must have been like this when Pa was young, him and his big brothers. Colum looked so astonishingly short, even seated at table, in the midst of the big O'Hara men.

The missing Bridie ran through the door just as Kathleen was ladling stew into blue and white bowls. Bridie was wet. Her shirt clung to her arms, and her hair dripped down her back. Scarlett looked through the door, but the sun was shining.

"Did you tumble into a well, then, Bridie?" asked the youngest brother, the one named Timothy. He was glad to deflect attention away from himself. His brothers had been teasing him about his weakness for an unnamed girl they referred to only as "Golden Hair."

"I was washing myself in the river," Bridie said. Then she began to eat, ignoring the uproar caused by her statement. Even Colum, who rarely criticized, raised his voice and banged the table.

"Look at me and not the rabbit, Brigid O'Hara. Do you not know the Boyne claims a life for every mile of its length every year?"

The Boyne. "Is that the same Boyne as the Battle of the Boyne, Colum?" Scarlett asked. The whole table fell silent. "Pa must have told me about that a hundred times. He said the O'Haras lost all their lands because of it." Bowls and spoons resumed their clatter.

692

"It is, and we did," Colum said, "but the river continued in its course. It marks the boundary of this land. I'll show it to you if you want to see, but not if you're thinking of using it like a washtub. Brigid, you've got better sense. What possessed you?"

"Kathleen told me Cousin Scarlett was coming, and Eileen told me a lady's maid must be washed every day before she touches the lady's clothes or her hair. So I went to wash." She looked full at Scarlett for the first time. "It's my intention to please, so you'll take me back to America with you." Her blue eyes were solemn, her soft rounded chin thrust out with determination. Scarlett liked the look of her. There'd be no homesick tears from Bridie, she was sure. But, she could only use her until the trip was over. No Southerner ever had a white maid. She looked for the right words to tell the girl.

Colum did it for her. "It was already decided you'd go to Savannah with us, Bridie, so you could have avoided risking your life . . . "

"Hoo-rah!" Bridie shouted. Then she blushed crimson. "I'll not be so rowdy when I'm in service," she said earnestly to Scarlett. And, to Colum, "I was only at the ford, Colum, where the water's barely to the knee. I'm not such a fool as all that."

"We'll find out just what manner of fool you are, then," Colum said. He was smiling again. "Scarlett will have the task of telling you what a lady's needs might be, but you'll not be after her for schooling before it's the hour to depart. There's two weeks and a day you'll be sharing quarters on the ship, time enough to learn all you're able to learn. Bide your time till then, with Kathleen and the house your better and your duty."

Bridie sighed heavily. "It's a mountain of burden, being the youngest."

Everyone hooted her loudly. Except Daniel, who spoke not at all throughout the meal. When it was over, he pushed back his chair and stood. "The ditching's best done in this dry spell," he said. "Finish your meal and get back to your labors." He bowed ceremoniously to Scarlett. "Young Katie Scarlett O'Hara, you honor my house and I bid you welcome. Your father was greatly loved and his absence has been a stone in my breast for all these fifty years and more."

She was too surprised to say a word. By the time she thought of something, Daniel was out of sight behind the barn, on his way to his fields.

Colum pushed back his chair, then moved it near the hearth. "There s no way for you to know it, Scarlett darling, but you've made your mark on this house. That's the first time I've heard Daniel O'Hara use words on anything that hadn't to do with the farm. You'd better watch your step or the widows and spinsters of the region will buy a spell to lay on you. Daniel's a widower, you know, and could use a new wife."

"Colum! He's an old man!"

"And isn't his mother still thriving at a hundred? He's got plenty of good years left. You'd better remind him you've got a husband back home."

"Maybe I'll remind my husband that he's not

the only man in the world. I'll tell him he's got a rival in Ireland." The thought made her smile, Rhett jealous of an Irish farmer. But why not, really? One of these days she might just mention it, not saying that it was her uncle, or that he was old as the hills. Oh, she was going to have a fine time when she had Rhett where she wanted him! An unexpected pang of longing struck her like physical pain. She wouldn't tease him about Daniel O'Hara or anything else. All she wanted was to be with him, to love him, to have this baby for them both to love.

"Colum's right about one thing," said Kathleen. "Daniel's given you the blessing of the head of the house. When you can't bear another minute of Molly, you'll have a place here if you want it."

Scarlett saw her chance. She'd been consumed with curiosity. "Where do you put everybody?" she asked bluntly.

"There's the loft, divided in two. The boys have their side, Bridie and me the other. And Uncle Daniel took the bed by the fire when Grandmother didn't want it. I'll show you." Kathleen pulled on the back edge of a wooden settle along the wall beyond the stairs, and it folded open and down to reveal a thick mattress covered by a woolen blanket. "He said that's why he was taking it, to show her she'd missed a good thing, but I've always thought he felt too lonely above the room after Aunt Theresa died."

" 'Above the room'?"

"Through there." Kathleen gestured toward the door. "We fitted it as a parlor, no sense wasting it. The bed's still there for you any time you've the mind."

Scarlett couldn't imagine that she ever would. Seven people in one small house were at least four or five too many in her opinion. Particularly such big people. No wonder Pa was called the runt of the litter, she thought, and no wonder he always carried on like he thought he was ten feet tall.

She and Colum visited her grandmother again before going back to Molly's, but Old Katie Scarlett was asleep by the fire. "Do you think she's all right?" Scarlett whispered.

Colum just nodded. He waited until they were outside before he spoke. "I saw the stewpot on the table, and it was almost empty. She'll have fixed Sean's dinner and shared it since we were there. She always has a small nap after meals."

The tall hedgerows that bordered the boreen were sweet with blossoms of hawthorn, and the singing of birds poured down from the branches at the top, two feet above Scarlett's head. It was wonderful to walk along, in spite of the wet ground. "Is there a boreen to the Boyne, Colum? You said you'd take me."

"And so I did. In the morning, if it please you. I promised Molly I'd have you home in good time today. She's having a tea party in your honor."

A party! For her! What a good idea it was, coming to meet her kinfolks before she settled in Charleston.

51

The food was good, but that's the only good thing I can find to say, Scarlett thought. She smiled brilliantly and shook hands with each of Molly's departing guests. God's nightgown! What limp droopy fingers these women have, and they all talk like they've got something stuck in their throat. I've never seen such a tacky bunch of people in all my born days.

The competitive overrefinement of provincial, would-be gentry was something Scarlett had never run into. There was an earthy forthrightness to Clayton County landowners and a true aristocracy that scorned pretension in Charleston and in the circle she'd thought of as "Melly's friends" in Atlanta. The elevated little finger of the hand lifting the teacup and the dainty, mouse-sized bites of scones and sandwiches that characterized Molly and her acquaintances seemed as ridiculous to her as in fact they were. She had eaten the excellent food with excellent appetite and ignored the hinted invitations to deplore the vulgarity of people who dirtied their hands with farm work. "What does Robert do, Molly—wear kid gloves all the time?" she'd asked, delighted to see that lines did show up in Molly's perfect skin when she frowned.

I reckon she'll have a few words to say to Colum about bringing me here, but I don't care. It served her right for talking about me like I wasn't an O'Hara at all, or her either. And where did she come up with that idea that a plantation is the same thing as—what did she call it?—an English manor. I might have to have a few words with Colum myself. Their faces were a treat, though, when I told them all our servants and field hands were always black. I don't think they've ever heard of dark skin, much less seen any. This is a strange place, all around.

"What a lovely party, Molly," said Scarlett. "I declare I ate till I could fairly pop. I think I might just take a little rest up in my room for a while."

"You must, naturally, do whatever you like, Scarlett. I had the boy bring around the trap so we could have a drive, but if you'd prefer to sleep . . ."

"Oh, no, I'd love to go out. Can we go to the river, do you think?" She'd planned to get away from Molly, but it was too good a chance to miss. The truth was she'd rather ride to see the Boyne than walk there. She didn't trust Colum one bit when he said it wasn't far.

Rightly so, as it turned out. Wearing yellow gloves to match the yellow spokes of the trap's tall wheels, Molly drove all the way back to the main road, then through the village. Scarlett looked at the row of dispirited-looking buildings with interest.

The trap rolled through the biggest gates Scarlett had ever seen, tremendous creations of wrought iron topped with gold spear points, each side centered by a gold-surrounded brightly colored plaque of intricate design. "The Earl's coat of arms," said Molly lovingly. "We'll drive to the Big House and see the river from the garden.

It's all right, he's not there, and Robert got permission from Mr. Alderson."

"Who's that?"

"The Earl's land agent. He manages the entire manor. Robert knows him."

Scarlett tried to look impressed. Clearly, she was supposed to be bowled over, though she couldn't think why. What could be so important about an overseer? They were only hired help.

Her question was answered after a long drive on a perfectly straight, wide, gravelled road through spreading expanses of clipped lawn that reminded her for a moment of the great sweeping terraces of Dunmore Landing. The thought was pushed aside by her first sight of the Big House.

It was immense, not one building, it seemed, but a cluster of crenellated roofs and towers and walls. It was more like a small city than like any house Scarlett had ever seen or even heard of. She understood why Molly was so respectful of the agent. Managing a place like this would take more people and more work than the biggest plantation that had ever been. She craned her neck to look up at the stone walls and marble-framed tracery windows. The mansion Rhett had built for her was the largest and—to Scarlett's mind—most impressive residence in Atlanta, yet it could be put down in one corner of this place and hardly take up enough room to be noticed. I'd love to see the inside . . .

Molly was horrified that Scarlett would even ask. "We have permission to walk in the garden. I'll tie the pony to that hitching post, and we'll go through the gate there." She pointed to a steeply pointed arched entry. The iron gate was ajar. Scarlett jumped down from the trap.

The archway led through to a gravelled terrace. It was the first time Scarlett had ever seen gravel raked into a pattern. She was almost timid about walking on it. Her footprints would ruin the perfection of the S-curves formed by the raking. She looked apprehensively at the garden beyond the terrace. Yes, the paths were gravel. And raked. Not in curves, thank heaven, but still there wasn't a footprint to be seen. I wonder how they do that? The man with the rake has to have feet. She took a deep breath and crunched boldly onto the terrace and across it to the marble steps into the garden. The sound of her boots on the gravel was as loud as gunfire to her ears. She was sorry she'd come.

Where was Molly anyway? Scarlett turned around as quietly as she could. Molly was walking carefully, fitting her steps into the prints Scarlett had left. It made her feel much better that her cousin—for all her airs—was even more intimidated than she was. She looked up at the house, waiting for Molly to catch up. It seemed much more human from this side. There were French windows from the terrace to the rooms. Closed and curtained, but not too big to walk in and out of, not overwhelming like the doors on the front of the house. It was possible to believe that people might live here, not giants.

"Which way is the river?" Scarlett called to her cousin. She wasn't going to let an empty house make her whisper.

But she didn't care to linger, either. She refused

Molly's suggestion that they walk through all the paths and all the gardens. "I just want to see the river. I'm bored sick of gardens; my husband makes too much fuss about them." She fended off Molly's transparent curiosity about her marriage while they followed the center path toward the trees that marked the end of the garden.

And then suddenly it was there, through an artfully natural-looking gap between two clumps of trees. Brown and gold, like no water Scarlett had ever seen. The sunlight lay on top of the river like molten gold swirling in slow eddies of water as dark as brandy. "It's beautiful," she said aloud, her voice soft. She hadn't expected beauty.

To hear Pa talk it should be red from all the blood that was spilled, and rushing and wild. But it hardly looks like it's moving at all. So this is the Boyne. She'd heard about it all her life and now she was close enough to reach down and touch it. Scarlett felt an emotion unknown to her, something she couldn't name. She searched for some definition, some understanding; it was important, if she could just find it . . .

"That's the view," Molly said in her cramped, most refined diction. "All the best houses have a view from their gardens."

Scarlett wanted to hit her. She'd never find it now, whatever she'd been looking for. She looked where Molly indicated and saw a tower on the other side of the river. It was like the ones she'd seen from the train, made of stone and part crumbled away. Moss stained the base of it and vines clung to its sides. It was much bigger than she'd thought they would be when she saw them at a distance; it looked like it might be as much as thirty feet across and twice that high. She had to agree with Molly that it was a romantic view.

"Let's go," she said after one more look at the river. All of a sudden she felt very tired.

"Colum, I think I'm going to kill dear cousin Molly. If you could have heard that horrible Robert last night at dinner telling us how privileged we were to walk on the Earl's dumb garden paths. He must have said it about seven hundred times, and every single time Molly chirped away for ten minutes about what a thrill it was.

"And then, this morning, she practically swooned when she saw me in these Galway clothes. No chirpy little lady voice then, let me tell you. She lectured me about ruining her position and being an embarrassment to Robert. To Robert! He should be embarrassed every time he sees his dumb fat face in a looking glass. How dare Molly lecture me about disgracing him?"

Colum patted Scarlett's hand. "She's not the best companion I'd wish for you, Scarlett darling, but Molly has her virtues. She did lend us the trap for the day, and we'll have a grand outing with no thought of her to cloud it. Look at the blackthorn flowers in the hedges, and the wild cherries blooming their hearts out in that farmyard. It's too fine a day to waste on rancor. And you look like a lovely Irish lass in your striped stockings and red petticoat."

Scarlett stretched out her feet and laughed. Colum was right. Why should she let Molly ruin her day?

They went to Trim, an ancient town with a rich history that Colum knew would interest Scarlett not at all. So he told her instead about Market Day every Saturday, just like Galway, only, he had to acknowledge, considerably smaller. But with a fortune-teller most Saturdays, something you seldom found in Galway, and a glorious fortune promised if you paid tuppence, reasonable happiness for a penny, and tribulation foretold only if your pocket could produce merely a ha'penny.

Scarlett laughed—Colum could always make her laugh—and touched the drawstring bag hanging between her breasts. It was hidden by her shirt and her Galway blue cloak. No one would ever know she was wearing two hundred dollars in gold instead of a corset. The freedom was almost indecent. She had not been out of the house without stays since she was eleven years old.

He showed her Trim's famous castle, and Scarlett pretended interest in the ruins. Then he showed her the store where Jamie had worked from the time he was sixteen until he went to Savannah at the age of forty-two, and Scarlett's interest was real. They talked with the shopkeeper, and of course nothing would do but to close the shop and accompany the owner upstairs to meet his wife, who would surely die from the sorrow of it if she couldn't hear the news from Savannah straight from Colum's own lips and meet the visiting O'Hara who was already the talk of the countryside for her beauty and her American charm.

Then neighbors had to be told what a special

day it was and who was there, and they hurried to the rooms above the shop until Scarlett was sure the walls must be bulging.

Then, "The Mahoneys will be wounded by the slight if we come to Trim without seeing them," Colum said when at last they left Jamie's former employer. Who? They're Maureen's family, to be sure, with the grandest bar in all Trim and had Scarlett ever tried a bit of porter? The number of people was even larger this time, with more arriving every minute, and soon there were fiddlers and food. The hours sped by, and the long twilight was setting in when they started the short journey to Adamstown. The first shower of the day—a phenomenon to have so much sun, said Colum—intensified the scent of the blossoms in the hedgerows. Scarlett pulled up the hood of her cloak, and they sang all the way to the village.

"I'll stop in here in the bar and learn if there's a letter for me," Colum said. He looped the pony's reins around the village pump. In an instant heads thrust through the open half doors of all the buildings.

"Scarlett," cried Mary Helen, "the baby's got another tooth, come have a cup of tea and admire it."

"No, Mary Helen, you come along here with babe and tooth and husband and all," said Clare O'Gorman, née O'Hara. "Isn't she my own first cousin and my Jim dying to meet her?"

"And my cousin, too, Clare," shouted Peggy Monaghan. "And me with a barm brack on my hearth because I learned her partiality for it. "

Scarlett didn't know what to do. "Colum!" she called.

It was easy enough, he said. They'd just go to each house in turn, starting with the closest, gathering friends as they went. When the entire village was in one of the houses, that's where they'd stay for a while.

"Not too long, mind you, because you'll have to get into your finery for Molly's dinner table. She has her imperfections, as do we all, but you cannot thumb your nose at her under her own roof. She's tried too hard to shed those kinds of petticoats to be able to support seeing them in her dining room."

Scarlett put her hand on Colum's arm. "Do you think I can stay at Daniel's?" she asked. "I truly hate being at Molly's . . . What are you laughing about, Colum?"

"I've been wondering how I could persuade Molly to let us have the trap one more day. Now I think she can be convinced to make it available for the rest of your visit. You take yourself in there to see the new tooth, and I'll go have a small talk with Molly. Don't take this wrong, Scarlett darling, but she'll likely promise anything if I promise to take you elsewhere. She'll never live down what you said about Robert's elegant kid gloves for cow tending. It's the most cherished story in every kitchen from here to Mullingar."

Scarlett was installed in the room "above" the kitchen by suppertime. Uncle Daniel even smiled when Colum told the tale of Robert's gloves. This remarkable occurrence was added to the tale, making it an even better story for the next telling.

Scarlett adjusted with astonishing ease to the simplicity of Daniel's two-room cottage. With a room of her own, a comfortable bed, and Kathleen's tireless unobtrusive cleaning and cooking, Scarlett had only to enjoy herself on her holiday. And she did—enormously.

52

During the following week Scarlett was busier and, in some ways, happier than she had ever been. She felt stronger physically than she could remember ever feeling. Freed from the constriction of fashionable tight lacing and the metal cage of corset stays, she could move more quickly and breathe deeply for the first time in many years. In addition, she was one of those women whose vitality increased in pregnancy as if in response to the needs of the life growing within her. She slept deeply and woke at cockcrow with a raging appetite for breakfast and for the day ahead.

Which always produced both the comfortable delight of familiar pleasures and the stimulation of new experience. Colum was eager to take her out "adventuring," as he called it, in Molly's pony trap. But first he had to tear her away from her new friends. They poked their heads in at Daniel's door immediately after breakfast. For a visit, to invite her to visit them, with a story she might not have heard yet, or a letter from America that could use some explanation of the meaning of some words or phrases. She was the expert on America and was begged to tell what it was like, over and over again. She was also Irish, though she'd suffered, poor dear, from the lack of knowing it, and there were dozens of things to tell her and teach her and show her.

There was an artlessness about the Irish women that disarmed her; it was as if they were from another world, as foreign as the world they all believed in where fairies of all kinds did magical and enchanting things. She laughed openly when Kathleen put a saucer of milk and a plate of crumbled bread on the doorstep every evening in case any "little people" passing by were hungry. And when both saucer and plate were empty and clean in the morning Scarlett said sensibly that one of the barn cats must have been at them. Her skepticism bothered Kathleen not at all, and Kathleen's fairy supper became, for Scarlett, one of the most charming things about living with the O'Haras.

Another was the time she spent with her grandmother. She's tough as shoe leather, Scarlett thought with pride, and she fancied that her grandmother's blood in her veins was what had gotten her through the desperate times in her life. She ran over to the little cottage often, and if Old Katie Scarlett was awake and willing to talk, she'd sit on a stool and ask for stories about her Pa growing up.

Eventually she'd give in to Colum's urgings and climb up into the trap for the day's adventure. Warm in her wool skirts, protected by cloak and hood, she learned within a few days to pay no attention to the gusting wind from the west or the brief light rains that so often rode on it.

Just such a rain was falling when Colum took her to "the real Tara." Scarlett's cloak billowed around her when she reached the top of the uneven stone steps up the side of the low hill where Ireland's High Kings had ruled and made music, and loved and hated, and feasted and battled and, in the end, been defeated.

There's not even a castle. Scarlett looked around her and saw nothing except a scattering of grazing sheep. Their fleece looked gray under the gray sky in the gray light. She shivered, surprising herself. A goose walked over my grave. The childhood explanation flickered in her mind, making her smile.

"It pleases you?" asked Colum.

"Um, yes, very pretty.

"Don't lie, Scarlett darling, and don't search for prettiness at Tara. Come with me." He held out his hand and Scarlett put hers in it.

Together they walked slowly across the rich grass to an uneven area of what looked to her like grassy lumps in the earth. Colum walked over some of them and stopped. "Saint Patrick himself stood where we are standing now. He was a man then, a simple missionary, no bigger, likely, than I am. Sainthood came later and he grew in people's minds to a giant of a man, invincible, armed with God's Holy Word. It's better, I believe, to remember that he was a man first. He must have been frightened—alone, in his sandals and frieze cloak, facing the power of the High King and his magicians. Patrick had only his faith and his mission of truth and the need to tell it. The wind must have been cold. His need must have been like a consuming flame. He had already broken the High King's law, lighting a great bonfire on a night when it was the law that all fires should be put out. He could have been killed for the trespass, he knew that. He had purposed the great risk to draw the eye of the King and prove to him the magnitude of the message he, Patrick, bore. He did not fear death; he feared only that he would fail God. That he did not do. King Laoghaire, from his ancient jewelled throne, gave the bold missionary the right to preach without hindrance. And Ireland became Christian."

There was, in Colum's quiet voice, something that compelled Scarlett to listen and to try to understand what he was saying and something more besides. She'd never thought about saints as people, as able to be afraid. She'd never really thought about saints at all; they were just names of holy days. Now, looking at Colum's short stocky figure and ordinary face and graying hair tousled by the wind, she could imagine the face and figure of another ordinary-looking man, in the same stance of readiness. He wasn't afraid to die. How could anyone not be afraid to die? What must it be like? She felt a human wrench of envy of Saint Patrick, of all the saints, even, somehow, of Colum. I don't understand, and I never will, she thought. The realization came slowly, a heavy weight. She had learned a great and painful and stirring truth. There are things too deep, too complex, too conflicted for explanation or everyday understanding. Scarlett felt alone and exposed to the western wind.

Colum walked on, leading her. It was only a few dozen paces to the place where he stopped. "There," he said, "that row of low mounds, do you see it?" Scarlett nodded.

"You should have music and a glass of whiskey to stave off the wind and open your eyes, but I have none to give you, so perhaps you should close them to see. That is all we have left of the banqueting hall of the thousand candles. The O'Haras were there, Scarlett darling, and the Scarletts, and everyone you know—Monaghan, Mahoney, Mac-Mahon, O'Gorman, O'Brien, Danaher, Donahue, Carmody—others you've yet to meet, as well. All the heroes were there. The food, it was grand and plentiful, and the drink. And music to lift the heart right out of your body. A thousand guests it held, lit by the thousand candles. Can you see it, Scarlett? The flames glowing twice, thrice, ten times over, reflected as they were in the gold bracelets on their arms and in the gold cups that travelled to their mouths, and in the deep reds and greens and blues of the great gold-clasped jewels that held their carmine cloaks across their shoulders. What mighty appetites they had—for the venison and boar and roast goose gleaming in its fat—for the mead and the poteen—for the music that brought their fists to pounding on the tables with gold plates jouncing and rattling one upon the next. Can you see your Pa? And Jamie? And that rascal young Brian with his side-looking gaze at the women? Ach, what revelry! Can you see it,

She laughed with Colum. Yes, Pa would have been bellowing out "Peg in a Low Back'd Car" and calling for his cup to be filled just one more time because singing put such a terrible thirst on a man. How he would have loved it. "There'd be horses," she said confidently. "Pa always had to have a horse."

"Horses as strong and beautiful as great waves rushing at the shore."

"And somebody patient to put him to bed after."

Colum laughed. He put his arms around her and hugged her, then let her go. "I knew you'd feel the glorious fact of it," he said. There was pride in his words, pride in her. Scarlett smiled at him, her eyes like living emeralds.

The wind blew her hood onto her shoulders, and warmth touched her bare head. The shower was past. She looked up at the clean-washed blue sky; clouds, dazzling white, moved like dancers before the gusting winds. So close they seemed, so warm and sheltering the Irish sky.

Then her gaze fell and she saw Ireland before her, green upon green of fresh-growth fields and tender new leaves and hedgerows thick with life. She could see so far, to the mist-edged curve of the earth. Something ancient and pagan stirred deep within her, and the barely tamed wildness that was her hidden being surged hotly through her blood. This was what it was to be a king, this height above the world, this nearness to the sun and the sky. She threw her arms wide to embrace being alive, on this hill, with the world at her feet.

"Tara," said Colum.

"I felt so strange, Colum, not like me at all." Scarlett stepped on one of the wheel's yellow spokes and then up onto the seat of the trap.

"It's the centuries, Scarlett darling. All the life lived there, all the joy and all the sorrow, all the feasts and battles, they're in the air around and the land beneath you. It's time, years beyond our counting, weighing without weight on the earth. You cannot see it or smell it or hear it or touch it, but you feel it brushing your skin and speaking without sound. Time. And mystery."

Scarlett pulled her cloak close around her in the warm sun. "It was like at the river, it made me feel peculiar, too, somehow. I almost could put a word to it, but then I lost it." She told him about the Earl's garden and the river and the view of the tower.

" 'The best gardens have views,' do they?" Colum's voice was terrible with anger. "Is that what Molly said?"

Scarlett drew her body deeper into the cloak. What had she said that was so wrong? She'd never seen Colum like this, he was a stranger, not Colum at all.

He turned to her and smiled, and she saw that she'd been mistaken. "How would you like to encourage me in my weakness, Scarlett darling? They'll be introducing the horses to the race course in Trim today. I'd like to look them over and choose one to carry a small wager for me in Sunday's race."

She'd like that very much.

It was almost ten miles to Trim—not far, Scarlett thought. But the road twisted and turned and veered off from time to time, in directions away from the one they wanted, only to twist and turn some more until finally they were going again where they wanted to go. Scarlett agreed enthusiastically when Colum suggested they stop in a village for a cup of tea and a bite. Back in the trap they went a short way to a crossroads, then turned onto a wider, straighter road. He whipped up the pony to a smart pace. A few minutes later he whipped it again, harder, and they raced through a large village so quickly that the trap teetered on its high wheels.

"That place looked deserted," she said when they slowed again. "Why is that, Colum?"

"No one will live in Ballyhara; it has a bad history."

"What a waste. It looked right handsome."

"Have you ever been horse racing, Scarlett?"

"Only once to a real one, in Charleston, but at home we had pick-up races all the time. Pa was the worst. He couldn't bear just to ride along and talk to the rider next to him. He made a race out of every mile of road."

"And why not?"

Scarlett laughed. Colum was so like Pa sometimes. "They must have closed Trim down," Scarlett commented when she saw the crowds at the race course. "Everybody's here." She saw a lot of familiar faces. "They've closed Adamstown, too, I reckon." The O'Hara boys waved and smiled. She didn't envy them if Old Daniel happened to see them. The ditching wasn't done yet.

The packed-earth oval was three miles long. Workmen were just completing installation of the final jump. The race would be a steeplechase. Colum hitched the pony to a tree some distance from the track, and they worked their way into the crowd.

Everyone was in high spirits, and everyone knew Colum; they all wanted to meet Scarlett, "the little lady that inquired about Robert Donahue's habit of wearing gloves for farming."

"I feel like the belle of the ball," she whispered to Colum.

"And who better for the position?" He led the way, with many stops, to the area where the horses were being led in circles by riders or trainers.

"But Colum, they're magnificent. What are horses like that doing in a pokey little town's race?"

He explained that the race was neither little nor "pokey." It had a purse of fifty pounds for the winner, more than many a shopowner or farmer earned in a year. Also, the jumps were a real test. A winner at Trim could hold his own against the field in the more famous races at Punchestown or Galway, or even Dublin. "Or win by ten lengths any race at all in America," he added with a grin. "Irish horses are the best in the world, it's accepted knowledge everywhere."

"Just like Irish whiskey, I suppose," said Gerald O'Hara's daughter. She'd heard both claims all her life. The hurdles looked impossibly high to her; maybe Colum was right. It should be an exciting race meet. And even before the races, there'd be Trim Market Day. Truly, no one could wish for a better vacation.

A sort of undercurrent rumble ran through the talking, laughing, shouting crowd. "Fight! Fight!" Colum climbed up on the rail to see. A big grin spread across his face, and his fisted right hand smacked into his cupped left palm.

"Will you be wanting to place a small wager, then, Colum?" invited the man next to him on the rail.

"That I will. Five shillings on the O'Haras."

Scarlett nearly toppled Colum when she grabbed his ankle. "What's happening?"

The crowd was flowing away from the oval toward the disturbance. Colum jumped down, took Scarlett by the wrist, and ran.

Three or four dozen men, young and old, were grunting and yelling in a melee of fists and boots and elbows. The crowd made a broad uneven circle around them, shouting encouragement. Two piles of coats to one side were testimony to the sudden eruption of the fight; many of the coats had been stripped off so quickly that their sleeves were inside out. Within the ring shirts were getting red with spilled blood, from the shirt's owner or the man he was hitting. There was no pattern, no order. Each man hit whoever was closest to him, then looked around for his next target. Anyone knocked down was pulled up roughly by the person nearest him and shoved back into the fray.

Scarlett had never seen men fighting with their fists. The sounds of blows landing and the spurting blood from mouths and noses horrified her. All four of Daniel's sons were there, and she begged Colum to make them stop.

"And lose my five shillings? Don't be daft, woman."

"You're awful, Colum O'Hara, just awful."

She repeated the words later, to Colum and to Daniel's sons and to Michael and Joseph, two of Colum's brothers she hadn't met before. They were all in the kitchen at Daniel's house. Kathleen and Brigid were calmly washing the wounds, ignoring the yelps of pain and accusations of rough handling. Colum was passing around glasses of whiskey.

I don't think it's funny at all, no matter what they claim, Scarlett said to herself. She couldn't believe that faction fights were part of the fun of fairs and public events for the O'Haras and their friends. "Just high spirits," indeed! And the girls were worse, if anything, the way they were tormenting Timothy because he had nothing worse than a black eye.

53

The next day Colum surprised her by showing up before breakfast riding a horse and leading a second. "You said you liked to ride," he reminded her. "I borrowed us some mounts. But they're to go back by noon Angelus, so grab us

716

what's left of last night's bread and come along before the house fills with visitors."

"There's no saddle, Colum."

"Whist, are you a rider or not? Get the bread, Scarlett darling, and Bridie'll make a hand for you to step on."

She hadn't ridden bareback and astride since she was a child. She'd forgotten the feeling of being one creature with the horse. It all came back, as if she'd never stopped riding this way, and soon she barely needed the reins at all; the pressure of her knees told the horse what they were going to do.

"Where are we going?" They were in a boreen she'd never walked.

"To the Boyne. I've something to show you."

The river. Scarlett's pulse quickened. There was something there that drew her and repelled her at the same time.

It began to rain, and she was glad Bridie had made her bring a shawl. She covered her head, then rode silently behind Colum, hearing the rain on the leaves of the hedge and the slow, walking clopping of the horses' hooves. So peaceful. She felt no surprise when the rain stopped. Now the birds in the hedges could come out again.

The boreen ended, and the river was there. The banks were so low that the water all but lapped over them. "This is the ford where Bridie does her washing," said Colum. "Would you fancy a bath?"

Scarlett shivered dramatically. "I'm not that brave. The water must be freezing."

"You'll find out, but only a bit of splashing. We're going across. Get your reins steady." His horse stepped cautiously into the water. Scarlett gathered up her skirts and tucked them under her thighs, then followed.

On the opposite bank, Colum dismounted. "Come down and have breakfast," he said. "I'll tie the horses to a tree." Trees grew close to the river here; Colum's face was dappled by their shade. Scarlett slid to the ground and handed him her reins. She found a sunny patch to sit in, her back sloped against a tree trunk. Small yellow flowers with heart-shaped leaves carpeted the bank. She closed her eyes and listened to the quiet voice of the river, the sibilant rustle of the leaves above her head, the songs of birds. Colum sat beside her, and she opened her eyes slowly. He broke the half loaf of soda bread in two pieces, gave her the larger.

"I've a story to tell you while we eat," he said. "This land we're on is called Ballyhara. Two hundred years ago, less a few, it was home to your people, our people. This is O'Hara land."

Scarlett sat up, suddenly wide awake. This? This was O'Hara land? And "Ballyhara"—wasn't that the name of the deserted village they had driven through so fast? She turned eagerly towards Colum.

"Quiet, now, and eat your good bread, Katie Scarlett. It's a longish story," he said. Colum's smile silenced the questions on her lips. "Two thousand years ago, plus a few, the first O'Haras settled here and made the land their own. One thousand years ago—you see how close we're

718

coming—the Vikings, Norsemen we'd call them now, discovered the green richness of Ireland and tried to take it for their own. Irish—like the O'Haras—watched the rivers where the dragon-headed long boats might invade and built strong protections against the enemy." Colum tore a corner of bread and put it in his mouth. Scarlett waited impatiently as he chewed. So many years . . . her mind couldn't grasp so many years. What came after a thousand years ago?

"The Vikings were driven away," said Colum, "and the O'Haras tilled their land and fattened their cattle for two hundred years and more. They built a strong castle with room for themselves and their servants, because the Irish have long memories and just as the Vikings had come before, invasion could come again. And so it did. Not Vikings but English who had once been French. More than half of Ireland was lost to them, but the O'Haras prevailed behind their strong walls, and tended their land for another five hundred years.

"Until the Battle of the Boyne, which piteous story you know. After two thousand years of O'Hara care, the land became English. The O'Haras were driven across the ford, those that were left, the widows and babes. One of those children grew up a tenant farmer for the English across the river. His grandson, farmer of the same fields, married our grandmother, Katie Scarlett. At his father's side he looked across the brown waters of the Boyne and saw the castle of the O'Haras torn down, saw an English house rise in its place. But the name remained. Ballyhara."

And Pa saw the house, knew this land was O'Hara land. Scarlett wept for her father, understood the rage and sorrow she'd seen in his face and heard in his voice when he roared about the Battle of the Boyne. Colum went to the river and drank from his hands. He washed them, then cupped them again and brought water to Scarlett. After she drank, he wiped the tears from her cheeks with his gentle wet fingers.

"I wanted not to tell you this, Katie Scarlett—"

Scarlett interrupted angrily. "I have a right to know."

"And so I believe also."

"Tell me the rest. I know there's more. I can tell by your face."

Colum was pale, as a man in pain beyond bearing. "Yes, there's more. The English Ballyhara was built for a young lord. He was as fair and handsome as Apollo, they say, and he thought himself a god, as well. He determined to make Ballyhara the finest estate in all Ireland. His village—for he possessed Ballyhara to the last stone and leaf—must be more grand than any other, more grand than Dublin herself. And so it was, though not so grand as Dublin, save for the single street of it, which was wider than the capital's widest street. His stables were like a cathedral, his windows as clear as diamonds, his gardens a soft carpet to the Boyne. Peacocks spread their jewelled fans on his lawns and beauteous ladies decked in jewels graced his entertainments. He was lord of Ballyhara.

"His only sorrow was that he had but one son, and he the only child. But he lived to see his grandson born, before he went to Hell. And that grandson, too, had neither brother nor sister. But he was handsome and fair, and he became lord of Ballyhara and its cathedral stable and grand village. As did his son after him.

"I remember him, the young lord of Ballyhara. I was but a child and I thought him all things wondrous and fine. He rode a tall roan horse, and when the gentry trampled our corn under the hooves of their horses as they hunted the fox, he always threw coins to us children. He sat so tall and slim in his pink coat and white breeches and high, shining boots. I couldn't understand why my father took the coins away, from us and broke them and cursed the lord for the giving of them."

Colum stood and began to pace the riverbank. When he continued his story, his voice was thin from the strain of controlling it. "The Famine came, and with it the starvation and death. 'I cannot stand to see my tenants under such suffering,' said the lord of Ballyhara. 'I will buy two strong ships and give them free and safe passage to America, where there is food in abundance. I care not that my cows lament because there is no one to milk them and my fields fill with nettles because there is no one to cultivate them. I care more for the people of Ballyhara than for the cattle or the corn.'

"The farmers and villagers kissed his hand for his goodness, and many of them prepared for their voyage. But not all could bear the pain of leaving Ireland. 'We will stay, though we starve,' they told the young lord. He sent word, then, through the countryside that any man or woman had but to ask, and the untaken berth would be given free, with gladness.

"My father cursed him again. He raged at his two brothers, Matthew and Brian, for accepting the Englishman's gift. But they were firm to go . . . They drowned, with all the rest, when the rotten ships sank in the first heavy sea. They gained the bitter name 'coffin ships.'

"A man of Ballyhara lay in wait in the stables, not caring that they were as beautiful as a cathedral. And when the young lord came to mount his tall roan horse, he seized him and he hanged the golden-haired lord of Ballyhara in the tower by the Boyne where once O'Haras watched for dragon ships."

Scarlett's hand flew to her mouth. Colum was so pale, pacing and talking in that voice that wasn't his voice. The tower! It must be the same. Her hand closed tight across her lips. She mustn't speak.

"No one knows," Colum was saying, "the name of the man in the stable. Some say one name, some say another. When the English soldiers came, the men left at Ballyhara would not point to him. The English hanged them all, in payment for the death of the young lord." Colum's face was white in the sun-spattered shade of the trees. A cry burst from his throat. Wordless and inhuman.

He turned to Scarlett, and she shrank away from his wild eyes and tormented face. "A VIEW?" he shouted; it was like a cannon firing. He sank to his knees on the yellow bank of flowers and bent forward to hide his face. His body shuddered.

Scarlett's hands reached toward him, then fell limply in her lap. She didn't know what to do.

"Forgive me, Scarlett darling," said the Colum she knew, and he raised his head. "Me sister Molly is the eejit of the Western world for saying such a thing. She always did have a talent for enraging me." He smiled, and the smile was almost convincing. "We have time to ride across Ballyhara if you want to see it. It's been deserted for near thirty years, but there's been no vandalism. No one will go near it."

He held out his hand, and the smile in his ashen face was real. "Come. The horses are just here."

Colum's horse broke a path through the brambles and tangled growth, and soon Scarlett could see the mammoth stone walls of the tower ahead of them. He held up his hand to alert her, then he reined in. He cupped his hands in a funnel around his mouth. *"Seachain,"* he shouted, *"seachain."* The strange syllables echoed from the stones.

He turned his head, and his eyes were merry. There was color in his cheeks. "That's Gaelic, Scarlett darling, the Old Irish. There's a *cailleach,* a wise woman, lives in a hut somewhere nearby. She's a witch as old as Tara, some say, and the wife that ran off from Paddy O'Brien of Trim twenty years back, if you listen to others. I called out to warn her we're passing. She might not like being surprised. I don't say I believe in witches, mind, but it never does any harm to be respectful."

They rode on to the clearing around the tower. Up close Scarlett could see that the stones had no mortar between them and yet they had not shifted even an inch from their places. How old did Colum say it was? A thousand years? Two thousand? No matter. She wasn't afraid of it, the way she'd been when Colum was talking in that unnatural way. The tower was only a building, the finest work she'd ever seen. It's not scary at all. In fact, it kind of invites me over. She rode closer, ran her fingers over the joins.

"You're very brave, Scarlett darling. I warned you, there are those who say the tower's haunted by a hanging man."

"Fiddle-dee-dee! There's no such thing as ghosts. Besides, the horse wouldn't come close if it was here. Everybody knows that animals can sense those things."

Colum chuckled.

Scarlett laid her hand against the stone. It was smooth from aeons of weathering. She could feel the warmth of the sun in it and the cold of the rain and the wind. An unaccustomed peacefulness entered her heart. "You can tell it's old," she said, knowing that her words were inadequate, knowing that it didn't matter.

"It survived," Colum said. "Like a mighty tree with roots that go deep to the center of the earth."

"Roots that go deep." Where had she heard that before? Of course. Rhett said that about Charleston. Scarlett smiled, stroking the ancient stones. She could tell him a thing or two about roots going deep. Just wait till the next time he started bragging about how old Charleston was.

The house at Ballyhara was built of stone as well, but its stone was dressed granite, each block a perfect rectangle. It looked strong, enduring; the broken windowpanes and paint-lost windowframes were a jarring incongruity in the untouched permanence of the stone. It was a big house, with flanking wings that were themselves bigger than almost any house Scarlett knew. Built to last, she said to herself. It was really a shame nobody lived in it, a waste. "Didn't the Ballyhara lord have any children?" she asked Colum.

"No." He sounded satisfied. "There was a wife, I believe, who went back to her own people. Or to an asylum. Some say she went mad."

Scarlett sensed she'd better not admire the house to Colum. "Let's look at the village," she said. It was a town, too large to be a village, and there was not a whole window anywhere, or an unbroken door. It was derelict and despised, and it made Scarlett's flesh crawl. Hatred had done this. "What's the best way home?" she asked Colum.

54

"The Old One's birthday is tomorrow," Colum said when he left Scarlett at Daniel's house. "A man with any judgment would be called away until then, and I like to pretend I am one of those men. Tell the family I'll be back on the morning."

Why was he so skittish? Scarlett wondered. There couldn't be all that much to do for one old woman's birthday. A cake, of course, but what else was there? She'd already decided to give her grandmother the lovely lace collar she'd bought in Galway. There'd be plenty of time to buy another on the way home. Good heavens, that's the end of this week!

Scarlett discovered as soon as she was through the door that what she was going to have was a lot of hard manual labor. Everything in Old Katie Scarlett's house had to be scrubbed and polished, even if it was already clean, and in Daniel's house as well. Then the farmyard outside the old cottage had to be weeded and swept clean, ready for the benches and chairs and stools to hold everyone who couldn't squeeze into the cottage itself. And the barn cleaned and scrubbed and fresh straw put down for all who would sleep the night. It was going to be a very big party; not many made it to a hundred years.

"Eat and be gone," Kathleen told the men when they came in for dinner. She put a pitcher of buttermilk and four loaves of soda bread and a bowl of butter on the table. They were as meek as lambs, ate more quickly than Scarlett had known a person could eat, and left, bending to go through the low door, without a word.

"Now we start," Kathleen announced when they were gone. "Scarlett, I'll need lots of water from the well. The buckets are there by the door."

Scarlett, like the O'Hara men, never thought of arguing.

After dinner all the village women came to the house, with their children, to help with the work. Everything was noisy, the work was sweaty, Scarlett got blisters on the ridge of soft flesh at the base of her fingers. And she enjoyed herself more than she could credit. Barefoot like the others, with her skirts tucked up, a big apron around her waist, her sleeves rolled to the elbow, she felt as if she were a child again, playing in the kitchen yard, infuriating Mammy because she was dirtying her pinafore and had taken off her shoes and stockings. Only now she had playmates who were fun, instead of whiny Suellen and baby Carreen who was too young to enter in.

How long ago that was . . . not when you think about something as old as the tower, I guess. Roots that go deep . . . Colum was frightening this morning . . . that awful story about the ships . . . Those were my uncles, Pa's own brothers drowning. Damn that English lord. I'm glad they hung him.

There had never been a party the likes of Old Katie Scarlett's birthday celebration. O'Haras from all over County Meath and beyond came in donkey carts and wagons, on horseback, on foot. Half the population of Trim was there, and every soul that lived in Adamstown. They brought gifts and stories and food made especially for the feast, although Scarlett had thought that there was already food enough for an army. Mahoney's wagon from Trim rolled up with kegs of ale, and so did Jim Daly's from Mullingar. Seamus, Daniel's eldest son, rode the plow horse into Trim and returned with a box of clay pipes strapped on his back like a huge angular hump, tobacco in two sacks hung like saddlebags. For every man—and many women, too—must be given a new pipe on such a momentous occasion.

Scarlett's grandmother received the stream of guests and gifts like a queen, sitting in her high-backed chair, wearing her new lace collar on her good black silk, dozing when it pleased her and drinking whiskey in her tea.

When the evening Angelus bell rang, there were over three hundred people standing in and outside the tiny cottage, come to do honor to Katie Scarlett O'Hara on her one hundredth birthday.

She'd asked for "the old ways," and there was an elderly man in the place of honor by the fire opposite hers. With loving gnarled fingers he turned back linen wrappings to reveal a harp; three hundred and more voices sighed with joy. This was MacCormac, the only true inheritor of the music of the bards now that the great O'Carolan was dead. He spoke, and his voice was like music already. "I tell you the words of the master Turlough O'Carolan: 'I spend my time in Ireland happy and contented, drinking with every strong man who is a real lover of music.' And I add these words of my own making: I drink with every strong man and every strong woman such as Katie Scarlett O'Hara." He bowed to her. "That is to say, when drink is offered." Two dozen hands filled glasses. He carefully chose the largest, which he raised to Old Katie Scarlett, then drained. "Now I will sing you the tale of the coming of Finn MacCool," he said. His worn bent fingers touched the strings of the harp and magic filled the air.

And forever after there was music. Two pipers had come with their *pibs willeann,* there were fiddlers beyond counting, and pennywhistles by the dozens, and concertinas, and hands leaping with clacking bones, and the stirring, inciting beat of *bodhrans* following the strong lead of Colum O'Hara.

Women filled plates with food, Daniel O'Hara presided over the small barrels of poteen, dancing filled the center of the farmyard, and no one slept at all, save Old Katie Scarlett whenever she had a mind to.

"I didn't know there could ever be such a party," Scarlett said. She was breathing in short gasps, catching up before rejoining the pink-washed dancing in the sunrise.

"You mean you've never celebrated May Day?" exclaimed shocked cousins from she knew not where.

"You'll have to stay for May Day, Young Katie Scarlett," Timothy O'Hara said. A chorus of urging echoed him.

"I can't. We've got to catch the ship."

"There'll be other ships, surely?"

Scarlett jumped up from the bench. She'd had enough rest, and the fiddlers were starting a new reel. While she danced herself breathless again, the question sang in her head with the rollicking tune. There must be other ships. Why not stay and have fun dancing the reel in her striped stockings a little longer? Charleston would still be there when she arrived—with the same tea parties in the same crumbling houses behind the same high, unfriendly walls.

Rhett would still be there, too. Let him wait. She'd waited for him long enough in Atlanta, but things were different now. The baby in her womb made Rhett hers any time she wanted to claim him.

Yes, she decided, she might just stay for May Day. She was having such a good time.

The next day she asked Colum if he knew about another sailing, after May Day.

There was indeed another sailing. A fine ship, that stopped first at Boston, where he had to go while he was in America. She and Bridie would do very well on their own for the balance of the journey to Savannah. "She sails the evening of the ninth. You'll only have a half day to do your shopping in Galway."

She didn't need even that long; she'd already thought about it. No one in Charleston would ever wear Galway stockings or Galway petticoats. They were too bright and vulgar. She was only going to keep a few of those she'd bought for herself. They'd be wonderful souvenirs. She'd give the others to Kathleen and her new friends in the village.

"May ninth. That's a lot later than we planned, Colum."

"It's but a week and a day after May Day, Katie Scarlett. No time at all, once you're dead."

It was true! She'd never have this chance again. Besides, it would be a nice thing to do for Colum.

The trip from Savannah to Boston and back would be a real hardship for him. After he'd been so nice to her, it was the least she should do for him . . .

On April 26 the *Brian Boru* sailed from Galway with two staterooms unoccupied. She had arrived on the twenty-fourth, a Friday, with passengers and mail. The mail was sorted in Galway on Saturday; Sunday being Sunday, the small bag for Mullingar left on Monday. On Tuesday the coach from Mullingar to Drogheda left a smaller bag at Navan, and on Wednesday a post rider set out with a packet of letters for the postmistress at Trim. There was a big thick envelope for Colum O'Hara from Savannah, Georgia. He got a lot of mail, did Colum O'Hara, a grand devoted family the O'Haras, and the Old One's birthday a night he wouldn't soon forget. The post rider dropped it off at the bar in Adamstown. "No reason to wait a further twenty-four hours I was thinking," he said to Matt O'Toole, who operated the bar and the tiny shop and post station in the corner of it. "At Trim they'll only put it in a slot marked 'Adamstown' until tomorrow, when another man will bring it." He accepted with alacrity the glass of porter Matt O'Toole offered him on Colum's behalf. Small and needing paint O'Toole's bar might be, but it served a fine dark glass.

Matt O'Toole called his wife in from the yard where she was spreading the wash to dry. "Mind the place, Kate, I'm walking up the boreen to Uncle Daniel's." Matt's father was the brother of Daniel O'Hara's dead wife, Theresa, God rest her soul.

"Colum! That's wonderful!" Included in Colum's envelope from Jamie was a letter from Tom MacMahon, the contractor for the Cathedral. The Bishop—with a little persuading—had agreed to allow Scarlett to redeem her sister's dowry. Tara. My Tara. I'll do such marvelous things.

Great balls of fire! "Colum, did you see this? That skinflint Bishop is asking five thousand dollars for Carreen's third of Tara! God's nightgown! You could buy the whole of Clayton County for five thousand dollars. He'll have to come down in his price."

Bishops of the Church did not haggle, Colum told her. If she wanted the dowry, and she had the money, she should pay it. She'd also be financing the work of the Church, if that made the transaction more palatable to her.

"You know it doesn't, Colum. I hate to be taken for a ride by anybody, even the Church. I'm sorry if that offends you. Still, I must have Tara, my heart's set on it. Oh, what a fool I was to let you talk me into staying over. We could be halfway to Savannah by now!"

Colum didn't bother to correct her. He left her looking for a piece of paper and a pen. "I've got to write to Uncle Henry Hamilton right this minute! He can handle everything; it'll all be done when I get there."

On Thursday Scarlett went to Trim by herself. It was annoying that Kathleen and Bridie were busy at the farm, and infuriating that Colum had just disappeared without telling a soul where he was going or when he'd be back. Still, it couldn't be helped once he was gone. And she had so much to do. She wanted some of those lovely pottery bowls that Kathleen used in the kitchen, and lots of the baskets—every shape, and there were so many of them—and piles and piles of the thick linen cloths and napkins; there was no linen like that in the stores at home. She was going to make the kitchen at Tara warm and friendly, like the Irish ones. After all, wasn't the name Tara just about as Irish as you could get?

As for Will and Suellen, she'd do something very generous for them, for Will anyhow, he deserved it. There was lots of good land just going begging in the County. Wade and Ella would come live with her and Rhett in Charleston. Rhett really was fond of them. She'd find a good school, one with a short vacation time. Rhett would probably frown the way he always did about the way she treated the children, but when the baby was born and he saw how much she loved it, he'd stop criticizing her all the time. And in the summer, they'd be at Tara, a Tara reborn and beautiful and home.

Scarlett knew she was building castles in the air. Maybe Rhett would never leave Charleston, and she'd have to be satisfied with occasional visits to Tara. But why not daydream all she wanted on a beautiful spring day like this, driving a smart pony cart and wearing stockings striped in red and blue? Why not?

She giggled, touched the whip to the pony's neck. Listen to me—I sound downright Irish.

May Day was everything that had been promised. There was food and dancing on every street in Trim, plus four tremendous Maypoles on the green within the walls of the ruined castle. Scarlett's ribbon was red, and she had a wreath of flowers for her hair, and an English officer asked her to walk down to the river, and she told him off in no uncertain terms.

They went home after the sun came up; Scarlett walked the four miles with the rest of the family because she didn't want the night to end, even though it was now day. And because she was already starting to miss her cousins, all the people she'd met. She was longing to get home, to settle the details about Tara, to begin the work on it, but she was still glad that she'd stayed for May Day. There was only a week left now. It seemed a very short time.

On Wednesday, Frank Kelly, the post rider from Trim, stopped at Matt O'Toole's for a pipe and a pint. "There's a bulging letter for Colum O'Hara," he said. "What do you fancy it could be about?" They speculated pleasantly, and wildly. In America, anything might be true. And they might just as well speculate. Father O'Hara was a friendly man, as everyone agreed, and a grand talker. But when all was said and over, he never told much.

Matt O'Toole didn't take Colum's letter to him. There was no need. He knew that Clare

O'Gorman was going to visit her old grand-mother that afternoon. She'd take the letter, if Colum didn't stop in before. Matt hefted the envelope in his hand. It must be exceptionally fine news to warrant spending that much money to send such a weight. Or else a truly major disaster.

"There's post for you, Scarlett. Colum put it on the table. And a cup of tea when you want it. Did you have a pleasant visit with Molly?" Kathleen's voice was rich with anticipation.

Scarlett didn't disappoint her. With a giggle in her voice, she described the visit. "Molly had the doctor's wife with her, and her teacup rattled fit to break when I walked in. She didn't know whether she could get away with saying I was the new hired girl or not, I reckon. So then the doctor's wife said in a little fluty voice, 'Oh, the rich American cousin. What an honor.' And she didn't bat an eye at my clothes. Molly jumped up like a scalded cat and rushed over to give me one of her double kisses on the cheek when she heard that. I promise you, Kathleen, she got tears in her eyes when I said I'd only come to fetch a travelling costume out of my trunk. She was just dying for me to stay, no matter what I looked like. I gave her the kiss-kiss when I got ready to leave. And the doctor's wife, too, for good measure. Might as well go the whole hog."

Kathleen was bent over with laughter, her sewing dropped in a heap on the floor. Scarlett dropped her travelling suit beside it. She was sure it was going to need easing through the waist. If the baby wasn't making her thicker through the middle, then wearing easy clothes and eating so much was to blame. Whichever it was, she had no intention of taking the long trip laced so tight she couldn't breathe.

She picked up the envelope and held it in the doorway so the light could fall on it. It was covered with writing and rubber-stamped dates. Honestly! Her grandfather was the nastiest man in the world. Or else that horrible Jerome was responsible, more likely him. The envelope had gone to her care of her grandfather and he hadn't sent it to Maureen's for weeks. She tore it open impatiently. It was from some government bureau in Atlanta, mailed originally to the Peachtree Street house. She hoped she hadn't missed paying some tax or something. Between the money to the Bishop for Tara and the cost of the houses she was building, her reserves were getting too low to throw money away on late payment penalties. And she was going to need a lot for the work on Tara. Not to mention buying a place for Will. Her fingers touched the pouch beneath her shirt. No, Rhett's money was Rhett's money.

The document was dated March 26, 1875. The day she'd sailed from Savannah on the *Brian Boru*. Scarlett's eyes skimmed over the first few lines, then stopped. It made no sense. She went back to the beginning and read more slowly. All the color drained from her face. "Kathleen, where's Colum, do you know?" Why, I sound perfectly ordinary. That's funny.

"He's with the Old One, I think. Clare came to get him. Can't it wait a bit? I'm nearly finished with fixing this dress of mine for Bridie to wear on the voyage, and I know she wants to try it on for you to comment."

"I can't wait." She had to see Colum. Something had gone terribly wrong. They had to leave today, this minute. She had to get home.

Colum was in the yard in front of the cottage. "There's never been a spring so sunny," he said. "The cat and I are basking a bit."

Scarlett's unnatural calm vanished when she saw him, and she was screaming when she reached his side. "Take me home, Colum. Damn you and all the O'Haras and Ireland. I should never have left home."

Her hand was clutched painfully, nails biting into flesh. Crumbled in it was a statement from the sovereign state of Georgia that it had entered into its permanent records the absolute decree of divorce granted to one Rhett Kinnicutt Butler on the grounds of desertion by his wife, one Scarlett O'Hara Butler, by the Military District of South Carolina administered by the Federal Government of the United States of America.

"There is no divorce in South Carolina," said Scarlett. "Two lawyers told me so." She said it again and again, always the same words, until her throat was raw and she could no longer force sound through it. Then her chapped lips formed the words silently while her mind said them. Again and again.

Colum led her to a quiet corner of the vegetable garden. He sat beside her and talked, but he couldn't make her listen, so he took her clenched hands in his for comfort and stayed quiet beside her. Through the light shower that came with twilight. Through the brilliant sunset. Into the darkness. Bridie came looking for them when supper was ready, and Colum sent her away.

"Scarlett's off her head, Bridie. Tell them in the house not to worry, she only needs a bit of time to get over the shock. The news came from America: her husband's grievously sick. She's afraid he'll die without her by his side."

Bridie ran back to report. Scarlett was praying, she said. The family prayed too; their supper was cold when they finally began to eat. "Take a lantern out, Timothy," said Daniel.

The light reflected from Scarlett's glazed eyes. "Kathleen sent a shawl, too," Timothy whispered. Colum nodded, placed it over Scarlett's shoulders, waved Timothy away.

Another hour went by. Stars glowed in the nearly moonless sky; they were brighter than the light from the lantern. There was a brief small cry from a nearby wheat field, then a nearly soundless flutter of wings. An owl had made a kill.

"What am I to do?" Scarlett's rasping voice was loud in the darkness. Colum sighed quietly and thanked God. The worst of the shock was over.

"We'll go home as we planned, Scarlett darling. There's nothing happened that can't be remedied." His voice was calm, certain, soothing.

"Divorced!" There was an alarming rise of hysteria in the cracked sound. Colum chafed her hands briskly.

"What's done can be undone, Scarlett."

"I should have stayed. I'll never forgive myself."

"Whist, now. Should-haves solve nothing. It's the next thing to happen that needs thinking about."

"He'll never take me back. Not if his heart's so hard that he'd divorce me. I kept waiting for him to come after me, Colum, I was so sure he would. How could I have been such a fool? You don't know the all of it. I'm pregnant, Colum. How can I have a baby when I don't have a husband?"

"There, there," said Colum quietly. "Doesn't that take care of it? You've only got to tell him."

Scarlett's hands flew to her belly. Of course! How could she have been such a fool? Jagged laughter tore at her throat. There was no piece of paper ever written that would make Rhett Butler give up his baby. He could have the divorce cancelled, erased from all the records. Rhett could do anything. He'd just proved it again. There was no divorce in South Carolina. Unless Rhett Butler made up his mind to get one.

"I want to go right now, Colum. There must be a ship sailing earlier. I'll go crazy waiting."

"We're leaving early Friday, Scarlett darling, and the ship sails Saturday. If we go tomorrow there'll still be a day to fill before the sailing. Wouldn't you rather spend it here?"

"Oh, no, I've got to know I'm going. Even if it's only partway, I'll be heading home to Rhett. Everything's going to work out, I'll make it work out. It's going to be all right . . . isn't it, Colum? Say that it's going to be all right."

"That it is, Scarlett darling. You should eat

now, at least a cup of milk. With a drop in it, perhaps. You need sleep, too. You have to keep up your strength, for the good of the baby."

"Oh, yes! I will. I'll take wonderful care of myself. But first I've got to see about my frock, and my trunk needs repacking. And, Colum, how will we find a carriage to get to the train?" Her voice was rising again. Colum got up and pulled her to her feet.

"I'll take care of it, with the help of the girls for the trunk. But only if you'll eat something while you see to your frock."

"Yes! Yes, that's what we'll do." She was a little calmer, but still perilously edgy. He'd have to see to it that she drank the milk and whiskey as soon as they reached the house. Poor creature. If only he knew more about women and babies he would feel a lot easier in his mind. She'd been going sleepless and dancing like a dervish of late. Could that bring on a baby too soon? If she lost it, he feared for her reason.

55

Like so many people before him, Colum underestimated the strength of Scarlett O'Hara. She insisted that her baggage be brought from Molly's that night, and she gave orders to Brigid to pack her things while Kathleen fitted her frock on her. "Watch the lacing, Bridie," she said sharply when she put her corset on. "You're going to have to do this on the ship, and I won't be able to see behind me to tell you what to do."

Her feverish manner and ragged voice had already put Bridie in a terror. Scarlett's sharp cry of pain when Kathleen yanked on the laces made Bridie cry out, too.

It doesn't matter that it hurts, Scarlett reminded herself, it always hurts, always has. I'd just forgotten how much. I'll get used to it again after a while. I'm not hurting the baby. I always wore stays as long as I could when I was pregnant, and it was always a lot later than this. I'm not even ten weeks gone yet. I've got to get into my clothes, I've just got to. I'll be on that train tomorrow if it kills me.

"Pull, Kathleen," she gasped. "Pull harder."

Colum walked to Trim and arranged to get the carriage a day earlier. Then he made the rounds, spreading the word about Scarlett's terrible worry. When he was finished it was late and he was tired. But now there'd be no one wondering why the American O'Hara had gone off like a thief in the night without saying goodbye.

She did very well with her goodbyes to the family. The previous day's shock had armored her in a shell of numbness. She broke down only once, when she said goodbye to her grandmother. Or, rather, when Old Katie Scarlett said goodbye to her. "God go with you," the old woman said, "and the saints guide your footsteps. It's happy I am you were here for my birthday, Gerald's girl. The only pity is you'll not be at my wake . . . What are you weeping for, girl? Do you not know there's no party for the living half as grand as a wake? It's a shame to miss it."

Scarlett sat silent in the carriage to Mullingar and in the train to Galway. Bridie was too nervous to speak, but her excited happiness showed in her bright cheeks and large fascinated eyes. She'd never been more than ten miles from her home in all her fifteen years.

When they reached the hotel Bridie stared open-mouthed at its grandeur. "I'll see you ladies to your room," said Colum, "and be back in time to escort you to the dining room. I'm just going to go down to the harbor and arrange about loading the trunks. I'd like to see which staterooms they've given us, too. Now's the time to change if they're not the best."

"I'll go with you," said Scarlett. It was the first time she'd spoken.

"There's no need, Scarlett darling."

"There is for me. I want to see the ship or I won't feel certain it's really there."

Colum humored her. And Bridie asked if she might come, too. The hotel was too overwhelming for her. She didn't want to stay there alone.

The early evening breeze off the water was sweet with salt. Scarlett breathed deeply of it, remembering that Charleston always had salted air. She was unaware of the slow tears rolling down her cheeks. If only they could sail now, at once. Would the captain consider? She touched the pouch of gold between her breasts.

"I'm looking for the *Evening Star,*" Colum said to one of the longshoremen.

"She's down there," the man gestured with his thumb. "Been in just under an hour."

Colum concealed his surprise. The ship had

been due to land thirty hours earlier. No reason to let Scarlett know that the delay might mean trouble.

Gangs were moving methodically to and from the *Evening Star*. She carried cargo as well as passengers. "This is no place for a woman right now, Scarlett darling. Let's go back to the hotel, and I'll come back later."

Scarlett's jaw set. "No. I want to talk to the Captain."

"He'll be too busy to see anyone, even someone as lovely as yourself."

She was in no mood for compliments. "You know him, don't you, Colum? You know everybody. Fix it so I can see him now."

"The man's a stranger to me; I've never laid eyes on him, Scarlett. How should I be knowing him? This is Galway, not County Meath."

A uniformed man came off the *Star*'s gangplank. The two big canvas sacks on his shoulders seemed to burden him not at all; his gait was light and quick, unusual for a man of his size and girth.

"And isn't that Father Colum O'Hara himself?" he bellowed when he came near them. "What finds you so far from Matt O'Toole's bar, Colum?" He heaved one of the sacks to the ground and took off his hat to Scarlett and Bridie. "Didn't I always say that the O'Haras have the devil's own luck with the ladies?" he roared, laughing at his own humor. "Did you tell them you were a priest, Colum?"

Scarlett's smile was perfunctory when she was introduced to Frank Mahoney, and she paid no attention at all to the chain of cousinships that connected him to Maureen's family. She wanted to talk to the Captain!

"I'm just taking the post from America over to the station for sorting tomorrow," said Mahoney. "Will you want a look, Colum, or will you wait till you're back home again to read your perfumed love letters?" He laughed uproariously at his wit.

"That's kind of you, Frank. I'll take a look if you'll let me." Colum untied the sack near his feet, pulled it nearer the tall gas lamp that lighted the pier. He found the envelope from Savannah with ease. "Luck's in my pocket today," he said. "I knew from his last letter that another'd be coming soon from my brother, but I'd given up hope of it. I thank you, Frank. Would you allow me to buy you a pint?" His hand reached into his pocket.

"There's no need. I did it for the pleasure of breaking the English rules." Frank hoisted the sack again. "The God-rotting supervisor will be looking at his gold watch, I can't tarry. Good evening to you, ladies."

There were a half dozen smaller letters in the envelope. Colum flicked through them, searching for Stephen's distinctive handwriting. "Here's one for you, Scarlett," he said. He put the blue envelope in her hand, found Stephen's letter, tore it open. He had just begun to read it when he heard a high, prolonged cry, and felt a weight sliding against him. Before he could throw out his arms, Scarlett was lying at his feet. The blue envelope and thin pages fluttered in her limp hand, then the breeze scattered them across the cobbles. While Colum lifted Scarlett's shoulders and held his fingers to the pulse in her throat, Bridie ran after the pages.

The hackney cab jounced and swayed from the speed of their race back to the hotel. Scarlett's head rolled grotesquely from side to side, even though Colum tried to hold her firmly in his arms. He carried her quickly through the hotel lobby. "Call a doctor," he shouted to the liveried attendants, "and get out of my way." Once in Scarlett's room, he laid her on the bed.

"Come on, Bridie, help me get her clothes off," he said. "We've got to get some breath into her." He took a knife from a leather sheath inside his coat. Bridie's fingers moved nimbly along the buttons on the back of Scarlett's dress.

Colum cut the corset laces. "Now," he said, "help me lift her head up on the pillows, and cover her with something warm." He rubbed Scarlett's arms roughly, slapped her cheeks gently. "Have you got smelling salts?"

"I don't, Colum, nor do she, far's I know."

"The doctor will. I hope it's only a faint."

"She fainted, that's all, Father," said the doctor when he left Scarlett's bedroom, "but it's a deep one. I've left some tonic with the girl for when she comes out of it. These ladies! They will cut off all their circulation for the sake of fashion. Nothing to worry about, though. She'll be fine."

Colum thanked him, paid him, saw him out.

Then he sat heavily on a chair by the lamplit table, put his head in his hands. There was a great deal to worry about, and he questioned whether Scarlett O'Hara would ever be "fine" again. The crumpled, water-spotted pages of the letter were strewn on the table beside him. In their midst was a neatly trimmed clipping from a newspaper. "Yesterday evening," it read, "in a private ceremony at the Confederate Home for Widows and Orphans Miss Anne Hampton was joined in matrimony to Mr. Rhett Butler."

56

Scarlett's mind spiralled up, up, spinning, swirling, up, up out of the black toward consciousness, but some instinct forced it downward again, sliding, slipping back into darkness, away from the unbearable truth lying in wait for her. Again and again it happened, the struggle tiring her so much that she lay exhausted, motionless and pale in the big bed, as if dead.

She dreamed, a dream full of movement and urgency. She was at Twelve Oaks, and it was whole again and beautiful, as it had been before Sherman's torches. The gracious curving staircase turned through space as if magically suspended, and her feet were lightly nimble on its treads. Ashley was ahead of her, climbing, unaware of her cries to stop. "Ashley," she called, "Ashley, wait for me," and she ran after him.

How long the staircase was. She didn't remember it being so tall; it seemed to be growing ever higher as she ran, and Ashley was so far above her. She had to reach him. She didn't know why, but she knew she must, and she ran faster, always faster, until her heart was pounding in her breast. "Ashley!" she cried. "Ashley!" He paused, and she found strength she didn't know she possessed; she climbed, running even faster.

Relief flooded her body and her soul when her hand touched his sleeve. Then he turned toward her, and she screamed without sound. He had no face, only a pale featureless blur.

Then she was falling, tumbling through space, her eyes fixed in terror on the figure above her, her throat straining to scream. But the only sound was laughter, from below, rising like a cloud to surround her and mock her muteness.

I'm going to die, she thought. Terrible pain will crush me and I'll die.

But suddenly, strong arms closed around her and drew her gently from the falling. She knew them, she knew the shoulder that pillowed her head. It was Rhett. Rhett had saved her. She was safe in his embrace. She turned her head, lifted it to look into his eyes. Icy terror paralyzed her whole body. His face was formless, like mist or smoke, like Ashley's. Then the laughter began again, from the blankness that should be Rhett's face.

Scarlett's mind jolted into consciousness, fleeing from horror, and she opened her eyes. Darkness surrounded her, and the unknown. The lamp had burned out, and Bridie was asleep in her chair, unseen in a corner of the huge room. Scarlett stretched out her arms over the expanse of the big, unfamiliar bed. Her fingers touched soft linen, nothing else. The sides of the mattress were too distant to reach. She seemed to be marooned on a strange vastness of softness, without definition. Perhaps it went on forever into the silent darkness— Her throat constricted with fear. She was alone and lost in the dark.

Stop it! Her mind forced panic away, demanded that she take hold of herself. Scarlett carefully pulled her legs up, turned over into a kneeling crouch. Her movements were slow, so as to make no sound. Anything might be out there in the darkness, listening. She crawled with agonized caution until her hands felt the edge of the bed, then down to the hard solidity of the wooden frame.

What a ninnyhammer you are, Scarlett O'Hara, she told herself when tears of relief ran over her cheeks. Of course the bed is strange, and the room. You fainted, like some silly weak vaporish girl, and Colum and Bridie brought you to the hotel. Stop this scaredy-cat nonsense.

Then, like a physical blow, memory attacked her. Rhett was lost to her . . . divorced from her . . . married to Anne Hampton. She couldn't believe it, but she had to, it was true.

Why? Why had he done such a thing? She'd been so sure he loved her. He couldn't have done it, he couldn't.

But he had.

I never knew him. Scarlett heard the words as if she'd spoken them aloud. I never knew him at all. Who was it that I loved? Whose child am I carrying?

748

What's going to become of me?

That night, in the frightening darkness of an unseen hotel room in a country thousands of miles from her homeland, Scarlett O'Hara did the most courageous thing she had ever been called on to do. She faced up to failure.

It's all my fault. I should have gone back to Charleston as soon as I knew I was pregnant. I chose to have fun, and those weeks of fun have cost me the only happiness I really care about. I just didn't think about what Rhett might believe when I ran away, I didn't think past the next day, the next reel. I didn't think at all.

I never have.

All the impetuous, unconsidered errors of her life crowded around Scarlett in the black silence of the night, and she forced herself to look at them. Charles Hamilton—she had married him to spite Ashley, she hadn't cared for him at all. Frank Kennedy—she'd been horrid to him, lied to him about Suellen so that Frank would marry her and give her money to save Tara. Rhett—oh, she'd made too many mistakes to count. She'd married him when she didn't love him, and she'd made no effort to make him happy, she'd never even cared that he wasn't happy—not until it was too late.

Oh, God, forgive me, I never thought once about what I was doing to them, about what they were feeling. I hurt and hurt and hurt all of them, because I didn't stop to think.

Melanie, too, especially Melly. I can't bear to remember how nasty I was to her. I never once felt grateful for the way she loved me and stood up for me. I never even told her I loved her, too, because I didn't think of it until the end, when there was no chance.

Have I ever in my life paid attention to what I was doing? Have I—even once—ever thought about the consequences?

Despair and shame gripped Scarlett's heart. How could she have been such a fool? She despised fools.

Then her hands clenched and her jaw hardened and she stiffened her spine. She would not wallow in picking at the past and feeling sorry for herself. She would not whine—not to anyone else, and not to herself.

She stared at the darkness above her through dry eyes. She wouldn't cry, not now. She'd have the rest of her life to cry. Now she had to think, and think carefully, before she decided what to do.

She had to think about the baby.

For a moment she hated it, hated her thickening waist and the clumsy, heavy body that lay ahead. It was supposed to have given Rhett back to her, and it hadn't. There were things a woman could do—she'd heard of women who had rid themselves of unwanted babies . . .

. . . Rhett would never forgive her if she did that. And what difference did that make? Rhett was gone, forever.

A forbidden sob broke from Scarlett's lips despite all her willpower.

Lost. I lost him. I'm beaten. Rhett won.

Then sudden anger coursed through her, cauterizing her pain, energizing her exhausted body and spirit.

I'm beaten, but I'll get even with you, Rhett Butler, she thought with bitter triumph. I'll hit you harder than you've hit me.

Scarlett laid her hands gently on her belly. Oh, no, she wasn't going to get rid of this baby. She'd take care of it better than any baby in the history of the whole world.

Her mind filled with images of Rhett and Bonnie. He always loved Bonnie more than he loved me. He'd give anything—he'd give his life to have her back. I'll have a new Bonnie, all my own. And when she's old enough—when she loves me, and only me, more than anything or anyone on earth, then I'll let Rhett see her, see what he's missed . . .

What am I thinking? I must be crazy. Only a minute ago I realized how much I hurt him, and I hated myself. Now I'm hating him and planning to hurt him worse. I won't be like that, I won't let myself imagine such things, I won't.

Rhett's gone; I've admitted it. I can't give in to regrets or revenge, that's a waste when what I have to do is make a new life from scratch. I've got to find something fresh, something important, something to live for. I can do it if I put my mind to it.

Throughout the remainder of the night, Scarlett's mind moved methodically along the avenues of possibility. She found dead ends, she found and overcame obstacles, she found surprising corners of memory and of imagination and of maturity.

She remembered her youth and the County and the days before the War. The memories were somehow painless, distant, and she understood that she was no longer that Scarlett, that she could let go of her, permit the old days and their dead to rest.

She concentrated on the future, on realities, on consequences. Her temples began to throb, then to pound, then her whole head ached abominably, but she continued to think.

Just when the first sounds began in the street outside, all the pieces fell into place inside her mind, and Scarlett knew what she was going to do. As soon as enough light filtered through the drawn curtains into the room, Scarlett called out, "Bridie?"

The girl jumped up from the chair, blinking sleep from her eyes. "Thanks be to God you're restored!" she exclaimed. "The doctor left this tonic. I'll just find the spoon, it's on this table somewhere."

Scarlett opened her mouth meekly for the bitter medicine. "There," she said firmly, "I'll have no more of being sick. Open the curtains, it must be day by now. I need some breakfast, my head is aching, and I've got to get my strength back."

It was raining. A real rain, not the misty showers that were customary. Scarlett felt a dark satisfaction.

"Colum will want to know you're better, he's been that worried. Can I tell him to come in?"

"Not now. Tell him I'll want to see him later,

I want to talk to him. But not yet. Go on. Tell him. And ask him to show you how to order up my breakfast."

57

Scarlett forced herself to swallow bite after bite of food, even though she wasn't even aware of what she was eating. As she'd said to Bridie, she needed her strength.

After breakfast she sent Bridie away, with instructions to return after two hours. Then she sat down at the writing table near the window and, with a small frown of concentration, rapidly filled sheet after sheet of thick, creamy, unmarked letter paper.

After she had written, folded, and sealed two letters, she stared at the blank paper in front of her for a long time. She had planned it all out in the dark hours of the night, she knew what she was going to write, but she couldn't bring herself to pick up the pen and begin. Her very marrow shrank from what she had to do.

Scarlett shivered and looked away from the page. Her eyes fell on a pretty little porcelain clock on a nearby table, and she drew in her breath, shocked. So late! Bridie would be back in only forty-five minutes.

I can't put it off any longer, it won't change things no matter how long I do. There's no other way. I've got to write to Uncle Henry, eat humble pie, and ask him sweetly to help me. He's the only one I can trust. Scarlett gritted her teeth and reached for the pen. Her usually neat handwriting was cramped and uneven from strained determination when she put the words on paper that would turn over control of her Atlanta businesses and her precious hoard of gold in the Atlanta bank to Henry Hamilton.

It was like cutting the ground out from under her feet. She felt physically ill, almost dizzy. There was no fear that the old lawyer would cheat her, but there was no chance that he would watch every penny the way she always had. It was one thing to have him collect and bank the receipts from the store and the rent from the saloon. It was another thing altogether to give him control of store inventory and prices, and the amount of rent to charge the saloonkeeper.

Control. She was giving up control of her money, her safety, her success. Just when control was most needed. Buying Carreen's share of Tara was going to dig a deep hole in her accumulated gold, but it was too late now to stop the deal with the Bishop, and Scarlett wouldn't stop it even if she could. Her dream of spending summers at Tara with Rhett was dead now, but Tara was still Tara, and she was determined to make it hers.

Building the houses on the edge of town was another drain on her resources, but it had to be done. If only she wasn't certain that Uncle Henry would agree with everything Sam Colleton suggested, without asking the cost.

Worst of all, she wouldn't know what was going on, for good or for ill. Anything might happen.

"I can't do it!" Scarlett groaned aloud. But she continued to write. She had to do it. She was going to take a long vacation, she wrote, do some travelling. She would be out of touch, with no address where mail could reach her. She looked at the words. They blurred, and she blinked the tears away. None of that, she told herself. It was absolutely essential to cut all ties, or Rhett would be able to track her down. And he must not know about the baby until she chose to tell him.

But how could she bear not knowing what Uncle Henry was doing with her money? Or if the Panic was getting worse, threatening her savings? Or if her house burned down? Or, worse, her store?

She had to bear it, so she would. The pen scratched hurriedly across the pages, detailing instructions and advice that Henry Hamilton would probably disregard.

When Bridie returned, all the letters were on the blotter, folded and sealed. Scarlett was sitting in an armchair, her ruined corset in her lap.

"Oh, I forgot," Bridie moaned. "We had to cut you out, to let the breath into you. What will you have me do? There might be a shop nearby I could go to—"

"Never mind, it's not important," Scarlett said. "You can baste me into a frock, and I'll wear a cloak to hide the stitches in the back. Come on, now, it's getting late, and I've got a lot to do."

Bridie looked at the window. Late, was it? Her country-accustomed eyes could tell it wasn't yet nine in the morning. She went obediently to unpack the sewing kit Kathleen had helped her put together for her new role as lady's maid.

Thirty minutes later, Scarlett knocked on the door of Colum's room. She was hollow-eyed from lack of sleep, but immaculately groomed and perfectly composed. She didn't feel at all tired. The worst was over; now she had things to do. It restored her strength.

She smiled at her cousin when he opened his door. "Will your collar protect your reputation if I come in?" she asked. "I have things to talk about that are private."

Colum bowed and swung the door wide. "A thousand welcomes," he said. "It's good to see you smiling, Scarlett darling."

"It won't be long before I'll be able to laugh, I hope . . . Did the letter from America get lost?"

"No. I have it. Private. I understand what happened."

"Do you?" Scarlett smiled again. "Then you're wiser than I am. I know, but I'll likely never understand. Still, that's neither here nor there." She put the three letters she'd written on a table. "I'll tell you about these in a minute. First I have to tell you that I'm not going with you and Bridie. I'm going to stay in Ireland." She held up her hand. "No, don't say anything. I've thought it all through. There's nothing for me in America any more."

"Ah, no, Scarlett darling, you're being too hasty. Didn't I tell you there's nothing done that can't be undone? Your husband got a divorce once, he'll do it again when you go back and tell him about the baby."

"You're wrong, Colum. Rhett will never divorce Anne. She's his kind, from his people, from Charleston. And besides she's like Melanie. That doesn't mean anything to you, you never knew Melly. But Rhett did. He knew how rare she was long before I did. He respected Melly. She was the only woman he ever did respect, except maybe his mother, and he admired her the way she deserved. This girl he's married is worth ten of me, the same as Melly was, and Rhett knows it. She's worth ten of Rhett, too, but she loves him. Let him carry that cross." There was a savage bitterness in the words.

Ach, the suffering, he thought. There must be a way to help her. "You've got your Tara now, Katie Scarlett, and you've such dreams for it. Won't that comfort you till your heart's healed? You can build the world you want for the child you're carrying, a grand plantation made by his grandfather and his mother. If it's a boy, he can be called Gerald."

"You're not thinking anything I haven't already thought. Thank you, but you can't find an answer if I couldn't, Colum, believe me. One thing, I already have a son, a child you don't know about, if there's inheritance to consider. But the main thing is this baby. I can't go back to Tara to have his baby, I can't take this baby to Tara after it's born. People would never believe it was made in wedlock. They've always thought—in the County and in Atlanta—that I was no better than I should be. And I left Charleston the day after—after the baby was started." Scarlett's face blanched with painful longing. "No one would ever believe it was Rhett's baby. We slept in separate rooms for years. They'd call me a whore and my baby a bastard, and they'd smack their lips with pleasure in the calling."

The ugly words were marked on her twisted mouth.

"Not so, Scarlett, not so. Your husband knows the truth. He'll acknowledge the baby."

Scarlett's eyes flamed. "Oh, he'd acknowledge it all right, and he'd take it from me. Colum, you can't imagine how Rhett is about babies, his babies. He's like a madman with love. And he's got to own the child, be the best loved, be the all. He'd take this baby soon as it had the first breath in its little body. Don't think he couldn't do it, either. He got the divorce when it couldn't be gotten. He'd change any law or make a new one. There's nothing he can't do." She was whispering hoarsely, as if afraid. Her face was contorted with hatred and a wild, unreasoned terror.

Then suddenly, like a veil falling, it changed. It became smooth, and tranquil, except for her blazing green eyes. A smile appeared on her lips; it made Colum O'Hara's spine chill. "This is my baby," said Scarlett. Her quiet low-pitched voice was like a giant cat's purr. "Mine alone. He'll never know about it till I want him to, when it's too late for him. I'm going to pray for a girl. A beautiful blue-eyed girl."

Colum crossed himself.

Scarlett laughed harshly. "Poor Colum. You must have heard about the woman scorned, don't be so shocked. Don't fret, I won't frighten you any more." She smiled, and he could almost believe he'd imagined what he'd seen in her face a moment earlier. Scarlett's smile was open and affectionate.

"I know you're trying to help me, and I'm grateful, Colum, I really am. You've been so good to me, such a good friend, probably the best friend I ever had except Melly. You're like a brother. I always wished I had a brother. I hope you'll always be my friend."

Colum assured her that he would. He thought to himself that he'd never seen a soul so in need of help.

"I want you to take these letters to America for me, please, Colum. This one's to my Aunt Pauline. I want her to know I got her letter so she'll get all the pleasure possible out of her love for telling people 'I told you so.' And this one's to my Atlanta lawyer, there's business I have to settle. Both should be posted in Boston, I don't want anyone to know where I really am. This one I want you to hand-deliver. It'll mean more travel for you, but it's terribly important. It's to the bank in Savannah. I have a pile of gold and my jewelry in their vault, and I'm counting on you to bring it back safe for me. Did Bridie give you the bag I had 'round my neck? Good. That'll do me to get started with. Now I need you to find me a lawyer I can trust, if there is such a thing. I'm going to use Rhett Butler's money. I'm going to buy Ballyhara, where the O'Haras began. This child's going to have a heritage he could never provide. I'll show him a thing or two about roots that go deep."

"Scarlett darling, I beseech you. Wait a bit. We can stay in Galway awhile, with Bridie and me to take care of you. You're not over the shocks. One right on top the other the way they came, it's been too much for you to be making such big decisions."

"You think I've gone crazy, I suppose. Maybe I have. But this is my way, Colum, and I mean to take it. With your help or without it. No reason for you and Bridie to stay, either. I plan to go back to Daniel's tomorrow and ask them to take me in again until Ballyhara's mine. If you're afraid I need looking after, you can surely trust Kathleen and them.

"Come on, Colum," Scarlett said, "admit it. I've got you beat."

He spread his hands and admitted it.

Later he escorted her to the office of an English lawyer with a reputation for successful completion of whatever he put his hand to, and the search for the owner of Ballyhara was set into motion.

The following day Colum went to the Market as soon as the first tables were set up. He took the purchases Scarlett wanted back to the hotel. "Here you are then, Mrs. O'Hara," he said. "Black skirts and shirts and shawl and cloak and stockings for the poor new widow, and I've told Bridie that's what the news was that gave you the collapse. Your husband was taken by sickness before there was time for you to reach his side. And here you are as well—a wee gift from me. I'm thinking that when widow's weeds pull your spirits down, you'll feel better for knowing you've got them on." Colum deposited a heap of bright colored petticoats in Scarlett's lap.

Scarlett smiled. Her eyes brimmed with emotion. "How did you know I was kicking myself for giving all my Irish clothes to the cousins in Adamstown?" She waved at her trunk and valises. "I won't need these things any more. Take them with you and give them to Maureen to dole out."

"That's foolish extravagance and impetuosity, Scarlett."

"Fiddle-dee-dee! I took out my boots and my shimmies. The frocks are no use to me. I'm never going to be squeezed into a corset again, never. I'm Scarlett O'Hara, an Irish lass with a free-swinging skirt and a secret red petticoat. Free, Colum! I'm going to make a world for myself by my rules, not anybody else's. Don't worry about me. I'm going to learn to be happy." Colum averted his eyes from the grimly determined expression on Scarlett's face.

58

The ship's sailing was delayed two days, so Colum and Bridie were able to escort Scarlett to the train station on Sunday morning. First they all went to Mass.

"You must have a word with her, now, Colum," Bridie whispered in his ear when they met in the hallway. She rolled her eyes toward Scarlett.

Colum hid his smile with a cough. Scarlett was dressed like a widowed peasant, even to wearing a shawl instead of a cloak.

"We'll go along with her, Brigid," he said firmly. "She has a right to mourn any way she sees fit."

"But, Colum—this grand English hotel, all the people will be staring, and talking."

"And don't they have their rights, too? Let them stare and say what they will. We'll give no notice." He took Bridie's arm in a firm grasp, offered his other hand to Scarlett. She rested hers elegantly on top of it, as if he were leading her into a ballroom.

When she was seated in her first-class compartment on the train, Colum watched with relish, Bridie with horror, as one group of English travellers after another opened the door to the compartment, then backed away.

"The authorities shouldn't allow those people to buy first-class tickets," one woman said loudly to her husband.

Scarlett's hand shot out to hold the door before the Anglo could close it. She called out to Colum, who was on the platform nearby. "Faith! I forgot my basket of boiled taties, Father. Will you say a prayer to the Blessed Virgin that there'll be a peddler selling some food on this train?" Her brogue was so exaggerated that Colum could barely understand the words. He was still laughing when a station attendant closed the door, and the train began to move. The English couple, he was pleased to see, abandoned all dignity in their scramble into another compartment.

Scarlett waved goodbye, smiling, as her window moved out of his sight.

Then she sat back in her seat and allowed her

face to relax, permitted a single tear to escape. She was bone tired and dreading the return to Adamstown. Daniel's two-room cottage had seemed quaint and delightfully different from all she was accustomed to, as long as she was on a vacation visit. Now it was a cramped, crowded house with no luxuries, and it was the only place she could call home—for who knew how long. The lawyer might not be able to find the owner of Ballyhara. The owner might not be willing to sell. The price might be more, even, than all the money Rhett had given her.

Her carefully thought-out plan was riddled with holes, and she had no certainty about anything.

I won't think about it now, there's nothing I can do about any of those things. At least nobody'll be crowding in here wanting to chatter at me. Scarlett folded up the arms separating the three deeply cushioned seats, stretched out with a sigh, and fell asleep, her ticket on the floor where the conductor could see it. She had made a plan, and she was going to see it through as far as she could. It would be a lot easier if she wasn't tired half to death.

The first step proceeded without a hitch. She bought a pony and trap in Mullingar and drove it home to Adamstown. It wasn't as stylish a rig as Molly's; the trap was distinctly shabby looking. But the pony was younger and larger and stronger. And she'd made a start.

The family were shocked when she returned, and sympathetic for her loss in the best possible way. Once expressed, they never again spoke of their feelings; instead they asked was there anything they could do for her.

"You can teach me," said Scarlett. "I want to learn about an Irish farm." She followed Daniel and his sons through their work routines. She even set her jaw and forced herself to learn how to handle cattle, including milking the cow. After she'd learned all she could about Daniel's farm, Scarlett put herself out to charm Molly, then Molly's loathsome husband, Robert. His farm was five times the size of Daniel's. After Robert it was the turn of his boss, Mr. Alderson, manager of the Earl's entire estate. Not even in the days when she was captivating every man in Clayton County had Scarlett been so charming. Or worked so hard. Or succeeded so well. She had no time to notice the austerity of the cottage. All that mattered was the soft mattress at the end of the long, long summer day of work.

After a month, she knew almost as much about Adamstown as Alderson, and she'd identified at least six ways it could be improved. It was just about that time that she received the letter from her Galway lawyer.

The widow of Ballyhara's deceased owner had remarried only a year after his death and had herself died five years ago. Her heir and eldest son, now twenty-seven, lived in England where he was also heir to the estate of his father, who was still living. He had said he would give consideration to any offer in excess of fifteen thousand pounds. Scarlett studied the copy of the survey map of Ballyhara that was attached to the letter. It was much bigger than she'd thought.

Why, it's both sides of the road to Trim. And there's another river. The boundary's the Boyne on this side and—she squinted at the tiny lettering—the Knightsbrook on the other. What an elegant name. Knightsbrook. Two rivers. I've got to have it. But—fifteen thousand pounds!

She already knew from Alderson that ten pounds was a price paid only for prime growing land, and a high price at that. Eight was more like it, seven and a half for a shrewd bargainer. Ballyhara had a sizable area of bog, too. Useful for fuel, there was enough peat to last a few centuries. But nothing grew on bog, and the fields around it were too acid for wheat. Plus the land had gone to ruin in thirty years. It all needed clearing of scrub growth and tap-rooted weeds. She shouldn't pay more than four, four and a half. For 1,240 acres, that came to £4,960 or £5,580 at the most. There was the house, of course; it was huge. Not that she cared. The buildings in the town were more important. Forty-six of them all told, plus two churches. Five of the houses were quite grand, two dozen were only cottages.

But all were deserted. Likely to stay that way, too, with no one tending to the estate. Taken all in all, ten thousand pounds would be more than fair. He'd be lucky to get it. Ten thousand pounds—that was fifty thousand dollars! Scarlett was horrified.

I've got to start thinking in real money, I get too careless otherwise. Ten thousand doesn't sound like all that much of anything, but fifty thousand dollars is different. I know that's a fortune. With all that scrimping and saving and sharp dealing at the lumber mills and the store . . . and selling the mills outright . . . and the rent for the saloon . . . and never spending a penny I didn't absolutely have to, year in and year out, in ten years I only managed to put together a little over thirty thousand dollars. And I wouldn't have half that if Rhett hadn't paid for everything for almost the last seven years. Uncle Henry says I'm a rich woman with my thirty thousand, and I reckon he's right. Those houses I'm building don't cost more than a hundred to put up. What on earth kind of people have fifty thousand dollars to pay for a ramshackle ghost town and unworked land?

People like Rhett Butler, that's who. And I've got five hundred thousand of his dollars. To buy back the land stolen from my people. Ballyhara wasn't just land, it was O'Hara land. How could she even think about what she should or shouldn't pay? Scarlett made a firm offer of fifteen thousand pounds—take it or leave it.

After her letter was in the post, she shook all over, from head to toe. Suppose Colum didn't come back with her gold in time? There was no way of knowing how long the lawyer would take or when Colum would return. She barely said goodbye to Matt O'Toole after she gave him the letter. She was in a hurry.

She walked as quickly as the uneven ground would allow, wishing for rain. The tall thick hedges held the June heat in the narrow path between them. She had no hat to keep her head cool and to protect her skin from the sun. She almost never wore one; the frequent showers and the clouds that preceded and followed them made hats unnecessary. As for parasols, they were only ornaments in Ireland.

When she reached the ford over the Boyne she tucked up her skirts and stood in the water until her body was cooled. Then she went to the tower.

During the month she'd been back at Daniel's, the tower had become very important to her. She always went there when she was worried about anything or bothered or sad. Its great stones held heat and cool both; she could lay her hands on them or her cheek against them and find the solace and comfort she needed in its enduring ancient solidity. Sometimes she talked to it as if it were her father. More rarely she stretched her arms over its stones and wept upon it. She never heard a sound other than her own voice and the song of birds and the whisper of the river. She never sensed the presence of the eyes that were watching her.

Colum returned to Ireland on June 18. He sent a telegram from Galway: WILL ARRIVE TWO FIVE JUNE WITH SAVANNAH GOODS. The village was in an uproar. There had never been a telegram in Adamstown. There had never been a rider from Trim who was so uninterested in Matt O'Toole's porter, or a horse so swift carrying a rider.

When, two hours later, a second rider galloped into the village on an even more noteworthy horse, people's excitement knew no bounds. An-

other telegram for Scarlett from Galway. OFFER
ACCEPTED STOP LETTER AND CONTRACT FOLLOW.

It took little discussion before the villagers
agreed to do the only sensible thing. O'Toole's
and the smithy would close. The doctor would
close his door. Father Danaher would be spokes-
man, and they would all walk up to Daniel
O'Hara's to find out what was going on.

Scarlett had driven out in her pony trap, they
learned, and no more, because Kathleen knew
no more than they did. But everyone got to hold
and read the telegrams. Scarlett had left them
on the table for all the world to see.

Scarlett drove the tortuous roads to Tara with
a jubilant heart. Now she could really begin. Her
plan was clear in her head, each step following
logically upon the previous one. This trip to Tara
was not one of the steps; it had come into her
mind when the second telegram arrived, more
as a compulsion than as an impulse. It was com-
pellingly necessary on this glorious sunlit day to
see from Tara's hill the sweet green land that was
now her chosen home.

There were many more sheep grazing today
than when she'd been here before. She looked
over their wide backs and thought about wool.
No one grazed sheep in Adamstown; she'd have
to learn about the problems and profits of raising
sheep from a fresh source.

Scarlett stopped in her tracks. There were
people on the mounds that had once been the
great banqueting hall of Tara. She'd expected
to be alone. They're English too, damn them

for the interlopers they are. Resentment of the English was part of every Irishman's life, and Scarlett had absorbed it with the bread she ate and the music she danced to. These picnickers had no right to spread rugs and a tablecloth where the High Kings of Ireland had once dined, or to talk in their honking voices where harps had played.

Particularly when that spot was where Scarlett O'Hara intended to stand, solitary, to look at her country. She glowered with frustration at the dandified men in their straw hats and the women with their flowered silk parasols.

I won't let them spoil my day, I'll go where they're out of my sight. She walked to the twice-ringed mound that had been the wall-encircled house of King Cormac, builder of the banquet hall. The Lia Fail was here, the stone of destiny. Scarlett leaned against it. Colum had been shocked when she did that the day he first brought her to Tara. The Lia Fail was the coronation test of the ancient kings, he told her. If it cried aloud, the man being tested was acceptable as Ireland's High King.

She'd been so strangely elated that day that nothing would have surprised her, not even if the weathered granite pillar had called her by name. As, of course, it had not. It was almost as tall as she was; the top made a good resting place for the hollow at the base of her skull. She looked dreamily at the racing clouds above her in the blue sky and felt the wind lifting the loose locks of hair from her forehead and temples. The English voices were now only muted background to the gentle tinkling bells on the necks of some of the sheep. So peaceful. Maybe that's why I needed to come to Tara. I've been so busy I'd forgotten to be happy, and that was the most important part of my plan. Can I be happy in Ireland? Can I make it my real home?

There is happiness here in the free life I live. And how much more there'll be when my plan is complete. The hard part is done, the part that other people controlled. Now it's all up to me, the way I want it. And there's so much to do! She smiled at the breeze.

The sun slipped in and out of the clouds, and the lush long grass smelled richly alive. Scarlett's back slid down the stone and she sat on the green. Maybe she'd find a shamrock; Colum said they grew more thickly here than any place in Ireland. She'd tried lots of grassy patches, but never yet seen the unmistakable Irish clover. On an impulse Scarlett rolled down her black stockings and took them off. How white her feet looked. Ugh! She pulled her skirts up above her knees to let the sun warm her legs and feet. The yellow and red petticoats under her black skirt made her smile again. Colum had been right about that.

Scarlett wiggled her toes in the breeze.

What was that? Her head snapped erect.

And the tiny stir of life moved again in her body. "Oh," she whispered, and again, "Oh." She placed her hands gently over the small swelling under her skirts. The only thing she could feel was the bulky folded wool. It was no surprise that the quickening wasn't touchable; Scarlett knew it would be many weeks before her hands could feel the kicking.

She stood, facing the wind, and thrust out her cradled belly. Green and gold fields and summer-thick green trees filled the world as far as her eyes could see. "All this is yours, little Irish baby," she said. "Your mother will give it to you. By herself!" Scarlett could feel the cool windblown grass beneath her feet, and the warm earth beneath the grass.

She knelt then and ripped up a tuft of grass. Her face was unearthly when she dug into the ground beneath it with her nails, when she rubbed the moist fragrant earth in circles over her belly, when she said, "Yours, your green high Tara."

They were talking about Scarlett in Daniel's house. That was nothing new; Scarlett had been the villagers' chief topic of conversation ever since she first arrived from America. Kathleen took no offense, why should she? Scarlett fascinated and mystified her too. She had no trouble understanding Scarlett's decision to stay in Ireland. "Wasn't I that heartsore my own self," she said to one and all, "missing the mists and the soft earth and all in that hot, closed-in city? When she saw what was better, she knew not to give it up."

"Is it true, then, Kathleen that her husband beat her something wonderful, and she ran from him to save her baby?"

"Not at all, Clare O'Gorman, and who'd be spreading such terrible lies as that?" Peggy Monaghan was indignant. "It's a well-known fact that the sickness that took him in the end was already upon him, and he sent her away lest it reach into her womb."

"It's a terrible thing to be a widow and all alone with a baby on the way," sighed Kate O'Toole.

"Not so terrible as it might be," said Kathleen, the knowledgeable one, "not when you're richer than the Queen of England."

Everyone settled more comfortably in their seats around the fire. Now they were coming to it. Of all the intriguing speculation about Scarlett, the most enjoyable was to talk about her money.

And wasn't it a grand thing to see a fortune in Irish hands for once instead of the English?

None of them knew that the richest days of gossip were just about to begin.

Scarlett flapped the reins of the pony's back. "Get a move on," she said, "this baby's in a hurry for a home." She was on her way to Ballyhara at last. Until everything was certain about buying it she hadn't allowed herself to go any farther than the tower. Now she could look closely, see what she had.

"My houses in my town . . . my churches and my bars and my post office . . . my bog and my fields and my two rivers . . . What a wonderful lot there is to do!"

She was determined that the baby would be born in the place that would be its home. The Big House at Ballyhara. But everything else had to be done, too. Fields were most important. And a smithy in town to repair hinges and fashion plows. And leaks mended, windows reglazed, doors replaced on their hinges. The deterioration would have to be stopped immediately, now that the property was hers.

And the baby's, of course. Scarlett concentrated on the life within her, but there was no movement. "Smart child," she said aloud. "Sleep while you can. We're going to be busy all the time from now on." She only had twenty weeks to work in before the birth. It wasn't hard to calculate the date. Nine months from February 14, Saint Valentine's Day. Scarlett's mouth twisted. What a joke that was . . . She wouldn't think about that now—or ever. She had to keep her mind on November 14 and the work to be done before then. She smiled and started to sing.

When first I saw sweet Peggy,
'twas on a market day.
A low backed car she drove
and sat upon a truss of hay.
But when that hay was blooming grass
and deck'd with flow'rs of spring,
No flow'r was there that could compare
to the blooming girl I sing.
As she sat in her low backed car
The man at the turnpike bar
Never asked for the toll
But just rubbed his ould poll
And look'd after the low backed car . . .

What a good thing it was to be happy! This

excited anticipation and these unexpected good spirits definitely added up to happiness. She'd said, back in Galway, that she was going to be happy, and she was.

"To be sure," Scarlett added aloud, and she laughed at herself.

59

Colum was surprised when Scarlett met his train in Mullingar. Scarlett was surprised when he stepped out of the baggage car and not the coach. And when his companion stepped out after him. "This is Liam Ryan, Scarlett darling, Jim Ryan's brother." Liam was a big man, as big as the O'Hara men—Colum excepted—and he was dressed in the green uniform of the Royal Irish Constabulary. How on earth could Colum befriend one of them? she thought. The Constabulary were even more despised than the English militia, because they policed and arrested and punished their own people, under orders from the English.

Did Colum have the gold, Scarlett wanted to know. He did, and Liam Ryan with his rifle to guard it. "I've escorted many a package in my day," Colum said, "but never a time have I been nervous until now."

"I've got men from the bank to take it," said Scarlett. "I'm using Mullingar for safety, it's got the biggest garrison of military." She'd learned to loathe the soldiers, but where the safety of her gold was involved she was glad to use them. She could use the bank in Trim for convenience—for small sums.

As soon as she saw the gold stored in the security of the vault and signed the papers for the purchase of Ballyhara, Scarlett took Colum's arm and hurried him out onto the street.

"I've a pony trap, we can get going right away. There's so much to do, Colum. I've got to find a blacksmith right away and get the smithy going. O'Gorman's no good, he's too lazy. Will you help me find one? He'll be well paid to move to Ballyhara and well paid after he gets there, for there'll be all the work he can handle. I've bought scythes and axes and shovels, but they'll need sharpening. Oh! I need workmen too, to clear the fields, and carpenters to mend the houses, and glaziers and roofers and painters—everything imaginable!" Her cheeks were pink with excitement, her eyes shining. She was incredibly beautiful in her peasant black clothing.

Colum extricated himself from her grasp, then took her arm in his firm hand. "All will be done, Scarlett darling, and almost as quickly as you'd like. But not on an empty stomach. We'll be going now to Jim Ryan's. It's seldom he gets to see his Galway brother, and it's rare to find as grand a cook as Mrs. Ryan."

Scarlett made an impatient gesture. Then she forced herself to calm down. Colum's authority was quietly impressive. Also, she did try to remember to eat properly and drink quantities of milk for the baby's sake. The subtle movements could be felt many times every day now.

But after dinner she couldn't contain her anger when Colum said he wouldn't come with her at once. She had so much to show him, to talk about, to plan, and she wanted it all now!

"I've things to do in Mullingar," he said with placid, unshakable firmness. "I'll be home in three days, you've my word on it. I'll even set the time. Two in the afternoon we'll meet at Daniel's."

"We'll meet at Ballyhara," said Scarlett. "I've already moved in. It's the yellow house halfway down the street." She turned her back on him then and strode angrily away to get her trap.

Late that evening, after Jim Ryan's bar was closed for the night, its door was left on the latch for the men who quietly slipped in one by one to meet in a room upstairs. Colum laid out in detail the things they had to do. "It's a God-sent opportunity," he said with incandescent fervor, "an entire town of our own. All Fenian men, all their skills concentrated in one place, where the English would never think to look. The whole world already thinks my cousin's daft for paying such a price for property she might have bought for nothing just to spare the owner paying the taxes on it. She's American, too, a race known to be peculiar. The English are too busy laughing at her to be suspicious of what goes on in her property. We've long needed a secure headquarters. Scarlett's begging us to take it, though she doesn't know it."

Colum rode into Ballyhara's weed-grown street

at 2:43. Scarlett was standing in front of her house, arms akimbo. "You're late," she accused.

"Ah, but sure and you'll forgive me, Scarlett darling, when I tell you that following me on the road comes your smith and his wagon with forge and bellows and all that."

Scarlett's house was a perfect portrait of her, work first and comfort later, if at all. Colum observed everything with deceptively lazy eyes. The parlor's broken windows were neatly covered with squares of oiled paper glued over the panes. Farm implements of new shiny steel were stacked in the corners of the room. The floors were swept clean but not polished. The kitchen had a plain narrow wooden bedstead with a thick straw mattress covered by linen sheets and a woolen blanket. There was a small turf fire in the big stone fireplace. The only cooking implements were an iron kettle and small pot. Above, on the mantelshelf, were tins of tea and oatmeal, two cups, saucers, spoons, and a box of matches. The only chair in the room was placed by a big table under the window. The table held a large account book, open, with entries in Scarlett's neat hand. Two large oil lamps, a pot of ink, a box of pens and pen wipes, and a stack of paper were at the back of the table. A larger stack of paper was near the front. The sheets were covered with notes and calculations, held down with a large washed stone. The surveyor's map of Ballyhara was nailed to the wall nearby. So was a mirror, above a shelf that held Scarlett's silver-backed comb and brushes, and silver-topped jars of hairpins, powder, rouge, and rosewater-glycerine cream. Colum restrained a smile when he saw them. But when he saw the pistol next to them, he turned angrily. "You could get jailed for owning that weapon," he said, too loudly.

"Fiddle-dee-dee," she said, "the Captain of the militia gave it to me. A woman living alone who's known to have a lot of gold should have some protection, he said. He'd have posted one of his sissy-britches soldiers at the door if I'd let him."

Colum's laughter made her eyebrows rise. She didn't think what she'd said was all that amusing.

The larder shelves held butter, milk, sugar, a rack with two plates in it, a bowl of eggs, a ham hanging from the ceiling, and a loaf of stale bread. Buckets of water stood in a corner with a tin of lamp oil and a washstand outfitted with bowl, pitcher, soap dish and soap, and a towel rack with one towel on it. Scarlett's clothes hung from nails on the wall.

"You're not using the upstairs, then," Colum commented.

"Why should I? I have all I need here."

"You've done wonders, Colum, I'm really impressed." Scarlett stood in the center of Ballyhara's famously wide street and looked at the activity everywhere along the length of it. Hammering could be heard from every direction; there was the smell of fresh paint; new windows sparkled in a dozen buildings; and in front of her, a man on a ladder was putting up a gold-lettered sign above the door of the building that Colum had first earmarked for work.

"Did we really need to finish the bar first?" Scarlett asked. She'd been asking the same thing ever since Colum made the announcement.

"You'll find more willing workers if there's a place for them to have a pint when their work's done," he said for the thousandth time.

"So you've said, every time you opened your mouth, but I still can't see why it won't just make them worse. Why, if I didn't keep after them, nothing would ever get done on time. They'd be just like them!" Scarlett jerked her thumb at the groups of interested observers along the street. "They should be back wherever they come from, doing their own work, not watching while other people work."

"Scarlett darling, it's the national character to take the pleasures life has to offer first and worry about duties later. It's what gives the Irish their charm and their happiness."

"Well, I don't think it's charming, and it doesn't make me one bit happy. It's practically August already and not one single field's been cleared yet. How can I possibly plant in the spring if the fields aren't cleared and manured in the fall?"

"You've got months yet, Scarlett darling. Just look what you've already done in only weeks."

Scarlett looked. The frown disappeared from her forehead and she smiled. "That's true," she said.

Colum smiled with her. He said nothing about the soothing and pressuring he had had to do to prevent the men putting down their tools and walking away. They didn't take well to being bossed by a woman, especially one as demanding as Scarlett. If the underground links of the Fenian Brotherhood hadn't committed them to the resurrection of Ballyhara, he didn't know how many would be left, even with Scarlett paying above-average wages.

He, too, looked along the busy street. It would be a good life for these men, and others too, he thought, when Ballyhara was restored. Already he had two more barkeepers asking to come in, and a man who owned a profitable dry-goods store in Bective wanted to relocate. The houses, even the smallest ones, were better than the hovels occupied now by most of the farm laborers he'd chosen. They were as eager as Scarlett for the roofs and windows to be repaired so that they could leave their landlords and get started on the fields of Ballyhara.

Scarlett darted into her house and out again, gloves and covered milk jug in her hand. "I hope you'll keep everybody working and not have a big celebration to open the bar while I'm gone," she said. "I'll ride over to Daniel's for some bread and milk." Colum promised to keep the work going. He said nothing about the folly of her jouncing along on a saddleless pony in her condition. She'd already bitten his head off for suggesting that it was unwise.

"For pity's sake, Colum, I'm barely past five months. That's hardly pregnant at all!"

She was more worried than she'd ever let him

know. None of her earlier babies had given her so much trouble. She had an ache in her lower back that never went away, and occasionally there were spots of blood on her underclothes or her sheets that made her heart turn over. She washed them out with the strongest soap she had, the one meant for floors and walls, as if she could wash out the unknown cause together with the spots. Dr. Meade had warned her after her miscarriage that the fall had injured her severely, and she had taken an unconscionably long time to recover, but she refused to admit there might be anything really wrong. The baby wouldn't be kicking so strong if it wasn't healthy. And she had no time to be vaporish.

Frequent trips had created a well-defined track through Ballyhara's overgrown fields to the ford. The pony followed it almost by itself now, and Scarlett had time to think. She'd better get a horse pretty soon, she was getting too heavy for the pony. That was different, too. She'd never gotten so big before when she was carrying a baby. Suppose she had twins! Wouldn't that just be something? That would really pay Rhett back. She already had two rivers on her place to his one at Dunmore Landing. Nothing would please her more than to have two babies, just in case Anne had one. The thought of Rhett giving Anne a baby was too painful to bear. Scarlett turned her eyes and her mind onto the fields of Ballyhara. She just had to get started on them, she just had to, no matter what Colum said.

As always she paused by the tower before she rode to the ford. What good builders those long-ago O'Haras were, and how smart. Old Daniel had actually talked for almost a full minute when she mentioned how sorry she was that the stairs were gone. There were never any stairs outside, he said, only inside. A ladder gave people access to the door, set twelve feet up from the ground. When danger came people could run to the tower, pull the ladder up behind them, and fire arrows or throw stones or pour hot oil down on the attackers from the narrow slit windows, safe from assault by enemies below them.

One of these days I'll haul a ladder back here and have a look inside. I hope there aren't any bats. I do hate bats. Why didn't Saint Patrick get rid of them too when he was cleaning out the snakes?

Scarlett looked in on her grandmother, found her asleep, then stuck her head in Daniel's door. "Scarlett! What a happy thing it is to see you. Come in, do, and tell us the latest wonders you've done at Ballyhara." Kathleen reached for the teapot. "I was hoping you'd come. There's warm barm brack." Three of the village women were there. Scarlett pulled up a stool and joined them.

"How's the baby?" asked Mary Helen.

"Perfect," said Scarlett. She looked around the familiar kitchen. It was friendly and comfortable but she could hardly wait for Kathleen to have her new kitchen, the one in the largest house in Ballyhara town.

Scarlett had already mentally designated the houses she was going to give the family. They'd all have grand, spacious homes. Colum's was the smallest, only one of the gate houses where the estate adjoined the town, but he had chosen it for himself so she wouldn't argue. And he'd never have a family anyhow, being a priest. But there were much bigger houses in the town. She'd chosen the best for Daniel because Kathleen was with him and they'd probably want Grandmother with them too, plus there had to be room for Kathleen's family when she married, which she'd easily do with the dowry Scarlett would give her, including the house. Then a house for each of Daniel's and Patrick's sons too, even spooky Sean who lived with Grandmother. Plus farmland, as much as they wanted, so that they'd be able to marry, too. She thought it was terrible the way that young men and women couldn't get married because they had no land and no money to get any. The English landlords were truly heartless, the way they kept the Irish ground down under their heels. The Irish did all the labor to grow the wheat or oats, fatten the cattle and sheep, and then they had to sell to the English, at the prices the English set, for the English to export the grain and stock to England, where they'd make more money for more Englishmen. No farmer ever had much left when his rent was paid, and that could be raised at the whim of the English. It was worse than sharecropping, it was like being under the Yankees after the War, when they took anything they wanted, then boosted the taxes on Tara sky high. No wonder the Irish hated the English so. She'd hate the Yankees till her dying day.

But soon the O'Haras would be free of all that.

They'd be so surprised when she told them! It wouldn't be much longer, either. When the houses were finished and the fields ready—she wasn't about to give them halfway-done presents, she wanted everything to be perfect. They'd been so good to her. And they were her family.

The gifts were her cherished secret; she hadn't even told Colum yet. She'd been hugging it to herself ever since the night in Galway when the plan came to her. It added to her pleasure every time she looked at Ballyhara's street that she knew just which houses would be O'Hara houses. She'd have lots of places to go then, lots of fires to pull up a stool to, lots of homes with cousins in them for her baby to play with and go to school with and have huge holiday celebrations with at the Big House.

Because naturally that's where she and the baby would be. In the huge, enormous, fantastically elegant Big House. Bigger than the house on East Battery, bigger than the house at Dunmore Landing, even before the Yankees burned nine-tenths of it. And with land that had been O'Hara land before anybody ever heard of Dunmore Landing or Charleston, South Carolina, or Rhett Butler. How his eyes would bug out, how his heart would break when he saw his beautiful daughter—oh, please let it be a girl—in her beautiful home, and she was an O'Hara and her mother's child alone.

Scarlett cherished the daydream of sweet revenge. But that was years away, and the O'Hara houses were soon. As soon as she could make them ready.

60

Colum appeared at Scarlett's door late in August when the sky was still rosy with dawn. Ten burly men stood silently behind him in the mist-heavy half light. "Here are the men to clear your fields," he said. "Are you happy at last?"

She screeched with delight. "Let me get my shawl against the damp," she said, "and I'll be right out. Take them down to the first field beyond the gate." She hadn't finished dressing yet, her hair was all tumbled and her feet were bare. She tried to hurry but excitement made her clumsy. She'd been waiting so long! And it was getting more difficult every day to get her boots on. My grief, I'm as big as a house already. I must be going to have triplets.

The devil take it! Scarlett piled her unbrushed hair into a wad and stabbed hairpins in it to hold it, then she grabbed her shawl and ran along the street with her feet bare.

The men were grouped glumly around Colum on the weed-choked drive inside the open gate. "Never seen such a sight . . . those be more like trees than weeds . . . looks like all nettles to me . . . a man could spend a lifetime an acre . . ."

"A fine lot you are," Scarlett said clearly. "Are you afraid to get your hands dirty?"

They looked at her with disdain. They'd all heard about the little woman with the driving ways, nothing womanly about her.

"We were discussing the best way to get started," Colum said soothingly.

Scarlett was in no mood to be placated. "You don't get started at all if you discuss long enough. I'll show you how you get started." She put her left hand on the lower curve of her distended belly to support it, then she leaned over, and her right hand grasped a big handful of nettles at the base. With a grunt and a heave she ripped them from the earth. "There," she said contemptuously, "now you're started." She threw the spiny plants at the men's feet. Blood was oozing from wounds all over her hand. Scarlett spit in her palm then wiped her hand on her black widow's skirt and walked heavily away on her pale, fragile-looking feet.

The men stared at her back. First one, then another, then all of them took their hats off.

They were not the only ones who had learned to respect Scarlett O'Hara. Painters had discovered that she would climb the tallest ladder they had, moving like a crab to accommodate her shape, in order to point out overlooked spots or uneven brush strokes. Carpenters who attempted to use inadequate numbers of nails would find her hammering when they came to work. She slammed newly made or newly hung doors with a bang "that would wake the dead" to test hinges, and stood up inside chimneys with a flaming bundle of rushes in her hand to look for soot and test how well they drew. The roofers reported with awe that "only Father O'Hara's strong arm kept her from walking the roof tree and counting the slates." She drove everyone hard and herself harder.

And when it grew too dark to work, there were three free pints at the bar for every man who had stayed on the job that late, and even when their drinking and bragging and complaining was done, they could see her through her kitchen window bending over her papers and writing by lamplight.

"Did you wash your hands?" Colum asked when he entered the kitchen.

"Yes, and put some salve on too. It was a mess. I just get so mad sometimes I don't think what I'm doing. I'm fixing breakfast. Want some?"

Colum sniffed the air. "Porridge without salt? I'd rather have some boiled nettles."

Scarlett grinned. "Then pick your own. I'm leaving out salt for a while, it'll keep my ankles from swelling the way they've taken to doing lately . . . not that it's going to make much difference soon. I can't see my boots to lace them now, I won't be able to reach them in a week or two. I've figured it out, Colum. I'm having a litter, not a baby."

"I've 'figured it out,' as you say, myself. You need a woman to help you." He expected Scarlett to protest; she automatically denied every suggestion that she couldn't do everything herself. But she agreed. Colum smiled; he had just the woman for the job, he said, someone who could help with everything, even the bookkeeping if necessary. An older woman, but not too old to accept Scarlett's rule, and not so spineless that she wouldn't stand up to her when necessary. She was experienced at managing work and people and money, too. In fact, she was housekeeper at a Big House of an estate near Laracor, on the other side of Trim. She had knowledge of childbirth, though she was no midwife. She'd had six children herself. She could come to Scarlett now, to take care of her and this house until the Big House was repaired. Then she'd hire the women needed to run it, and she'd run them.

"You'll admit, Scarlett darling, that you've nothing in America quite like a Big House in Ireland. It needs a practiced hand. You'll need a steward, too, to manage the butler and the footmen and like that, plus a head stableman to rule the grooms, and a dozen or so gardeners with one to boss them—"

"Stop!" Scarlett was shaking her head furiously. "I'm not planning to start a kingdom here. I need a woman to help me, I grant you that, but I'll only be using a few rooms of that pile of stone up there to start with. So you'll have to ask this paragon of yours if she's willing to give up her high-and-mighty position. I doubt if she'll say yes."

"I'll ask her, then." Colum was sure she would agree, even if she had to scrub floors. Rosaleen Mary Fitzpatrick was the sister of a Fenian who'd been executed by the English, and the daughter and granddaughter of men who'd gone down in the Ballyhara coffin ships. She was the most passionate and dedicated member of his inner circle of insurgents.

Scarlett took three boiled eggs out of the bubbling water in the kettle, then poured water into the teapot. "You could have an egg or two if you're too proud to eat my porridge," she offered. "Without salt, of course."

Colum declined.

"Good, I'm hungry." She spooned porridge onto a plate, cracked the eggs and added them. The yolks were runny. Colum averted his eyes.

Scarlett ate hungrily and efficiently, talking rapidly between mouthfuls. She told him her plan for the whole family, to have all the O'Haras living in moderate luxury at Ballyhara.

Colum waited until she finished eating before he said, "They won't do it. They've been farming the land they're on for nearly two hundred years."

"Of course they will. Everybody always wants better than they've got, Colum."

He shook his head in reply.

"I'll prove you wrong. I'll ask them right now! No, that's not in my plan. I want to have everything ready first."

"Scarlett, I brought you your farmers. This morning."

"Those lazybones!"

"You didn't tell me what you were planning. I hired those men. Their wives and children are on their way here right now to move into the cottages at the end of the street. They've quit the landlords they had before."

Scarlett bit her lip. "That's all right," she said after a minute. "I'm putting the family in houses, anyhow, not cottages. These men can work for the cousins."

Colum opened his mouth, then closed it. There

was no point in arguing. And he was certain that Daniel would never move.

Colum called Scarlett down from the ladder she was on, inspecting fresh plaster, in midafternoon. "I want you to see what your 'lazybones' have done," he said.

Scarlett was so overjoyed that tears came to her eyes. There was a scythed and sickled path wide enough to drive the trap where she had ridden the pony before. Now she could visit Kathleen again, and get milk for her tea and her oatmeal. She'd felt too heavy to ride for the past week and more.

"I'll go this very minute," she said.

"Then let me lace up your boots."

"No, they press on my ankles. I'll go barefoot, now that I've got a cart to ride in and a road to ride on. You can hitch up the pony, though."

Colum watched her drive off with a feeling of relief. He went back to his gate house and his books, his pipe, and his glass of good whiskey with a sense of a reward well earned. Scarlett O'Hara was the most exhausting individual of any gender, any age, any nationality he'd ever met.

And why, he wondered, does my mind always add "poor lamb" to every opinion I have of her?

She looked like a poor lamb indeed when she burst in on him just before summer's late darkness fell. The family had—very kindly and very often—turned down her invitation and then her appeals to come to Ballyhara.

Colum had come to believe that Scarlett had become almost incapable of tears. She had not cried when she'd received the notice of the divorce, nor even when the ultimate blow fell with the announcement that Rhett had married again. But on this warm rainy night in August, she sobbed and wept for hours, until she fell asleep on his comfortable couch, a luxury unknown in her Spartan two rooms. He covered her with a lightweight coverlet and went to his bedroom. He was glad that she had found release for her grief, but he feared she would not see her outburst in the same light. So he left her alone; she might prefer not to see him for a few days. Strong people didn't like witnesses to their weak moments.

He was mistaken. Again, he thought. Would he ever really get to know this woman? In the morning, he found Scarlett was sitting at his kitchen table, eating the only eggs he had. "You're right, you know, Colum. They are a lot better with salt . . . And you might start thinking about good tenants for my houses. They'll have to be prosperous because everything in those houses is the best there is, and I expect a good rent."

Scarlett was profoundly hurt, even though she didn't show it again and never referred to it. She continued to ride over to Daniel's in the trap several times a week, and she worked just as hard as ever on Ballyhara, although her pregnancy was increasingly burdensome. By the end of September the town was done. Every building was clean, freshly painted inside and out, with strong doors and good chimneys and tight roofs. The population was growing by leaps and bounds.

There were two more bars, a cobbler's shop for boots and harness, the dry-goods store that had moved from Bective, an elderly priest for the small Catholic church, two teachers for the school, which would begin classes as soon as authorization came from Dublin, a nervous young lawyer who was hoping to build a practice, with an even more nervous young wife who peered from behind her lace curtains at the people on the street. The farmers' children played games in the street, their wives sat on their doorsteps and gossiped, the post rider from Trim came every day to leave the mail with the scholarly gentleman who had opened a shop with books and writing paper and ink in the one-room annex to the dry-goods store. There was a promise that an official post office would be designated after the first of the year, and a doctor had taken the lease on the largest of the houses, to begin occupancy the first week of November.

This last was the best news of all for Scarlett. The only hospital in the area was at the Work House in Dunshauglin, fourteen miles away. She'd never seen a Work House, the last refuge of the penniless, and she hoped she never would. She firmly believed in work instead of begging, but she'd rather not have to look at the unfortunates who ended up there. And it was certainly no way for a baby to start life.

Her own doctor. That was more her style. He'd be right at hand, too, for croup and chicken pox and all those things babies always got. Now all she had to do was put out word that she'd want a wet nurse in mid-November.

And get the house ready.

"Where is this perfect Fitzpatrick woman of yours, Colum? I thought you told me she'd agreed to come a month ago.

"She did agree a month ago. And gave a month's notice, like any responsible person has to do. She'll be here on October first, that's Thursday next. I've offered her the use of my house."

"Oh, have you? I thought she was supposed to housekeep me. Why doesn't she stay here?"

"Because, Scarlett darling, your house is the only building in Ballyhara that hasn't been repaired."

Scarlett looked around her kitchen-workroom in surprise. She had never paid any attention before to how it looked; it was only temporary, a convenient spot for watching the work on the town.

"It is disgusting, isn't it?" she said. "We'd best get the house done fast so I can move." She smiled, but with difficulty. "The truth is, Colum, I'm nearly worn out. I'll be glad to be done with the work so I can rest some."

What Scarlett didn't say was that the work had become just that—work—after the cousins said they wouldn't move. It had taken the joy out of rebuilding the O'Hara lands when the O'Haras wouldn't be enjoying them. She'd tried and tried to figure out why they'd turned her down. The only answer that made sense to her was that they didn't want to be too close to her, that they didn't really love her, despite all their kindnesses and warmth. She felt alone now, even when she was with them, even when she was with Colum. She'd believed he was her friend, but he'd told her they'd never come. He knew them, was one of them.

Her back hurt all the time now. Her legs, too, and her feet and ankles were so swollen that walking was agony. She wished she wasn't having the baby. It was making her ill, and it had given her the idea of buying Ballyhara in the first place. And she had six—no, six and a half—more weeks of this.

If I had the energy, I'd bawl, she thought despondently. But she found another weak smile for Colum.

He looks like he wants to say something and doesn't know what to say. Well, I can't help him. I'm clean out of conversation.

There was a knock on the street door. "I'll go," Colum said. That's right, run like a rabbit.

He came back to the kitchen with a package in his hand and an unconvincing smile on his face. "That was Mrs. Flanagan, from the store. The tobacco you ordered for Grandmother came in, she brought it over. I'll take it to her for you."

"No." Scarlett heaved herself to her feet. "She asked me to get it. It's the only thing she's ever asked for. You hitch up the pony and help me into the trap. I want to take it to her."

"I'll come with you."

"Colum, there's barely room on the seat for me, let alone the two of us. Just bring me the trap and get me in it. Please."

794

And how I'll get out of it, God only knows.

Scarlett wasn't very happy when her cousin Sean came out from her grandmother's cottage at the sound of her arrival. "Spooky Sean" she called him to herself, just as she always thought of her cousin Stephen in Savannah as "Spooky Stephen."

They gave her the shivers because they always watched silently while the other O'Haras were talking and laughing. She didn't care much for people who didn't talk and laugh. Or for people who seemed to be thinking secret thoughts. When Sean offered his arm to help her walk into the house, she sidestepped clumsily to avoid him.

"No need," she said gaily, "I can manage just fine." Even more than Stephen, Sean made her nervous. All failure made Scarlett nervous, and Sean was the O'Hara who had failed. He was Patrick's third son. The eldest died, Jamie worked in Trim instead of farming, so when Patrick died in 1861, Sean inherited the farm. He was "only" thirty-two at the time, and the "only" was an excuse he thought adequate for all his troubles. He mismanaged everything so badly that there was a real chance the lease would be lost.

Daniel, as the eldest, called Patrick's children together. Although he was sixty-seven, Daniel had more faith in himself than in Sean or in his own son Seamus, who was also "only" thirty-two. He'd worked beside his brother all his life; now that Patrick was gone, he wouldn't hold his tongue and watch their life's work go, too. Sean would have to go instead.

Sean went. But not away. He had lived with his grandmother for twelve years now, letting her take care of him. He refused to do any work on Daniel's farm. He made Scarlett's hackles rise. She walked away from him as fast as her bare swollen feet would carry her.

"Gerald's girl!" said her grandmother. "It's glad I am to see you, Young Katie Scarlett."

Scarlett believed her. She always believed her grandmother. "I've brought your tobacco, Old Katie Scarlett," she said with genuine cheerfulness.

"What a grand thing to do. Will you have a pipe with me?"

"No, thank you, Grandmother. I'm not quite that Irish yet."

"Ach, that's a shame. Well, I'm as Irish as God makes them. Fill a pipe for me, then."

The tiny cottage was quiet except for the sound of her grandmother's soft sucking pulls on the stem of her pipe. Scarlett put her feet up on a stool and closed her eyes. The peacefulness was balm.

When she heard shouting outside, she was furious. Couldn't she have a half hour's quiet? She hurried as best she could into the farmyard, ready to scream at whoever was making the racket.

What she saw was so terrifying that she forgot her anger, the pain in her back, the agony in her feet, everything except her fear. There were soldiers in Daniel's farmyard, and constables, and an officer on a curvetting horse with a naked saber in his hand. The soldiers were setting up a tripod of tree trunks. She hobbled across to join Kathleen, who was weeping in the doorway.

"Here's another one of them," said one of the soldiers. "Look at her. These miserable Irish breed like rabbits. Why don't they learn to wear shoes instead?"

"You don't need shoes in bed," another said, "or under a bush." The Englishman laughed. The constables looked down at the ground.

"You!" Scarlett called loudly. "You on the horse. What are you and those common creatures doing at this farm?"

"Are you addressing me, girl?" The officer looked down his long nose.

She lifted her chin and stared at him with cold green eyes.

"I am not a girl, sir, and you are not a gentleman, even if you pretend to be an officer."

His mouth dropped open. Now his nose is hardly noticeable at all. I guess that's because fish don't have noses, and he looks like a landed fish. The hot joy of combat filled her with energy.

"But you're not Irish," said the officer. "Are you that American?"

"What I am is none of your concern. What you're doing here is my concern. Explain yourself."

The officer remembered who he was. His mouth closed and his back stiffened. Scarlett noticed that the soldiers were stiff all over, and staring, first at her, then at their officer. The constables were looking from the corners of their eyes.

"I am executing an order of Her Majesty's Government to evict the people resident on this farm for nonpayment of rent." He waved a scrolled paper.

Scarlett's heart was in her throat. She lifted her chin higher. Beyond the soldiers she could see Daniel and his sons running from the fields with pitchforks and cudgels, ready to fight.

"There's obviously been a mistake," Scarlett said. "What amount is supposed to be unpaid?" Hurry, she thought, for God's sake hurry, you long-nosed fool. If any O'Hara man—or men—hit a soldier, they'd be sent to prison, or worse.

Everything seemed to slow down. The officer took forever to open the scroll. Daniel and Seamus and Thomas and Patrick and Timothy moved as if they were under water. Scarlett unbuttoned her shirt. Her fingers felt like sausages, the buttons like uncontrollable lumps of suet.

"Thirty-one pounds eight shillings and nine pence," said the officer. It was taking him an hour to say every word, Scarlett was sure. Then she heard the shouting from the field, saw the big O'Hara men running, waving fists and weapons. She clawed frantically at the string around her neck, at the pouch of money when it appeared, at its tightly closed neck.

Her fingers felt the coins, the folded bank notes, and she breathed a silent prayer of thanks.

She was carrying the wages of all the workers at Ballyhara. More than fifty pounds. Now she was as cool and unhurried as melting ice cream.

She lifted the cord from her neck, over her head, and she jingled the pouch in her hand. "There's extra for your trouble, you ill-bred cad," she said. Her arm was strong and her aim true. The pouch struck the officer in the mouth. Shillings and pence scattered down the front of his tunic and onto the ground. "Clean up the mess you've made," said Scarlett, "and take away that trash you brought with you!"

She turned her back on the soldiers. "For the love of God, Kathleen," she whispered, "get over in the field and stop the men before there's real trouble."

Later Scarlett confronted Old Daniel. She was livid. Suppose she hadn't brought the tobacco? Suppose it hadn't come in today? She glared at her uncle, then burst out, "Why didn't you tell me you needed money? I'd have been glad to give it to you."

"The O'Haras don't take charity," said Daniel.

" 'Charity'? It's not charity when it's your own family, Uncle Daniel."

Daniel looked at her with old, old eyes. "What isn't earned by your own hands is charity," he said. "We've heard your history, Young Scarlett O'Hara. When my brother Gerald lost his wits, why did you not call upon his brothers in Savannah? They're all your own family."

Scarlett's lips trembled. He was right. She hadn't asked or accepted help from anyone. She had had to carry the burden alone. Her pride wouldn't permit any yielding, any weakness.

"And in the Famine?" She had to know. "Pa would have sent you all he had. Uncle James and Uncle Andrew too."

"We were wrong. We thought it, would end. When we learned what it was, we'd left it too late."

She looked at her uncle's thin straight shoulders, the proud tilt of his head. And she understood. She would have done the same. She understood, too, why she'd been wrong to offer Ballyhara as a substitute for land he'd farmed all his life. It made all his work meaningless, and the work of his sons, his brothers, his father, his father's father.

"Robert raised the rent, didn't he? Because I made that smart remark about his gloves. He was going to pay me back through you."

"Robert's a greedy man. There's no saying that it's anything to do with you."

"Will you allow me to help? It would be an honor."

Scarlett saw approval in Old Daniel's eyes. Then a glint of humor. "There's Patrick's boy Michael. He works in the stables at the Big House. He has grand ideas about breeding horses. He could apprentice in the Curragh did he have the fee."

"I thank you," said Scarlett formally.

"Will anybody be wanting supper or should I throw it to the pigs?" Kathleen said with pretended anger.

"I'm so hungry I could cry," said Scarlett. "I'm

a truly terrible cook, you should know." I'm happy, she thought. I hurt from head to toe, but I'm happy. If this baby isn't proud to be an O'Hara, I'll wring its neck.

61

"You need a cook," said Mrs. Fitzpatrick. "I do not myself cook well."

"Me neither," said Scarlett. Mrs. Fitzpatrick looked at her. "I don't cook well either," Scarlett said hastily. She didn't think she was going to like this woman, no matter what Colum said. Right off the bat when I asked her what her name was, she answered "Mrs. Fitzpatrick." She knew I meant her first name. I've never called a servant "Mrs." or "Mr." or "Miss." But then I've never had a white servant. Kathleen as lady's maid doesn't count, or Bridie. They're my cousins. I'm glad Mrs. Fitzpatrick is no kin of mine.

Mrs. Fitzpatrick was a tall woman, at least half a head taller than Scarlett. She was not thin, but there was no fat on her; she looked solid as a tree. It was impossible to tell how old she was. Her skin was flawless, like the skin of most Irish women, product of the constant soft moisture in the air. It had the look of heavy cream. The color in her cheeks was dramatic, a streak of deep rose rather than an all-over blush. Her nose was thick, a peasant's nose, but with prominent bone, and her lips were a thin wide slash. Most startling and distinctive of all were her dark, surprisingly delicate eyebrows. They formed a perfect thin feathered arch above her blue eyes, strange contrast to her snow-white hair. She was wearing a severe gray gown with plain white linen collar and cuffs. Her strong capable hands were folded in her lap. Scarlett felt like sitting on her own roughened hands. Mrs. Fitzgerald's were smooth, her short nails buffed, her cuticles perfect white half-moons.

There was an English seasoning in her Irish voice. Still soft, but it had lost some music to clipped consonants.

I know what she is, Scarlett realized, she's businesslike. The thought made her feel better. She could deal with a businesswoman whether she liked her or not.

"I am confident that you will find my services useful, Mrs. O'Hara," said Mrs. Fitzpatrick, and there was no possible doubt that Mrs. Fitzpatrick was confident about everything she did or said. Scarlett felt irritated. Was this woman challenging her? Did she intend to run things?

Mrs. Fitzpatrick was still speaking: "I would like to express my pleasure at meeting you and in working for you. I shall be honored to be housekeeper for The O'Hara."

What did she mean?

The dark brows arched. "Do you not know? Everyone is talking of nothing else." Mrs. Fitzgerald's thin wide mouth parted in a gleaming smile. "No woman in our lifetime has ever done it, perhaps no woman in many hundreds of years. They're calling you The O'Hara, head of the family O'Hara, in all its branches and ramifications. In the days of the High Kings, each family had its leader, representative, champion. Some distant ancestor of yours was The O'Hara who stood for all the valor and pride of all other O'Haras. Today that designation has been reborn for you."

"I don't understand. What do I have to do?"

"You've already done it. You're respected and admired, trusted and honored. The title's awarded, not inherited. You have only to be what you are. You are The O'Hara."

"I think I'll have a cup of tea," said Scarlett weakly. She didn't know what Mrs. Fitzpatrick was talking about. Was she joking? Mocking? No, she could tell this was not a woman who made jokes. What did it mean, "The" O'Hara? Scarlett tried it silently on her tongue. The O'Hara. It was like a drumbeat. Deep, hidden, buried, primitive, something within her kindled. The O'Hara. A light grew in her pale tired eyes, making them glow green, fire emerald. The O'Hara.

"I'll have to think about that tomorrow . . . and every day for the rest of my life. Oh, I feel so different, so strong ". . . only be what you are . . . " she said. What does that mean? The O'Hara.

"Your tea, Mrs. O'Hara."

"Thank you, Mrs. Fitzpatrick." Somehow the intimidating self-confidence of the older woman had become admirable, not irritating. Scarlett took the cup and looked into the other woman's eyes. "Please have some tea with me," she said. "We need to talk about a cook and other things. We have only six weeks, and a lot to do."

Scarlett had never been in the Big House. Mrs.

Fitzpatrick hid her astonishment and her own curiosity about it. She'd been housekeeper to a prominent family, directress of a very big house, but it had not approached the Big House at Ballyhara in magnificence. She helped Scarlett turn the huge tarnished brass key in the great rusted lock and threw her weight against the door. "Mildew," she said when the smell hit them. "We'll need an army of women with pails and scrubbing brushes. Let's have a look at the kitchen first. No cook worth having is going to come to a house without a first-class kitchen. This part of the house can be done later. Just ignore the paper falling off the walls and the animal droppings on the floor. The cook won't even see these rooms."

Curved colonnades connected two large wing buildings to the main block of the house. They followed the one to the east first and found themselves in a large corner room. Doors opened onto interior corridors that led to more rooms and a staircase to yet more rooms. "You'll put your steward to work here," said Mrs. Fitzpatrick when they returned to the large corner room. "The other rooms will do for servants and storerooms. Stewards do not live in the Big House; you'll have to give him a dwelling in the town, a large one, in keeping with his position as manager of the estate. This is obviously the Estate Office."

Scarlett didn't reply at once. She was seeing another office in her mind, and the wing of another Big House. "Bachelor guests" had used the wing at Dunmore Landing, Rhett had said. Well, she didn't plan to have a dozen rooms' worth of bachelor guests, or any other kind of guests. But she could certainly use an office, just like Rhett's. She'd get the carpenter to make her a big desk, twice as big as Rhett's, and she'd hang the estate maps on the walls, and she'd look out the window just the way he did. But she would see the clean-cut stones of Ballyhara, not a pile of burnt bricks, and she'd have fields of wheat, not a passel of flower bushes.

"I'll be the steward at Ballyhara, Mrs. Fitzpatrick. I don't intend to have a stranger manage my place."

"I mean no disrespect, Mrs. O'Hara, but you don't know what you're saying. It's a full-time occupation. Not only maintaining the stores and supplies, but also listening to complaints and settling disputes between workers and farmers and the people of the town."

"I'll do it. We'll put benches along that hallway for people to sit on, and I'll see anyone with a problem on the first Sunday of every month after Mass." Scarlett's firm jaw told the housekeeper that there was no point in arguing.

"And Mrs. Fitzpatrick—there will be no spittoons, is that clear?"

Mrs. Fitzpatrick nodded, even though she had never heard the word before. In Ireland, tobacco was smoked in a pipe, not chewed.

"Good," said Scarlett. "Now let's find this kitchen you're so worried about. It must be in the other wing."

"Do you feel up to walking all that way?" asked Mrs. Fitzpatrick.

"It has to be done," said Scarlett. Walking was torture for her feet and her back, but there was no question about doing it. She was appalled by the condition of the house. How would it ever be done in six weeks? It has to be, that's all. The baby must be born in the Big House.

"Magnificent," was Mrs. Fitzpatrick's pronouncement about the kitchen. The room was cavernous and two stories high, with broken skylights in the roof. Scarlett was sure she'd never been in a ballroom half as large. A tremendous stone chimney nearly covered the wall at the far end of the room. Doors on each side of it led to a stone-sinked scullery on the north side, an empty room on the south. "The cook can sleep here, that's good and that"—Mrs. Fitzpatrick pointed upward—"is the most intelligent arrangement I've ever seen." A balustraded gallery ran the length of the kitchen wall at the second-story level. "The rooms above the cook's and the scullery will be mine. The kitchen maids and the cook will never know when I might be watching them. That should keep them alert. The gallery must connect to the second floor of the house itself. You can come over, too, to see what's going on in the kitchen below. They'll keep working all the time."

"Why couldn't I just go in the kitchen and see?"

"Because they'd stop working to curtsey and wait for orders while the food scorched."

"You keep talking about 'they' and 'maids,' Mrs. Fitzpatrick. What happened to the cook? I thought we were going to get one woman."

Mrs. Fitzpatrick's hand gestured to the expanses of floor and wall and windows. "One woman couldn't manage all this. No competent woman would try. I'd like to see the storerooms and laundry, probably in the basement. Do you want to come down?"

"Not really. I'll sit outside, away from the smell." She found a door. It led out into an overgrown walled garden. Scarlett backed into the kitchen. A second door opened onto the colonnade. She lowered herself to the paved floor and leaned against a column. A heavy fatigue pressed on her. She'd no idea the house would need so much work. From the outside it looked as if it was almost intact.

The baby kicked and she absentmindedly pushed the foot or whatever back down. "Hey, little baby," she murmured, "what do you think of this? They're calling your mother 'The O'Hara.' I hope you're impressed. I sure am." Scarlett closed her eyes to take it all in.

Mrs. Fitzpatrick came out, brushing cobwebs from her clothes. "It will do," she said succinctly. "Now what we both need is a good meal. We'll go to Kennedy's bar."

"The bar? Ladies don't go unescorted to bars."

Mrs. Fitzpatrick smiled. "It's your bar, Mrs. O'Hara. You can go there whenever you please. You can go anywhere at all, whenever you like. You are The O'Hara."

Scarlett turned the thought over in her mind. This wasn't Charleston or Atlanta. Why shouldn't she go to the bar? Hadn't she nailed down half the floorboards herself? And didn't everyone say that Mrs. Kennedy, the barkeeper's wife, made a pastry for her meat pies that would melt in your mouth?

The weather turned rainy, not the brief showers or misty days that Scarlett had gotten used to, but real torrents of rain that lasted sometimes for three to four hours. The farmers complained about the soil compacting if they walked on the newly cleared fields to spread the cartloads of manure Scarlett had bought. But Scarlett, forcing herself to walk daily to check the progress at the Big House, blessed the mud on the ungravelled drive because it cushioned her swollen feet. She gave up boots altogether and kept a bucket of water inside her front door to rinse her feet when she came in. Colum laughed when he saw it. "The Irish in you is strengthening every day, Scarlett darling. Did you learn that from Kathleen?"

"From the cousins when they came in from the fields. They always washed the earth off their feet. I figured it was because Kathleen would be mad if they tracked up her clean floor."

"Not a bit of it. They did it because Irishmen— and women too—have done it as long as anyone's great-grandfather can remember. Do you shout 'seachain' before you throw the water out?"

"Don't be silly, of course not. I don't put a bowl of milk on the doorstep every night either. I don't believe I'm likely to drench any fairies or give them supper. That's all childish superstition."

"So you say. But one day a pooka's going to

get you for your insolence." He looked nervously under her bed and pillow.

Scarlett had to laugh. "All right, I'll bite, Colum. What's a pooka? Second cousin to a leprechaun, I suppose."

"The leprechauns would shudder at the suggestion. A pooka is a fearful creature, malicious and sly. He'll curdle your cream in an instant or tangle your hair with your own brush."

"Or swell my ankles, I guess. That's as malicious as anything I've ever been through."

"Poor lamb. How much longer?"

"About three weeks. I've told Mrs. Fitzpatrick to clean out a room for me and order in a bed."

"Are you finding her helpful, Scarlett?"

She had to admit she was. Mrs. Fitzpatrick wasn't so taken with her position that she minded working hard herself. Plenty of times Scarlett had found her scrubbing the stone floor and stone sinks in the kitchen herself to show the maids how to do it.

"But Colum, she's been spending money like there's no end to it. Three maids I've got up there already, just to get things nice enough so that a cook will be willing to come. And a stove the likes of which I've never seen, all kinds of burners and ovens and a well thing for hot water. It cost almost a hundred pounds, and ten more to haul it from the railroad. Then, after all that, nothing would do but to have the smith make all kinds of cranes and spits and hooks for the fireplace. Just in case the cook doesn't like stove ovens for some things. Cooks must be more spoiled than the Queen."

"More useful, too. You'll be glad when you sit down to your first good meal in your own dining room."

"So you say. I'm happy enough with Mrs. Kennedy's meat pies. I ate three last night. One for me and two for this elephant inside me. Oh, I'll be so happy when this is over . . . Colum?" He'd been away, and Scarlett didn't feel as easy with him as she used to, but she needed to ask him anyhow. "Have you heard about this 'The O'Hara' business?"

He had and he was proud of her and he thought it was deserved. "You're a remarkable woman, Scarlett O'Hara. No one who knows you thinks otherwise. You've ridden over blows that would fell a lesser woman—or a man as well. And you've never moaned or asked pity." He smiled roguishly. "You've done what's near miraculous, too, getting all these Irish to work the way they have. And spitting in the eyes of the English officer— well, they say you put out the sight in one of them from a hundred paces."

"That's not true!"

"And why should a grand tale be tarnished by the truth? Old Daniel himself was the first who called you The O'Hara, and he was there."

Old Daniel? Scarlett flushed with pleasure.

"You'll be swapping stories with Finn Mac-Cool's ghost one day soon, to hear the talk. The whole countryside's richer for having you here." Colum's light tone darkened. "There's one thing I want to caution you about, Scarlett. Don't turn up your nose at people's beliefs; it's insulting to them."

"I never do! I go to Mass every Sunday, even though Father Flynn looks like he might fall asleep any minute."

"I'm not speaking of the Church. I'm talking about the fairies and the pookas and that. One of the mighty deeds you're praised for is moving back to the O'Hara land when everyone knows it's haunted by the ghost of the young lord."

"You can't be serious."

"I can, and I am. It matters not whether you believe or not. The Irish people do. If you mock what they believe in, you're spitting in their eyes."

Scarlett could see that, silly as it all was. "I'll hold my tongue, and I won't laugh, unless it's at you, but I'm not going to holler before I empty the bucket."

"You don't have to. They're saying you're so respectful you whisper real soft."

Scarlett laughed until she disturbed the baby and was kicked mightily. "Now look what you did, Colum. My insides are black and blue. But it's worth it. I haven't laughed like that since you went away. Stay home for a while, will you?"

"That I will. I want to be one of the first to see this elephant child of yours. I'm hoping you'll name me a godfather."

"Can you do that? I'm counting on you to baptize him or her or them."

Colum's smile vanished. "I cannot do that, Scarlett darling. Anything else you ask me, though it be to fetch you the moon for a bauble. I do not perform the sacraments."

"Whyever not? That's your job."

"No, Scarlett, that's the job of a parish priest

or on special occasions a bishop or archbishop or more. I'm a missionary priest, working to ease the sufferings of the poor. I perform no sacraments."

"You could make an exception."

"That I could not, and that's an end of it. But the grandest of godfathers I'll be, if asked, and see to it that Father Flynn doesn't drop the babe in the font or on the floor, and I'll teach him his catechism with such eloquence that he'll think he's learning a limerick instead. Do ask me, Scarlett darling, or you'll break my yearning heart."

"Of course I'll ask you."

"Then I've got what I came for. Now I can go beg a meal in a house that adds salt."

"Go on, then. I'm going to rest until the rain stops then go see Grandmother and Kathleen while I can. The Boyne's almost too high to ford already."

"One more promise, and I'll stop fussing you. Stay in your house Saturday evening with your door shut tight and your curtains drawn. It's All Hallows' Eve, and the Irish believe all the fairies are out from all the time since the world began. And, as well, goblins and ghosts and spirits carrying their heads under their arms and all manner of unnatural things. Pay heed to the customs and close yourself in safe from seeing them. None of Mrs. Kennedy's meat pies. Boil some eggs. Or, if you're really feeling Irish, have a supper of whiskey washed down with ale."

"No wonder they see spooks! But I'll do as you say. Why don't you come over?"

"And be in the house all night with a seductive lass like you? I'd have me collar taken away."

Scarlett stuck out her tongue at him. Seductive, indeed. To an elephant maybe.

The trap wobbled alarmingly when she crossed the ford and she decided not to stay long at Daniel's. Her grandmother was looking drowsy, so Scarlett didn't sit down. "I just stopped in for a second, Grandmother, I won't keep you from your nap."

"Come kiss me goodbye, then, Young Katie Scarlett. You're a lovely girl to be sure." Scarlett embraced the tough tiny body gently, kissed the old cheek firmly. Almost at once her grandmother's chin dropped on her chest.

"Kathleen, I can't stay long, the river's rising so. By the time it's down I doubt I'll be able to get in the trap at all. Have you ever seen such a giant baby?"

"Yes, I have, but you don't want to hear it. Every baby's the only baby is my observation of mothers. You'll have a minute for a bite and a cup of tea?"

"I shouldn't but I will. May I take Daniel's chair? It's the biggest."

"You're welcome to it. Daniel's never been so warm towards any of us as he is to you."

The O'Hara, thought Scarlett. It warmed her even more than the tea and the smoke-smelling clean fire.

"Have you the time to see Grandmother, Scarlett?" Kathleen put a stool beside Daniel's chair with tea and cake on it.

"I went there first. She's napping now."

"That's grand, then. It would be a pity if she missed telling you goodbye. She's taken out her shroud from the box where she keeps her treasures. She'll be dead ere long."

Scarlett stared at Kathleen's serene face. How can she say things like that in the same tone of voice as talking about the weather or something? And then drink tea and eat cake as calm as you please?

"We're all hoping for a few dry days first," Kathleen went on. "The roads are that deep in mud people will have trouble getting to the wake. But we'll have to take what comes." She noticed Scarlett's horror and misinterpreted it.

"We'll all miss her, Scarlett, but she's ready to go, and those that live as long as Old Katie Scarlett have a way of knowing when their time is on them. Let me fill your cup, what's left must be cold."

It clattered in its saucer as Scarlett put it down. "I really can't, Kathleen, I've got to cross the ford, I have to go."

"You'll send word when the pains start? I'll be happy to stay with you."

"I will, and thank you. Will you give me a hand up in the trap?"

"Will you take a bit of cake for later? I can wrap it in no time."

"No, no, thank you, truly, but I'm worried about the water."

I'm more fretful about going crazy, Scarlett thought when she drove off. Colum was right, the Irish are all spook-minded. Who'd have thought it of Kathleen? And my own grandmother having a shroud all ready. Heaven only knows what they get up to on Halloween. I'm going to lock the door and nail it shut, too. This stuff is giving me the shivers.

The pony lost its footing for a long terrifying moment crossing the ford.

Might as well face it, no more travel for me until after the baby. I wish I'd accepted the cake.

62

The three country girls stood in the wide doorway of the Big House bedroom Scarlett had chosen for her own. All were wearing big homespun aprons and wide-ruffled mobcaps, but that was the only thing about them that was the same. Annie Doyle was as small and round as a puppy, Mary Moran as tall and ungainly as a scarecrow, Peggy Quinn as neat and pretty as an expensive doll. They were holding hands and crowded together. "We'll be going now if it's all the same to you, Mrs. Fitzpatrick, before the heavy rain starts in," said Peggy. The other girls nodded vigorously.

"Very well," said Mrs. Fitzpatrick, "but come in early Monday to make up the time."

"Oh, yes, miss," they chorused, dropping clumsy curtseys. Their shoes made a racket on the stairs.

"Sometimes I despair," sighed Mrs. Fitzpatrick, "but I've made good maids out of sorrier material than that. At least they're willing. Even the rain wouldn't have bothered them if today wasn't Halloween. I suppose they think if clouds darken the sky it's the same as nightfall." She looked at the gold watch pinned on her bosom. "It's only a little after two . . . Let's get back where we were. I'm afraid that all this wet will keep us from finishing, Mrs. O'Hara. I wish it weren't so, but I'm not going to lie to you. We've got all the old paper off the walls and everything scrubbed and fresh. But you need new plaster in some spots, and that means dry walls. Then time for the plaster to dry afterwards before the wall is painted or papered. Two weeks just isn't enough."

Scarlett's jaw hardened. "I am going to have my baby in this house, Mrs. Fitzpatrick. I told you that from the beginning."

Her anger flowed right off Mrs. Fitzpatrick's sleekness. "I have a suggestion—" said the house-keeper.

"As long as it's not to go someplace else."

"On the contrary. I believe with a good fire on the hearth and some cheerful thick curtains at the windows, the bare walls won't be offensive at all."

Scarlett looked at the gray, waterstained, cracked plaster with gloom. "It looks horrible," she said.

"A rug and furniture will make a great differ-ence. I've got a surprise for you. We found it in the attic. Come look." She opened the door to an adjoining room.

Scarlett walked heavily to the door, then

burst out laughing. "God's nightgown! What is it?"

"It's called a State Bed. Isn't it remarkable?" She laughed with Scarlett while they stared at the extraordinary object in the center of the room. It was immense, at least ten feet long and eight wide. Four enormously thick dark oak posts carved to look like Greek goddesses supported a tester frame on their laurel-wreathed heads. The head and footboards were carved in deep relief with scenes of toga-clad men in heroic postures beneath bowers of intertwined grapes and flowers. At the rounded peak of the tall headboard there was a flaking, gold-leafed crown.

"What kind of giant do you reckon slept in it?" asked Scarlett.

"It was probably made especially for a visit from the Viceroy."

"Who's that?"

"The head of the government in Ireland."

"Well, I'll say this for it, it's big enough for this giant baby I'm having. If the doctor can reach far enough to catch it when it comes."

"Then shall I order the mattress made? There's a man in Trim who can do it in two days."

"Yes, do. Sheets, too, or else sew some together. My grief, I could sleep for a week in that thing and never hit the same spot twice."

"With a tester and curtains on it, it will be like a room in itself."

"Room? It'll be like a house. And you're right, once I'm in it I won't notice the nasty walls at all. You're a marvel, Mrs. Fitzpatrick. I feel better than I have in months. Can you imagine what it'll do to a baby to enter the world in that? It'll probably grow to be ten feet tall!"

Their laughter was companionable as they walked slowly down the scrubbed granite staircase to the ground floor. This'll have to be carpeted first thing, Scarlett thought. Or maybe I'll just close up the second floor altogether. These rooms are so big I'd have a huge house on the one floor alone. If Mrs. Fitzpatrick and the cook will allow it. Why not? No sense being The O'Hara if I can't have things my way. Scarlett stood aside to let Mrs. Fitzpatrick open the heavy front door.

They looked out into a sheet of water. "Damn," said Scarlett.

"This is a downpour, not a rain," the housekeeper said. "It can't last at this rate. Would you like a cup of tea? The kitchen's warm and dry; I've had the stove going all day to test it."

"Might as well." She followed Mrs. Fitzpatrick's thoughtfully slow steps to the kitchen.

"This is all new," said Scarlett suspiciously. She didn't like any spending without her approval. And the cushioned chairs by the stove looked too cozy altogether for cooks and maids who were supposed to be working. "What did this cost?" She tapped the big heavy wood table.

"A few bars of soap. It was in the tack room, filthy dirty. The chairs are from Colum's house. He suggested we woo the cook into comfort before she sees the rest of the house. I've made a list of furniture for her room. It's on the table there for your approval."

Scarlett felt guilty. Then she suspected that she

was supposed to feel guilty, and she felt cross. "What about all those lists I approved last week? When are those things coming?"

"Most of them are here, in the scullery. I was planning to unpack them next week, with the cook. Most of them have their own systems for arranging utensils and such."

Scarlett felt cross again. Her back was hurting worse than usual. She put her hands over the pain. Then a new pain ripped through her side and down her leg, shoving the back pain into insignificance. She grabbed the side of the table for support and stared dumbly at the liquid streaming down her legs and across her bare feet to pool on the scrubbed stone floor.

"The water broke," she said at last, "and it's red." She looked at the window and the heavy rain outside. "Sorry, Mrs. Fitzpatrick, you're going to get very wet. Get me up on this table and give me something to soak up the water . . . or the blood. Then high-tail it to the bar or the store and tell somebody to ride hell for leather for a doctor. I'm about to have a baby."

The ripping pain was not repeated. With the chair cushions under her head and the small of her back, Scarlett was quite comfortable. She wished she had something to drink, but she decided she'd better not get off the table. If the pain came back she might fall and hurt herself.

I probably shouldn't have sent Mrs. Fitzpatrick off to scare people to death like that. I've only had three pains since she left, and they were hardly anything. I'd really feel fine if there wasn't so much blood. Every pain and every time the baby kicks it just gushes out. That's never happened before. When the water breaks, it's clear, not bloody.

Something's wrong.

Where is the doctor? Another week and there'd have been one right on the doorstep. Now it'll be some stranger from Trim, I guess. How do, Doctor, you'd never know it but it wasn't supposed to be like this, I was going to be in a bed with a gold crown on it, not on a table from the tack room. What kind of start is this for a baby? I'll have to name it "Foal" or "Jumper" or something else horsey.

There's the blood again. I don't like this. Why isn't Mrs. Fitzpatrick back—at least I could have a cup of water for pity's sake, I'm dry as a bone. Stop that kicking, baby, you don't have to act like a horse just because we're on a tack table. Stop it! You just make me bleed. Wait till the doctor comes, then you can get out. Truth to tell, I'll be glad to be rid of you.

It sure was easier starting you than it is finishing you . . . No, I mustn't think about Rhett, I'll go crazy if I do.

Why doesn't it stop raining? Pouring, more like it. Wind's rising, too. This is an honest to goodness storm. Fine time I picked to have a baby, to have my water break . . . why is it red? Am I going to bleed to death on a tack table, for God's sake, without so much as a cup of tea? Oh, how I'd love some coffee. Sometimes I miss it so much I want to scream . . . or cry . . . oh Lord, more gushing. At least it doesn't hurt.

Hardly a contraction at all, more a twitch or something . . . Then why does so much blood gush out? What's going to happen when the real labor starts? Dear God, there'll be a river of blood, all over the floor. Everybody'll have to wash their feet. I wonder if Mrs. Fitzpatrick has a bucket of feet water. I wonder if she hollers before she throws it out? I wonder where the hell she is? As soon as this is over I'm going to fire her—no references, either, at least nothing she'll want to show anybody. Running off and leaving me dying of thirst here all by myself.

Don't kick like that. You're more like a mule than a horse. Oh, God, the blood . . . I'm not going to lose hold of myself, I'm not. I won't. The O'Hara doesn't do that kind of thing. The O'Hara. I like that a lot . . . What was that? The doctor?

Mrs. Fitzpatrick came in. "Are you doing all right, Mrs. O'Hara?"

"Just fine," said The O'Hara.

"I've brought sheets and blankets and soft pillows. Some men are coming with a mattress. Can I do anything for you?"

"I'd like some water."

"Right away."

Scarlett propped herself on an elbow and drank thirstily. "Who's getting the doctor?"

"Colum. He tried to cross the river for the doctor in Adamstown, but he couldn't make it. He's gone to Trim."

"I figured. I'd like some more water please, and a fresh sopper. This one's soaked through."

Mrs. Fitzpatrick tried to hide the horror on

her face when she saw the blood-soaked towel between Scarlett's legs. She wadded it up and hurried to one of the stone sinks with it. Scarlett looked at the trail of bright red drops on the floor. That's part of me, she told herself, but she couldn't believe it. She'd had lots of cuts in her life, as a child playing, when she was hoeing cotton at Tara, even when she pulled up the nettles. Put them all together and they'd never bled as much as that towel had in it. Her abdomen contracted and blood gushed onto the table.

Stupid woman, I told her I needed another towel.

"What time does your watch say, Mrs. Fitzpatrick?"

"Five-sixteen."

"I reckon the storm's making travel slow. I'd like some water and another towel, please. No, come to think of it, I'd like some tea, with plenty of sugar." Give the woman something to do and maybe she'll quit hanging over me like an umbrella. I'm sick and tired of making conversation and brave smiles. I'm scared half-witted if truth be known. The contractions aren't any stronger, or closer together, either. I'm not getting anywhere at all. At least the mattress feels better than the table, but what's going to happen when it gets soaked through, too? Is the storm getting worse or am I just spooked?

Rain was buffeting the windows now, propelled by a mighty wind. Colum O'Hara was nearly knocked down by a branch torn from a tree in the wood near the house. He climbed over it and moved on, bent against the wind. Then he remembered, turned around, was blown onto the limb, fought for a foothold in the quagmire mud of the drive, dragged the limb to one side, fought against the wind again towards the house.

"What time is it?" said Scarlett.

"Almost seven."

"Towel, please."

"Scarlett darling, is it very bad?"

"Oh, Colum!" Scarlett pushed herself to half sitting. "Is the doctor with you? The baby's not kicking as much as before."

"I found a midwife in Dunshaughlin. There's no getting to Trim, the river's over the road. Lie back, now, like a good mother. Don't tire yourself more than you have to."

"Where is she?"

"On the way. My horse was faster, but she's close behind. She's brought hundreds of babies, you'll be in good hands."

"I've had babies before, Colum. This is different. There's something bad wrong."

"She'll know what to do, lamb. Try not to fret."

The midwife bustled in just after eight. Her starched uniform was limp with wet, but her competent manner was as crisp as if she hadn't been rushed on an emergency at all.

"A baby, is it? Ease your mind, missus, I know everything there is to know about helping the little dear things into this vale of tears." She took off her cape and handed it to Colum. "Spread that out near the fire so it can dry," she said in a voice accustomed to command. "Soap and warm water, missus, for me to wash my hands. This will do over here." She walked briskly to the stone sink. At the sight of the blood-soaked towels she wilted, gestured frantically to summon Mrs. Fitzpatrick. They had a whispered conference.

The brightness that had come to Scarlett's eyes faded. She lowered the lids over her sudden tears.

"Let's just see what we have here," said the midwife with false cheer. She lifted Scarlett's skirts, felt her abdomen. "A fine strong baby. He just greeted me with a kick. We'll see about inviting him to come out now and give his Ma a little rest." She turned to Colum. "You'd better leave us to our women's work, sir. I'll call you when your son is born."

Scarlett giggled.

Colum removed his Balmacaan overcoat. His collar gleamed in the lamplight. "Oh," said the midwife. "Forgive me, Father."

"For I have sinned," Scarlett said in a shrill voice.

"Scarlett," Colum said quietly.

The midwife pulled him towards the sink. "It may be you should stay, Father," she said, "for the last rites."

She spoke too loudly. Scarlett heard her. "Oh, dear God," she cried.

"Help me," the midwife ordered Mrs. Fitzpatrick. "I'll show you how to hold her legs."

Scarlett screamed when the woman's hand thrust into her womb. "Stop! Jesus, the pain, make it stop." When the examination was over

824

she was moaning from the hurt. Blood covered the mattress and her thighs, was spattered on Mrs. Fitzpatrick's dress, the midwife's uniform, the floor for three feet on each side of the table. The midwife pushed up the sleeve on her left arm. Her right arm was red halfway to the elbow.

"I'll have to try it with both hands," she said.

Scarlett groaned. Mrs. Fitzpatrick stepped in front of the woman. "I have six children," she said. "Get out of here. Colum, get this butcher out of this house before she kills Mrs. O'Hara and I kill her. So help me God, that's what will happen."

The room was lit suddenly by a flash of brilliance through skylight and windows, and a heavier torrent of rain slashed against the glass.

"I'm not going out in that," the midwife howled. "It's full dark."

"Put her in another room, then, but get her out of here. And when she's away, Colum, go bring the smith. He doctors animals; a woman can't be that different."

Colum had the cringing midwife by the upper arm. Lightning scored the sky above, and she screamed. He shook her like a rag. "Quiet yourself, woman." He looked at Mrs. Fitzpatrick with dull hopeless eyes. "He'll not come, Rosaleen, no one will come now it's dark. Have you forgot what night this is?"

Mrs. Fitzpatrick wiped Scarlett's temples and cheeks with a cool damp cloth. "If you don't bring him, Colum, I'll do it. I've a knife and a pistol in the desk at your house. It only needs showing him there's more certain things to fear than ghosts."

Colum nodded. "I'll go."

Joseph O'Neill, the blacksmith, crossed himself. His face glistened with sweat. His black hair was plastered to his head from walking through the storm, but the sweat was fresh. "I've doctored a horse once, same as this, but a woman I cannot do such violence to." He looked down at Scarlett and shook his head. "It's against nature, I cannot."

There were lamps along the edges of all the sinks, and lightning flashing one jagged bolt after another. The huge kitchen was brighter than day, save for the shadowed corners. The storm raging outside seemed to be attacking the thick stone walls of the house.

"You've got to do it, man, else she'll die."

"She will that, and the babe too, if it's not dead some time past. There's no movement."

"Don't wait, then, Joseph. For the love of God, man, it's her only hope." Colum kept his voice steady, commanding.

Scarlett stirred feverishly on the bloody mattress. Rosaleen Fitzpatrick sponged her lips with water, squeezed a few drops between them. Scarlett's eyelids quivered then opened. Her eyes were glazed with fever. She moaned piteously.

"Joseph! I order you."

The smith shuddered. He raised his thick muscled arm over Scarlett's mounded belly. Lightning glittered on the blade of the knife in his hand.

"Who is that?" said Scarlett distinctly.

"Saint Patrick preserve me!" cried the smith.

"Who's that lovely lady, Colum, in the beautiful white gown?"

The smith dropped the knife on the floor and backed away. His hands were stretched in front of him, palms outward, fending off his terror.

The wind swirled, caught a branch, hurled it crashing through the window above the sink. Shards of glass cut Joseph O'Neill's arms, now crossed over his head. He fell to the floor, screaming, and through the open window the wind screamed in above him. Shrieking noise was everywhere—outside, inside, within the smith's screaming, around and on the howling wind, in the storm, in the distance beyond the storm, a wailing in the wind.

The flames in the lamps jumped and wavered and some went out. Quietly in the midst of the storm's intrusion the kitchen door was opened and closed again. A wide shawled figure walked across the kitchen, among the terrorized people, to the window. It was a woman with a creased round face. She reached into the sink and twisted one of the towels, wringing out the blood.

"What are you doing?" Rosaleen Fitzpatrick snapped out of her terror, stepped toward the woman. Colum's outstretched arm halted her. He recognized the *cailleach,* the wise woman who lived near the tower.

One by one the wise woman piled blood-stained towels atop one another until the hole in the window was filled. Then she turned. "Light the lamps again," she said. Her voice was hoarse, as if she had rust in her throat.

She took off her wet black shawl, folded it neatly, placed it on a chair. Beneath it she was wearing a brown shawl. That, too, came off and was folded, put on the chair. Then a dark blue one with a hole on one shoulder. And a red one with more holes than wool. "You haven't done as I told you," she scolded Colum. Then she walked to the smith and kicked him sharply in the side. "You're in the way, smith, go back to your forge." She looked at Colum again. He lit a lamp, looked for another, lit it, until a steady flame burned in each.

"Thank you, Father," she said politely. "Send O'Neill home, the storm is passing. Then come hold two lamps high by the table. You," she turned to Mrs. Fitzpatrick, "do the same. I'll ready The O'Hara."

A cord around her waist held a dozen or more pouches made of different-colored rags. She reached into one and withdrew a vial of dark liquid. Lifting Scarlett's head with her left hand, she poured the liquid into her mouth with her right. Scarlett's tongue reached out, licked her lips. The *cailleach* chuckled and lowered the head onto the pillow.

The rusty voice began to hum a tune that was no tune. Gnarled stained fingers touched Scarlett's throat, then her forehead, then pulled up and released her eyelids. The old woman took a folded leaf from one of her pouches and put it on Scarlett's belly. Then she extracted a tin snuff box from another and put it beside the leaf.

Colum and Mrs. Fitzpatrick stood like statues with the lamps, but their eyes followed every move.

The leaf, unfolded, contained a powder. The woman sprinkled it over Scarlett's belly. Then she took a paste from the snuff box and rubbed it over the powder and into Scarlett's skin.

"I'm going to tie her down lest she injure herself," the woman said, and she lashed ropes from around her waist below Scarlett's knees, across her shoulders, around the sturdy table legs.

Her small old eyes looked first at Mrs. Fitzpatrick, then at Colum. "She will scream, but she will not feel pain. You will not move. The light is vital."

Before they could reply she took a thin knife, wiped it with something from one of her pouches, and stroked it the length of Scarlett's belly. Scarlett's scream was like the cry of a lost soul.

Before the sound was gone the *cailleach* was holding a blood-covered baby in her two hands. She spit something she was holding in her mouth onto the floor, then blew into the baby's mouth, once, twice, thrice. The baby's arms jerked, then its legs.

Colum whispered the Hail Mary.

A whisk of the knife cut the cord, the baby was laid on the folded sheets and the woman was back beside Scarlett. "Hold the lamps closer," she said.

Her hands and fingers moved quickly, sometimes with a flash of the knife, and bloody bits of membrane fell to the floor beside her feet. She poured more dark fluid between Scarlett's lips, then a colorless one into the horrible wound in her belly. Her cracked humming accompanied the small precise movements as she sewed the wound together.

"Wrap her in linen then in wool while I wash the babe," she said. Her knife slashed through the ropes binding Scarlett.

When Colum and Mrs. Fitzpatrick were finished, the woman returned with Scarlett's baby swaddled in a soft white blanket. "The midwife forgot this," the *cailleach* said. Her chuckle brought an answering throaty sound from the baby, and the infant girl opened her eyes. The blue irises looked like pale tinted rings around the black, unfocused pupils. She had long black lashes and two tiny lines for eyebrows. She was not red and misshapen like most newborns because she had not passed through the birth canal. Her tiny nose and ears and mouth and soft pulsing skull were perfect. Her olive skin was very dark against the white blanket.

63

Scarlett struggled towards the voices and the light her sedated mind vaguely perceived. There was something . . . something important . . . a question . . . Firm hands held her head, gentle fingers parted her lips, a cooling sweet liquid bathed her tongue, trickled down her throat, and she slept again.

The next time she fought for consciousness she remembered what the question was, the vital, the all-important question. The baby. Was it dead? Her hands fumbled to her abdomen, and burning pain leapt at her touch. Her teeth bruised her lips, her hands pressed harder, fell away. There was no kicking, no firm rounded lumpiness that was a questing foot. The baby had died. Scarlett uttered a weak cry of misery, no louder than a mew, and the releasing sweet draught poured into her mouth. Throughout her drugged sleep slow weak tears seeped from her closed eyes.

Semiconscious for the third time, she tried to hold on to the darkness, to stay asleep, to push the world away. But the pain grew, tore at her, made her move to flee it, and the moving gave it such strength that she whimpered helplessly. The cool glass vial tipped, and she was freed. Later, when she floated again to the edges of consciousness, she opened her mouth in readiness, eager for the dreamless darkness. Instead there was a cold wet cloth wiping her lips, and a voice she knew but couldn't remember. "Scarlett darling . . . Katie Scarlett O'Hara . . . open your eyes . . ."

Her mind searched, faded, strengthened— Colum. It was Colum. Her cousin. Her friend . . . Why didn't he let her sleep if he was her friend? Why didn't he give her the medicine before the pain came back?

"Katie Scarlett . . ."

She opened her eyes halfway. Light hurt them, and she closed the lids.

"That's a good girl, Scarlett darling. Open your eyes, I've something for you." His coaxing tone was insistent. Scarlett's eyes opened. Someone had moved the lamp, and the dimness was easy.

There's my friend Colum. She tried to smile, but memory flooded her mind, and her lips crumpled into childlike bubbling sobs. "The baby's dead, Colum. Put me to sleep again. Help me forget. Please. Please, Colum."

The wet cloth stroked her cheeks, wiped her mouth. "No, no, no, Scarlett, no, no, the baby's here, the baby's not dead."

Slowly the meaning became clear. Not dead, said her mind. "Not dead?" said Scarlett.

She could see Colum's face, Colum's smile. "Not dead, mavourneen, not dead. Here. Look."

Scarlett turned her head on the pillow. Why was it so hard, just to turn her head? A pale bundle in someone's hands was there. "Your daughter, Katie Scarlett," said Colum. He parted the folds of the blanket, and she saw the tiny sleeping face.

"Oh," Scarlett breathed. So small and so perfect and so helpless. Look at the skin, like rose petals, like cream—no, she's browner than cream, the rose is only a hint of rose. She looks sunbrowned, like . . . like a baby pirate. She looks exactly like Rhett!

Rhett! Why aren't you here to see your baby? Your beautiful dark baby.

My beautiful dark baby. Let me look at you.

Scarlett felt a strange and frightening weakness, a warmth that washed through her body like a strong, low, enveloping wave of painless burning.

The baby opened her eyes. They stared directly

into Scarlett's. And Scarlett felt love. Without conditions, without demands, without reasons, without questions, without bounds, without reserve, without self.

"Hey, little baby," she said.

"Now drink your medicine," said Colum. The tiny dark face was gone.

"No! No, I want my baby. Where is she?"

"You'll have her next time you wake up. Open your mouth, Scarlett darling."

"I won't," she tried to say, but the drops were on her tongue, and in a moment the darkness closed over her. She slept, smiling, a glow of life under her deathly paleness.

Perhaps it was because the baby looked like Rhett; perhaps it was because Scarlett always valued most what she fought hardest for; or perhaps it was because she'd had so many months with the Irish, who adored children. More likely it was one of the wonders that life gives for no cause at all. Whatever the origin, pure consuming love had come to Scarlett O'Hara after a lifetime of emptiness, not knowing what she lacked.

Scarlett refused to take any more pain-killer. The long red scar on her body was like a streak of white-hot steel, but it was forgotten in the overwhelming joy she felt whenever she touched her baby or even looked at her.

"Send her away!" Scarlett said when the healthy young wet nurse was brought in. "Time after time I had to bind my breasts and suffer agonies while the milk dried up, all to be a lady and keep my figure. I'm going to nurse this baby, have her close to me. I'll feed her and make her strong and see her grow."

When the baby found her nipple the first time and nursed greedily with a tiny wrinkle of concentration on her brow, Scarlett smiled down at her with triumph. "You're a Momma's girl, all right, hungry as a wolf and fixed on getting what you want."

The baby was baptized in Scarlett's bedroom, because Scarlett was too weak to walk. Father Flynn stood near the Viceregal bed where she was propped up against lace-trimmed pillows holding the baby in her arms until she had to give her over to Colum, who was godfather; Kathleen and Mrs. Fitzpatrick were godmothers. The baby wore an embroidered linen gown, thin from washings, that had been worn by hundreds of O'Hara babies for generation after generation. She was named Katie Colum O'Hara. She waved her arms and kicked her legs when the water touched her, but she didn't cry.

Kathleen wore her best blue frock with a lace collar, although she should have been in mourning. Old Katie Scarlett was dead. However, everyone agreed that Scarlett should not be told until she was stronger.

Rosaleen Fitzpatrick watched Father Flynn from hawk-like eyes, poised to snatch the baby if he faltered for a second. She'd been speechless for a long minute after Scarlett asked her to serve as godmother. "How did you guess how I feel about this baby?" she asked when her voice returned.

"I didn't," said Scarlett, "but I know I wouldn't have a baby if you hadn't stopped that monster woman from killing her. I remember a good bit about that night."

Colum took Katie from Father Flynn when the ceremony was over and put her in Scarlett's outstretched hands. Then he poured a tot of whiskey for the priest and the godparents and made a toast: "To the health and happiness of mother and child, The O'Hara and the newest of the O'Haras." After that, he escorted the doddering saintly old man to Kennedy's bar where he bought a few rounds for all there in honor of the occasion. He hoped against hope that it would stop the rumors that were already flying all over County Meath.

Joe O'Neill, the blacksmith, had cowered in a corner of Ballyhara's kitchen until daylight, then scuttled to his smithy to drink himself brave. "Though Saint Patrick himself would have needed more than all the prayers at his beckoning on that night," he told anyone who would listen, and there were many.

"Ready was I to save the life of The O'Hara when the witch come through the stone wall and throws me with terrible force onto the floor. Then kicks me—and I could feel in my flesh that the foot was no human foot but a cloven hoof. She cast a spell on The O'Hara then and ripped the babe from the womb. All bloody was the babe, and blood on the floors and the walls and in the air. A lesser man would have sheltered his eyes from such a fearful sight. But Joseph O'Neill saw the babe's fine strong form beneath the blood, and I'm telling you it was a manchild, with manhood plain between its limbs.

" 'I'll wash the blood away,' says the demon, and she turns her back, then presents to Father O'Hara a spindly frail near-lifeless creature—female and brown as the earth of the grave. Now who will tell me? If I didn't see a changeling, what was it I saw that terrible night? There's no good will come of it, not to The O'Hara nor any man who's touched by the shadow of the fairy babe left in place of The O'Hara's stolen boy."

The story from Dunshaughlin got to Ballyhara after a week. The O'Hara was dying, said the midwife, and could only be saved by ridding her of the dead babe in her womb. Who would know these things, pitiful though they were, better than a midwife who'd seen all there was to see of childbirth? Of a sudden the suffering mother sat up on her bed of pain. "I see it," says she, "the banshee! Tall and clad all in white with the fairy beauty on its face." Then the devils drove a spear from Hell through the window and the banshee flew out to wail the call to death. It was calling the soul of the lost babe, but the dead babe was restored among the living by sucking out the soul of the good old woman who was grandmother to The O'Hara. It was the devil's work and no mistaking and the babe The O'Hara takes for her own is nought but a ghoul.

"I feel that I should warn Scarlett," Colum said to Rosaleen Fitzpatrick, "but what can I tell her? That people are superstitious? That All Hallows' Eve is a dangerous birth date for a baby? I cannot find any advice to give her, there's no way to protect the baby from talk."

"I'll see to Katie's safety," Mrs. Fitzpatrick said. "No one and nothing enters this house unless I say so, and no harm will come near that tiny child. Talk will be forgotten in time, Colum, you know that. Something else will come along to weave tales about and everyone will see that Katie's only a little girl like any other little girl."

A week later Mrs. Fitzpatrick took a tray of tea and sandwiches to Scarlett's room and stood patiently while Scarlett bombarded her with the same plaint she'd been making for days.

"I don't see why I have to stay stuck up here in this room forever. I feel plenty well enough to be up and about. Look at the lovely sunshine today, I want to take Katie out for a ride in the trap, but the best I can do is sit by the window and look out at the leaves falling. I'm sure she's watching. Her eyes look up and then follow them floating down— Oh, look! Come look! Look at Katie's eyes here in the light. They're changing from blue. I thought they'd turn brown like Rhett's because she's the spit of him. But I can see the first little specks, and they're green. She's going to have my eyes!"

Scarlett nuzzled the baby's neck. "You're Momma's girl, aren't you, Katie O'Hara? No, not Katie. Anybody can be a Katie. I'm going to call you Kitty Cat, with your green eyes." She lifted the solemn baby up to face the housekeeper.

"Mrs. Fitzpatrick, I'd like to introduce you to Cat O'Hara." Scarlett's smile was like sunlight.

Rosaleen Fitzpatrick felt more frightened than at any time in her life.

64

The enforced idleness of her convalescence gave Scarlett many hours to think, since her baby spent most of the day and the night sleeping, exactly like all other infants. Scarlett tried reading, but she had never cared for it, and she had not changed in that way.

What had changed was what she thought about.

First and foremost, there was her love for Cat. Only weeks old, the baby was too young to be responsive, except in reacting to her own hunger and the satisfaction of Scarlett's warm breast and milk. It's loving that's making me so happy, Scarlett realized. It has nothing to do with being loved. I like to think Cat loves me, but the truth is she loves to eat.

Scarlett was able to laugh at the joke on herself. Scarlett O'Hara, who'd made men fall in love with her as a sport, as an amusement, was nothing more than a source of food to the one person she loved more than she'd ever loved in her life.

Because she hadn't really loved Ashley; she'd known that for a long time. She'd only wanted what she couldn't have and called that love.

I threw away over ten years on the false love, too, and I lost Rhett, the man I really loved.

. . . Or did I?

She searched her memory, in spite of the pain.

It always hurt to think about Rhett, about losing him, about her failure. It eased the pain some when she thought about the way he'd treated her and hatred burned away the hurt. But for the most part, she managed to keep him out of her mind; it was less disturbing.

During these long days with nothing to do, however, her mind kept going back over her life, and she couldn't avoid remembering him.

Had she loved him?

I must have, she thought, I must love him still, or my heart wouldn't ache the way it does when I see his smile in my mind, hear his voice.

But for ten years she had conjured up Ashley in the same way, imagining his smile and his voice.

And I wanted Rhett most after he left me, Scarlett's deep core of honesty reminded her.

It was too confusing. It made her head ache, even more than her heart. She wouldn't think about it. It was much better to think about Cat, to think about how happy she was.

To think about happiness?

I was happy even before Cat came. I was happy from the day I went to Jamie's house. Not like now, I didn't dream anybody could ever feel as happy as I do every time I look at Cat, every time I hold her, or feed her. But I was happy, all the same, because the O'Haras took me just the way I was. They never expected me to be just like them, they never made me feel I had to change, they never made me feel I was wrong.

Even when I was wrong. I had no call to expect

Kathleen to do my hair and mend my clothes and make my bed. I was putting on airs. With people who never did anything so tacky as put on airs themselves. But they never said, "Oh, stop putting on airs, Scarlett." No, they just let me do what I was doing and accepted me, airs and all. Just like I was.

I was awful wrong about Daniel and all moving to Ballyhara. I was trying to make them be a credit to me. I wanted them to live in grand houses and be grand farmers with lots of land and hired hands to do most of the work. I wanted to change them. I never wondered what they wanted. I didn't take them just the way they were.

Oh, I'm never going to do that to Cat. I'm never going to make her different from what she is. I'm always going to love her like I do now— with my whole heart, no matter what.

Mother never loved me like I love Cat. Or Suellen or Carreen, either. She wanted me to be different from me, she wanted me to be just like her. All of us, that's what she wanted from all three of us. She was wrong.

Scarlett recoiled from what was in her head. She'd always believed her mother was perfect. It was unthinkable that Ellen O'Hara could ever be wrong about anything.

But the thought would not go away. It returned again and again when she was unprepared to shut it out. It returned in different guises, with different embellishments. It would not leave her alone.

Mother was wrong. Being a lady like her isn't

the only way to be. It isn't even always the best way to be. Not if it doesn't make you happy. Happy is the best way to be because then you can let other people be happy, too. Their own way.

Mother wasn't happy. She was kind and patient and caring—for us children, for Pa, for the darkies. But not loving. Not happy. Oh, poor Mother. I wish you could have felt the way I feel now, I wish you could have been happy.

What was it Grandfather had said? That his daughter Ellen had married Gerald O'Hara to run away from a disappointment in love. Was that why she was never happy? Was she pining over someone she couldn't have the way I pined over Ashley? The way I pine now over Rhett when I can't help it.

What a waste! What a horrible, senseless waste. When happiness was so wonderful, how could anyone cling to a love that made them unhappy? Scarlett vowed that she wouldn't do it. She knew what it was to be happy, and she would not ruin it.

She caught her sleeping baby up in her arms and hugged her. Cat woke and waved her helpless hands in protest. "Oh, Kitty Cat, I'm sorry. I just had to hug you some."

They were all wrong! The idea was so explosive that it woke Scarlett from a sound sleep. They were wrong! All of them—the people who cut me dead in Atlanta, Aunt Eulalie and Aunt Pauline, and just about everybody in Charleston. They wanted me to be just like them, and because

I'm not, they disapproved of me, made me feel like there was something terribly wrong with me, made me think I was a bad person, that I deserved to be looked down on.

And there was nothing I did that was as terrible as all that. What they punished me for was that I wasn't minding their rules. I worked harder than any field hand—at making money, and caring about money isn't ladylike. Never mind that I was keeping Tara going and holding the aunts' heads above water and supporting Ashley and his family and paying for almost every piece of food on the table at Aunt Pitty's plus keeping the roof fixed and the coal bin filled. They all thought I shouldn't have dirtied my hands with the ledgers from the store or put on a smile when I sold lumber to the Yankees. There were plenty enough things I did that I shouldn't have done, but working for money wasn't one of them, and that's what they blamed me for most. No, that's not quite it. They blamed me for being successful at it.

That and pulling Ashley back from breaking his neck flinging himself into the grave after Melly. If it had been the other way around, and I'd saved her at Ashley's burial, it would have been all right. Hypocrites!

What gives people whose whole life is a lie the right to judge me? What's wrong with working as hard as you can, and then more besides? Why is it so terrible to push in and stop disaster from happening to anyone, especially a friend?

They were wrong. Here in Ballyhara I worked as hard as I could, and I was admired for it. I kept Uncle Daniel from losing his farm, and they started calling me The O'Hara.

That's why being The O'Hara makes me feel so strange and so happy all at the same time. It's because The O'Hara is honored for all the same things that I've been thinking were bad all these years. The O'Hara would have stayed up late doing the books for the store. The O'Hara would have grabbed Ashley away from the grave.

What was it Mrs. Fitzpatrick said? "You don't have to do anything, you only have to be what you are." What I am is Scarlett O'Hara, who makes mistakes sometimes and does things right sometimes, but who never pretends any more to be what she's not. I'm The O'Hara, and I'd never be called that if I was as bad as they make me out to be in Atlanta. I'm not bad at all. I'm not a saint, either, God knows. But I'm willing to be different, I'm willing to be who I am, not pretend to be what I'm not.

I'm The O'Hara, and I'm proud of it. It makes me happy and whole.

Cat made a gurgling noise to indicate that she was awake, too, and ready to be fed. Scarlett lifted her from her basket and settled the two of them in the bed. She cupped the tiny unprotected head in one hand and guided Cat to her breast.

"I promise you on my word of honor, Cat O'Hara. You can grow up to be whatever you are, even if it's as different from me as day from night. If you have a leaning towards being a lady, I'll even show you how, never mind what I think about it. After all, I know all the rules even if I can't abide them."

65

"I'm going out, and there's no more to be said about it." Scarlett glowered mulishly at Mrs. Fitzpatrick.

The housekeeper stood in the open doorway like an immovable mountain. "No, you are not."

Scarlett changed her tactics. "Please do let me," she coaxed, with the sweetest smile in her arsenal. "The fresh air will do me a world of good. It'll perk up my appetite, too, and you know how you've been after me about not eating enough."

"That will improve. The cook has arrived."

Scarlett forgot that she was being beguiling. "And high time, too! Is her high-and-mightiness bothering to say what took her so long."

Mrs. Fitzpatrick smiled. "She started out on time, but her piles bothered her so badly she had to stop overnight every ten miles on the way here. It seems we won't have to worry about her lazing in a rocking chair when she should be on her feet working."

Scarlett tried not to laugh, but she couldn't help it. And she couldn't really stay mad at Mrs. Fitzpatrick; they had grown too close for that. The older woman had moved into the housekeeper's apartment the day after Cat was born. She was Scarlett's constant companion while she was ill. And readily available afterwards.

Many people came to visit Scarlett in the long convalescent weeks after Cat was born. Colum almost daily, Kathleen almost every other day, her big O'Hara men cousins after Mass each Sunday, Molly more often than Scarlett liked. But Mrs. Fitzpatrick was always there. She brought tea and cakes to the visitors, whiskey and cakes to the men, and after the visitors left she stayed with Scarlett to hear the news the visitors had brought and finish off the refreshments. She brought news herself—about the happenings in the town of Ballyhara and in Trim—and gossip she'd heard in the shops. She kept Scarlett from being too lonely.

Scarlett invited Mrs. Fitzpatrick to call her "Scarlett" and asked, "What's your first name?"

Mrs. Fitzpatrick never told her. It wouldn't do for any informality to develop, she said firmly, and she explained the strict hierarchy of an Irish Big House. Her position as housekeeper would be undermined if the respect accorded to it was diminished by familiarity on anyone's part, even the mistress's. Perhaps especially the mistress's.

It was all too subtle for Scarlett, but Mrs. Fitzpatrick's pleasant unyieldingness made it clear to her that it was important. She settled for the names the housekeeper suggested. Scarlett could call her "Mrs. Fitz," and she would call Scarlett "Mrs. O." But only when they were alone together. In front of other people, full formality had to be maintained.

"Even Colum?" Scarlett wanted to know. Mrs. Fitz considered, then yielded. Colum was a special case.

Scarlett tried to take advantage now of Mrs.

Fitz's partiality to him. "I'll only walk down to Colum's," she said. "He hasn't been to see me for ages, and I miss him."

"He's away on business and you know it. I heard him tell you he was going."

"Bother!" Scarlett muttered. "You win." She went back to her chair by the window and sat down. "Go talk to Miss Piles."

Mrs. Fitz laughed aloud. "By the way," she said as she left, "her name is Mrs. Keane. But you can call her Miss Piles if you like. You'll likely never meet her. That's my job."

Scarlett waited until she was sure Mrs. Fitz wouldn't catch her and then she got ready to go out. She'd been obedient long enough. It was an accepted fact that after childbirth a woman recuperated for a month, most of the time in bed, and she'd done that. She didn't see why she should have to add three more weeks to it just because Cat's birth hadn't been normal. The doctor at Ballyhara struck her as a good man, even reminded her a little of Dr. Meade. But Dr. Devlin himself admitted that he had no experience of babies brought by knife. Why should she listen to him? Particularly when there was something she really had to do.

Mrs. Fitz had told her about the old woman who had appeared, as if by magic, to deliver Cat in the middle of the Halloween tempest. Colum had told her who the woman was—the *cailleach* from the tower. Scarlett owed the wise woman her life, and Cat's. She had to thank her.

The cold took Scarlett by surprise. October had

been warm enough, how could one month make so much difference? She wrapped the folds of her cloak around the well-blanketed baby. Cat was awake. Her large eyes looked at Scarlett's face. "You darling thing," said Scarlett softly. "You're so good, Cat, you never cry, do you?" She walked through the bricked stableyard to the route she'd used so often in the trap.

"I know you're there someplace," Scarlett shouted at the thicket of undergrowth beneath the trees that bordered the tower's clearing. "You might as well come on out and talk to me, because I'm going to stand right here freezing to death until you do. The baby, too, if that matters to you." She waited confidently. The woman who had brought Cat into the world would never let her be exposed for long to the cold damp in the shadow of the tower.

Cat's eyes left Scarlett's face to move from side to side as if she were looking for something. A few minutes later Scarlett heard a rustling in the thick growth of holly bushes to her right. The wise woman stepped out between two of them. "This way," she said, and stepped back.

There was a path, Scarlett saw when she got near. She'd never have found it if the wise woman hadn't held back the spiny holly branches with one of her shawls. Scarlett followed the path until it disappeared in a grove of low-branched trees. "I give up," she said, "where to now?"

There was a rusty laugh behind her. "This way," said the wise woman. She walked around Scarlett and bent low under the branches. Scarlett did the same. After a few steps she could straighten. The clearing in the center of the grove held a small mud hut thatched with reeds. A thin plume of gray smoke curled upward from its chimney. "Come in," said the woman. She opened the door.

"She's a fine child," said the wise woman. She had examined every aspect of Cat's body, down to the nails on her smallest toes. "What have you named her?"

"Katie Colum O'Hara." It was only the second time Scarlett had spoken. Once inside the door, she'd begun thanking the wise woman for what she'd done, but the woman had stopped her.

"Let me have the babe," she'd said, hands outstretched. Scarlett had passed Cat over at once, then kept silent during the detailed examination.

" 'Katie Colum,' " the woman repeated. " 'Tis a weak soft sound for this strong child. My name is Grainne. A strong name."

Her rough voice made the Gaelic name sound like a challenge. Scarlett shifted on her stool. She didn't know how she should reply.

The woman wrapped Cat in her napkin and blankets. Then she lifted her and whispered so quietly in her little ear that Scarlett couldn't hear, even though she strained for the words. Cat's fingers caught hold of Grainne's hair. The wise woman held Cat against her shoulder.

"You would not have understood even if you had heard, O'Hara. I spoke in the old Irish. It was a charm. You have heard that I know magic as well as herbs."

Scarlett admitted she had.

"Perhaps I do. I have some knowledge of the old words and the old ways, but I do not say they are magic. I look and I listen and I learn. To some it may be like magic that another sees, where he is blind, or hears, when he is deaf. It lies largely in the believing. Do not hope that I can do magic for you."

"I never said I came here for that."

"Only to speak thanks? Is that the all of it?"

"Yes, it is, and now I've done it and I must go before I'm missed at the house."

"I ask your forgiveness," the wise woman said. "There are few feel thankful when I enter their lives. I wonder you don't feel anger at what I did to your body."

"You saved my life and my baby's too."

"But I took life away from all other babes. A doctor might have known how to do more."

"Well, I couldn't get a doctor, or I would have had one!" Scarlett closed her lips firmly over her quick tongue. She'd come to say thank you, not to insult the wise woman. But why was she talking riddles in her raspy scary voice? It gave a person gooseflesh.

"I'm sorry," said Scarlett, "that was rude of me. I'm sure no doctor could have done any better. More likely not even half as well. And I don't know what you mean about other babies. Are you saying I was having twins and the other one died?" It was certainly a possibility, Scarlett thought. She'd been so big when she was pregnant. But surely Mrs. Fitz or Colum would have told her. Maybe not. They hadn't told her about

Old Katie Scarlett dying until two weeks after it happened.

A feeling of unbearable loss squeezed Scarlett's heart. "Was there another baby? You've got to tell me!"

"Shhh, you're bothering Katie Colum," said Grainne the wise woman. "There was no second child in the womb. I did not know you would mistake my words. The woman with white hair looked knowledgeable, I believed she understood and would tell you. I lifted the womb with the baby, and I had not the skills to restore it. You will never have another child."

There was a terrible finality in the woman's words and the way she said them, and Scarlett knew absolutely that they were true. But she couldn't believe them, she wouldn't. No more babies? Now, when she'd finally discovered the encompassing joy of being a mother, when she'd learned—so late—what it was to love? It couldn't be. It was too cruel.

Scarlett had never understood how Melanie could have knowingly risked her life to have another baby, but she did now. She would do the same. She'd go through the pain and the fear and the blood again and again to have that moment of seeing her baby's face for the first time.

Cat made a soft mewing sound. It was her warning that she was getting hungry. Scarlett felt her milk begin to flow in response. What am I taking on so for? Don't I already have the most wonderful baby in the whole world? I'm not going to lose my milk fretting about imaginary babies when my Cat is real and wants her mother.

"I've got to go," said Scarlett. "It's close to time to feed the baby." She held out her hands for Cat.

"One more word," said Grainne. "A warning."

Scarlett felt afraid. She wished she hadn't brought Cat. Why didn't the woman give her back?

"Keep your babe close, there are those who say she was brought by a witch and must be bewitched therefrom."

Scarlett shivered.

Grainne's stained fingers gently undid Cat's grasp. She brushed her soft wisp-covered head with a kiss and a murmur. "Go well, Dara." Then she gave the baby to Scarlett. "I will call her 'Dara' in my memory. It means oak tree. I am grateful for the gift of seeing her, and for your thanks. But do not bring her again. It is not wise for her to have aught to do with me. Go now. Someone is coming and you should not be seen . . . No, the path the other takes is not yours. It is the one from the north used by foolish women who buy potions for love or beauty or harm to those they hate. Go. Guard the babe."

Scarlett was glad to obey. She plodded doggedly through the cold rain that had begun to fall. Her head and back were bent to protect her baby from harm. Cat made sucking noises beneath the shelter of Scarlett's cloak.

Mrs. Fitzpatrick eyed the wet cloak on the floor by the fire, but she made no comment. "Miss Piles seems to have a nice light hand with a batter," she said. "I've brought scones with your tea.

"Good, I'm starving." She'd fed Cat and had a nap and the sun was shining again. Scarlett was confident now that the walk had done her a world of good. She wouldn't take no for an answer the next time she wanted to go out.

Mrs. Fitz didn't attempt to stop her. She recognized futility when she met it.

When Colum came home Scarlett walked down to his house for tea. And advice.

"I want to buy a small closed buggy, Colum. It's too cold to go around in the trap, and I need to do things. Will you pick one out for me?"

He'd be willing, said Colum, but she could do her own choosing if she'd prefer. The buggy makers would bring their wares to her. As would the makers of anything else she fancied. She was the lady of the Big House.

"Now why didn't I think of that?" said Scarlett.

Within a week she was driving a neat black buggy with a thin yellow stripe on its side, behind a neat gray horse that lived up to the seller's promise that it had good go in it with hardly a mention of the whip ever needed.

She also had a "parlor suite" of green-upholstered shiny oak furniture with ten extra chairs that could be pulled near the hearth, and a marble-topped round table large enough to seat six for a meal. All these sat on a Wilton carpet in the room adjoining her bedroom. No matter what outrageous tales Colum might tell about French women entertaining crowds while they lounged in their beds, she was going to have a proper place to see her visitors. And no matter what Mrs. Fitz said, she saw no reason at all to use the downstairs rooms for entertaining when there were plenty of empty rooms upstairs and handy.

She didn't have her big desk and chair yet because the carpenter in Ballyhara was making them. What point was there in having a town of your own if you weren't smart enough to support the businesses in it? You could be sure of getting your rent if they were earning money.

Cat's padded basket was beside her on the buggy seat everywhere Scarlett went. She made baby noises and blew bubbles and Scarlett was sure that they were singing duets when she drove along the road. She showed Cat off at every shop and house in Ballyhara. People crossed themselves when they saw the dark-skinned baby with the green eyes and Scarlett was pleased. She thought they were blessing the baby.

As Christmas came nearer, Scarlett lost much of the elation she'd felt when she was freed from the captivity of convalescence. "I wouldn't be in Atlanta for all the tea in China, even if I was invited to all the parties, or in Charleston, either, with their silly dance cards and receiving lines," she told Cat, "but I'd like to be somewhere that's not so damp all the time."

Scarlett thought it would be nice to be living in a cottage so that she could whitewash it and paint the trim the way Kathleen and the cousins were doing. And all the other cottagers too, in Adamstown and beside the roads. When she walked over to Kennedy's bar on December 22 and saw the shops and houses being limed and painted over the almost-new jobs done in the autumn, she pranced with delight. Her pleasure in the neat prosperity of her town took away the slight sadness that she often felt when she went to her own bar for companionship. It sometimes seemed as if the conversation turned stiff as soon as she entered.

"We've got to decorate the house for Christmas," she announced to Mrs. Fitz. "What do the Irish do?"

Holly branches on mantels and over doors and windows, said the housekeeper. And a big candle, usually red, in one window to light the Christ Child's way. We'll have one in every window, Scarlett declared, but Mrs. Fitz was firm. One window. Scarlett could have all the candles she wanted on tables—or the floor, if it made her happy—but only one window should have a candle. And that one could only be lighted on Christmas Eve when the Angelus rang.

The housekeeper smiled. "The tradition is that the youngest child in the house lights a rush from the coals on the hearth as soon as the Angelus is heard, then lights the candle with the flame from the rush. You might have to help her a bit."

Scarlett and Cat spent Christmas at Daniel's house. There was nearly enough admiration for Cat to satisfy even Scarlett. And enough people coming through the open door to keep her mind off the Christmases at Tara in the old days when the family and house servants went out onto the wide porch after breakfast in response to the cry,

"Christmas Gift." When Gerald O'Hara gave a drink of whiskey and a plug of tobacco to every field hand as he handed him his new coat and new boots. When Ellen O'Hara said a brief prayer for each woman and child as she gave them lengths of calico and flannel together with oranges and stick candy. Sometimes Scarlett missed the warm slurrings of black voices and the flashing smiles on black faces almost more than she could bear.

"I need to go home, Colum," Scarlett said.

"And aren't you home now, on the land of your people that you made O'Hara land again?"

"Oh, Colum, don't be Irish at me! You know what I mean. I'm homesick for Southern voices and Southern sunshine and Southern food. I want some corn bread and fried chicken and grits. Nobody in Ireland even knows what corn is. That's just a word for any kind of grain to them."

"I do know, Scarlett, and I'm sorry for the heartache you're feeling. Why not go for a visit when good sailing weather comes? You can leave Cat here. Mrs. Fitzpatrick and I will take care of her."

"Never! I'll never leave Cat."

There was nothing to be said. But from time to time the thought popped up in Scarlett's head: it's only two weeks and a day to cross the ocean, and sometimes the dolphins play alongside for hours on end.

On New Year's Day, Scarlett got her first hint

of what it really meant to be The O'Hara. Mrs. Fitz came to her room with morning tea instead of sending Peggy Quinn with the breakfast tray. "The blessings of all the saints on mother and daughter in the new year to come," she said cheerily. "I must tell you about the duty you have to do before your breakfast."

"Happy New Year to you, too, Mrs. Fitz, and what on earth are you talking about?"

A tradition, a ritual, a requirement, said Mrs. Fitz. Without it there'd be no luck all year. Scarlett might have a taste of tea first, but that was all. The first food eaten in the house must be the special New Year's barm brack on the tray. Three bites had to be eaten, in the name of the Trinity.

"Before you start, though," Mrs. Fitz said, "come into the room I've got ready. Because after you have the Trinity bites you have to throw the cake with all your might against a wall so that it breaks into pieces. I had the wall scrubbed yesterday, and the floor."

"That's the craziest thing I ever heard. Why should I ruin a perfectly good cake? And why eat cake for breakfast anyhow?"

"Because that's the way it's done. Come do your duty, The O'Hara, before the rest of the people in this house die of hunger. No one can eat before the barm brack is broken."

Scarlett put on her wool wrapper and obeyed. She had a swallow of tea to moisten her mouth, then bit three times into the edge of the rich fruited cake as Mrs. Fitz directed. She had to hold it in both hands because it was so big. Then she repeated the prayer against hunger during the year that Mrs. Fitz taught her and heaved with both arms, sending the cake flying and crashing against the wall. Bits flew all over the room.

Scarlett laughed. "What an awful mess. But the throwing part was fun."

"I'm glad you liked it," said the housekeeper. "You've got five more to do. Every man, woman, and child in Ballyhara has to get a little piece for good luck. They're waiting outside. The maids will take the pieces down on trays after you finish."

"My grief," said Scarlett. "I should have taken littler bites."

After breakfast Colum accompanied her through the town for her next ritual. It was good luck for the whole year if a dark-haired person visited a house on New Year's Day. But the tradition required that the person enter, then be escorted out, then be escorted back in again.

"And don't you dare laugh," Colum ordered. "Any dark-haired person is good luck. The head of a clan is ten times over good luck."

Scarlett was staggering when it was over. "Thank goodness there are still so many empty buildings," she gasped. "I'm awash with tea and foundering from all the cake in my stomach. Did we really have to eat and drink in every single place?"

"Scarlett darling, how can you call it a visit if there's no hospitality offered and received? If you were a man, it would have been whiskey and not tea."

Scarlett grinned. "Cat might have loved that."

February 1 was considered the beginning of the farm year in Ireland. Accompanied by everyone who worked and lived in Ballyhara, Scarlett stood in the center of a big field and, after saying a prayer for the success of the crops, sank a spade into the earth, lifted and turned the first sod. Now the year could begin. After the feast of applecake—and milk, of course, because February 1 was also the feast day of Saint Brigid, Ireland's other patron saint, who was also patron saint of the dairy.

When everyone was eating and talking after the ceremony, Scarlett knelt by the opened earth and took up a handful of the rich loam. "This is for you, Pa," she murmured. "See, Katie Scarlett hasn't forgotten what you told her, that the land of County Meath is the best in the world, better even than the land of Georgia, of Tara. I'll do my best to tend it, Pa, and love it the way you taught me. It's O'Hara soil, and it's ours again."

The age-old progression of plowing and harrowing, planting and praying had a simple, hardworking dignity that won Scarlett's admiration and respect for all who lived by the land. She had felt it when she lived in Daniel's cottage and she felt it now for the farmers at Ballyhara. For herself as well, because she was, in her own way, one of them. She hadn't the strength to drive the plow, but she could provide it. And the horses to pull it. And the seed to plant in the furrows it made.

The Estate Office was her home even more than her rooms in the Big House. There was another cradle for Cat by her desk, identical to the one in her bedroom, and she could rock it with her foot while she worked on her record books and her accounts. The disputes that Mrs. Fitzpatrick had been so gloomy about turned out to be simple matters to settle. Especially if you were The O'Hara, and your word was law. Scarlett had always had to bully people into doing what she wanted; now she had only to speak quietly, and there was no argument. She enjoyed the first Sunday of the month very much. She even began to realize that other people occasionally had an opinion worth listening to. The farmers really did know more about farming than she did, and she could learn from them. She needed to. Three hundred acres of Ballyhara land were set aside as her own farm. The farmers worked it and paid only half the usual rent for the land they leased from her. Scarlett understood sharecropping; it was the way things were done in the South. Being an estate landlord was still new to her. She was determined to be the best landlord in all Ireland.

"The farmers learn from me, too," she told Cat. "They'd never even heard of fertilizing with phosphates until I handed out those sacks of it. Might as well let Rhett get a few pennies of his money back if it'll mean a better wheat crop for us."

She never used the word "father" in Cat's hearing. Who could tell how much a tiny baby took in and remembered? Especially a baby who was so clearly superior in every way to every other baby in the world.

As the days lengthened, breezes and rain became softer and warmer. Cat O'Hara was becoming more and more fascinating; she was developing individuality.

"I certainly named you right," Scarlett told her, "you're the most independent little thing I ever saw." Cat's big green eyes looked at her mother attentively while she was talking, then returned to her absorbed contemplation of her own fingers. The baby never fussed, she had an infinite capacity to amuse herself. Weaning her was hard on Scarlett, but not on Cat. She enjoyed examining her porridge with fingers and mouth. She seemed to find all experience extremely interesting. She was a strong baby with a straight spine and high-held head. Scarlett adored her. And, in a special way, respected her. She liked to scoop Cat up and kiss her soft hair and neck and cheeks and hands and feet; she longed to hold Cat in her lap and rock her. But the baby would tolerate only a few minutes of cuddling before she pushed herself free with her feet and fists. And Cat's small dark-skinned face could have such an outraged expression that Scarlett was forced to laugh even when she was being forcefully rejected.

The happiest times for both of them were at the end of the day when Cat shared Scarlett's bath. She patted the water, laughing at its splashes, and Scarlett held her, jounced her up and down, and sang to her. Then there was the sweetness of drying the perfect tiny limbs, each finger and toe individually, and spreading powder over Cat's silky skin and into each baby wrinkle.

When Scarlett was twenty years old, war had forced her to give up her youth overnight. Her will and endurance had hardened and so had her face. In the spring of 1876, when she was thirty-one, the gentle softness of hope and youth and tenderness gradually returned. She was unaware of it; her preoccupation with the farm and the baby had replaced her life-long concentration on her own vanity.

"You need some clothes," Mrs. Fitz said one day. "I've heard there's a dressmaker who wants to rent the house you lived in if you'll fresh paint the inside. She's a widow and well-fixed enough to pay a fair rent. The women in the town would like it, and you need it, unless you're willing to find a woman in Trim."

"What's wrong with the way I look? I wear decent black, the way a widow should. My petticoats hardly ever peek out."

"You don't wear decent black at all. You wear earth-stained, rolled-sleeves, peasant women clothes, and you're the lady of the Big House."

"Oh, fiddle-dee-dee, Mrs. Fitz. How could I ride out to see if the timothy grass is growing if I had on lady-of-the-house clothes? Besides, I like being comfortable. As soon as I can go back into colored skirts and shirts I'll start worrying about whether they have stains on them. I've always hated mourning, I don't see any reason to try and make black look fresh. No matter what you do to it, it's still black."

"Then you aren't interested in the dress-maker?"

"Of course I'm interested. Another rent is always interesting. And one of these days I'll order some frocks. After the planting. The fields should be ready for the wheat this week."

"There's another rent possible," the housekeeper said carefully. She'd been surprised more than once by unexpected astuteness on Scarlett's part. "Brendan Kennedy thinks he could do well if he added an inn to his bar. There's the building next to him could be used."

"Who on earth would come to Ballyhara to stay at an inn? That's crazy. Besides, if Brendan Kennedy wants to rent from me, he should carry his hat in his hand and come talk to me himself, not pester you to do it."

"Ach, well. Likely it was only talk." Mrs. Fitzgerald gave Scarlett the week's household account book and abandoned talk of the inn for the moment. Colum would have to work on it; he was much more persuasive than she was.

"We're getting to have more servants than the Queen of England," said Scarlett. She said the same thing every week.

"If you're going to have cows, you're going to need hands to milk them," said the housekeeper.

Scarlett picked up the refrain ". . . and to separate the cream and make the butter—I know. And the butter's selling. I just don't like cows, I guess. I'll go over this later, Mrs. Fitz. I want to take Cat down to watch them cutting peat in the bog."

"You'd better go over it now. We're out of

money in the kitchen and the girls need paying tomorrow."

"Bother! I'll have to get some cash from the bank. I'll drive in to Trim."

"If I was the banker, I'd never give money to a creature dressed like you."

Scarlett laughed. "Nag, nag, nag. Tell the dressmaker I'll order the painting done."

But not the inn opened, thought Mrs. Fitzpatrick. She'd have to talk to Colum tonight.

The Fenians had been steadily growing in strength and numbers throughout Ireland. With Ballyhara, they now had what they most needed: a secure location where leaders from every county could meet to plan strategy, and where a man who needed to flee the militia could safely go, except that strangers were too noticeable in a town that was hardly larger than a village. Militia and constabulary patrols from Trim were few, but one man with sharp eyes was enough to destroy the best-laid plans.

"We really need the inn," Rosaleen Fitzpatrick said urgently. "It makes sense that a man with business in Trim would take a room this close but cheaper than in town."

"You're right, Rosaleen," Colum soothed, "and I'll talk to Scarlett. But not right away. She's too quick-minded for that. Give it a rest for a bit. Then when I bring it up, she won't wonder why we're both pressing."

"But Colum, we mustn't waste time."

"We mustn't lose everything by hurry, either. I'll do it when I believe the moment's right." Mrs.

Fitzpatrick had to settle for that. Colum was in charge. She consoled herself by remembering that at least she'd gotten Margaret Scanlon in. And she hadn't even had to make up a tale to do it. Scarlett did need some clothes. It was a shocking disgrace the way she insisted on living— the cheapest clothes, two rooms lived in out of twenty. If Colum weren't Colum, Mrs. Fitzpatrick would doubt what he'd said, that not so long ago Scarlett had been a very fashionable woman.

" '. . . *and if that diamond ring turns brass, Momma's gonna buy you a looking glass,'* " Scarlett sang. Cat splashed vigorously in the sudsy water of the bath. "Momma's gonna buy you some pretty frocks, too," said Scarlett, "and buy Momma some. Then we'll go on the great big ship."

There was no reason to put it off. She had to go to America. If she left soon after Easter, she could be back in plenty of time for the harvest.

Scarlett made up her mind on the day she saw the delicate haze of green on the meadow where she'd turned the first sod. A fierce surge of excitement and pride made her want to cry aloud, "This is mine, my land, my seeds burst into life." She looked at the barely visible young growth and pictured it reaching up, becoming taller, taller, stronger, then flowering, perfuming the air, intoxicating the bees until they could hardly fly. The men would cut it then, scythes flashing silver, and make tall ricks of sweet golden hay. Year after year the cycle would turn—sow and reap—

the annual miracle of birth and growth. Grass would grow and become hay. Wheat would grow and become bread. Oats would grow and become meal. Cat would grow—crawl, walk, talk, eat the oatmeal and the bread and jump onto the stacked hay from the loft of the barn just as Scarlett had done when she was a child. Ballyhara was her home.

Scarlett squinted up at the sun, saw the clouds racing towards it, knew that soon it would rain, and soon after that it would clear again, and the sun would warm the fields until the next rain, followed by the next warming sunlight.

I'll feel the baking heat of Georgia sun one more time, she decided, I'm entitled to that. I miss it sometimes so terribly. But, somehow, Tara's more like a dream than a memory. It belongs in the past, like the Scarlett I used to be. That life and that person don't have anything to do with me any more. I've made my choice. Cat's Tara is the Irish Tara. Mine will be too. I'm The O'Hara of Ballyhara. I'll keep my shares of Tara for Wade and Ella's inheritance, but I'll sell everything in Atlanta and cut those ties. Ballyhara's my home now. Our roots go deep here, Cat's and mine and Pa's. I'll take some O'Hara land with me when I go, some earth to mix into the Georgia clay of Gerald O'Hara's grave.

Her mind touched briefly on the business she had to deal with. All that could wait. What she must concentrate on was the best way to tell Wade and Ella about their wonderful new home. They wouldn't believe she wanted them—why should they? In truth she never had. Until she discovered what it felt like to love a child, to be a real mother.

It's going to be hard, Scarlett told herself many times, but I can do it. I can make up for the past. I've got so much love in me that it just spills over. I want to give some to my son and my daughter. They might not like Ireland at first, it's so different, but once we go to Market Day a couple of times, and the races, and I buy them their own ponies . . . Ella should look darling in skirts and petticoats, too. All little girls love to dress up . . . They'll have millions of cousins, with all the O'Haras around, and the children in Ballyhara town to play with . . .

66

"You cannot leave until after Easter, Scarlett darling," said Colum. "There's a ceremony on Good Friday that only The O'Hara can do."

Scarlett didn't argue. Being The O'Hara was too important to her. But she was annoyed. What difference could it possibly make who planted the first potato? It irritated her, too, that Colum wouldn't go with her. And that he was away so much lately. "On business," he said. Well, why couldn't he do his fundraising in Savannah again, instead of wherever else he went to?

The truth was that everything irritated her. Now that she had decided to go, she wanted to be gone. She was snappish with Margaret Scanlon, the dressmaker, because it took so long to have her dresses made. And because Mrs. Scanlon looked so interested when Scarlett ordered dresses in colorful silks and linens as well as mourning black.

"I'll be seeing my sister in America," Scarlett said airily, "the colors are a gift for her." And I don't care whether you believe that or not, she thought crossly. I'm not really a widow, and I'm not about to go back to Atlanta looking drab and dowdy. Suddenly her utilitarian black skirt and stockings and shirt and shawl had become unspeakably depressing to her. She could hardly wait for the moment when she could put on the green linen frock with the wide ruffles of thick creamy lace. Or the pink and navy striped silk . . . If Margaret Scanlon ever finished them.

"You'll be surprised when you see how pretty your Momma looks in her new dresses," Scarlett told Cat. "I've ordered some wonderful little frocks for you, too." The baby smiled, showing her small collection of teeth.

"You're going to love the big ship," Scarlett promised her. She had reserved the largest and best stateroom on the *Brian Boru* for departure from Galway on the Friday following Easter.

On Palm Sunday the weather turned cold, with hard slanting rain that was still falling on Good Friday. Scarlett was soaking wet and chilled to the bone after the long ceremony on the open field.

She hurried to the Big House as soon after as she could, longing for a hot bath and a pot of tea. But there was not even time for her to put on dry clothes. Kathleen was waiting for her with an urgent message. "Old Daniel is calling for you, Scarlett. He took sick in the chest, and he's dying."

Scarlett drew in her breath sharply when she saw Old Daniel. Kathleen crossed herself. "He's slipping," she said quietly.

Daniel O'Hara's eyes were sunken in their sockets, his cheeks so hollow that his face looked like a skull covered by skin. Scarlett knelt by the austere fold-out bed and took his hand. It was hot, papery dry and weak. "Uncle Daniel, it's Katie Scarlett."

Daniel opened his eyes. The tremendous effort of will it required made Scarlett want to weep. "I've a favor to ask," he said. His breathing was shallow.

"Anything."

"Bury me in O'Hara earth."

Don't be silly, you're a long way from that, Scarlett meant to say, but she couldn't lie to the old man. "I will that," she said, the Irish way of affirmation.

Daniel's eyes closed. Scarlett began to weep. Kathleen led her to a chair by the fire. "Will you help me brew the tea, Scarlett? They'll all be coming." Scarlett nodded, unable to speak. She hadn't realized until this moment how important her uncle had become in her life. He seldom spoke, she almost never talked to him, he was simply there—solid, quiet, unchanging and strong. Head of the household. In her mind Uncle Daniel was The O'Hara.

Kathleen sent Scarlett home before dark fell.

"You've your baby to tend, and there's nothing more to do here. Come back tomorrow."

On Saturday everything was much the same. People came to pay their respects in a steady stream all day. Scarlett fixed pot after pot of tea, sliced the cakes people brought, buttered bread for sandwiches.

On Sunday she sat with her uncle while Kathleen and the O'Hara men went to Mass. When they returned she went to Ballyhara. The O'Hara must celebrate Easter in the Ballyhara church. She thought Father Flynn would never finish his sermon, thought she'd never get away from the townspeople, all of whom asked about her uncle and expressed their hopes for his recovery. Even after forty days of stringent fasting—there was no dispensation for O'Haras of Ballyhara—Scarlett had no appetite for the big Easter dinner.

"Take it to your uncle's house," suggested Mrs. Fitzpatrick. "There are big men there still getting the farm work done. They'll need food, and poor Kathleen that busy with Old Daniel."

Scarlett hugged and kissed Cat before she left. Cat patted her little hands on her mother's tear-stained cheeks. "What a thoughtful Kitty Cat. Thank you, my precious. Momma will be better soon, then we'll play and sing in the bath. And then we'll go for a wonderful ride on the big ship." Scarlett despised herself for having the thought, but she hoped they wouldn't miss the *Brian Boru*.

That afternoon Daniel rallied a little. He recognized people and spoke their names. "Thank God," Scarlett said to Colum. She thanked God, too, that Colum was there. Why did he have to go away so much? She'd missed him this long weekend.

It was Colum who told her Monday morning that Daniel had died during the night. "When will the funeral be? I'd like to make the sailing on Friday." It was so comfortable to have a friend like Colum; she could tell him anything without worrying that he'd misunderstand or disapprove.

Colum shook his head slowly. "That cannot be, Scarlett darling. There are many who respected Daniel and many O'Haras with distance to come over mud-mired roads. The wake will last at least three days, more likely four. After, there's the burial."

"Oh, no. Colum! Say I don't have to go to the wake; it's too morbid, I don't think I could bear it."

"You must go, Scarlett. I'll be with you."

Scarlett could hear the keening even before the house was in sight. She looked at Colum with desperation, but his face was set.

There was a crowd of people outside the low door. So many had come to mourn Daniel that there wasn't enough room for all of them. Scarlett heard the words "The O'Hara," saw a path open for her. She wished with all her heart that the honor would go away. But she walked in with her head bent, determined to do the right thing by Daniel.

"He's in the parlor," said Seamus. Scarlett steeled herself. The eerie wailing was coming from there. She walked in.

Tall thick candles burned on tables at the head and foot of the big bed. Daniel lay on top of the coverlet in a white garment trimmed in black. His work-worn hands were crossed on his chest, the beads of a rosary between them.

"Why did you leave us? Ochón!
Ochón Ochón, Ullagón Ó!"

The woman swayed from side to side as she lamented. Scarlett recognized her cousin Peggy, who lived in the village. She knelt by the bed to say a prayer for Daniel. But the keening filled her mind with such confusion that she couldn't think.

Ochón, Ochón.

The plaintive, primitive cry twisted her heart, frightened her. She got to her feet and went into the kitchen.

She looked with disbelief at the mass of men and women that filled the room. They were eating and drinking and talking as if nothing unusual was happening at all. The air was thick with smoke from the men's clay pipes in spite of the open door and windows. Scarlett approached the group around Father Danaher. "Yes, he woke to call people by name and to make his end with a clean soul. Ah, it was a grand confession he made, I've never heard a better. A fine man Daniel O'Hara was. We'll not see his like again in our lifetimes." She edged away.

"And do you not remember, Jim, the time Daniel and his brother Patrick, God rest his soul, took the Englishman's prize pig and carried it down into the peat bog to farrow? Twelve little ones and all of them squealing, and the sow as fierce as any wild boar? The land agent was shaking and the Englishman cursing and all the rest of the world laughing at the show."

Jim O'Gorman laughed, swatted the tale teller's shoulder with his big blacksmith's hand. "I do not remember, Ted O'Hara, no more do you, and that's the truth of it. We were neither of us born when the adventure of the sow had its happening, and well you know it. You heard it from your father same as I heard it from mine."

"But wouldn't it be a fine thing to have seen, Jim? Your cousin Daniel was a grand man, and that's the truth of it."

Yes, he was, thought Scarlett. She moved around, listening to a score of stories of Daniel's life. Someone noticed her. "And tell us, if you will, Katie Scarlett, about your uncle refusing the farm with the hundred cattle you gave him."

She thought quickly. "This was the way of it," she began. A dozen eager listeners leaned toward her. Now what am I going to say? "I . . . I said to him, 'Uncle Daniel' . . . I said, 'I want to give you a present.'" Might as well make it good. "I said, 'I've got a farm with . . . a hundred acres and . . . a quick stream and a bog of its own and . . . a hundred bullocks and fifty milk cows and three hundred geese and twenty-five pigs and . . . six teams of horses.' " The audience sighed at the grandeur. Scarlett felt inspiration on her tongue. " 'Uncle Daniel,' I said, 'this is all for you, and a bag of gold besides.' But his voice thundered at me till I quaked. 'I'll not touch it, Katie Scarlett O'Hara.' "

Colum grabbed her arm and pulled her outside

the house, through the crowd, behind the barn. Then he let himself laugh. "You're always surprising me, Scarlett darling. You've just made Daniel into a giant—but whether it's a giant fool or a giant too noble to take advantage of a fool woman, I don't know."

Scarlett laughed with him. "I was just getting the hang of it, Colum, you should have let me stay." Suddenly she put her hand over her mouth. How could she be laughing at Uncle Daniel's wake?

Colum took her wrist, lowered her hand. "It's all right," he said, "a wake's supposed to celebrate a man's life and the importance of him to all who come. Laughter's part of it, as much as lamentation."

Daniel O'Hara was buried on Thursday. The funeral was almost as big as Old Katie Scarlett's had been. Scarlett led the procession to the grave his sons had dug in the ancient walled graveyard at Ballyhara that she and Colum had found and cleaned up.

Scarlett filled a leather pouch with soil from Daniel's grave. When she spread it on her father's grave, it would be almost as if he was buried near his brother.

When the funeral was over, the family went to the Big House for refreshments. Scarlett's cook was delighted to have an occasion to show off. Long trestle tables stretched the length of the unused drawing room and library. They were covered with hams, geese, chickens, beef, mountains of breads and cakes, gallons of porter, barrels of whiskey, rivers of tea. Hundreds of

O'Haras had made the trip in spite of the muddy roads.

Scarlett brought Cat down to meet her kinfolk. The admiration was all that Scarlett could have wished for, and more.

Then Colum supplied a fiddle and his drum, three cousins found pennywhistles, and the music went on for hours. Cat waved her hands to the music until she was worn out, then fell asleep in Scarlett's lap. I'm glad I missed the ship, Scarlett thought; this is wonderful. If only Daniel's death wasn't the reason for it.

Two of her cousins came over to her and bent down from their great height to speak quietly. "We have need of The O'Hara," said Daniel's son Thomas.

"Will you come to the house tomorrow after breakfast?" asked Patrick's son Joe.

"What's it about?"

"We'll tell you tomorrow when there's quiet for you to think."

The question was: who should inherit Daniel's farm? Because of the long-past crisis when Old Patrick died, two O'Hara cousins were claiming the right. Like his brother Gerald, Daniel had never made a will.

It's Tara all over again, thought Scarlett, and the decision was easy. Daniel's son Seamus had worked hard on the farm for thirty years while Patrick's son Sean lived with Old Katie Scarlett and did nothing. Scarlett gave the farm to Seamus. Like Pa should have given Tara to me.

She was The O'Hara, so there was no argument. Scarlett felt elated, confident that she had given more justice to Seamus than anyone had ever given her.

The next day a far-from-young woman left a basket of eggs on the doorstep of the Big House. Mrs. Fitz found out that she was Seamus' sweetheart. She'd been waiting for almost twenty years for him to ask her to marry him. An hour after Scarlett's decision, he had.

"That's very sweet," Scarlett said, "but I hope they don't get married real soon. I'll never get to America at the rate I'm going." She now had a cabin booked on a ship sailing April 26, a year exactly after the date she was originally supposed to have ended her "vacation" in Ireland.

The ship wasn't the luxurious *Brian Boru*. It wasn't even a proper passenger ship. But Scarlett had her own superstition—if she delayed again until after May Day, she'd somehow never leave at all. Besides, Colum knew the ship and its captain. It was a cargo ship, true, but it was carrying only bales of best Irish linen, nothing messy. And the captain's wife always travelled with him, so Scarlett would have female companionship and a chaperone. Best of all, the ship had no paddlewheel, no steam engine. She'd be under sail all the way.

67

The weather was beautiful for more than a week. The roads were dry, the hedgerows were full of flowers, Cat's feverish sleeplessness one night turned out to be only a new tooth coming in. On the day before she was to leave Scarlett ran, half-dancing, to Ballyhara town to pick up the last of Cat's frocks from the dressmaker. She was confident that nothing could go wrong now.

While Margaret Scanlon wrapped the frock in tissue paper Scarlett looked out at the deserted dinner-time town and saw Colum going into the abandoned Protestant Church of Ireland on the other side of the wide street.

Oh, good, she thought, he's going to do it after all. I thought he'd never listen to reason. It makes no sense at all for the whole town to be squashed into that dinky little chapel for Mass every Sunday when there's that great big church standing empty. Just because it was built by Protestants is no reason for Catholics not to take it over. I don't know why he's been so stubborn so long, but I won't fuss at him. I'll just tell him how happy it makes me that he's changed his mind.

"I'll be right back," she told Mrs. Scanlon. She hurried along the weed-ridden path that led to the small side entrance, tapped on the door and pushed it open. A loud noise sounded, then another, and Scarlett felt something sharp hit her sleeve, heard a shower of pebbles on the ground at her feet, a booming reverberation inside the church.

A shaft of light from the open door fell directly onto a strange man who had spun to face her. His stubbled face was twisted into a snarl, and his dark, shadowed eyes were like a wild animal's.

He was half crouching, and he was pointing

a pistol at her, held out from his rag-clothed body in his two dirty, rock-steady hands.

He shot at me. The knowledge filled Scarlett's mind. He's already killed Colum and now he's going to kill me. Cat! I'll never see Cat again. White-hot anger freed Scarlett from the physical paralysis of shock. She raised her fists and lunged forward.

The sound of the second shot was an explosion that echoed deafeningly from the vaulted stone ceilings for a time that seemed forever. Scarlett threw herself to the floor, screaming.

"I'll ask you to be quiet, Scarlett darling," said Colum. She knew his voice, and yet it was not his voice. There was steel in this voice, and ice.

Scarlett looked up. She saw Colum's right arm around the neck of the man, Colum's left hand around the man's wrist, the pistol pointing at the ceiling. She got slowly to her feet.

"What is going on here?" she enunciated carefully.

"Close the door if you please," said Colum. "There's light enough from the windows."

"What . . . is . . . going . . . on . . . here?"

Colum gave her no answer. "Drop it, Davey boy," he said to the man. The pistol fell with a metallic crash onto the stone floor. Slowly Colum lowered the man's arm. Quickly he moved his own arm from its stranglehold around the man's neck, made two fists with his hands and clubbed the man with them. The unconscious form fell at Colum's feet.

"He'll do," Colum said. He walked briskly past

Scarlett and quietly closed the door, slid the bolt across. "Now, Scarlett darling, we have to talk."

Colum's hand closed around her upper arm from behind her. Scarlett jerked away, whirled to face him. "Not 'we,' Colum. You. You tell me what is going on here."

The warmth and lilt was back in his voice. "It's an unfortunate happening to be sure, Scarlett darling . . ."

"Don't you 'Scarlett darling' me. I'm not buying any charm, Colum. That man tried to kill me. Who is he? Why are you sneaking around to meet him? What is going on here?"

Colum's face was only a pale blur in the shadows. His collar was startlingly white. "Come where we can see," he said quietly, and he walked to a place where thin slats of sunlight slanted down from the boarded-over windows.

Scarlett couldn't believe her eyes. Colum was smiling at her. "Ach, the pity of it is, if we'd had the inn this would never have happened. I wanted to keep you out of it, Scarlett darling, it's a worrisome thing once you know."

How could he smile? How did he dare? She stared, too horrified to speak.

Colum told her about the Fenian Brotherhood.

When he finished, she found her voice. "Judas! You filthy, lying traitor. I trusted you. I thought you my friend."

"I said it was a worrisome thing."

She felt too heartsick to be angry at his smiling, rueful response. Everything was a betrayal, all of it. He'd been using her, deceiving her from

878

the moment they met. They all had—Jamie and Maureen, all her cousins in Savannah and Ireland, all the farmers on Ballyhara, all the people in Ballyhara town. Even Mrs. Fitz. Her happiness was a delusion. Everything was a delusion.

"Will you listen now, Scarlett?" She hated Colum's voice, the music of it, the charm. I won't listen. Scarlett tried to close her ears, but his words crept between her fingers. "Remember your South, with the boots of the conqueror upon her, and think of Ireland, her beauty and her life's blood in the murdering hands of the enemy. They stole our language from us. Teaching a child to speak Irish is a crime in this land. Can you not see it, Scarlett, if your Yankees were speaking in words you did not know, words you learned at the point of a sword because 'stop' must be a word you knew to the very pit of your knowing, else you would be killed for not stopping. And then your child being taught her tongue by those same Yankees, and your child's tongue not your own so that she knew not what words of love you said to her, you knew not what need she told you in the Yankee tongue and could not give her her desire. The English robbed us of our language and with that robbing they took our children from us.

"They took our land, which is our mother. They left us nothing when our children and our mother were lost. We knew defeat in our souls.

"Do you but think of it now, Scarlett, when your Tara was being taken from you. You battled for it, you've told me how. With all your will, all your heart, all your wit, all your might. Were

879

lies needed, you could lie, deceptions, you could deceive, murder, you could kill. So it is with us who battle for Ireland.

"And yet we are more fortunate than you. Because we have yet time for the sweetnesses of life. For music and dance and love. You know what it is to love, Scarlett. I watched the growth and the blossoming with your babe. Do you not see that love feeds without gluttony on itself, that love is an always brimming cup, from which drinking fills again and still more.

"So it is with our love for Ireland and her people. You are loved by me, Scarlett, by us all. You are not unloved because Ireland is our love of loves. Must you not care for your friends because you care for your child? One does not deny the other. You thought I was your friend, you say, your brother. And so I am, Scarlett, and will be until time ends. Your happiness gladdens me, your sorrow is my grief. And yet Ireland is my soul; I can hold nothing traitorous if it be done to free her from her bondage. But she does not take away the love I have for you; she makes it more."

Scarlett's hands had slid on their own volition from her ears down to where they now hung limply by her sides. Colum had enthralled her as he always did when he spoke that way, though she understood no more than half of what he was saying. She felt as if she were somehow wrapped 'round in gossamer which warmed and bound at the same time.

The unconscious man on the floor groaned. Scarlett looked at Colum with fear. "Is that man a Fenian?"

"Yes. He's on the run. A man he thought his friend denounced him to the English."

"You gave him that gun." It was not a question.

"Yes, Scarlett. You see, I keep no more secrets from you. I have concealed weapons throughout this English church. I am the armorer for the Brotherhood. When the day arrives, as soon it will, many thousands of Irishmen will be armed for the uprising, and those arms will come from this English place."

"When?" Scarlett dreaded his reply.

"There's no date set. We need five more shipments, six if it can be done."

"That's what you do in America."

"It is. I raise the money, with help from many, then others find a way to buy weapons with it, and I bring them into Ireland."

"On the *Brian Boru.*"

"And others."

"You're going to shoot the English."

"Yes. We will be more merciful, though. They have killed our women and children as well as our men. We will kill soldiers. A soldier is paid to die."

"But you're a priest," she said, "you can't kill."

Colum was still for several minutes. Dust motes turned lazily in the stripes of light from the window to his bowed head. When he lifted it, Scarlett saw that his eyes were dark with sorrow.

"When I was a boy of eight," he said, "I watched the wagons of wheat and the droves of cattle on the road from Adamstown toward Dublin and the English banquet tables there. I also watched my sister die of hunger because she was but two years old and had no strength to carry her without food. Three, my brother was, and he, too, had too little strength. The smallest always were the first to die. They cried because they were hungry and were too young to understand when they were told there was no food. I understood, for I was eight and wiser. And I did not cry because I knew that crying uses strength needed to survive without food. Another brother died, he was seven, and then the six-year-old and the one who was five, and to my eternal shame I have forgot which was the girl and which the boy. My mother went then, but I have always thought she died more from the pain of her broken heart than from the pain of her empty belly.

"It takes many months to starve to death, Scarlett. It is not a merciful death. For all those months the wagons of food rolled past us." Colum's voice sounded lifeless. Then it livened.

"I was a likely lad. Once ten, and the Famine years past and with food to fill me, I was quick at my studies, good at my books. Our priest thought me full of promise and he told my father that perhaps, with diligence, I might in time be accepted in the seminary. My father gave me everything he could give. My older brothers did more than their share of work on the farm so that I need do none and could be diligent at my books. No one grudged me for 'tis a great honor to a family to have a son who is a priest. And I took from them without thought for I had pure, encompassing faith in the goodness of God and the wisdom of Holy Mother Church, which I believed to be a vocation, a call to the priesthood." His voice rose.

"Now I will learn the answer, I believed. The seminary contains many holy books and holy men and all the wisdom of the Church. I studied and I prayed and I searched. I found ecstasy in prayer, knowledge in studies. But not the knowledge I was seeking. 'Why?' I asked my teachers, 'why must little children die from hunger?' But the only answer given me was, 'Trust in God's wisdom and have faith in His love.' "

Colum raised his arms above his tortured face, raised his voice to a shout. "God, my Father, I feel Your presence and Your almighty power. But I cannot see Your face. Why have You turned away from Your people the Irish?" His arms dropped.

"There is no answer, Scarlett," he said brokenly, "there has never been an answer. But I saw a vision, and I have followed it. In my vision the starving children came together and their weakness was less weak in their numbers. They rose up in their thousands, their fleshless small arms reaching out, and they overturned the carts heaped with food, and they did not die. It is my vocation now to turn over those carts, to drive out the English from their banqueting tables, to give Ireland the love and mercy that God has denied her."

Scarlett gasped at his blasphemy. "You'll go to Hell."

"I am in Hell! When I see soldiers mocking a mother who must beg to buy food for her children, it is a vision from Hell. When I see old men pushed into the muck of the street so that soldiers will have the sidewalks, I see Hell. When I see evictions, floggings, the groaning carts of grain passing the family with a square meter of potatoes to keep them from death, I say that all Ireland is Hell, and I will gladly suffer death and then torment for all eternity to spare the Irish one hour of Hell on earth."

Scarlett was shaken by his vehemence. She groped for understanding. Suppose she hadn't been there when the English came with the battering ram to Daniel's house? Suppose all her money was gone, and Cat was hungry? Suppose the English soldiers really were like Yankees and stole her animals and burned the fields she'd watched greening?

She knew what it was to be helpless before an army. She knew the feeling of hunger. They were memories no amount of gold could ever quite erase.

"How can I help you?" she asked Colum. He was fighting for Ireland, and Ireland was the home of her people and her child.

68

The ship captain's wife was a stout, red-faced woman who took one look at Cat and held out her arms. "Will she come to me?" Cat reached out in reply. Scarlett was sure Cat was interested in the eyeglasses hanging on a chain around the woman's neck, but she didn't say so. She loved to hear Cat admired, and the captain's wife was doing just that. "What a little beauty she is—no, sweetheart, they go on your nose, not in your mouth—with such lovely olive skin. Was her father Spanish?"

Scarlett thought quickly. "Her grandmother," she said.

"How nice." She extracted the glasses from Cat's fingers and substituted a ship's biscuit.

"I'm a grandmother four times over, it's the most wonderful thing in the world. I started sailing with the captain when the children were grown because I couldn't stand the empty house. But now there's the added pleasure of the grandchildren. We'll go to Philadelphia for cargo after Savannah, and I'll have two days there with my daughter and her two."

She's going to talk me to death before we're out of the bay, Scarlett thought. I'll never be able to stand two weeks of this.

She discovered very soon that she needn't have worried. The captain's wife repeated the same things so often that Scarlett had only to nod and say "My goodness" at intervals without listening at all. And the older woman was wonderful with Cat. Scarlett could take her exercise on deck without worry about the baby.

She did her best thinking then, with the salt wind in her face. Mostly she planned. She had a lot to do. She had to find a buyer for her store. And there was the house on Peachtree Street. Rhett paid for the upkeep, but it was ridiculous to have it sitting there empty when she'd never use it again . . .

So she'd sell the Peachtree Street house and

the store. And the saloon. That was sort of too bad. The saloon produced excellent income and was no trouble at all. But she'd made up her mind to cut herself free of Atlanta, and that included the saloon.

What about the houses she was building? She didn't know anything at all about that project. She had to check and make sure the builder was still using Ashley's lumber . . .

She had to make sure Ashley was all right. And Beau. She'd promised Melanie.

Then, when she was done with Atlanta, she would go to Tara. That must be last. Because once Wade and Ella learned they were going home with her, they'd be anxious to get going. It wouldn't be fair to keep them dangling. And saying goodbye to Tara would be the hardest thing she had to do. Best to do it quickly; it wouldn't hurt so much then. Oh, how she longed to see it.

The long slow miles up the Savannah River from the sea to the city seemed to go on forever. The ship had to be towed by a steam-powered tugboat through the channel. Scarlett walked restlessly from one side of the deck to the other with Cat in her arms, trying to enjoy the baby's excited reaction to the marsh birds' sudden eruption into flight. They were so close now, why couldn't they get there? She wanted to see America, hear American voices.

At last. There was the city. And the docks. "Oh, and listen, Cat, listen to the singing. Those are black folks' songs, this is the South, feel the sun?

It will last for days and days. Oh, my darling, my Cat, Momma's home."

Maureen's kitchen was just as it had been, nothing had changed. The family was the same. The affection. The swarms of O'Hara children. Patricia's baby was a boy, almost a year old, and Katie was pregnant. Cat was embraced at once into the daily rhythms of the three-house home. She regarded the other children with curiosity, pulled their hair, submitted to hers being pulled, became one of them. Scarlett was jealous. She won't miss me at all, and I cannot bear to leave her, but I have to. Too many people in Atlanta know Rhett and might tell him about her. I'd kill him before I'd let him take her from me. I can't take her with me. I have no choice. The sooner I go, the sooner I'll be back. And I'll bring her own brother and sister as a gift for her.

She sent telegrams to Uncle Henry Hamilton at his office, and to Pansy at the house on Peachtree Street, and took the train for Atlanta on the twelfth of May. She was both excited and nervous. She'd been gone so long—anything might have happened. She wouldn't fret about it now, she'd find out soon enough. In the meantime she'd simply enjoy the hot Georgia sun and the pleasure of being all dressed up. She'd had to wear mourning on the ship, but now she was radiant in emerald green Irish linen.

But Scarlett had forgotten how dirty American trains were. The spittoons at each end of the car were soon surrounded by evil-smelling tobacco juice. The aisle became a filthy debris trap before twenty miles were done. A drunk lurched unevenly past her seat and she suddenly realized that she should not be travelling alone. Why, anybody at all could move my little hand valise and sit next to me! We do things an awful lot better in Ireland. First Class means what it says. Nobody intrudes on you in your own little compartment. She opened the Savannah newspaper as a shield. Her pretty linen suit was already rumpled and dusty.

The hubbub at the Atlanta Depot and the shouting daredevil drivers in the maelstrom at Five Points made Scarlett's heart race with excitement, and she forgot the grime of the train. How alive it all was, and vital, and always changing. There were buildings she'd never seen before, new names above old storefronts, noise and hurry and push.

She looked eagerly out the window of her carriage at the houses on Peachtree Street, identifying the owners to herself, noting the signs of better times for them. The Merriwethers had a new roof, the Meades a new color paint. Things weren't nearly as shabby as they'd been when she left a year and a half back.

And there was her house! Oh. I don't remember it being so crowded on the lot like that. There's hardly any yard at all. Was it always so close to the street? For pity's sake, I'm just being silly. What difference does it make? I've already decided to sell it anyhow.

This was no time to sell, said Uncle Henry Hamilton. The depression was no better, business was bad everywhere. The hardest hit market of all was real estate, and the hardest hit real estate was the big places like hers. People were moving down, not up.

The little houses, now, like the ones she'd been building on the edge of town, they were selling as fast as people could put them up. She was making a fortune there. Why did she want to sell anyhow? It wasn't as if the house cost her anything, Rhett paid all the bills with money left over, too.

He's looking at me like I smelled bad or something, Scarlett thought. He blames me for the divorce. For a moment she felt like protesting, telling her side of the story, telling what had really happened. Uncle Henry was the only one left who was on my side. Without him there won't be a soul in Atlanta who doesn't look down on me.

And it doesn't matter a bit. The idea burst in her mind like a Roman candle. Henry Hamilton's wrong in judging me just like everybody else in Atlanta was wrong in judging me. I'm not like them, and I don't want to be. I'm different, I'm me. I'm The O'Hara.

"If you don't want to bother with selling my property, I won't take it against you, Henry," she said. "Just tell me so." There was a simple dignity in her manner.

"I'm an old man, Scarlett. It would probably be better for you to hook up with a younger lawyer."

Scarlett rose from her chair, held out her hand, smiled with real fondness for him.

It was only after she was gone that he could put words to the difference in her. "Scarlett's grown up. She didn't call me 'Uncle Henry.' "

"Is Mrs. Butler at home?"

Scarlett recognized Ashley's voice immediately. She hurried from the sitting room into the hall; a quick gesture of her hand dismissed the maid who'd answered the door. "Ashley, dear, I'm so happy to see you." She held out both her hands to him.

He clasped them tightly in his, looking down at her. "Scarlett, you've never looked lovelier. Foreign climates agree with you. Tell me where you've been, what you've been doing. Uncle Henry said you'd gone to Savannah, then he lost touch. We all wondered."

I'll just bet you all wondered, especially your adder-tongued old sister, she thought. "Come in and sit down," she said, "I'm dying to hear all the news."

The maid was hovering to one side. Scarlett said quietly as she passed her, "Bring us a pot of coffee and some cakes."

She led the way into the sitting room, took one corner of a settee, patted the seat beside her. "Sit here beside me, Ashley, do. I want to look at you." Thank the Lord, he's lost that hangdog look he had. Henry Hamilton must have been right when he said that Ashley was doing fine. Scarlett studied him through lowered lashes while she busied herself clearing room on a table for the coffee tray. Ashley Wilkes was still a handsome man. His thin aristocratic features had become more distinguished with age. But he looked older than his years. He can't be more than forty, Scarlett thought, and his hair's more silver than gold. He must spend a lot more time in the lumberyard than he used to, he's got a nice color to his skin, not that office gray look he had before. She looked up with a smile. It was good to see him. Especially looking so fit. Her obligation to Melanie didn't seem so burdensome now.

"How's Aunt Pitty? And India? And Beau? He must be practically a grown man!"

Pitty and India were just the same, said Ashley with a quirk of his lips. Pitty got the vapors at every passing shadow and India was very busy with committee work to improve the moral tone of Atlanta. They spoiled him abominably, two spinsters trying to see which one was the best mother hen. They tried to spoil Beau, too, but he'd have none of it. Ashley's gray eyes lit up with pride. Beau was a real little man. He'd be twelve soon, but you'd take him for almost fifteen. He was president of a sort of club the neighborhood boys had formed. They'd built a tree house in Pitty's backyard, made from the best lumber the mill turned out, too. Beau had seen to that; he already knew more about the lumber business than his father, said Ashley with a mixture of ruefulness and admiration. And, he added with intensified pride, the boy might have the makings of a scholar. He'd already won a school prize for Latin composition, and he was reading books far above his age level—

"But you must be bored by all this, Scarlett. Proud fathers can be very tedious."

"Not a bit, Ashley," Scarlett lied. Books, books, books, that was exactly what was wrong with the Wilkeses. They did all their living out of books, not life. But maybe the boy would be all right. If he knew lumber already, there was hope for him. Now, if Ashley would just not get all stiff-necked, she had one more promise to Melly that she could settle. Scarlett put her hand on Ashley's sleeve. "I've got a big favor to beg," she said. Her eyes were wide with entreaty.

"Anything, Scarlett, you should know that." Ashley covered her hand with his.

"I'd like for you to promise that you'll let me send Beau to University and then with Wade on a Grand Tour. It would mean a lot to me—after all, I think about him as practically my son, too, seeing that I was there when he was born. And I've come into really a lot of money lately, so that's no problem. You can't be so mean that you'd say no."

"Scarlett—" Ashley's smile was gone. He looked very serious.

Oh, bother, he's going to be difficult. Thank goodness, here's that slowpoke girl with the coffee. He can't talk in front of her and I'll have a chance to jump in again before he has a chance to say no.

"How many spoons of sugar, Ashley? I'll fix your cup."

Ashley took the cup from her hand, put it on the table. "Let the coffee wait for a minute, Scarlett." He took her hand in his. "Look at me, dear." His eyes were softly luminous. Scarlett's thoughts were distracted. Why, he looks almost like the old Ashley, Ashley Wilkes of Twelve Oaks.

"I know how you came into that money, Scarlett. Uncle Henry let it slip. I understand how you must feel. But there's no need. He was never worthy of you, you're well rid of Rhett, never mind how. You can put it all behind you, as if it never happened."

Great balls of fire, Ashley's going to propose!

"You're free from Rhett. Say you'll marry me, Scarlett, and I'll pledge my life to making you happy the way that you deserve to be."

There was a time when I would have traded my soul for those words, Scarlett thought, it's not fair that now I hear them and don't feel anything at all. Oh, why did Ashley have to do that? Before the question was formed in her mind, she knew the answer. It was because of the old gossip, so long ago it seemed to be now. Ashley was determined to redeem her in the eyes of Atlanta society. If that wasn't just like him! He'll do the gentlemanly thing even if it means tearing up his whole life.

And mine, too, by the way. He didn't bother to think of that, I don't suppose. Scarlett bit her tongue to keep from unleashing her anger on him. Poor Ashley. It wasn't his fault he was the way he was. Rhett said it: Ashley belonged to that time before the War. He's got no place in the world today. I can't be angry or mean. I don't want to lose anyone who was part of the glory days. All that's left of that world is the memories and the people who share them.

"Dearest Ashley," Scarlett said, "I don't want

to marry you. That's the all of it. I'm not going to play belle games with you and tell lies and keep you panting after me. I'm too old for that, and I care for you too much. You've been a big piece of my life all along, and you always will be. Say you'll let me keep that."

"Of course, my dear. I'm honored you feel that way. I won't distress you by referring again to marriage." He smiled, and he looked so young, so much like the Ashley of Twelve Oaks that Scarlett's heart turned over. Dearest Ashley. He mustn't ever guess that she'd clearly heard relief in his voice. Everything was all right. No, better than all right. Now they could truly be friends. The past was neatly finished.

"What are your plans, Scarlett? Are you home for good, as I hope?"

She'd prepared for this question even before she sailed from Galway. She must make sure that no one in Atlanta could know how to find her, it made her too vulnerable to Rhett, to losing Cat. "I'm selling up, Ashley, I don't want to be tied down at all for a while. After I visited in Savannah, I paid a visit to some of Pa's family in Ireland, then I went travelling." She had to be careful what she said. Ashley had been abroad, he'd catch her out in a minute if she claimed she'd been to places she hadn't been. "Somehow or other I never got around to seeing London. I figure I might settle there for a while. Do help me out, Ashley. Do you think London's a good idea?" Scarlett knew, from Melanie, that he considered London as perfect as a city could be. He'd talk his head off, and forget to ask any more questions.

"I enjoyed the afternoon so much, Ashley. You'll come again, won't you? I'll be here for a while settling things."

"As often as I can. It's a rare pleasure." Ashley accepted his hat and gloves from the maid. "Goodbye, Scarlett."

"Goodbye. Oh—Ashley, you will grant my favor I asked, won't you? I'll be miserable if you don't."

"I don't think—"

"I swear to you, Ashley Wilkes, if you don't let me set up a little fund for Beau, I'll cry like a river over its banks. And you know as well as I do that no gentleman ever deliberately makes a lady cry."

Ashley bowed over her hand. "I was thinking how much you'd changed, Scarlett, but I was wrong. You can still wrap men around your little finger and make them like it. I'd be a bad father to deny Beau a gift from you."

"Oh, Ashley, I do love you and I always will. Thank you."

And run to the kitchen and tell that, Scarlett thought as she watched the maid close the door behind Ashley. Might as well give all the old cats something good to gossip about. Besides, I do love Ashley and always will, in a way they'd never understand.

It took much longer than she'd expected for Scarlett to accomplish her business in Atlanta. She didn't leave for Tara until June 10.

Almost a month away from Cat already! I can't

bear it. She might forget me. I probably missed a new tooth, maybe two. Suppose she was fretful and nobody knew that she'd feel better if she could splash in the water? It's so hot, too. She might have prickly heat. A little Irish baby doesn't know anything about hot weather.

During her final week in Atlanta Scarlett was so jumpy with nerves that she could hardly sleep. Why wouldn't it rain? Red dust covered everything only a half hour after it had been wiped away.

But once on the train to Jonesboro she was able to relax. In spite of the delays she had done everything she'd set out to do, and done it better than both Henry Hamilton and her new lawyer said it could be done.

Naturally enough the saloon had been the easiest. The depression increased its business and its value. She was sad about the store. It was worth more for the land it was on than as a business; the new owners were going to tear it down and put up a building eight stories tall. Five Points, at least, was still Five Points, depression or no depression. She'd realized enough from those two sales to buy another fifty acres and put up another hundred houses on the edge of the city. That would keep Ashley prosperous for a couple of years. Plus the builder had told her that other builders were starting to buy only from Ashley too. They could trust him not to sell green lumber, something that couldn't be said for the other yards in Atlanta. It really looked as if he was going to be a success in spite of himself.

And she was going to make a fortune. Henry

Hamilton was right about that. Her little houses sold as fast as they were finished.

They had made a profit. A lot of profit. She was downright shocked when she saw how much money had accumulated in her bank account. Enough to cover all the expenses she'd been worried about at Ballyhara all these months with everything going out and so little coming in. Now she was even. The harvest would be all income, free and clear, plus provide seed for next year. And the rent rolls from the town were bound to keep growing. Before she left, a cooper was asking about one of the empty cottages, and Colum said he had a tailor in mind for another.

She would have done the same thing even if she hadn't made so much money, but it was much easier to do since she had. The builder was instructed to send all the future profits to Stephen O'Hara in Savannah. He'd have all the money he needed to carry out Colum's instructions.

It was funny about the Peachtree Street house, Scarlett thought. You'd think it would hurt to part with it. After all, it was where I lived with Rhett, the place where Bonnie was born and spent her terribly brief life. But the only thing I felt was relief. When that girls' school made an offer I could have kissed the old prune-faced headmistress. It felt like lifting chains off me. I'm free now. No more obligations in Atlanta. Nothing binding me in.

Scarlett smiled to herself. Just like her corsets. She had never been laced up again after Colum and Kathleen cut her free in Galway. Her waist was a few inches bigger, but she was still slimmer than most of the women she saw on the street who were laced until they could hardly breathe. And she was comfortable—at any rate as comfortable as a person could be in this heat. She could dress herself, too, not be dependent on a maid. And the thick chignon she wore was no trouble to do on her own. It was wonderful to be self-sufficient. It was wonderful not to care about what other people did or did not do or what they approved or disapproved. It was most wonderful of all to be going home to one Tara and then taking her children home to another one. Soon she'd be with her precious Cat. Soon after that back again in the fresh, sweet, rain-washed cool of Ireland. Scarlett's hand stroked the soft leather pouch in her lap. She'd take the earth from Ballyhara to her father's grave first thing.

Can you see from where you are, Pa? Do you know? You'd be so proud of your Katie Scarlett, Pa. I'm The O'Hara.

69

Will Benteen was waiting for her at the Jonesboro depot. Scarlett looked at his weather-worn face and deceptively slack-looking body and grinned from ear to ear. Will must be the only man God ever made who could look like he was lounging on a peg leg. She hugged him ferociously.

"Landsake, Scarlett, you ought to warn a man. Nearly knocked me off my pin. It's good to see you."

"It's good to see you, Will. I expect I'm gladder to see you than anybody else this whole trip." It was true. Will was more dear to her than even the Savannah O'Haras. Maybe because he'd been through the bad times with her, maybe because he loved Tara as much as she did. Maybe simply because he was such an honest good man.

"Where's your maid, Scarlett?"

"Oh, I don't fool with a maid any more, Will. I don't fool with a lot of things I used to fool with."

Will shifted the straw in his mouth. "I noticed," he said laconically. Scarlett laughed. She'd never thought before of what it must feel like to a man when he hugged a girl without stays.

"No more cages for me, Will, not ever, not any kind," she said. She wished she could tell him why she was so happy, tell him about Cat, about Ballyhara. If it was only Will, she'd tell him in a second, she trusted him. But he was Suellen's husband, and she wouldn't trust her sister as far as she could throw her—with an anvil tied on besides. And Will might feel duty bound to tell his wife everything. Scarlett had to hold her tongue. She climbed up onto the seat of the wagon. She'd never known Will to use their buggy. He could combine buying stores in Jonesboro with meeting the train. The wagon was loaded with sacks and boxes.

"Tell me the news, Will," Scarlett said when they were on the road. "I haven't heard anything for such a long time."

"Well, let me see. I reckon you want to hear about the kids first. Ella and our Susie are thick as thieves. Susie being a mite younger kind of gives Ella the upper hand, and that's done her a world of good. You ain't hardly going to know Wade when you see him. He started shooting up about the day he hit fourteen last January, and it don't look like he's ever going to stop. For all the weedy look, though, he's strong as a mule. Works like one, too. Thanks to him there's twenty fresh acres under crops this year."

Scarlett smiled. What a help he'd be at Ballyhara, and how he'd love it. A born farmer, she'd never have thought it. Must take after Pa. The leather pouch was warm in her lap.

"Our Martha's seven now, and Jane, the baby, was two last September. Suellen lost a baby, last year, another little girl it was."

"Oh, Will, I'm so sorry."

"We decided not to try again," Will said. "It was real hard on Suellen, the doctor advised it. We've got three healthy girls and that's more than most people get to bring them happiness. 'Course I'd have liked a boy, any man would, but I'm not complaining. Besides, Wade's been all the son any man could hope for. He's a fine boy, Scarlett."

She was happy to hear it. And surprised. Will was right, she wasn't going to know Wade. Not if he was anything close to the boy Will made him out to be. She remembered a cowardly, frightened, pale little boy.

"I'm that fond of Wade, I agreed to talk to you for him, though I don't generally cotton to sticking my nose into other folks' business. He's always been kind of scared of you, Scarlett, you know that. Any road, what he wants me to tell you is he don't want no more schooling. He's done with the school 'round here this month, and the law won't make him do no more."

Scarlett shook her head. "No, Will. You can tell him or I'll do it. His daddy went to University and so will Wade. No offense, Will, but a man can't go very far without an education."

"No offense taken. And none given, but I figure you're wrong. Wade can read and write and do all the calculations a farmer's ever going to need. And that's what he wants. Farming. Farming Tara, to put a finger on it. He says his grandpa built Tara with no more schooling than he's got and he don't see why he should have to be any different. The boy's not like me, Scarlett. Hell, I can't hardly do more than write my name. He had four years at the fancy school you had him at in Atlanta and three more here in the school-house and on the land. He knows all a country boy needs to know. That's what he is, Scarlett, a country boy, and he's happy at it. I'd hate to see you mess him up."

Scarlett bristled. Who did Will Benteen think he was talking to? She was Wade's mother, she knew what was best for him.

"Long as you've got your dander up, I might as well finish what I've got to say," Will continued in his slow Cracker drawl. He looked directly ahead at the dusty red road. "They showed me the new papers about Tara over to the County Court House. Seems like you done got hold of Carreen's share. I don't know what your thinking is, Scarlett, and I ain't asking. But I'm telling you this. If anybody comes up the road flapping something legal at me 'bout taking Tara, I plan to meet 'em at the end of the drive with a shotgun in my hand."

"Will, I swear on a stack of Bibles, I'm not planning to do anything to Tara." Scarlett was grateful it was the truth. Will's softspoken nasal drawl was more frightening than the loudest shout could ever be.

"I'm glad to hear it. My figuring is it should be Wade's. He's your pa's only grandson, and land should stay in the family. I'm hoping you'll leave him where he is, Scarlett, to be my right hand and like a son to me, just the way he is now. You'll do what you want to do. You always did. I gave Wade my word I'd talk to you, and now I have. We'll leave it there, if you don't mind. I said all I got to say."

"I'll think about it," Scarlett promised. The wagon creaked along the familiar road and she saw that the land she'd known as cultivated fields was now all gone back to scrub trees and rough weed grasses. She felt like crying. Will saw the slope of her shoulders and the droop of her mouth.

"Where you been this last couple of years, Scarlett? If it wasn't for Carreen we wouldn't have known where you'd gone to at all, but then she lost track, too."

Scarlett forced herself to smile. "I've been having adventures, Will, travelling all over the place. I visited my O'Hara kinfolks, too. A bunch of them are in Savannah, the nicest people you'd ever want to meet. I stayed with them ever so long. And then I went to Ireland to meet some more. You can't imagine how many O'Haras there are." Her throat clogged with tears. She held the leather pouch to her breast.

"Will, I brought something for Pa. Will you let me off at the graveyard and keep everybody away for a little while?"

"Glad to."

Scarlett knelt in the sun by Gerald O'Hara's grave. The black Irish soil filtered through her fingers to mix with the red clay dust of Georgia. "Ach, Pa," she murmured, and the meter of her words was Irish, "it's a grand place to be sure, County Meath. You're remembered well, Pa, by all of them. I didn't know, Pa, I'm sorry. I didn't know you should be having a fine wake and all the stories told about when you were a boy." She lifted her head and the sunlight gleamed in the flood of tears down her face. Her voice was cracked, clogged with weeping, but she did the best she could, and her grief was strong.

"Why did you leave me? Ochón!
Ochón, Ochón, Ullagón Ó!"

Scarlett was glad she hadn't told anyone in Savannah about her plan to take Wade and Ella back to Ireland with her. Now she didn't have to explain why she'd left them at Tara; it would have been so humiliating to tell the truth, that her own children didn't want her, that they were strangers to her and she to them. She couldn't admit to anyone, not even herself, how much it hurt and how much she blamed herself.

She felt small and mean; she could hardly even be glad for Ella and Wade, who were so obviously happy.

Everything had hurt at Tara. She'd felt like a stranger. Except for Grandma Robillard's portrait, she hardly recognized anything in the house. Suellen had used the money every month to buy new furniture and furnishings. The unscarred wood of the tables was glaringly shiny to Scarlett's eyes, the colors in the rugs and curtains too bright. She hated it. And the baking heat she'd longed for in the Irish rains gave her a headache that lasted the whole week she was there. She'd enjoyed visiting Alex and Sally Fontaine, but their new baby only reminded her how much she missed Cat.

It was only at the Tarletons' that she had a good time. Their farm was doing well, and Mrs. Tarleton talked nonstop about her mare in foal and her expectations for the three-year-old she insisted that Scarlett admire.

The easy, no-invitation-required visiting back and forth had always been the best thing about the County.

But she'd been glad to leave Tara, and that hurt, too. If she didn't know how much Wade loved it, it would have broken her heart that she could hardly wait to get away. At least her son was taking her place. She saw her new lawyer in Atlanta after the Tara visit, and she made a will, leaving her two-thirds share of Tara to her son. She wasn't going to do like her father, and her Uncle Daniel, and leave a mess behind her. And if Will died first, she didn't trust Suellen an inch. Scarlett signed the document with a flourish, and then she was free.

To go back to her Cat. Who healed all Scarlett's hurts in a second. The baby's face lit up when she saw her, and the little arms reached out to her, and Cat even wanted to be hugged, and tolerated being kissed a dozen times.

"She looks so brown and healthy!" Scarlett exclaimed.

"And no wonder to it," said Maureen. "She loves the sunshine that much, she takes off her bonnet the minute your back is turned. Little gypsy is what she is, and a joy every hour of the day."

"Of the day and the night," Scarlett amended, holding Cat close.

Stephen gave Scarlett her instructions for the trip back to Galway. She didn't like them. Truth to tell, she didn't much like Stephen either. But Colum had told her Stephen was in charge of all arrangements, so she donned her mourning clothes and kept her complaints to herself.

The ship was named *The Golden Fleece* and it was the latest thing in luxury. Scarlett had no quibble with the size or the comfort of her suite. But it did not make a direct crossing. It took a week longer, and she was anxious to get back to Ballyhara to see how the crops were faring.

It was not until she was actually on the gangplank that she saw the big Notice of Departure with the ship's itinerary, or she would have refused to go, no matter what Stephen said. *The Golden Fleece* loaded passengers in Savannah,

Charleston, and Boston, disembarked them in Liverpool and Galway.

Scarlett turned in panic, ready to run back to the dock. She couldn't go to Charleston, she just couldn't! Rhett would know she was on the ship—Rhett always knew everything, somehow— and he'd walk right into her stateroom and take Cat away.

I'll kill him first. Anger drove away her panic, and Scarlett turned again to walk up onto the ship's deck. Rhett Butler wasn't going to make her turn tail and run. All her luggage was already on board, and she was sure that Stephen was smuggling guns to Colum in her trunks. They were depending on her. Also, she wanted to get back to Ballyhara, and she wouldn't let anything or anybody stand in her way.

By the time Scarlett reached her suite, she had built up a consuming fury against Rhett. More than a year had passed since he had divorced her, then immediately married Anne Hampton. During that year Scarlett had been so busy, had experienced such changes in her life, that she'd been able to block out the pain he had caused her. Now it tore her heart, and with the pain was a deep fear of Rhett's unpredictable power. She transformed them into rage. Rage was strengthening.

Bridie was travelling with Scarlett part way. The Boston O'Haras had found her a good position as a lady's maid. Until she learned the ship was going to stop in Charleston, Scarlett had been glad at the prospect of Bridie's company.

But the thought of stopping in Charleston made Scarlett so nervous that her young cousin's constant chatter nearly drove her crazy. Why couldn't Bridie leave her alone? Under Patricia's tutelage Bridie had learned all the duties of her job, and she wanted to try them all out on Scarlett. She was loudly distressed when she learned that Scarlett had stopped wearing corsets, and vocally disappointed that none of Scarlett's gowns needed mending. Scarlett longed to tell her that the first requirement for a lady's maid was to speak only when spoken to, but she was fond of Bridie, and it wasn't the girl's fault that they were going to stop in Charleston. So she forced herself to smile and act as if nothing was bothering her.

The ship sailed up the coast during the night, entering Charleston Harbor at first light. Scarlett hadn't slept at all. She went out on deck for the sunrise. There was a rose-tinted mist on the wide waters of the harbor. Beyond it the city was blurred and insubstantial, like a city in a dream. The white steeple of Saint Michael's Church was palest pink. Scarlett imagined that she could hear its familiar chimes faintly in the distance between the slow strokes of the ship's engine. They must be unloading the fishing boats at the Market now, no it's a little early yet, they must still be coming in. She strained her eyes, but the mist hid the boats if they were there ahead.

She concentrated on remembering the different kinds of fish, the vegetables, the names of the coffee vendors, the sausage man—anything to keep her mind occupied, to fend off memories she didn't dare confront.

But as the sun cleared the horizon behind her, the tinted mist lifted and she saw the pocked walls of Fort Sumter to one side. The *Fleece* was entering the waters where she'd sailed with Rhett and laughed at the dolphins with him and been struck by the storm with him.

Damn him! I hate him—and his damned Charleston—

Scarlett told herself she should go to her stateroom, lock herself in with Cat; but she stood as if rooted to the deck. Slowly the city grew larger, more distinct, glowing white and pink and green, pastel in the shimmering morning air. She could hear Saint Michael's chimes, smell the heavy tropical sweetness of blooming flowers, see the palm trees in White Point Gardens, the opalescent glitter of crushed oyster shell paths. Then the ship was passing the promenade along East Battery. Scarlett could see above it from the ship's deck. There were the treetop-tall columns of the Butler house, the shadowed piazzas, the front door, the windows to the drawing room, her bedroom— The windows! And the telescope in the card room. She picked up her skirts and ran.

She ordered breakfast served in her suite, insisted that Bridie stay with her and Cat. The only safety was there, locked in, out of sight. Where Rhett couldn't find out about Cat and take her away.

The steward spread a glistening white cloth on the round table in Scarlett's sitting room, then rolled in a cart with two tiers of silver domed plates. Bridie giggled. While he meticulously set places and floral centerpiece he talked about Charleston. It was all Scarlett could do not to correct him, he had so many things wrong. But he was Scottish, on a Scottish ship, why should anyone expect him to know anything?

"We'll be sailing again at five o'clock," said the steward, "after cargo's loaded and the new passengers board. You ladies might want to take an excursion to see the town." He began placing platters and lifting off their covers. "There's a nice buggy with a driver who knows all the places to see. Only fifty pence or two dollars fifty American. Waiting at the foot of the gangplank. Or if you'd like some cooler air off the water there's a boat over at the next wharf south that goes up the river. There was a big civil war in America some ten years back. You can see the ruins of big mansion houses burnt by the armies fighting over them. You'd have to hurry, though, she leaves in forty minutes."

Scarlett tried to eat a piece of toast, but it stuck in her throat. The gilded clock on the desk ticked the minutes away. It sounded very loud to her. At the end of a half hour she jumped up. "I'm going out, Bridie, but don't you dare stir a step. Open the portholes, use that palmetto fan over there, but you and Cat stay in here with the door locked no matter how hot it gets. Order anything you want to eat and drink."

"Where are you going, Scarlett?"

"Never mind about that. I'll be back before the ship sails."

The excursion boat was a small rear-wheel paddle boat painted in bright red, white, and blue. Its name, in gold letters, was *Abraham Lincoln*. Scarlett remembered it well. She'd seen it passing Dunmore Landing.

July was not a month when many people toured the South. She was one of only a dozen passengers. She sat under an awning on the upper deck fanning herself and cursing mourning dress for its long-sleeved, high-necked sweltering effect in the Southern summer heat.

A man in a tall top hat striped red and white bellowed commentary through a megaphone. It made her angrier by the minute.

Look at all those fat-faced Yankees, she thought with hatred, they're just lapping this up. Cruel slave owners, indeed! Sold down the river, my foot! We loved our darkies just like family, and some of them owned us more than we owned them. *Uncle Tom's Cabin*. Fiddle-dee-dee! No decent person would read that kind of trash.

She wished she hadn't given in to the impulse to come. It was only going to upset her. It was already upsetting her, and they weren't even out of the harbor and into the Ashley River yet.

Mercifully, the commentator ran out of things to say and for a long while the only sound was the thunk-thunk of the pistons and the splash of water as it fell from the wheel. Marsh grass was green and gold on both sides with wide moss-hung oaks on the riverbank behind it. Dragonflies darted through the midge-dancing air above the grass; occasionally a fish leapt from the water, then flopped back in. Scarlett sat quietly, removed from the other passengers, nursing her rancor. Rhett's plantation was ruined, and he was doing nothing to save it. Camellias! At Ballyhara, she had hundreds of acres of healthy crops where she had found rank weeds. And she had rebuilt an entire town, while he just sat and stared at his burnt chimneys.

That's why she had come on the paddleboat, she told herself. It would make her feel good to see how far she was outstripping him. Scarlett tensed before each bend, relaxed when it was past and Rhett's house had not appeared.

She'd forgotten Ashley Barony. Julia Ashley's big square brick house looked magnificently forbidding in the center of its unadorned lawn. "This is the only plantation the heroic Union forces did not destroy," bawled the man in the absurd hat. "It was not in the tender heart of their commander to injure the frail spinster woman who lay ill inside."

Scarlett laughed aloud. "Frail spinster," indeed! Miss Julia must have scared the pants off him! The other passengers looked at her curiously, but Scarlett was unaware of their scrutiny. The Landing would be next . . .

Yes, there was the phosphate mine. So much bigger! There were five barges being loaded. She searched under the wide-brimmed hat of the man on the dock. It was that white-trash soldier—she couldn't remember his name, something like

911

Hawkins—no matter, around that bend, past that big live oak . . .

The angle of the sunlight sculpted the great grass terraces of Dunmore Landing into green velvet giant steps and scattered sequins on the butterfly lakes beside the river. Scarlett's involuntary cry was lost in the exclamations of the Yankees crowded around her along the rail. At the top of the terraces the scorched chimneys were tall sentinels against the painfully bright blue sky; an alligator was sunning itself on the grass between the lakes. Dunmore Landing was like its owner: cultivated, damaged, dangerous. And unreachable. The shutters were closed on the wing that remained, the place that Rhett used for his office and his home.

Her eyes darted avidly from spot to spot, comparing her memory to what she saw. Much more of the garden was cleared and everything looked as if it was thriving. Some building was going up behind the house; she could smell raw lumber, see the top of a roof. The shutters of the house were fixed, or maybe new. They didn't sag at all, and they glistened with green paint. He'd done a lot of work over the fall and winter.

Or they had. Scarlett tried to look away. She didn't want to see the newly cleared gardens. Anne loves those flowers as much as Rhett does. And the fixed-up shutters must mean a fixed-up house where the two of them live together. Does Rhett fix breakfast for Anne?

"Are you all right, miss?" Scarlett pushed past the concerned stranger.

"The heat—" she said. "I'll go over there,

deeper in the shade." For the remainder of the excursion she looked only at the unevenly painted deck. The day seemed to last forever.

70

Five o'clock was striking when Scarlett ran pell-mell down the ramp from the *Abraham Lincoln.* Damn fool boat. She stopped to catch her breath on the dock. She could see that the gangplank of *The Golden Fleece* was still in place. No harm done. But still, the master of the excursion boat should be horsewhipped. She'd been half out of her mind ever since four o'clock.

"Thank you for waiting for me," she said to the ship's officer at the head of the gangplank.

"Oh, there are more to come," he said, and Scarlett transferred her anger to the captain of the *Fleece.* If he said five o'clock, he should sail at five o'clock. The sooner she got away from Charleston, the happier she would be. This must be the hottest place on the face of the earth. She shaded her eyes with her hand to look at the sky. Not a cloud in sight. No rain, no wind. Just heat. She started along deck towards her rooms. Poor baby Cat must be practically cooked. As soon as they got out of the harbor she'd bring her up on deck for whatever breeze the ship's movement might cause.

Clattering hoofbeats and feminine laughter caught her attention. Maybe this was who they were waiting for. She glanced down at an open victoria. With three fabulous hats on the women in it. They weren't like any hats she'd ever seen, and even from a distance she could tell they were very expensive. Wide brimmed, decorated with clusters of feathers or plumes held by sparkling jewels and swirled with airy tulle netting, from Scarlett's perspective the hats were like wonderful parasols or fantastic confections of pastry on big trays.

I'd look simply wonderful in a hat like that. She leaned slightly over the rail to look at the women. They were elegant, even in the heat, wearing pale organdy or voile trimmed with—it looked like wide silk ribbon or was it ruching?—on cuirass fronts and—Scarlett blinked—no bustle at all, not even a hint of one, and no train either. She hadn't seen anything like that in Savannah or Atlanta. Who were these people? Her eyes devoured the pale kid gloves and folded parasols, lace, she thought, but she couldn't be sure. Whoever they were, they certainly were having a good time laughing their heads off and not hurrying to get on the ship they were holding up either.

The Panama-hatted man with them stepped down into the street. With his left hand he took off his hat. His right hand reached upward to hand the first woman down.

Scarlett's hands clutched the railing. Dear God, it's Rhett. I've got to run inside. No. No. If he's on this ship I've got to get Cat off, find a place to hide, find another ship. But I can't do that. I've got two trunks in the hold with frilly dresses and Colum's rifles in them. What in the name of God am I going to do? Her mind raced

914

from one impossible idea to another while she stared blindly at the group below her.

Slowly her brain registered what she was seeing: Rhett was bowing, kissing one gracefully extended hand after another. Her ears opened to the repeated "goodbye and thank you" of the women. Cat was safe.

But Scarlett was not. Her protective rage had disappeared, and her heart was exposed.

He doesn't see me. I can look at him all I want. Please, please don't put your hat back on, Rhett.

How well he looked. His skin was brown, his smile as white as his linen suit. He was the only man in the world who didn't wrinkle linen. Ah, that lock of hair that annoyed him so was falling down on his forehead again. Rhett flicked it back with two fingers in a gesture that Scarlett knew so well she felt weak-kneed with possessive memory. What was he saying? Something outrageously charming, she was sure, but he was using that low intimate voice he saved for women. Curse him. And curse those women. She wanted that voice murmuring to her, only her.

The ship's captain walked down the gangplank, adjusting the set of his gold epauletted jacket. Don't make them hurry, Scarlett wanted to shout. Stay, stay just a little longer. It's my last chance. I'll never see him again. Let me store up the sight of him.

He must have just had his hair cut, there's the tiniest pale line above his ears. Is that more gray at the temples? It looks so elegant, the silver streaking his crow-black hair. I remember how it felt under my fingers, crisp and shockingly soft at the same time. And the muscles in his shoulders and his arms, sliding so smoothly under the skin, stretching the skin when they hardened. I want—

The ship's whistle shrieked loudly. Scarlett jumped. She could hear rapid footsteps, the rumble of the gangplank, but she kept her eyes fixed on Rhett. He was smiling, looking over there to her right, looking up. She could see his dark eyes and slashing brows and impeccably groomed mustache. His entire strong, masculine, unforgettable pirate's face. "My beloved," she whispered, "my love."

Rhett bowed once again. The ship was moving away from the dock. He put his hat on and turned away. His thumb tilted the hat to the back of his head.

Don't go, cried Scarlett's heart.

Rhett glanced over his shoulder as if there had been a sound. His eyes met hers, and surprise stiffened his lithe body. For a long, immeasurable moment the two of them looked at each other while the space between them widened. Then blandness smoothed Rhett's face as he touched two fingers to his hat brim in salute. Scarlett lifted her hand.

He was still standing there on the dock when the ship turned into the channel to the sea. When Scarlett could see him no longer, she sank numbly into a deck chair.

"Don't be silly, Bridie, the steward will sit right outside the door. He'll come get us if Cat so much as turns over. There's no reason for you not to come to the dining saloon. You can't have your dinner in here every night."

"There's reason enough for me, Scarlett. I don't feel easy among fancy gentlemen and ladies, pretending to be one of them."

"You're just as good as they are, I told you that."

"And I heard you say it, Scarlett, but you don't hear me. I prefer to have me meal in here with all the silver hats on the dishes and my manners my own business. 'Tis soon enough I'll have to go where the lady I'm maiding tells me to go and do what I'm told to do. It's certain that having a grand meal in private comfort won't be one of my instructions. I'll take it now while I can."

Scarlett had to agree with Bridie. But she couldn't possibly have dinner in the suite herself. Not tonight. She had to find out who those women were and why they were with Rhett, or she'd go mad.

They were English, she learned as soon as she entered the dining saloon. The distinctive accent was dominating the captain's table.

Scarlett told the steward that she would like to change her seating to the small table near the wall. The table near the wall was also near the captain's table.

There were fourteen at his table: a dozen English passengers, the captain, and his first officer. Scarlett had a keen ear and could tell almost at once that the passengers' accents were different from the ship's officers, although to her they were all English and therefore to be despised by anyone with a drop of Irish blood.

They were talking about Charleston. Scarlett gathered that they didn't think much of it. "My dears," one of the women trumpeted, "I've never seen anything as dreary in my life. How my darling Mama could have told me that it was the only civilized place in America! It simply makes me worry that she's gone dotty without our noticing."

"Now, Sarah," said the man to her left, "you do have to take that war of theirs into consideration. I found the men to be very decent. Down to their last shilling, I'm sure, but never a mention, and the liquor was first rate. Single malt at the club bar."

"Geoffrey, my love, you'd think the Sahara was civilized if there was a club with drinkable whiskey. Heaven only knows it couldn't be any hotter. Beastly climate."

There was a chorus of agreement.

"On the other hand," said a youthful female voice, "that terribly attractive Butler man said the winters are quite delightful. He invited us back."

"I'm sure he invited you back, Felicity," said an older woman. "You behaved disgracefully."

"Frances, I did no such thing," protested Felicity. "I was only having some fun for the first time on this dreary trip. I cannot credit why Papa sent me to America. It's a wretched place."

A man laughed. "He sent you, sister dear, to get you out of the clutches of that fortune hunter."

"But he was so attractive. I don't see any point in having a fortune if you have to fend off every

918

attractive man in England simply because he's not rich."

"At least you're supposed to fend them off, Felicity," said a girl. "That's easy enough to do. Think of our poor brother. Roger's supposed to draw American heiresses like flies, and marry a fortune to refill the family coffers." Roger groaned and everyone laughed.

Talk about Rhett, Scarlett implored silently.

"There's simply no market for Honourables," Roger said. "I can't get it through Papa's head. Heiresses want tiaras."

The older woman they called Frances said that she thought they were all disgraceful and that she couldn't understand young people today. "When I was a gel—" she began.

Felicity giggled. "Frances, dear, when you were a 'gel' there were no young people. Your generation were born forty years old and disapproving of everything."

"Your impertinence is intolerable, Felicity. I shall speak to your father."

A brief silence fell. Why on earth doesn't that Felicity person say something more about Rhett? Scarlett thought.

It was Roger who brought up the name. Butler, he said, offered some good shooting if he came back in the autumn. Seems he had rice fields gone to grass and the ducks practically landed on the barrel of your gun.

Scarlett tore a roll into fragments. Who gave two cents about ducks? The other Englishmen did, it seemed. They talked about shooting throughout the main course of dinner. She was thinking she'd have done better to stay with Bridie when her ears picked up a low-toned private conversation between Felicity and her sister, whose name turned out to be Marjorie. Both of them thought Rhett one of the most intriguing men they'd ever met. Scarlett listened with mixed feelings of curiosity and pride.

"A shame he's so devoted to his wife," Marjorie said and Scarlett's heart sank.

"Such a colorless little thing, too," Felicity said. Scarlett felt a little bit better.

"Out and out rebound, I heard. Didn't anyone tell you? He was married before, to an absolute tearing beauty. She ran off with another man and left Rhett Butler flat. He's never gotten over it."

"Gracious, Marjorie, can you imagine what the other man must be like if she'd leave the Butler man for him?"

Scarlett smiled to herself. She was enormously gratified to know that gossip had her leaving Rhett and not the other way around.

She felt much better than when she'd sat down. She might even have some dessert.

The following day the English discovered Scarlett. The three young people agreed that she was a superbly romantic figure, a mysterious young widow. "Damned nice looking, too," Roger added. His sisters told him he must be going blind. With her pale skin and dark hair and those green eyes, she was fantastically beautiful. The only thing she needed was some decent clothes and she'd turn heads wherever she went. They decided they'd "take her up." Marjorie made the approach by admiring Cat when Scarlett had her on deck for an airing.

Scarlett was more than willing to be "taken up." She wanted to hear every detail of every hour they'd spent in Charleston. It wasn't difficult for her to invent a tragic story of her marriage and bereavement that satisfied all their cravings for melodrama. Roger fell in love with her within the first hour.

Scarlett had been taught by her mother that genteel discretion about family matters was one of the hallmarks of a lady. Felicity and Marjorie Cowperthwaite shocked her with their casual unveiling of family skeletons. Their mother, they said, was a pretty and clever woman who had trapped their father into marriage. She managed to be run down by his horse when he was out riding. "Poor Papa is so dim," Marjorie laughed, "that he thought he'd probably ruined her because her frock was torn and he saw her bare breasts. We're certain that she tore it herself before she ever left the vicarage. She married him like a shot before he could puzzle out what she was up to."

To add to Scarlett's confusion, Felicity and Marjorie were ladies. Not simply "ladies" as opposed to "women." They were Lady Felicity and Lady Marjorie and their "dim papa" was an earl.

Frances Sturbridge, their disapproving chaperone, was also a "Lady," they explained, but she was Lady Sturbridge, not Lady Frances, because she wasn't born a "Lady" and she'd married a man who was "only a baronet."

"Whereas I could marry one of the footmen

and Marjorie could run off with the boot boy, and we'd still be Lady Felicity and Lady Marjorie in the foul sinks of Bristol where our husbands robbed poor boxes to support us."

Scarlett could only laugh. "It's too complicated for me," she admitted.

"Oh, but my dear, it can be ever so much more complicated than our boring little family. When you get into widows and horrid little viscounts and third son's wives and so on, it's like a labyrinth. Mama has to hire advice every time she gives a dinner or she'd be guaranteed to insult someone fearfully important. You simply must not seat the daughter of an earl's younger son, like Roger, below somebody like poor Frances. It's all too foolish for words."

The Cowperthwaite Ladies were more than a little giddy and rattlebrained, and Roger seemed to have inherited some of Papa's dimness, but they were a cheerful and warmhearted trio who genuinely liked Scarlett. They made the trip fun for her, and she was sorry when they left the ship at Liverpool.

Now she had almost two full days before she got to Galway, and she wouldn't be able to delay any longer thinking about the meeting with Rhett in Charleston, that was really no meeting at all.

Had he felt the same shock of recognition she had when their eyes met? It was, for her, as if the rest of the world disappeared and they were alone in some place and time separate from everything and everyone that existed. It wasn't possible that she could feel so bound to him by a look and that he would not feel the same way. Was it?

She worried and relived the moment until she began to think she'd dreamed it or even imagined it.

When the *Fleece* entered Galway Bay she was able to store the memory with her other prized memories of Rhett. Ballyhara was waiting, and harvest time was near.

But first she had to smile and whisk her trunks past the customs inspectors. Colum was expecting the weapons.

It was hard to remember that the English were all such bad people when the Cowperthwaites were so charming.

71

Colum was waiting at the end of the gangplank when Scarlett left *The Golden Fleece*. She hadn't expected him, she'd known only that someone would meet her and take care of her trunks. At the sight of his stocky figure in worn black clericals and smiling Irish face, Scarlett felt that she'd come home. Her luggage went past customs without any questions other than, "And how are things in America?" to which she answered, "Awful hot," and, "How old is that grand beautiful baby, then?" to which Scarlett replied proudly, "Three months shy of a year, and already trying to walk."

It took nearly an hour to drive the short distance from the port to the train station. Scarlett had never seen such traffic snarls, not even at Five Points.

It was because of the Galway Races, said Colum. Before Scarlett could remember what had happened to her the previous year in Galway, he quickly added details. Steeplechase and flat racing, five days' worth every July. It meant that the militia and constabulary were too busy in the city to be wasting time idling around the docks. It also meant that there was not a hotel room to be had at any price. They'd be taking the afternoon train to Ballinasloe and spending the night there. Scarlett wished there was a train all the way to Mullingar. She wanted to get home.

"How are the fields, Colum? Is the wheat nearly ripe? Is the hay cut yet? Has there been plenty of sun? And what about the peat that was cut? Was there enough? Did it dry out like it was supposed to? Is it good? Does it burn hot?"

"Wait and see, Scarlett darling. You'll be pleased with your Ballyhara, I'm certain of it."

Scarlett was much more than pleased. She was overcome. The townspeople had erected arches covered with fresh greenery and gold ribbon over her route through Ballyhara town. They stood outside the arches waving handkerchiefs and hats, cheering her return. "Oh, thank you, thank you, thank you," she cried over and over, with tears brimming from her eyes.

At the Big House Mrs. Fitzpatrick and the three ill-assorted maids and the four dairymaids and the stablemen were lined up to greet her. Scarlett could barely keep herself from hugging Mrs. Fitz, but she obeyed the housekeeper's rules and maintained her dignity. Cat was bound by no rules. She laughed and held out her arms to Mrs. Fitzpatrick and was immediately caught up in an emotion-ridden embrace.

Less than an hour later Scarlett was dressed in her Galway peasant clothes striding quickly over her fields, Cat in her arms. It felt so good to be moving, stretching her legs. There'd been too many hours, days, weeks of sitting. On trains, and ships, in offices and armchairs. Now she wanted to walk, ride, bend, reach, run, dance. She was The O'Hara, home again, and the sun was warm between gentle, cooling, swiftly passing Irish rains.

Fragrant mounds of golden hay stood in field cocks seven feet tall on the meadows. Scarlett made a cave in one and crawled inside it with Cat to play house. Cat shrieked with delight when she pulled part of the "roof" down on them. And then when the dust made her sneeze. She picked off dried blossoms and put them in her mouth. Her expression of disgust when she spat them out made Scarlett laugh. Scarlett's laughter made Cat frown. Which made Scarlett laugh all the more. "Better get used to being laughed at, Miss Cat O'Hara," she said, "because you're a wonderfully silly little girl and you make your Momma very, very happy, and when people are happy they laugh a lot."

Scarlett took Cat back to the house when she started yawning. "Pick the hay out of her hair while she naps," she told Peggy Quinn. "I'll be back in time to give her supper and a bath." She interrupted the slow, chewing contemplation of one of the plow horses in the stable to ride him, bareback and astride, over Ballyhara in the lingering, slowly dimming twilight. The wheat fields were richly yellow, even in the blue-hued light. There would be a bounteous harvest. Scarlett rode home, content. Ballyhara would probably never deliver the kind of profit she'd earned from building and selling cheap houses, but there were satisfactions beyond earning money. The land of the O'Haras was fruitful again; she had brought it back, at least in part, and next year there'd be more acres tilled; the year after, still more.

"It's so good to be back," Scarlett said to Kathleen next morning. "I have about a million messages from everybody in Savannah." She settled herself happily beside the hearth and put Cat down to explore the floor. Before long the heads began to appear above the half door, everyone eager to hear about America and Bridie and all the rest.

At the Angelus the women hurried back down the boreen to the village, and the O'Hara men came in from the fields for their dinner.

Everyone except Seamus, and, of course, Sean who'd always taken his meals in the small cottage with Old Katie Scarlett O'Hara. Scarlett didn't notice at the time. She was too busy greeting Thomas and Patrick and Timothy and persuading Cat to give up the big spoon she was trying to eat.

It was only after the men had gone back to their work that Kathleen told her how much things had changed while she was away.

"It's sorry I am to say it, Scarlett, but Seamus took it hard that you didn't stay for his wedding."

"I wish I could have, but I couldn't. He must have known that. I had business in America."

"I've a feeling it's more Pegeen who bears the bad will. Did you not remark that she wasn't in the visitors this morning?"

The truth was, Scarlett admitted, that she hadn't noticed at all. She'd only met Pegeen once, she didn't really know her. What was she like? Kathleen chose her words carefully. Pegeen was a dutiful woman, she said, who kept a clean house and set a good table and saw to every comfort for Seamus and Sean in the small cottage. It would be a kindness to the whole family if Scarlett would go to call on her and admire the home she was making. She was that tender of her dignity that she was waiting to be visited before she'd do any visiting herself.

"My grief," Scarlett said, "how silly. I'll have to wake Cat up from her nap."

"Leave her, I'll keep watch while I do the mending. It's better I don't go with you."

So Kathleen didn't much like her cousin's new wife, thought Scarlett, that was interesting. And Pegeen was keeping house separately instead of going in with Kathleen in the larger cottage, at least for dinner. Tender of her dignity indeed! What a waste of energy to fix two meals instead of one. She had an idea she wasn't likely to take to Pegeen, but she made up her mind to be nice. It couldn't be easy coming into a family that had so many shared years, and she knew all too well what it felt like to be the outsider.

Pegeen made it hard for Scarlett to stay sympathetic. Seamus' wife had a prickly disposition. And she looks like she's been drinking vinegar, Scarlett thought. Pegeen poured out tea that had been stewed so long it was almost undrinkable. Wants me to know I kept her waiting, I reckon. "I wish I'd been here for the wedding," said Scarlett bravely. Might as well take the bull by the horns. "I've brought best wishes from all the O'Haras in America to add to mine. I hope you and Seamus will be very happy." She was pleased with herself. Gracefully said, she thought.

Pegeen nodded stiffly. "I'll tell Seamus about your kindness," she said. "He's wanting to have a word with you. I told him to stay nearby. I'll call him now."

Well! Scarlett said to herself, I've felt more welcome in my life. She wasn't sure at all that she wanted Seamus to "have a word" with her. She'd hardly exchanged ten words with Daniel's oldest son in all the time she'd been in Ireland.

After she heard Seamus' "word," Scarlett was quite sure she wished she hadn't. He expected her to pay the rent that was coming due on the farm and he believed it was only just that he and Pegeen have the bigger cottage because he was now in Daniel's place as owner. "Mary Margaret's proper willing to do the cooking and washing for my brothers as well as me. Kathleen can do for Sean over here, seeing she's his sister."

"I'll be glad to pay the rent," said Scarlett. But she'd have liked to be asked, not told. "But I don't see why you're talking to me about who lives where. You and Pegeen—I mean, Mary

Margaret—should discuss that with your brothers and Kathleen."

"You're The O'Hara," Pegeen nearly shouted, "you've got the say."

"She's got the truth of it, Scarlett," said Kathleen when Scarlett complained to her. "You are The O'Hara." Before Scarlett could say anything, Kathleen smiled and told her it made no differnce anyhow. She was going to be leaving Daniel's cottage soon; she was going to marry a boy from Dunsany. He'd asked her only the Saturday before, Market Day in Trim. "I haven't told the others yet, I wanted to wait for you."

Scarlett hugged Kathleen. "How exciting! You'll let me give the wedding, won't you? We'll have a wonderful party."

"So I got off the hook," she told Mrs. Fitz that night. "But only by the skin of my teeth. I'm not so sure being The O'Hara is exactly what I thought it would be."

"And what was that, exactly, Mrs. O?"

"I don't know. More fun, I guess."

In August the potatoes were harvested. It was the best crop they'd ever had, the farmers said. Then they began to reap the wheat. Scarlett loved to watch them. The shiny sickles flashed in the sun and the golden stalks fell like rippling silk. Sometimes she took the place of the man who followed the reaper. She'd borrow the staff with a curved end that the farmers called the loghter-hook and draw up the fallen wheat into small sheaves. She couldn't master the quick twisting movement the man made to tie each sheaf with a stalk of wheat, but she became very handy with the loghter-hook.

It sure beats picking cotton, she told Colum. Yet there were still moments when sharp pangs of homesickness caught her off guard. He understood her feelings, he said, and Scarlett was sure he did. He truly was the brother she'd always wanted.

Colum seemed preoccupied, but he said it was nothing more than his impatience that the wheat took precedence over finishing the work on the inn that Brendon Kennedy was making in the building next to his bar. Scarlett remembered the desperate man in the church, the man Colum had said was "on the run." She wondered if there were more of them, what Colum did for them. But she'd really rather not know, and she didn't ask.

She preferred to think about happy things, like Kathleen's wedding. Kevin O'Connor wasn't the man Scarlett would have picked for her, but he was clearly head over heels in love, and he had a good farm with twenty cows at grass, so he was considered a very good catch. Kathleen had a substantial dowry, in cash saved up from selling butter and eggs, and in her owning all the kitchen implements of Daniel's house. She sensibly accepted a gift of a hundred pounds from Scarlett. It wasn't necessary to add it to her dowry, she said with a conspiratorial wink.

The great disappointment for Scarlett was that she couldn't hold the wedding party at the Big House. Tradition demanded that the wedding take place in the house the couple would live in. The best Scarlett could do was contribute several geese and a half dozen barrels of porter to the wedding feast. Even that was going over the edge a bit, Colum warned her. The groom's family were the hosts.

"Well, if I'm going to go over the edge, I might as well go way over," Scarlett told him. She warned Kathleen, too, in case she wanted to object. "I'm coming out of mourning. I'm sick to death of wearing black."

She danced every reel at the wedding party, wearing bright blue and red petticoats under a dark green skirt, and stockings striped in yellow and green.

Then she cried all the way home to Ballyhara. "I'm going to miss her so much, Colum. I'll miss the cottage, too, and all the visitors. I'll never go there again, not with nasty Pegeen handing out her nasty old tea."

"Twelve miles isn't the end of the earth, Scarlett darling. Get yourself a good riding horse instead of driving your buggy, and you'll be in Dunsany in no time at all."

Scarlett could see the sense to that, although twelve miles was still a long way. What she refused to consider at all was Colum's quiet suggestion that she start thinking about marrying again.

She woke up in the night sometimes, and the darkness in her room was like the dark mystery of Rhett's eyes meeting hers when her ship was leaving Charleston. What had he been feeling?

Alone in the silence of the night, alone in the vastness of the ornate bed, alone in the black blankness of the unlit room, Scarlett wondered, and dreamed of impossible things, and sometimes wept from the ache of wanting him.

"Cat," said Cat clearly when she saw her reflection in the mirror.

"Oh, thank God," Scarlett cried aloud. She'd been afraid her baby was never going to talk. Cat had rarely gurgled and cooed like other babies, and she looked at people who talked baby talk to her with an expression of profound astonishment. She walked at ten months, which was early, Scarlett knew, but a month later she was still practically mute except for her laughter. "Say 'ma-ma,' " Scarlett begged. To no avail.

"Say 'ma-ma,' " she tried again after Cat spoke, but the little girl wriggled out of her grasp and plunged recklessly across the floor. Her walking was more enthusiastic than skillful.

"Conceited little monster," Scarlett called after her. "All babies say 'ma-ma' for their first word, not their own name."

Cat staggered to a halt. She looked back at Scarlett with a smile that Scarlett said later was "positively diabolical." "Mama," she said casually. Then she lurched off again.

"She probably could have said it all along if she'd wanted to," Scarlett, bragged to Father Flynn. "She tossed it to me like a bone to a dog."

The old priest smiled tolerantly. He had listened to many proud mothers in his long years. "It's a grand day," he offered pleasantly.

"A grand day in every way, Father!" exclaimed

932

Tommy Doyle, the youngest of Ballyhara's farmers. "It's sure that we've made the harvest of harvests." He refilled his glass, and Father Flynn's. A man was entitled to relax and enjoy himself at the Harvest Home celebration.

Scarlett allowed him to give her a glass of porter, too. The toasts would be starting soon and it would be bad luck if she didn't share them with at least a sip. After the good luck that had blessed Ballyhara all year, she wasn't about to risk inviting any bad.

She looked at the long, laden tables set up the length of Ballyhara's wide street. Each was decorated with a ribbon-tied sheaf of wheat. Each was surrounded by smiling people enjoying themselves. This was the best part of being The O'Hara. They had all worked, each in his or her own way, and now they were all together, the whole population of the town, to celebrate the results of that work.

There was food and drink, sweets and a small carousel for the children, a wooden platform for dancing later in front of the unfinished inn. The air was golden with afternoon light, the wheat was golden on the table, a golden feeling of happiness bathed everyone in shared repletion. It was exactly what Harvest Home was meant to be.

The sound of horses coming made mothers look for their younger children. Scarlett's heart stopped for a moment when she couldn't find Cat. Then she saw her sitting on Colum's knee at the end of the table. He was talking to the man beside him. Cat was nodding as if she understood every word. Scarlett grinned. What a funny little girl her daughter was.

A group of militia rode into the end of the street. Three men, three officers, their polished brass buttons more golden than the wheat. They slowed their horses to a walk, and the noise around the tables died away. Some of the men rose to their feet.

"At least the soldiers have the decency not to gallop past, stirring up dust," said Scarlett to Father Flynn. But when the men reined in before the deserted church she fell silent, too.

"Which way to the Big House?" said one of the officers. "I'm here to talk to the owner."

Scarlett stood up. "I am the owner," she said. She was amazed that her suddenly dry mouth could make any sound at all.

The officer looked at her tumbled hair and bright peasant clothes. His lips curled in a sneer. "Very amusing, girl, but we're not here to play games."

Scarlett felt an emotion that had become almost a stranger to her, a wild, elated anger. She stepped up onto the bench she'd been sitting on and put her hands on her hips. She looked insolent and she knew it.

"No one invited you here—soldier—to play games or anything else. Now what do you want? I am Mrs. O'Hara."

A second officer walked his horse forward a few steps. He dismounted and came on foot to stand in front of and below Scarlett's position on the bench. "We're to deliver this, Mrs. O'Hara." He removed his hat and one of his white gauntlets and handed a scrolled paper up to Scarlett. "The garrison is going to second a detachment to Ballyhara for its protection."

Scarlett could feel tension, like a storm, in the warm end-of-summer atmosphere. She unrolled the paper and read it slowly, twice. She could feel the knots in her shoulders relax when the full meaning of the document was clear to her. She lifted her head and smiled so everyone could see her. Then she turned the full force of her smile on the officer looking up at her. "That's mighty sweet of the colonel," she said, "but I'm really not interested, and he can't send any soldiers to my town without my agreement. Will you tell him for me? I don't have any unrest here in Ballyhara at all. We get along real fine." She held the vellum sheet down to the officer. "You-all look a mite parched, would you like a glass of ale?" The admiring expression on her face had enchanted men just like this officer from the day she turned fifteen. He blushed and stammered exactly like dozens of young men she'd beguiled in Clayton County, Georgia.

"Thank you, Mrs. O'Hara, but—uh—regulations—that is, personally I'd like nothing better—but the colonel wouldn't—um—he'd think—"

"I understand," said Scarlett kindly. "Maybe some other time?"

The first toast of Harvest Home was to The O'Hara. It would have been the first toast anyway, but now the salute was a loud roar.

72

Winter made Scarlett restless. Except for riding there was nothing active to do, and she needed to be busy. The new fields were cleared and manured by the middle of November, and then what did she have to think about? There weren't even many complaints or disputes brought to her office on First Sundays. True, Cat could walk across the room herself to light the Christmas candle and there were the New Year's Day ceremonies of barm brack against the wall and being the dark-haired visitor in town, but even so the short days seemed too long to her. She was warmly welcomed in Kennedy's bar now that she was known to be supporting the Fenians, but she quickly tired of the songs about the blessed martyrs to Irish freedom and the loud-voiced threats to run the English out. She went down to the bar only when she was starved for company. She was overjoyed when Saint Brigid's Day arrived on February 1 and the growing year had begun again. She turned the first sod with such enthusiasm that soil flew out in a wide circle around her. "This year will be even better than last," she predicted rashly.

But the new fields put an impossible burden on the farmers. There was never enough time to do everything that needed doing. Scarlett nagged at Colum to move some more laborers into the town. There were still plenty of vacant cottages. He wouldn't agree to let strangers in.

Scarlett backed down. She understood the need for secrecy about the Fenians. Finally Colum found a compromise. She could hire men just for the summer. He'd take her to the hiring fair at Drogheda. The horse fair would be on, too, and she could buy the horses she thought she needed.

" 'Thought,' my foot, Colum O'Hara. I must have been blind and half-witted too when I paid good money for the plow horses we've got. They don't go any faster than a box turtle on a rocky road. I'm not going to be cheated again that way."

Colum smiled to himself. Scarlett was an astonishing woman, amazingly competent at many things. But she was never going to best an Irish horse trader, he was sure of that.

"Scarlett darling, you look like a village lass, not landed gentry. No one will believe you can pay for a merry-go-round ride, let alone a horse."

Her frown was meant to intimidate. She didn't understand that she really did look like a girl dressed up for a fair. Her green shirt made her eyes even greener and her blue skirt was the color of the spring sky. "Will you please do me the kindness, *Father* Colum O'Hara, to get this buggy moving? I know what I'm doing. If I look rich, the dealer will think he can stick me with any old broken-down thing he has. I'll do much better in village clothes. Now come on. I've been waiting for weeks and weeks. I don't see any reason why the hiring fair can't be on Saint Brigid's Day when the work starts."

Colum smiled at her. "Some of the lads go

to school, Scarlett darling." He flicked the reins and they were on their way.

"A fat lot of good that'll do them, ruining their eyes on books when they could be out in the air earning a good wage besides." She was cranky with impatience.

The miles rolled by, and the hedgerows were sweet with blackthorn blossoms. Once they were really on their way Scarlett began to enjoy herself. "I've never been to Drogheda, Colum. Will I like it?"

"I believe you will. It's a very big fair, this, much bigger than any you've seen." He knew that Scarlett didn't mean the city when she asked about Drogheda. She liked the excitement of fairs. The intriguing possibilities in a crooked old city street were incomprehensible to her. Scarlett liked things to be obvious and easily understood. It was a trait that often made him uneasy. He knew she had no real understanding of what danger she courted with her involvement in the Fenian Brotherhood, and ignorance could lead to disaster.

But today he was on her business, not his. He intended to enjoy the fair as much as Scarlett.

"Look, Colum, it's enormous!"

"Too big, I fear. Will you choose the lads first or the horses? They're at different ends."

"Oh, bother! The best ones will get snapped up in the beginning, they always do. I'll tell you what—you pick out the boys and I'll go straight for the horses. You come to me when you finish.

You're sure the boys will go to Ballyhara on their own?"

"They're here for hiring and they're used to walking. Some of them likely walked a hundred miles to be here."

Scarlett smiled. "Better look at their feet, then, before you sign anything. I'll be looking at teeth. Which way do I go?"

"Back in that corner, where the banners are. You'll see some of the best horses in Ireland at Drogheda Fair. I've heard of a hundred guineas and more paid."

"Fiddle-dee-dee! What a tale teller you are, Colum. I'll get three pair for under that, you'll see."

There were big canvas tents that served as temporary stables for the horses. Ha! thought Scarlett, nobody's going to sell me an animal in bad light. She pushed into the noisy crowd that was milling around inside the tent.

My grief, I've never seen so many horses in one place in my life! How smart of Colum to bring me here. I'll have all the choice I need. She elbowed her way from one place to another, looked over one horse after another. "Not yet," she said to the traders. She didn't like the system in Ireland at all. You couldn't just walk up to the owner and ask him what he wanted for his animal. No, that was too easy. The minute there was any interest one of the traders jumped in to name a price that was way out of line one end or another and then badger buyer and seller into an agreement in the end. She'd learned the hard way about some of their tricks. They'd grab your hand and slap down on it so sharp it hurt, and that meant you might have bought yourself a horse if you weren't careful.

She liked the looks of a pair of roans that the dealer shouted were perfectly matched three-year-olds and only seventy pounds the pair. Scarlett put her hands behind her back. "Walk them out in the light where I can see them," she said.

Owner and dealer and people nearby all protested furiously. "Takes all the sport out," said a small man in riding breeches and a sweater.

Scarlett insisted, but very sweetly. Catch more flies with honey, she reminded herself. She looked at the horses' gleaming coats, rubbed her hand over them and looked at the pomade on her palm. Then she caught expert hold of one horse's head and examined his teeth. She burst out laughing. Three-year-old, my maiden aunt! "Take 'em in," she said, with a wink at the dealer. "I've got a grandfather younger than them." She was enjoying herself very much.

After an hour, though, she'd only found three horses that she liked both as animal and as a good buy. Every single time she had to coax and charm the owner into letting her examine the horse in the light. She looked enviously at the people buying hunters. There were jumps set up in the open, and they could get a good look at what they were buying, doing what they were buying it to do. They were such beautiful horses, too. For a plow horse, looks weren't important. She turned away from the view of the jumping. She needed three more plow horses. While her eyes accustomed themselves to the shaded interior of the tent, Scarlett leaned against one of the thick tent supports. She was starting to get tired. And she was only half done.

"Where is this Pegasus of yours, Bart? I don't see anything flying over the jumps."

Scarlett's hands reached for the thick support. I'm losing my mind. That sounded like Rhett's voice.

"If you brought me on a wild goose chase—"

It is! It is! I can't be mistaken. No one else in the world sounds like Rhett. She turned quickly, looking into the sunlit square, blinking.

That's his back. Isn't it? It is, I'm sure it is. If only he'd say something else, turn his head. It can't be Rhett. He's got no reason to be in Ireland. But I couldn't be wrong about that voice.

He turned to speak to the slightly built fair-haired man beside him. It was Rhett. Her knuckles were white against her hands, so tightly was she holding on to the post. She was trembling.

The other man said something, pointed with his crop, and Rhett nodded. Then the fair-haired man walked away, out of her sight, and Rhett was there alone. Scarlett stood in the shadow, looking out to the light.

Don't move, she ordered herself when he started to walk away. But she couldn't obey. She burst from the shadows and ran after him. "Rhett!"

He stopped awkwardly, Rhett who was never clumsy, and he spun around. An expression she couldn't recognize flickered on his face, and his dark eyes seemed very bright beneath the shading bill of his cap. Then he smiled the mocking smile she knew so well. "You do turn up in the most unexpected places, Scarlett," he said.

He's laughing at me, and I don't care. I don't care about anything as long as he'll say my name and stand near me. She could hear her own heart beating.

"Hello, Rhett," she said, "how are you?" She knew it was a foolish, inadequate thing to say, but she had to say something.

Rhett's mouth twitched. "I'm remarkably well for a dead man," he drawled, "or was I mistaken? I thought I glimpsed a widow at the dock in Charleston."

"Well, yes. I had to say something. I wasn't married, I mean I didn't have a husband—"

"Don't try to explain, Scarlett. It's not your forte."

"Forty? What are you talking about?" Was he being mean? Please don't be mean, Rhett.

"It's not important. What brings you to Ireland? I thought you were in England."

"What made you think that?" Why are we standing here making conversation about nothing at all? Why can't I think? Why am I saying these stupid things?

"You didn't get off the ship in Boston."

Scarlett's heart leapt to the meaning of what he'd said. He'd taken the trouble to find out where she was going, he cared about her, he wanted to keep her from disappearing. Happiness flooded her heart.

"May I assume from your cheerful attire that you're no longer mourning my death?" said

Rhett. "Shame on you, Scarlett, I'm not yet cold in my grave."

She looked down in horror at her peasant clothes, then up at his impeccably tailored hacking jacket and perfectly tied white stock. Why did he always have to make her feel like a fool? Why couldn't she at least feel angry?

Because she loved him. Whether he believed it or didn't, it was the truth.

Without planning or thought of consequences, Scarlett looked at the man who had been her husband for so many years of lies. "I love you, Rhett," she said with simple dignity.

"How unfortunate for you, Scarlett. You always seem to be in love with another woman's husband." He lifted his cap politely. "I have another commitment, please excuse me if I leave you now. Goodbye." He turned his back on her and walked away. Scarlett looked after him. She felt as if he had slapped her face.

For no reason. She'd made no demands on him, she'd made a gift of the greatest thing she'd learned to give. And he'd trampled it into the muck. He'd made a fool of her.

No, she'd made a fool of herself.

Scarlett stood there, a brightly colored, small isolated figure amid the noise and movement of the horse fair, for a measureless time. Then the world came back into focus, and she saw Rhett and his friend near another tent, in a circle of intent spectators. A different tweed-clad man was holding a restless bay by the bridle, and a red-faced man wearing a plaid vest was swooping his right arm down, in the familiar motions of the horse trade. Scarlett imagined she could hear the slapping palms as he exhorted Rhett's friend, and the horse's owner, to come to a deal.

Her feet moved by themselves, marching across the space separating her from them. There must have been people in her way, but she was unconscious of them, and somehow they melted away.

The dealer's voice was like some ritual chant, cadenced and hypnotic: ". . . a hundred and twenty, sir, you know that's a handsome price, even for a beast as grand as this one . . . and you, sir, you can go twenty-five, isn't that the fact of it, to add a noble animal like this to your stables . . . one-forty? Sure, you must add a little reasonableness to your thinking, the gentleman's come up to one twenty-five, it's only the way of the world for you to take a small step to meet him; say one-forty's your price down from forty-two and we'll be making a deal before the day's out . . . One-forty it is, now see the generous nature of the man, you'll prove you can match him, won't you now? Say one-thirty instead of one twenty-five and there's only a breath between you, no more than can be managed for the cost of a pint or two . . ."

Scarlett stepped into the triangle of seller, buyer, and dealer. Her face was shockingly white above her green shirt, her eyes greener than emeralds. "One-forty," she said clearly. The dealer stared confused, his rhythm broken. Scarlett spit into her right hand and slapped it loudly against his. Then she spit again, looking at the seller. He lifted his hand and spat into the palm, then slapped once, twice against hers in the age-old seal of deal made. The dealer could only spit and seal in acquiescence.

Scarlett looked at Rhett's friend. "I hope you're not too disappointed," she said in a honeyed tone.

"Why, of course not, that is to say—"

Rhett broke in. "Bart, I'd like you to meet . . ." he paused.

Scarlett did not look at him. "Mrs. O'Hara," she said to Rhett's bewildered companion. She held out her spit-wet right hand. "I'm a widow."

"John Morland," he said, and took her grimy hand. He bowed, kissed it, then smiled ruefully into her blazing eyes. "You must be something to see taking a fence, Mrs. O'Hara. Talk about leaving the field behind! Do you hunt around here?"

"I . . . um . . ." Dear heaven, what had she done? What could she say? What was she going to do with a thoroughbred hunter in Ballyhara's stable? "I confess, Mr. Morland, I just gave in to a woman's impulse. I had to have this horse."

"I felt the same way. But not quickly enough, it seems," said the cultivated English voice. "I'd be honored if you'd join me some time, join the hunt from my place, that is. It's near Dunsany, if you're familiar with that part of the County."

Scarlett smiled. She'd been in that part of the County not so long ago, at Kathleen's wedding. No wonder the name John Morland was familiar. She'd heard all about "Sir John Morland" from Kathleen's husband. "He's a grand man, for all that he's a landlord," said Kevin O'Connor a dozen times. "Didn't he tell me himself to drop five pounds from the rent as a gift for my wedding?"

Five pounds, she thought. How very generous. From a man who'll pay thirty times that for a horse. "I'm familiar with Dunsany," Scarlett said. "It's not far from the friends I'm visiting. I'd dearly love to hunt with you sometime. I can hack over any day you name."

"Saturday next?"

Scarlett smiled wickedly. She spit in her palm and lifted her hand. "Done!"

John Morland laughed. He spit in his, slapped hers once, twice. "Done! Stirrup cup at seven and breakfast after."

For the first time since she'd pushed in on them, Scarlett looked at Rhett. He was looking at her as if he'd been looking for a long time. There was amusement in his eyes and something else that she couldn't define. Great balls of fire, you'd think he'd never met me before or something. "Mr. Butler, a pleasure to see you," she said graciously. She dangled her dirty hand elegantly in front of him.

Rhett removed his glove to take it. "Mrs. O'Hara," he said with a bow.

Scarlett nodded to the staring dealer and the grinning former owner of her horse. "My groom will be here shortly to make the necessary arrangements," she said airily, and she hiked up her skirts to take a bundle of banknotes from the garter above her red-and-green striped knee. "Guineas, is that right?" She counted the money into the seller's hand.

Her skirts swirled when she turned and walked away.

"What a remarkable woman," said John Morland.

Rhett smiled with his lips. "Astonishing," he said in agreement.

"Colum! I was afraid you'd got lost," said Scarlett when her cousin emerged from the crowds near the tents.

"Not a bit of it, Scarlett. I got hungry. Have you eaten?"

"No, I forgot."

"Are you pleased with your horses?"

Scarlett looked down at him from her perch on the rail of the jumping ring. She began to laugh. "I think I bought an elephant. You've never seen such a big horse in your life. I had to, but I don't know why." Colum put a steadying hand on her arm. Her laughter was ragged and her eyes were bright with pain.

73

"Cat will go out," said the little voice.

"No, sweetheart, not today. Soon, but not today." Scarlett felt a terrifying vulnerability. How could she have been so reckless? How could she have ignored the danger to Cat? Dunsany was not that far away, not nearly far enough to be sure that people wouldn't know about The O'Hara and her dark-skinned child. She kept Cat with her day and night, upstairs in their two rooms while she looked worriedly out the window above the drive.

Mrs. Fitz was her go-between for the things that had to be done, and done faster than fast. The dressmaker raced back and forth for fittings of Scarlett's riding habit, the cobbler worked like a leprechaun far into the night on her boots, the stableman labored with rags and oil over the cracked and dry sidesaddle that had been left in the tack room thirty years before Scarlett arrived, and one of the boys from the hiring fair who had quiet hands and an easy seat exercised the powerful big bay hunter. When Saturday dawned, Scarlett was as ready as she'd ever be.

Her horse was a bay gelding named Half Moon. He was, as she'd told Colum, very big, nearly seventeen hands, with a deep chest and long back and powerfully muscled thighs. He was a horse for a big man; Scarlett looked tiny and fragile and very feminine on him. She was afraid she looked ridiculous.

And she was quite certain that she'd make a fool of herself. She didn't know Half Moon's temperament or peculiarities, and there was no chance to get to know them because she was riding sidesaddle, as all ladies did. When she was a girl, Scarlett had loved riding sidesaddle. It produced a graceful fall of skirts that emphasized her tiny waist. Also, in those days she seldom went faster than a walk, the better to flirt with men riding alongside.

But now the sidesaddle was a serious handicap. She couldn't communicate with the horse through pressure of her knees because one knee was hooked around the sidesaddle's pommel, the other one rigid because only by pressing on the one stirrup could a lady counterbalance her un-balanced position. I'll probably fall off before I even get to Dunsany, she thought with despair, and I'll certainly break my neck if I get as far as the first fence. She knew from her father that jumping fences and ditches and hedges and stiles and walls was the thrilling part of hunting. Colum had made things no better when he told her that ladies frequently avoided active hunting altogether. The breakfast was the social part and riding clothes were very becoming. Serious accidents were much more likely when riding side-saddle and no one blamed the ladies for being sensible.

Rhett would be glad to see her cowardly and weak, she was convinced. And she'd much prefer to break her neck than to give him that satis-faction. Scarlett touched her crop to Half Moon's neck. "Let's try a trot and see if I can balance on this stupid saddle," she sighed aloud.

Colum had described a fox hunt to Scarlett, but she wasn't prepared for the first impact of it. Morland Hall was an amalgamation of building over more than two centuries, with wings and chimneys and windows and walls attached higgledy-piggledy to one another around the stone-walled courtyard that had been the keep of the fortified castle erected by the first Morland baronet in 1615. The square courtyard was filled with mounted riders and excited hounds. Scarlett forgot her apprehensions at the sight. Colum had omitted to mention that the men wore "pinks," misnamed bright red jackets. She had never seen anything so glamorous in her life.

"Mrs. O'Hara!" Sir John Morland rode over to her, his gleaming top hat in his hand. "Welcome. I didn't believe you'd come."

Scarlett's eyes narrowed. "Did Rhett say that?"

"On the contrary. He said wild horses wouldn't keep you away." There was no guile in Morland. "How do you like Half Moon?" The Baronet stroked the big hunter's sleek neck. "What a beauty he is."

"Um? Yes, isn't he?" said Scarlett. Her eyes were moving quickly, searching for Rhett. What a lot of people! Damn this veil anyhow, everything looks blurred. She was wearing the most conservative riding clothes fashion allowed. Unrelieved black wool with a high neck, and low black top hat with a face veil pulled tight and tied over the netted thick knot of hair at the nape of her neck. It was worse than mourning, she thought, but respectable as all get-out, a real antidote to bright-colored skirts and striped stockings. Scarlett was rebellious in only one matter: she would not wear a corset under her habit. The sidesaddle was torture enough.

Rhett was looking at her. She looked away quickly when she finally saw him. He's counting on me to make a spectacle of myself. I'll show Mr. Rhett Butler. I might break every bone in my body, but nobody's going to laugh at me, especially not him.

"Ride along easy, well back, and watch what

the others do," Colum had said. Scarlett began as he advised. She felt her palms sweating inside her gloves. Up ahead the pace was picking up, then beside her a woman laughed and whipped her horse, breaking into a gallop. Scarlett looked briefly at the panorama of red and black backs streaming down the slope in front of her, at the horses jumping effortlessly over the low stone wall at the base of the hill.

This is it, she thought, it's too late now to worry about it. She shifted her weight without knowing she should and felt Half Moon moving faster, faster, sure-footed veteran of a hundred hunts. The wall was behind her and she had hardly noticed the jump. No wonder John Morland wanted Half Moon so much. Scarlett laughed aloud. It made no difference that she'd never hunted in her life, that she hadn't sat sidesaddle for more than fifteen years. She was all right, better than all right. She was having fun. No wonder Pa never opened a gate. Why bother when you could go over the fence?

The specters of her father and Bonnie that had plagued her were gone. Her fear was gone. There was only the excitement of the misty air streaking past her skin and the power of the animal that she controlled.

That and the new determination to overtake and pass and leave Rhett Butler far behind.

Scarlett stood with the muddy train of her habit looped over her left arm and a glass of champagne in her right hand. The paw of the fox that she'd been awarded would be mounted on a silver base, if she'd allow it, said John Morland.

"I'd love it, Sir John."

"Please call me Bart. All my friends do."

"Please call me Scarlett. Everybody does, whether they're friends or not." She was giddy and pink-cheeked from the exhilaration of the hunt and her success. "I've never had a better day," she told Bart. It was almost true. Other riders had congratulated her, she saw the unmistakable admiration in the men's eyes, jealousy in the women's. Everywhere she looked there were handsome men and beautiful women, silver trays of champagne, servants, wealth; people having a good time, a good life. It was like life before the War, only now she was grown up, she could do and say what she liked, and she was Scarlett O'Hara, country girl from North Georgia, in a baronet's castle partying with Lady this and Lord that and even a countess. It was like a story in a book, and Scarlett's head was turned.

She could almost forget that Rhett was there, almost erase the memory of being insulted and despised.

But only almost. And her treacherous mind kept remembering things she had seen and heard as she rode back to the house after the hunt: Rhett acting like it didn't matter that she'd beaten him to the kill . . . teasing the Countess as if she were just anybody at all . . . looking so damned at ease and comfortable and not impressed . . . being so . . . so Rhett. Damn him, anyhow.

"Congratulations, Scarlett." Rhett was at her side, and she hadn't seen him approaching.

Scarlett's arm jerked, and champagne spilled on her skirts.

"Dammit, Rhett, do you have to sneak up on people like that?"

"I'm sorry." Rhett offered her a handkerchief. "And I'm sorry for my boorish behavior at the horse fair. My only excuse is that I was shocked to see you there."

Scarlett took the handkerchief and bent over to wipe at the dampness on her skirts. There was no point to it; her habit was already spattered with mud from the wild cross-country chase. But it gave her a chance to collect her thoughts and to hide her face for a moment. I will not show how much I care, she vowed silently. I will not show how much he hurt me.

She looked up, and her eyes were sparkling, her lips curved in a smile. "You were shocked," she said. "Imagine what I was. What on earth are you doing in Ireland?"

"Buying horses. I'm determined to win at the races next year. John Morland's stables have a reputation for producing likely yearlings. I go to Paris Tuesday to look at some more. What brought you to Drogheda in local costume?"

Scarlett laughed. "Oh, Rhett, you know how I love to dress up. I borrowed those clothes from one of the maids at the house I'm visiting." She looked from side to side, searching for John Morland. "I've got to make my manners and get going," she said over her shoulder. "My friends will be furious if I'm not back pretty soon." She looked at Rhett for an instant, then hurried off. She didn't dare stay. Not close to him like that. Not even in the same room . . . the same house.

The rain began when she was a little more than five miles from Ballyhara. Scarlett blamed it for the wetness on her cheeks.

On Wednesday she took Cat to Tara. The ancient mounds were just high enough for Cat to feel triumphant when she climbed them. Scarlett watched Cat's recklessness on the run down the mound and forced herself not to warn her that she might fall.

She told Cat about Tara, and her family, and the banquets of the High Kings. Before they left she held the little girl as high as she could to look out over the country of her birth. "You're a little Irish Cat, your roots go deep here . . . Do you understand anything I'm saying?"

"No," said Cat.

Scarlett put her down so she could run. The strong little legs never walked now, always ran. Cat fell often. There were ancient hidden irregularities under the grass. But she never cried. She got to her feet and ran some more.

Watching her was healing for Scarlett. It made her whole again.

"Colum, who's this man Parnell? People were talking about him at the hunt breakfast, but I couldn't make any sense out of what they were saying."

A Protestant, said Colum, and an Anglo. Nobody to concern them.

Scarlett wanted to argue but she'd learned it was a waste of time. Colum never discussed the English, especially not the English landowners in Ireland, who were known as the Anglo-Irish. He would manage to change the subject before she knew he was doing it. It bothered her that he wouldn't even admit that some of the English might be nice people. She'd liked the sisters on the ship from America, and everyone had been nice to her at the hunt. Colum's intransigence made her feel a distance between them. If he'd only talk about it instead of snapping her head off.

She asked Mrs. Fitz the other question that had been on her mind. Who were the Irish Butlers that everyone hated so much?

The housekeeper brought her a map of Ireland. "Do you see this?" She swept her hand over an entire county, as big as County Meath. "That's Kilkenny. Butler country. The Dukes of Ormonde they are. They're probably the strongest Anglo family in Ireland." Scarlett looked closely at the map. Not far from the city of Kilkenny she saw the name Dunmore Cave. And Rhett's plantation was called Dunmore Landing. There had to be a connection.

Scarlett started to laugh. She'd been feeling so superior because the O'Haras were rulers of twelve hundred acres, and here were the Butlers with their own county. Without lifting a finger Rhett had won again. He always won. How could any woman be blamed for loving a man like that?

"And what's so amusing, Mrs. O?"

"I am, Mrs. Fitz. Thank God I can laugh about it."

Mary Moran poked her head around the door without knocking. Scarlett didn't bother to say anything. The gangly, nervous girl would be even worse for weeks if anyone criticized her. Servants. A problem even when you hardly had any. "What is it, Mary?"

"A gentleman to see ye." The maid held out a card. Her eyes were even rounder than usual.

Sir John Morland, Bart.

Scarlett ran down the stairs. "Bart! What a surprise. Come in, we can sit on the steps. I don't have any furniture." She was genuinely pleased to see him, but she couldn't take him up to her sitting room. Cat was having her nap next door.

Bart Morland sat down on the stone steps as if it were the most natural thing in the world to have no furniture. He'd had the devil of a time finding her, he said, until he ran into the postman in the bar. That was his only excuse for being so late delivering her trophy from the hunt.

Scarlett looked at the silver plaque with her name and the date of the hunt. The fox pad was no longer bloody, that was something, but it was not a thing of beauty.

"Disgusting, isn't it?" said Bart cheerfully.

Scarlett laughed. No matter what Colum said, she liked John Morland. "Would you like to say hello to Half Moon?"

"Thought you'd never suggest it. I was wondering how to drop a really weighty hint. How is he?"

Scarlett made a face. "Underexercised, I'm afraid. I feel guilty about it, but I've been very busy. It's haying time."

"How's your crop?"

"So far, so good. If we don't get a real rain."

They walked through the colonnade and out to the stable. Scarlett was going to pass it on the way to the pasture and Half Moon, but Bart stopped her. Could he go inside? Her stables were famous, and he'd never seen them. Scarlett was puzzled, but she agreed readily. The horses were at work or pasture, so there was nothing to see except empty stalls, but if he wanted to see them—

The stalls were separated by granite columns with Doric capitals. Tall vaulting sprang up from the columns to meet and cross and create a ceiling of stone that looked as light and weightless as air and sky.

John Morland cracked his knuckles, then apologized. When he was really excited, he said, he did it without thinking. "You don't find it extraordinary to have a stable that looks like a cathedral? I'd put an organ in it and play Bach to the horses all day."

"Probably give them strangles."

Morland's whooping laugh made Scarlett laugh, too; he sounded so comic. She filled a small bag with oats for him to feed Half Moon.

Walking beside Morland, Scarlett searched her mind for some way to interrupt his admiring

957

chatter about her stables, something casual she could say to start him talking about Rhett.

There was no need. "I say, what luck for me that you're friends with Rhett Butler," Bart exclaimed. "If he hadn't introduced us, I'd never have gotten a look at those stables of yours."

"I was so surprised to run into him like that," Scarlett said quickly. "How do you happen to know him?"

He didn't really know Rhett at all, Bart replied. Some old friends had written to him a month ago, saying that they were sending Rhett to look at his horses. Then Rhett had arrived, bearing a letter of introduction from them. "He's a remarkable fellow, really serious about horses. Knows a lot, too. I wish he could have stayed longer. Are you old friends? He never quite got around to telling me."

Thank goodness, thought Scarlett. "I have some family in Charleston," she said. "I met him when I was visiting there."

"Then you must have met my friends the Brewtons! When I was at Cambridge I'd go down to London for the Season just in hopes that Sally Brewton might have come over. I was mad for her, just like everybody else."

"Sally Brewton! That monkey face?" Scarlett blurted before she thought.

Bart grinned. "The very same. Isn't she marvelous? She's such an original."

Scarlett nodded enthusiastically, and smiled. But in truth she'd never understand how men could be mad for anyone that ugly.

John Morland assumed that everyone who

958

knew Sally must certainly adore her, and he talked about her for the next half hour while he leaned on the pasture fence and tried to entice Half Moon to come get the oats he held in his palm.

Scarlett half-listened while she thought her own thoughts. Then Rhett's name captured her full attention. Bart chuckled as he recounted the gossip Sally had included in her letter. Rhett had fallen into the oldest snare in history, it seemed. Some orphanage was having an outing at his country place, and one of the orphans turned up missing when it was time to leave. So what did he do but go off with the schoolteacher to search for it. All ended well, the child was found, but not until after dark. Which meant, of course, that the spinster teacher was compromised, and Rhett had to marry her.

The best part was that he'd been run out of town years before when he refused to make an honest woman out of another girl he'd been indiscreet with.

"You'd think he would have learned to be careful after the first time," Bart chortled. "He must be a lot more absentminded than he appears. Don't you find that hilarious, Scarlett? Scarlett?"

She gathered her wits. "Speaking as a female, I'd say it serves Mr. Butler right. He has the look of a man who's caused a lot of girls a lot of trouble when he wasn't being absentminded."

John Morland whooped with laughter. The sound attracted Half Moon, who approached the fence warily. Bart shook the bag of oats.

Scarlett was elated, and yet she felt like crying.

So that was why Rhett had been so quick to divorce and remarry. What a sly boots Anne Hampton is. She had me fooled good and proper. Or maybe not. Maybe it was just wretched luck for me that it took so long to find the stray orphan. And that Anne is Miss Eleanor's special favorite. And that she looks so much like Melly.

Half Moon backed away from the oats. John Morland reached into a pocket of his jacket and found an apple. The horse nickered in anticipation.

"Look here, Scarlett," Bart said as he broke the apple. "I've got something a bit ticklish to talk to you about." He extended his open palm with one quarter of the apple on it for Half Moon.

"A bit ticklish!" If he only knew how ticklish his conversation had already been. Scarlett laughed. "I don't mind you spoiling that animal rotten, if that's what you mean," she said.

Heavens no! Bart's gray eyes widened. What could have put such a thought in her head?

It was something truly delicate, he explained. Alice Harrington—she was the stoutish one at the hunt who'd ended up in the ditch—was having a house party at Midsummer Night, and she wanted to invite Scarlett but didn't have the nerve. He'd been appointed diplomat to sound her out about it.

Scarlett had a hundred questions. Essentially they boiled down to when, where, and what to wear. Colum would be furious, she was sure, but she didn't care. She wanted to get dressed up and drink champagne and ride like the wind again over streams and fences following the hounds and the fox.

74

Harrington House was a huge block of a house made of Portland stone. It wasn't far from Ballyhara, just past a crossroads village named Pike Corner. The entrance was hard to find; there were no gates and no gatehouse, only a pair of unadorned and unmarked stone columns. The gravel drive skirted a broad lake then turned into a plain gravelled area in front of the stone house.

A footman came out of the front door at the sound of the buggy's wheels. He handed Scarlett down, then turned her over to a maid who was waiting in the hallway. "My name is Wilson, miss," she said with a curtsey. "Will you be wanting to rest a bit after your journey or will you be joining the others?" Scarlett chose to join the others, and the footman led her the length of the hall to an open door onto a lawn.

"Mrs. O'Hara!" shouted Alice Harrington. Now Scarlett remembered her vividly. "Ended up in a ditch" hadn't been much of a description, nor had "stout." Fat and loud would have identified Alice Harrington for her at once. She moved toward Scarlett with a surprisingly light step and bellowed that she was happy to see her. "I do hope you like croquet, I'm terrible, and my team would adore to lose me."

"I've never played," Scarlett said.

"All the better! You'll have beginner's luck."

She held out her mallet. "Green stripes, it's perfect for you. You have such unusual eyes. Let me introduce everyone, then you can take my place and give my team a chance."

Alice's team—now Scarlett's—was made up of an elderly man in tweeds introduced as General Smyth-Burns, and a couple in their early twenties who both wore spectacles, Emma and Chizzie Fulwich. The General presented the opponents to her, Charlotte Montague, a tall, thin woman with beautifully dressed gray hair, Alice's cousin Desmond Grantley, who was as rotund as she, and an elegant pair named Genevieve and Ronald Bennet. "Watch out for Ronald," said Emma Fulwich, "he cheats."

The game was fun, Scarlett thought, and the scent of freshly mowed lawn was better than flowers. Her competitive instincts were at their full height before her third turn came around, and she earned a "Well done!" and a pat on the shoulder from the General when she whacked Ronald Bennet's ball far out onto the lawn.

When the game was over Alice Harrington halloed them an invitation to tea. The table was set up under a tremendous beech tree; its shade was welcome. So was the sight of John Morland. He was listening attentively to the young woman sitting beside him on the bench, but he waggled his fingers at Scarlett in greeting. The rest of the house party was there, too. Scarlett met Sir Francis Kinsman, a handsome rakehell type, and his wife, and she pretended convincingly that she remembered Alice's husband Henry, from the hunt at Bart's.

Bart's companion was clearly not pleased to be interrupted for introductions, but she was icily gracious. "This is Louisa Ferncliff," said Alice with determined cheerfulness. "She's an Honourable," Alice whispered to Scarlett.

Scarlett smiled, said, "How do you do," and let it go at that. She had a pretty good idea that the frosty young woman wouldn't take kindly to being called Louisa right off the bat, and surely you didn't call people Honourable. Especially when they looked like they hoped John Morland would suggest a little dishonorable kissing behind a bush.

Desmond Grantley held a chair for Scarlett and asked if she would permit him to bring her an assortment of sandwiches and cakes. Scarlett generously said she would. She looked at the circle of what Colum scornfully called "gentry" and thought again that he shouldn't be so pigheaded. These people were really very nice. She was sure she was going to have a good time.

Alice Harrington took Scarlett up to her bedroom after tea. It was a long way, through rather shabby reception rooms, up a wide staircase with a worn runner and along a broad hall with no rug at all. The room was big, but sparsely furnished, Scarlett thought, and the wallpaper was definitely faded. "Sarah has unpacked for you. She'll be up to do your bath and help you dress at seven, if that's all right. Dinner's at eight."

Scarlett assured Alice that the arrangements were fine.

"There's writing material in the desk, and some

books on that table, but if you'd rather have something different—"

"Heavens no, Alice. Now don't let me take up your time, when you have guests and all." She snatched up a book at random. "I can hardly wait to read this. I've been wanting to for ages."

What she'd really been wanting was escape from Alice's incessant noisy recital of the virtues of her fat cousin Desmond. No wonder she was nervous about inviting me, Scarlett thought; she must know that Desmond's nothing to make a girl's heart beat faster. I guess she found out I'm a rich widow and she wants to help him get his licks in first, before anybody else finds out about me. Too bad, Alice, there's not a chance, not in a million years.

As soon as Alice was gone, the maid assigned to Scarlett tapped on the door and entered. She curtseyed, smiling eagerly. "Me name is Sarah," she said. "I'm honored to be dressing The O'Hara. When will the trunks be arriving, then?"

"Trunks? What trunks?" Scarlett asked.

The maid covered her mouth with her hand and moaned through her fingers.

"You'd better sit down," Scarlett said. "I have an idea I need to ask you a bunch of questions."

The girl was happy to oblige. Scarlett's heart grew heavier by the minute as she learned how much she didn't know.

The worst thing was there'd be no hunt. Hunting was for autumn and winter. The only reason Sir John Morland had arranged one was to show off his horses to his rich American guest.

Almost as bad was the news that ladies dressed

964

for breakfast, changed for lunch, changed for afternoon, changed for dinner, never wore the same thing twice. Scarlett had two daytime frocks, one dinner gown, and her riding habit. There was no point in sending to Ballyhara for any more, either. Mrs. Scanlon, the dressmaker, had gone without sleep to finish the things she had with her. All her clothes made new for the trip to America were hopelessly out of fashion.

"I think I'll leave first thing in the morning," said Scarlett.

"Oh, no," Sarah cried, "you mustn't do that, The O'Hara. What do you care what the others do? They're only Anglos."

Scarlett smiled at the girl. "So it's us against them, Sarah, is that what you're telling me? How did you know I was The O'Hara?"

"Everyone in County Meath knows about The O'Hara," said the girl proudly, "everyone Irish."

Scarlett smiled. She felt better already. "Now, Sarah," she said, "tell me all about the Anglos who are here." Scarlett was sure the servants in the house must know everything about everybody. They always did.

Sarah didn't disappoint her. When Scarlett went downstairs for dinner, she was armored against any snobbishness she might meet. She knew more about the other guests than their own mothers did.

Even so, she felt like a backwoods Cracker. And she was furious at John Morland. All he'd said was "light frocks in the daytime and something rather naked for dinner at night." The other women were gowned and jewelled like queens,

965

she thought, and she'd left her pearls and her diamond earbobs at home. Also, she was sure that her gown fairly screamed aloud that a village dressmaker had made it.

She gritted her teeth and made up her mind that she was going to have a good time anyhow. *Might as well, I'll never get invited any place else.*

In fact there were many things she enjoyed. In addition to croquet, there was boating on the lake, plus contests shooting at targets with bow and arrows and a game called tennis, both of them quite the latest rage, she was told.

After dinner Saturday everyone rummaged through big boxes of costumes that had been brought to the drawing room. There was buffoonery and uninhibited laughter and a lack of self-consciousness that Scarlett envied. Henry Harrington draped Scarlett in a long-trained silk cloak glittering with tinsel and put a crown of fake jewels on her head. "That makes you tonight's Titania," he said. Other men and women draped or clothed themselves from the boxes, shouting out who they were and racing through the big room in a free-for-all game of hiding behind chairs and chasing one another.

"I know it's all very silly," John Morland said apologetically through a huge papier-mâché lion's head. "But it is Midsummer Night, we're all allowed to go a bit mad."

"I'm mighty put out with you, Bart," Scarlett told him. "You're no help to a lady at all. Why didn't you tell me I needed dozens of dresses?"

"Oh, Lord, do you? I never notice what ladies have on. I don't understand why they fuss so."

By the time everyone tired of the game they were playing, the long, long Irish twilight was done.

"It's dark," Alice shouted. "Let's go look at the fires."

Scarlett felt a wave of guilt. She should be at Ballyhara. Midsummer Night was almost as important as Saint Brigid's Day in farming tradition. Bonfires marked the turning point in the year, its shortest night, and gave mystical protection for the cattle and the crops.

When the house party went out onto the dark lawn they could see the glow of a distant fire, hear the sound of an Irish reel. Scarlett knew she should be at Ballyhara. The O'Hara should be at the bonfire ceremony. And there, too, when the sun rose and the cattle were run through the dying coals of the fire. Colum had told her she shouldn't go to an Anglo house party. Whether she believed in them or not, the ancient traditions were important to the Irish. She'd gotten angry with him. Superstitions couldn't run her life. But now she suspected she was wrong.

"Why aren't you at the Ballyhara fire?" asked Bart.

"Why aren't you at yours?" Scarlett snapped angrily.

"Because I'm not wanted there," said John Morland. His voice in the darkness sounded very sad. "I did go once. I thought there might be one of those folk wisdom things behind running the cattle through the ashes. Good for the hooves or something. I wanted to try it on the horses."

"Did it work?"

"I never found out. All the joy went out of the celebration when I arrived, so I left."

"I should have left here," Scarlett blurted.

"What an absurd thing to say. You're the only real person here. An American, too. You're the exotic bloom in the patch of weeds, Scarlett."

She hadn't thought of it that way. It made sense, too. People always made much over guests from far away. She felt much better, until she heard The Honourable Louisa say, "Aren't they entertaining? I do adore the Irish when they go all pagan and primitive like this. If only they weren't so lazy and stupid, I wouldn't mind living in Ireland."

Scarlett vowed silently to apologize to Colum the minute she got back home. She should never have left her own place and her own people.

"And hasn't any other living soul ever made a mistake, Scarlett darling? You had to learn the way of them for yourself else how would you know? Dry your eyes, now, and ride out to see the fields. The hired lads have started building the haycocks."

Scarlett kissed her cousin's cheek. He hadn't said, "I told you so.

In the weeks that followed, Scarlett was invited to two more house parties, by people she had met at Alice Harrington's. She wrote stilted, proper refusals for both. When the haycocks were finished she had the hired lads start working on the ruined lawn behind the house. It could be back in good grass by next summer, and Cat would love to play croquet. That part had been fun.

The wheat was ripe yellow, almost ready to harvest, when a rider brought a note to her and invited himself into the kitchen for a cup of tea "or something more manly" while he waited for her to write a reply for him to take back.

Charlotte Montague would like to call on her if it was convenient.

Who on earth was Charlotte Montague? Scarlett had to rack her brain for nearly ten minutes before she recalled the pleasant, unobtrusive older woman at the Harringtons'. Mrs. Montague, she remembered, had not raced around like a wild Indian on Midsummer Night. She'd sort of disappeared after dinner. Not that it made her any less English.

But what could she want? Scarlett's curiosity was piqued. The note said "a matter of considerable interest to us both."

She went to the kitchen herself to give Mrs. Montague's messenger the note inviting her to tea that afternoon. She knew she was trespassing on Mrs. Fitz's territory. The kitchen was supposed to be viewed only from the bridge-like gallery above. But it was her kitchen, wasn't it? And Cat had started spending hours there every day, why couldn't she?

Scarlett nearly put on her pink frock for Mrs. Montague's call. It was cooler than her Galway skirts and the afternoon was very warm, for Ireland. Then she put it back in the wardrobe. She wouldn't pretend to be what she was not.

She ordered barm brack for tea instead of the scones she usually had.

Charlotte Montague was wearing a gray linen jacket and skirt with a lace jabot that Scarlett's fingers itched to touch. She'd never seen lace so thick and elaborate.

The older woman took off her gray kid gloves and gray feathered hat before she sat in the plush-covered chair next to the tea table.

"Thank you for receiving me, Mrs. O'Hara. I doubt that you want to waste time talking about the weather; you'd prefer to know why I'm here, is that correct?" Mrs. Montague had an interesting wryness in her voice and her smile.

"I've been dying of curiosity," said Scarlett. She liked this beginning.

"I have learned that you're a successful businesswoman, both here and in America . . . Don't be alarmed. What I know, I keep to myself; it's one of my most valuable assets. Another, as you can imagine, is that I have means of learning things that others do not. I'm a businesswoman, too. I would like to tell you about my business, if I may."

Scarlett could only nod dumbly. What did this woman know about her? And how?

To put it at its most basic level, she arranged things, said Mrs. Montague. She was born the youngest daughter of a younger son of a good family, and she had married a younger son of another. Even before he died in a hunting accident she had grown tired of being always on the edge of things, always trying to keep up appearances and lead the life expected of well-bred ladies and gentlemen, always in need of money. After she was widowed she found herself in the position of poor relation, a position that was intolerable.

What she had was intelligence, education, taste, and entrée to all the best houses in Ireland. She built on them, adding discretion and information to the attributes she began with.

"I am—in a manner of speaking—a professional houseguest and friend. I give generously of advice—in clothing, in entertaining, in decorating houses, in arranging marriages or assignations. And I am paid generous commissions by dressmakers and tailors, bootmakers and jewelers, furniture dealers and rug merchants. I am skillful and tactful, and it is doubtful that anyone suspects that I am being paid. Even if they do suspect, either they don't want to know or they are so satisfied with the outcome that they don't care, particularly since it costs them nothing."

Scarlett was shocked and fascinated. Why was the woman confessing all of this, to her of all people?

"I'm telling you this because I am sure you're no fool, Mrs. O'Hara. You would wonder—and rightly—if I offered to help you, as the saying goes, out of the goodness of my heart. There is no goodness in my heart, except insofar as it adds to my personal well-being. I have a business proposal for you. You deserve better than a shabby little party given by a shabby little woman like Alice Harrington. You have beauty and brains and money. You can be an original. If you put yourself in my hands, under my tutelage, I will make you the most admired, the most sought-after woman in Ireland. It will take two to three years. Then the whole world will be open to you, to do with as you will. You will be famous. And I will have enough money to retire in luxury."

Mrs. Montague smiled. "I've been waiting nearly twenty years for someone like you to come along."

75

Scarlett hurried across the kitchen bridge to Mrs. Fitzpatrick's rooms as soon as Charlotte Montague left. She didn't care that she was supposed to send for the housekeeper to come to her; she had to talk to someone.

Mrs. Fitz came out of her room before Scarlett could knock on the door. "You should have sent for me, Mrs. O'Hara," she said in a low voice.

"I know, I know, but it takes so long, and what I have to tell you just won't wait!" Scarlett was extremely agitated.

Mrs. Fitzpatrick's cold look calmed her down rapidly. "It will have to wait," she said. "The kitchen maids will hear every word you say and repeat it with embellishments. Walk slowly with me, and follow my lead."

Scarlett felt like a chastised child. She did as she was told.

Halfway across the gallery above the kitchen Mrs. Fitzpatrick stopped. Scarlett stopped with her and contained her impatience while Mrs. Fitz talked about improvements that had been made in the kitchen. The wide balustrade was plenty big enough to sit on, Scarlett thought idly, but she stood as erect as Mrs. Fitz, looking down at the kitchen and the exceedingly busy-looking maids far below.

Mrs. Fitzpatrick's progress was stately, but she did move. When they reached the house, Scarlett started talking as soon as the door to the bridge closed behind them.

"Of course it's ridiculous," she said after she reported what Mrs. Montague had said. "I told her so, too. 'I'm Irish,' I said, 'I don't want to be sought after by the English.' " Scarlett was talking very fast, and her color was high.

"Quite right you were, too, Mrs. O. The woman's no better than a thief, by the words out of her own mouth."

Mrs. Fitzpatrick's vehemence silenced Scarlett. She didn't repeat Mrs. Montague's response. "Your Irishness is one of the intriguing things about you. Striped stockings and boiled potatoes one day, partridge and silks the next. You can have both; it will only add to your legend. Write to me when you decide."

Rosaleen Fitzpatrick's account of Scarlett's visitor infuriated Colum. "Why did Scarlett even let her in the door?" he raged.

Rosaleen tried to calm him. "She's lonely, Colum. No friends save you and me. A child is all the world to its mother, but not much company. I'm thinking some fancy socializing might be good for her. And for us, if you put your mind on it. Kennedy's Inn is nearly finished. We'll have men coming and going soon. What better than to have other comings and goings to distract the eyes of the English?

"I took this Montague woman's measure at a glance. She's a cold, greedy sort. Mark my words, the first thing she will do is tell Scarlett that the Big House must be furnished and furbished. This Montague will play games with the cost of everything, but Scarlett can well afford it. And there will be strangers coming through Trim to Ballyhara every day of the year with their paints and velvets and French fashions. No one will pay heed to one or two more travelling this way.

"There's wonder already about the pretty American widow. Why isn't she looking for a husband? I say we'll do better to send her out to the English at their parties. Otherwise, the English officers may start coming here to court her."

Colum promised to "put his mind on it." He went out that night and walked for miles, trying to decide what was best for Scarlett, what was best for the Brotherhood, how they could be reconciled.

He'd been so worried of late that he didn't always think clearly. There had been reports of some men losing their commitment to the Fenian movement. Good harvests for two years in a row were making men comfortable, and comfort made it harder to risk everything. Also, Fenians who had infiltrated the constabulary were hearing rumors about an informer in the Brotherhood. Underground groups were perpetually in danger from informants. Twice in the past an uprising had been destroyed by treachery. But this one had been so carefully, so slowly planned. Every precaution taken. Nothing left to chance. It mustn't go wrong now. They were so close. The highest councils had planned to give the signal for action in the coming winter, when three-fourths of the English militia would be away from their garrisons for fox hunting. Instead the word had come down: delay until the informer is identified and disposed of. The waiting was eating away at him.

When the sunrise came, he walked through the rose-tinted ground mist to the Big House, let himself in with a key, and went to Rosaleen's room. "I believe you're right," he told her. "Does that earn me a cup of tea?"

Mrs. Fitzpatrick made a graceful apology to Scarlett later that day, admitting that she had been too hasty and too prejudiced. She urged Scarlett to start creating a social life for herself with Charlotte Montague's help.

"I've decided it's a silly idea," Scarlett replied. "I'm too busy."

When Rosaleen told Colum, he laughed. She slammed the door when she left his house.

Harvest, Harvest Home celebration, golden autumn days, golden leaves beginning to fall. Scarlett rejoiced in the rich crops, mourned the end of the growing year. September was the time for the half-yearly rents, and she knew her tenants would have profit left over. It was a grand thing, being The O'Hara.

She gave a big party for Cat's second birthday. All the Ballyhara children ten and under played in the big empty rooms on the ground floor, tasted ice cream for probably the first time, ate barm brack with tiny favors baked in it as well as currants and raisins. Every one of them went home with a shiny coin. Scarlett made sure they went home early because of all the superstitions about Halloween. Then she took Cat upstairs for her nap.

"Did you like your birthday, darling?"

Cat smiled drowsily. "Yes. Sleepy, Momma."

"I know you are, angel. It's way past your nap time. Come on . . . into bed . . . you can nap in Momma's big bed because this is a big birthday."

Cat sat up as soon as Scarlett laid her down. "Where's Cat's present?"

"I'll get it, darling." Scarlett brought the big china dollbaby from its box where Cat had left it.

Cat shook her head. "The other one." She turned on her stomach and slid down under the eiderdown to the floor, landing with a thump. Then she crawled under the bed. She backed out with a yellow tabby cat in her arms.

"For pity's sake, Cat, where did that come from? Give it to me before it scratches you."

"Will you give it back?"

"Of course, if you want it. But it's a barn cat, baby, it might not want to stay in the house."

"It likes me."

Scarlett gave in. The cat hadn't scratched Cat, and she looked so happy with it. What harm could it possibly do to let her keep it? She put the two of them in her bed. I'll probably end up sleeping with a hundred fleas, but a birthday is a birthday.

Cat nestled into the pillows. Her drooping eyes opened suddenly. "When Annie brings my milk," she said, "my friend can drink mine." Her green eyes closed and she went limp with sleep.

Annie tapped on the door, came in with a cup of warm milk. She told them when she got back to the kitchen that Mrs. O'Hara had laughed and laughed, she couldn't think why. She'd said something about cats and milk. If anybody wanted to know what she thought, said Mary Moran, she thought it would be a lot more seemly for that baby to have a decent Christian name, may the saints protect her. All three maids and the cook crossed themselves three times.

Mrs. Fitzpatrick saw and heard from the bridge. She crossed herself, too, and said a silent prayer. Cat would soon be too big to keep protected all the time. People were afraid of fairy changelings, and what people feared, they tried to destroy.

Down in Ballyhara town, mothers were scrubbing their children with water in which angelica root had steeped all day. It was a known protection against witches and spirits.

The horn did it. Scarlett was exercising Half Moon when both of them heard the horn and then the hounds. Somewhere close by in the countryside people were hunting. For all she knew, Rhett might even be with them. She put Half Moon over three ditches and four hedges on Ballyhara, but it wasn't the same. She wrote to Charlotte Montague the next day.

Two weeks later three wagons rolled heavily up the drive. The furniture for Mrs. Montague's rooms had arrived. The lady followed in a smart carriage, along with her maid.

She directed the disposition of the furniture in a bedroom and sitting room near Scarlett's, then left her maid to see to her unpacking. "Now we begin," she said to Scarlett.

"I might just as well not be here at all," Scarlett complained. "The only thing I'm allowed to do is sign bank drafts for scandalous amounts of money." She was talking to Ocras, Cat's tabby. The name meant "hungry" in Irish and had been given by the cook in an exasperated moment. Ocras ignored Scarlett, but she had no one else to talk to. Charlotte Montague and Mrs. Fitzpatrick seldom asked her opinion about anything. Both of them knew what a Big House should be, and she didn't.

Nor was she very interested. For most of her life the house she lived in had simply been there, already as it was, and she'd never thought about it. Tara was Tara, Aunt Pittypat's was Aunt Pitty's, even though half of it belonged to her. Scarlett had involved herself only with the house Rhett built for her. She'd bought the newest and most expensive furnishings and decorations, and she'd been pleased with them because they proved how rich she was. The house itself never gave her pleasure; she hardly saw it. Just as she didn't really see the Big House at Ballyhara. Eighteenth-century Palladian, Charlotte said, and what, pray tell, was so important about that? What mattered to Scarlett was the land, for its richness and its crops, and the town, for its rents and services and because no one, not even Rhett, owned his own town.

However, she understood perfectly well that accepting invitations placed an obligation on her to return them, and she couldn't invite people to a place that had furniture in only two rooms. She was lucky, she supposed, that Charlotte Montague wanted to transform the Big House for her. She had more interesting things to do with her time.

Scarlett was firm about the points that mattered to her: Cat must have a room next to her own, not in some nursery wing with a nanny; and Scarlett would do her own accounts, not turn all her business over to a bailiff. Other than that, Charlotte and Mrs. Fitz could do whatever they liked. The costs made her wince, but she had agreed to give Charlotte a free hand and it was too late to back out once she'd shaken hands on it. Besides, money just didn't matter to her now the way it used to.

So Scarlett took refuge in the Estate office and Cat made the kitchen her own while workmen did unknown, expensive, noisy, smelly things to her house for months on end. At least she had the farm to run, and her duties as The O'Hara. Also she was buying horses.

"I know little or nothing about horses," said Charlotte Montague. It was a statement that made Scarlett's eyebrows skid upwards. She'd come to believe that there was nothing on earth Charlotte didn't claim to be an expert on. "You'll need at least four saddle horses and six hunters, eight would be better, and you must ask Sir John Morland to assist you in selecting them."

"Six hunters! God's nightgown, Charlotte, you're talking about, more than five hundred pounds!" Scarlett shouted. "You're crazy." She brought her voice down to normal sound, she'd learned that shouting at Mrs. Montague was a waste of energy; nothing bothered the woman. "I'll educate you a little about horses," she said with venomous sweetness. "You can only ride one. Teams are for carriages and plows."

She lost the argument. As usual. That was why she didn't bother to argue about John Morland's help, she told herself. But Scarlett knew that really she had been hoping to have a reason to see Bart. He might have some news of Rhett. She rode over to Dunsany the next day. Morland was delighted by her request. Of course he'd help her find the best hunters in all Ireland . . .

"Do you ever hear from your American friend, Bart?" She hoped the question sounded casual, she'd waited long enough to get it in. John Morland could talk about horses even longer than Pa and Beatrice Tarleton.

"Rhett, do you mean?" Scarlett's heart turned over at the sound of his name. "Yes, he's much more responsible about his correspondence than I am." John gestured towards the untidy pile of letters and bills on his desk.

Would the man just get on with it? What about Rhett?

Bart shrugged, turned his back to the desk. "He's determined to enter the filly he bought from me in the Charleston races. I told him she was bred for hurdles and not for the flat, but he's sure her speed will compensate. I'm afraid he's going to be disappointed. In another three or four years, perhaps he might prove right, but when you remember that her dam was out of . . ."

Scarlett stopped listening. John Morland would talk bloodlines all the way back to the Flood! Why couldn't he tell her what she wanted to know? Was Rhett happy? Had he mentioned her?

She looked at the young Baronet's animated, intense face and forgave him. In his own eccentric way, he was one of the most charming men in the world.

John Morland's life was built around horses. He was a conscientious landlord, interested in his estate and his tenants. But breeding and training race horses was his true passion, followed closely by fox hunting in the winter on the magnificent hunters he kept for himself.

Possibly they compensated for the romantic tragedy of Bart's absolute devotion to the woman who had gained possession of his heart when they were both not much more than children. Her name was Grace Hastings. She'd been married to Julian Hastings for nearly twenty years. John Morland and Scarlett shared a bond of hopeless love.

Charlotte had told her what "everyone in Ireland" knew—John was relatively immune to husband-hunting women because he had little money.

His title and his property were old—impressively old—but he had no income except his rents, and he spent almost every shilling of that on his horses. Even so, he was very handsome in an absentminded way, tall and fair with warm, interested gray eyes and a breathtakingly sweet smile that accurately reflected his goodhearted nature. He was strangely innocent for a man who had spent all of his forty-some years in the worldly circles of British society. Occasionally a woman with money of her own, like the Honourable Louisa, fell in love with him and made a determined pursuit that embarrassed Morland and amused everyone else. His eccentricities became more pronounced then; his absentmindedness bordered on vacancy, his waistcoats were often buttoned wrong, his contagious whooping laughter became sometimes inappropriate, and he rearranged his collection of paintings by George Stubbs so often that the walls of his house became peppered with holes.

A beautiful portrait of the famous horse Eclipse was balanced perilously on a stack of books, Scarlett noticed. It made no difference to her, she wanted to know about Rhett. I'll go ahead and ask, she decided. Bart won't remember anyhow. "Did Rhett say anything about me?"

Morland blinked, his mind on the filly's forebears. Then her question registered. "Oh, yes, he asked me if you might possibly sell Half Moon. He's thinking about starting up the Dunmore Hunt again. He wants me to keep my eye open for any more like Half Moon, too."

"He'll have to come back to buy them, I guess,"

Scarlett said, praying for affirmation. Bart's answer sunk her in despair.

"No, he'll have to trust me. His wife's expecting, you see, and he won't leave her side. But now that I'll be aiming you at the cream of the crop, I couldn't help Rhett anyhow. I'll write and tell him so as soon as I find the time."

Scarlett was so preoccupied with Bart's news that he had to shake her arm to get her attention. When did she want to start the search for her hunters, he asked.

Today, she answered.

Throughout the winter she went every Saturday with John Morland to one hunt or another in County Meath, trying out hunters that were for sale. It wasn't easy to find mounts that suited her, for she demanded that the horse be as fearless as she was. She rode as if demons were chasing her, and the riding eventually made it possible for her to stop imagining Rhett as father to any child but Cat.

When she was home, she tried to give the little girl extra attention and affection. As usual, Cat scorned embraces. But she would listen to stories about the horses for as long as Scarlett would talk.

When February came, Scarlett turned the first sod with the same happy excitement as in earlier years. She had succeeded in relegating Rhett to the past and seldom thought of him at all.

It was a new year, full of good things to come. If Charlotte and Mrs. Fitz ever got finished with whatever they were doing to her house, she might even be able to give a party. She missed Kathleen, and the rest of the family. Pegeen made visits so uncomfortable that she almost never saw her cousins any more.

That could wait, it would have to. There was planting to be done.

In June Scarlett spent a long, exhausting day being measured by the dressmaker Charlotte Montague had brought over from Dublin. Mrs. Sims was merciless. Scarlett had to hold her arms up, out, in front, at her sides, one up one down, one forward one back, in every imaginable position and some she would never have imagined. For what seemed like hours. Then the same thing sitting. Then in every position of the quadrille, the waltz, the cotillion. "The only thing she didn't measure me for was my shroud," Scarlett groaned.

Charlotte Montague gave one of her infrequent smiles. "She probably did, without your knowing it. Daisy Sims is very thorough."

"I refuse to believe that terrifying woman's name is Daisy," Scarlett said.

"Don't you ever call her that, unless she invites you to. No one below the rank of Duchess is ever allowed to be familiar with Daisy. She's the best at her trade; they wouldn't dare risk offending her."

"You called her Daisy."

"I'm the best at my trade, too."

Scarlett laughed. She liked Charlotte Montague, and respected her as well. Though she wouldn't call her exactly cozy to have for a friend.

She put on her peasant clothes then and had

supper—Charlotte reminded her it was dinner—before she went out to the hill near Knightsbrook River for the lighting of the Midsummer Night bonfire. When she was dancing to the familiar music of the fiddles and pipes and Colum's *bodhran*, she thought how lucky she was. If what Charlotte had promised was true, she was going to have both worlds, Irish and Anglo. Poor Bart, she remembered, wasn't welcome at his own estate's bonfire.

Scarlett thought of her good fortune again, when she presided at the Harvest Home banquet. Ballyhara had another good crop, not as good as the two previous years, but still enough to make every man's pocket jingle. Everyone in Ballyhara celebrated their good fortune. Everyone except Colum, Scarlett noticed. He looked as if he hadn't slept in a week. She wished she could ask him what was wrong, but he'd been cross as a bear with her for weeks. And he never seemed to go to the bar any more, according to Mrs. Fitz.

Well, she wasn't going to let his gloom ruin her good mood. Harvest Home was a party.

Also, the hunting season would be starting any day now, and her new riding habit was the most enchanting design Scarlett had ever seen. Mrs. Sims was everything Charlotte had said she was.

"If you're ready we will take a tour," said Charlotte Montague. Scarlett put down her teacup. She was more eager than she wanted to admit.

"Mighty kind of you, Charlotte, seeing as how every door except my rooms has been locked for practically a year." She sounded as cranky as she could, but she suspected that Charlotte was too smart to be fooled. "I'll just find Cat to go with us."

"If you like, Scarlett, but she saw everything as it was done. She's a remarkable child, just appears when a door or window is left open. It made some of the painters quite nervous when they found her on top of their scaffolding."

"Don't tell me things like that, I'll have a seizure. Little monkey, she climbs everything." Scarlett called for Cat and looked for Cat to no avail. Sometimes the little girl's independence annoyed her, like now. Usually she was proud. "I guess she'll catch up with us if she's interested," she said at last. "Let's go, I'm dying to see." Might as well admit it. She wasn't fooling anybody.

Charlotte led the way upstairs first to long corridors lined with bedrooms for guests, then back down again to what Scarlett still had trouble calling the first floor instead of, in American usage, the second. Charlotte took her to the end of the house away from the rooms she'd been using. "Your bedroom, your bath, your boudoir, your dressing room, Cat's playroom, bedroom, nursery." The doors flew open as Charlotte unveiled her labors. Scarlett was enchanted with the feminine pale-green-and-gilt furniture in her rooms and the frieze of alphabet animal paintings in Cat's playroom. The child-size chairs and tables made her clap her hands. Why hadn't she thought of it? There was even a child-size tea set on Cat's table and a child-size chair by the hearth.

"Your private rooms are French," said Charlotte, "Louis Sixteenth, if you care. They represent your Robillard self. Your O'Hara self dominates the reception rooms on the ground floor."

The only ground floor room that Scarlett knew was the marble-floored hall. She used its door to the drive and the broad stone staircase to the upper floors. Charlotte Montague led her quickly through it. She opened tall double doors on one side of it and ushered Scarlett into the dining room. "My stars," Scarlett exclaimed, "I don't know enough people to fill up all those chairs."

"You will," said Charlotte. She led Scarlett through the long room to another tall door. "Now this is your breakfast room and morning room. You may want to have dinner in here as well when you are a small number." She walked across the room to more doors. "The great salon and ballroom," she announced. "I admit to being very pleased with this."

One long wall was made up of widely spaced French doors with tall gilt mirrors between them. The wall opposite was centered by a fireplace surmounted by another gilt-framed mirror. All the mirrors were infinitesimally tilted so that they reflected not only the room but also the high ceiling. It was painted with scenes from the heroic legends of Irish history. The High Kings' buildings on the hill of Tara looked rather like Roman temples. Scarlett loved it.

"The furniture throughout this floor is Irish-made, so are the fabrics—all wools and linens—and the silver, china, glass, almost everything.

This is where The O'Hara is hostess. Come, there's only the library still to see."

Scarlett liked the leather-covered chairs and Chesterfield, and she recognized that the leather-backed books were very handsome. "You've done a wonderful job, Charlotte," she said sincerely.

"Yes, well it wasn't as difficult as at first I feared. The people who lived here must have used a Capability Brown design for the gardens, so there was only pruning and cleaning to do. The kitchen garden will be very productive next year, though it may be two years before the wall fruits come back. They had to be pruned back to leaders."

Scarlett hadn't the remotest idea what Charlotte was talking about, nor the faintest interest. She was wishing Gerald O'Hara could see the ceiling in the ballroom and Ellen O'Hara could admire the furniture in her boudoir.

Charlotte opened more doors. "Here we are in the hall again," she said. "Excellent circular movement for large parties. The Georgian architects knew precisely what, they were doing . . . Come through to the entrance door, Scarlett."

She escorted Scarlett onto the top of the steps that led down to the freshly gravelled drive. "Your staff, Mrs. O'Hara."

"My grief," Scarlett said weakly.

Two long rows of uniformed servants were facing her. To her right Mrs. Fitzpatrick stood slightly in front of the cook, four kitchen maids, two parlor maids, four upstairs maids, three dairymaids, the head laundress, and three laundry maids.

To her left she saw a haughty-looking man who could only be a butler, eight footmen, two nervous-footed boys, the stableman she knew and six grooms, and five men she guessed were gardeners by their earth-stained hands.

"I believe I need to sit down," she whispered.

"First you smile and welcome them to Ballyhara," Charlotte said. Her tone would permit no remonstrance. Scarlett did as she was told.

Back inside the house—which had now become an establishment—Scarlett began to giggle. "They're all better dressed than I am," she said. She looked at Charlotte Montague's expressionless face. "You're about to bust out laughing, Charlotte, you can't fool me. You and Mrs. Fitz must have had a high old time planning this."

"We did rather," Charlotte admitted. A smile was the nearest thing to "bust out laughing" that Scarlett could get from her.

Scarlett invited all the people from Ballyhara and Adamstown to come up to see the revived Big House. The long dining room table was spread with refreshments, and she darted from room to room, urging everyone to help themselves, dragging them to see the High Kings. Charlotte Montague stood quietly to one side of the big staircase, quietly disapproving. Scarlett ignored her. She tried to ignore the discomfort and embarrassment of her cousins and villagers, but within a half hour of their arrival, she was close to tears.

"It goes against tradition, Mrs. O," Rosaleen Fitzpatrick murmured to her, "it's naught to do with you. No farmer's boot has ever crossed the threshold of a Big House in Ireland. We're a people ruled by the old ways, and we're not ready for change."

"But I thought the Fenians wanted to change everything."

Mrs. Fitz sighed. "That is so. But the change is for a return to even older ways than the ones that keep the boots out of a Big House. I wish I could explain more clearly."

"Don't bother, Mrs. Fitz. I've just made a mistake, that's all. I won't do it again."

"It was the error of a generous heart. Take credit for that."

Scarlett forced a smile. But she was bewildered and upset. What was the point of having all these Irish-decorated rooms if the Irish didn't feel comfortable in them? And why did her own cousins treat her like a stranger in her own house?

After everyone left and the servants removed all traces of the party, Scarlett went from room to room alone.

Well, I like it, she decided. I like it a lot. It was, she thought, a damn sight prettier than Dunmore Landing would ever be, or ever was.

She stood in the midst of the reflected images of the High Kings and imagined Rhett there with her, full of envy and admiration. It would be years from now, when Cat was grown, and he would be heartsick that he had missed seeing his daughter grow up to become the beautiful heiress of the home of the O'Haras.

Scarlett ran to the stairs and up them and

through the corridor to Cat's room. "Hello," said Cat. She was sitting at her little table, carefully pouring milk into a cup for her big tabby. Ocras was watching attentively from his commanding position in the center of the table. "Sit down, Momma," Cat invited. Scarlett lowered herself onto a small chair.

If only Rhett were there to join the tea party. But he wasn't, and he never would be, and she had to accept it. He would have tea parties with his other child, his other children—by Anne. Scarlett resisted the impulse to grab Cat in her arms. "I'd like two lumps of sugar, please, Miss O'Hara," she said.

That night Scarlett couldn't sleep. She sat upright in the center of her exquisite French bed with her silk-covered eiderdown wrapped closely around her for warmth. But the warmth and comfort she wanted was to feel Rhett's arms around her, to hear his deep voice mocking the disastrous party until she could laugh at it and at the error of giving it.

She wanted comfort for her disappointment. She wanted love, grown-up caring and understanding. Her heart had learned to love, it was overflowing with love, and she had nowhere to spend it.

Damn Rhett for getting in the way! Why couldn't she love Bart Morland? He was kind, he was attractive, Scarlett enjoyed being with him. If she really wanted him, she didn't doubt for a minute that she could make him forget Grace Hastings.

But she didn't want him, that was the problem. She didn't want anybody except Rhett.

It's not fair! she thought, like a child. And, like a child, eventually she cried herself to sleep.

When she woke, she was in control of herself once more. So what if everyone had hated her party? So what if Colum hadn't stayed more than ten minutes? She had other friends, and she was going to make lots more. Now that the house was finally done, Charlotte was busy as a spider spinning a web with plans about the future. And in the meantime, the weather was perfect for hunting, and Mrs. Sims had made a tremendously becoming riding habit for her.

76

Scarlett rode to Sir John Morland's hunt in style. She was riding a saddle horse and was accompanied by two grooms leading Half Moon and Comet, one of her new hunters. The skirts of her new habit flowed elegantly over her new side-saddle, and she was very pleased with herself. She had had to fight Mrs. Sims like a tiger, but she had won. No corsets. Charlotte had been amazed. No one, she said, ever argued with Daisy Sims and won. No one till me, maybe, Scarlett thought. I won the argument with Charlotte, too.

Bart Morland's hunt was no place for Scarlett to make her emergence into the world of Irish society, said Charlotte. He himself was beyond reproach and, except for his lack of money, one of the most eligible bachelors around. But he didn't keep a grand household at all. The footmen at his breakfasts were really stable grooms in livery for a few hours. Charlotte had secured a much more important invitation for Scarlett. It would do exactly what was needed to prepare for her real debut. Scarlett couldn't possibly go first to Morland Hall instead of Charlotte's selection.

"I can and I will," Scarlett said firmly. "Bart is my friend." She repeated it until Charlotte gave in. She didn't tell Charlotte the rest. She needed to go someplace where she felt at least a little bit comfortable. Now that it was getting close, the prospect of "Society" scared her even more than it enticed her. She kept thinking of what Mammy had said about her once: "Just a mule in horse's harness." As the Paris-inspired wardrobe from Mrs. Sims came into the house Scarlett thought of the saying more and more often. She could imagine hundreds of lords and ladies and earls and countesses whispering it when she went to her first important party.

"Bart, I'm glad to see you."

"I'm glad to see you, too, Scarlett. Half Moon is looking ready for a good run. Come along over here and have a stirrup cup with my special guest. I've been lion-hunting. I'm proud as Lucifer."

Scarlett smiled graciously at the young Member of Parliament for County Meath. He was very handsome, she thought, even though usually she didn't much like men who wore beards, even well-trimmed ones like this Mr. Parnell. She'd heard the name before—oh, yes, at Bart's breakfast. She remembered now. Colum really detested this Parnell. She'd have to pay attention so she could tell Colum all about him. After the hunt. For now Half Moon was eager to go and so was she.

"I can't for the life of me understand how you can be so stubborn, Colum." Scarlett had passed from enthusiasm to explanation to rage. "You've never even bothered to go hear the man speak, for pity's sake. Well, I heard him, he was fascinating, everybody was hanging on his every word. And he wants exactly what you always talked about—Ireland for the Irish, and no evictions, and even no rent and no landlords. What more can you ask?"

Colum's patience cracked. "I can ask that you not be such a trusting fool! Do you not know that your Mr. Parnell is a landlord himself? And a Protestant. And educated at the English Oxford University. He's looking for votes, not justice. The man's a politician, and his Home Rule policy, that you've swallowed for the sugar coating of his earnest manner and handsome face, is nothing more nor less than a stick for him to shake at the English and a carrot to tempt the poor ignorant Irish donkey."

"There's simply no talking to you! Why, he said right out that he supports the Fenians."

Colum grabbed Scarlett's arm. "Did you say anything?"

She jerked away from him. "Of course not. You take me for a fool and lecture me like I'm a fool, but I am not a fool. And I know this much. There's no reason to smuggle in guns and start a war if you can get what you want without it. I lived through a war that a bunch of hotheads started because of some high-faluting principles. All it did was kill most of my friends and ruin everything. For nothing. I'm telling you right now, Colum O'Hara, there's a way to get Ireland back for the Irish without killing and burning, and that's what I'm for. No more money for Stephen to buy guns with, do you hear? And no more guns hidden away in my town. I want them out of that church. I don't care what you do with them, sink them in the bog for all it matters to me. But I want to be rid of them. Right away."

"And rid of me as well, are you saying?"

"If you insist, then—" Scarlett's eyes filled with tears. "What am I saying? What are you saying? Oh, Colum, don't let this happen. You're my best friend, my almost brother. Please, please, please Colum, don't be so hardheaded. I don't want to fight." The tears spilled over.

Colum took her hand in his and held it very tight. "Ach, Scarlett darling, it's the Irish temper in the two of us talking, not Colum and Scarlett. The fearful pity of it, the two of us scowling and shouting. Forgive me, *aroon*"

"What does that mean, '*aroon*'?" she asked between sobs.

"It means 'darling' like Scarlett darling in English. In Irish you're my Scarlett *aroon.*"

"That's pretty."

"All the better as a name for you, then."

"Colum, you're charming the birds from the trees again, but I'm not going to let you charm me into forgetting. Promise me you'll get rid of those guns. I'm not asking you to vote for Charles Parnell, just promise me you won't start a war."

"I promise you, Scarlett *aroon.*"

"Thank you. I feel worlds better. Now I've got to go. Will you come up to the house for dinner in my fancy morning room though it's at night?"

"I cannot, Scarlett aroon. I'm meeting a friend."

"Bring him, too. With the cook fixing food for those nine million servants I've got all of a sudden, I'm sure there'll be enough to feed you and your friend."

"Not tonight. Another time."

Scarlett didn't press him, she had gotten what she wanted. Before she went home she detoured to the little chapel and made her confession to Father Flynn. Losing her temper with Colum was part of it, but not the main part. She was there to be absolved of the sin that made her own blood run cold. She had thanked God when John Morland told her that six months earlier Rhett's wife had lost her baby.

Not long after Scarlett left, Colum O'Hara entered the confessional. He had lied to her, a heavy sin. After doing his penance he went to the arsenal in the Anglican church to make sure the arms were sufficiently well concealed in the event she decided to investigate.

Charlotte Montague and Scarlett left for the house party that was Scarlett's debut after she went to early Mass on Sunday. The party was to last a week. Scarlett didn't like being away from Cat for so long, but the birthday party was only just over—Mrs. Fitz was still in a tight-lipped fury about the damage all the running children had done to the parquet in the ballroom—and she was certain that Cat wouldn't miss her. With all the new furnishings to inspect and new servants to investigate, Cat was a very busy little girl.

Scarlett, Charlotte, and Evans, Charlotte's maid, rode in Scarlett's elegant brougham to the train station in Trim. The house party was in County Monaghan, too far to go by road.

Scarlett was more excited than nervous. Going to John Morland's first had been a good idea. Charlotte was nervous enough for both of them, although it didn't show; Scarlett's future in the fashionable world would be decided by the way she impressed people this week. Charlotte's future, also. She glanced at Scarlett to reassure herself. Yes, she looked lovely in her green merino travelling costume. Those eyes of hers were a gift from God, so distinctive and memorable. And her slim uncorseted body was sure to set tongues wagging and the pulses of men racing. She looked precisely like what Charlotte had insinuated to chosen friends: a beautiful, not-too-young American widow with fresh Colonial looks and charm; somewhat gauche, but refreshing as a result; romantically Irish, as only a foreigner could be; substantially, perhaps even phenomenally wealthy, so much so that she could afford to be a free spirit; well bred, with an aristocratic French bloodline, but vigorous and exuberant from her American background; unpredictable but well-mannered, naive yet experienced; all in all an intriguing and amusing addition to the circles of people who knew too much about one another and were avid for someone new to talk about.

"Perhaps I should tell you again who is likely to be at the party," Charlotte suggested.

"Please don't, Charlotte, I'll forget again anyhow. Besides, I know the important part. A duke is more important than a marquess, then comes an earl, and after that viscount, baron, and baronet. I may call all the men 'sir' just like in the South, so I needn't worry about that 'milord' and 'your grace' business, but I must never call the ladies 'ma'am' the way we do in America, because that's reserved for Queen Victoria, and she's definitely not going to be there. So, unless I'm asked to use the Christian name, I just smile and avoid using anything. A plain old 'mister' or 'miss' is hardly worth bothering with at all unless they're 'honourable.' I do think that's funny. Why not 'respectable' or something else like that?"

Charlotte shuddered inside. Scarlett was too confident, too breezy. "You haven't paid attention, Scarlett. There are some names with no title at all, not even 'honourable,' that are equally as important as any non-royal dukes. The Herberts, Burkes, Clarkes, Lefroys, Blennerhassetts—"

Scarlett giggled. Charlotte stopped. What would be, would be.

The house was an immense Gothic-style structure with turrets and towers, stained-glass windows as tall as a cathedral's, corridors that extended for more than a hundred yards. Scarlett's confidence ebbed when she saw it. "You're The O'Hara," she reminded herself and she marched up the stone entrance steps with her chin at an angle that dared anyone to challenge her.

By the end of dinner that night she was smiling at everyone, even the footman behind her tall-backed chair. The food was excellent, copious, exquisitely presented, but Scarlett barely tasted it. She was feasting on admiration. There were forty-six guests in the house party, and they all wanted to know her.

". . . and on New Year's Day, I have to knock on every single door in the town, go in, go out, go in again and drink a cup of tea. I declare, I don't know why I don't turn yellow as a China-man, drinking half the tea in China the way I do," she said gaily to the man on her left. He was fascinated by the duties of The O'Hara.

When the hostess "turned" the table, Scarlett enchanted the retired general on her right with a day-by-day account of the siege of Atlanta. Her Southern accent was not at all what one expected an American to sound like, they reported later to anyone who'd listen, and she's a damn'd intelligent woman.

She was also a "damn'd attractive woman." The excessively big diamond-and-emerald engagement ring she'd received from Rhett sparkled impressively on her bare-but-not-too-bare bosom. Charlotte had ordered it remade into a pendant that hung from a white gold chain so fine that it was nearly invisible.

After dinner Scarlett played whist with her customary skill. Her partner won enough money to cover her losses at three previous house parties, and Scarlett became a sought-after companion among ladies as well as gentlemen.

The following morning, and for five mornings after, there was a hunt. Even on a mount from her host's stables Scarlett was adept and fearless. Her success was assured. The Anglo-Irish gentry as a whole admired nothing quite as much as they did a fine rider.

Charlotte Montague had to be vigilant, or she'd be caught looking like a cat who'd just finished a bowl of thick cream.

"Did you enjoy yourself?" she asked Scarlett on the way back to Ballyhara.

"Every minute, Charlotte! Bless you for getting me invited. Everything was perfect. It's so thoughtful having those sandwiches in the bedroom. I always get hungry late at night, I guess everybody does."

Charlotte laughed until her eyes were streaming with tears. It made Scarlett huffy. "I don't see what's so funny about a healthy appetite. With the card game lasting until all hours, it's a long time after dinner when you go to bed."

When Charlotte could speak, she explained. At the more sophisticated houses the ladies' bedrooms were supplied with a plate of sandwiches that could be used as a signal to admirers. Set on the floor of the corridor outside a lady's room, the sandwiches were an invitation for a man to come in.

Scarlett blushed crimson. "My grief, Charlotte, I ate every crumb. What must the maids think?"

"Not just the maids, Scarlett. Everyone in the house party must be wondering who the fortunate man was. Or men. Naturally no gentleman would claim the title, or he wouldn't be a gentleman."

"I'll never be able to look anyone in the face again. That's the most scandalous thing I ever heard. It's disgusting! And I thought they were all such nice people."

"But my dear child, it's precisely the nice people who devise these discretions. Everyone knows the rules, and no one refers to them. People's amusements are their own secrets, unless they choose to tell."

Scarlett was about to say that where she came from people were honest and decent. Then she remembered Sally Brewton in Charleston. Sally had talked the same way, all about "discretion" and "amusements" as if infidelity and promiscuity were a normal, accepted thing.

Charlotte Montague smiled complacently. If any one thing had been needed to create a legend for Scarlett O'Hara, the mistake about the sandwiches had accomplished it. Now she'd be known as refreshingly Colonial, but satisfactorily sophisticated.

Charlotte began to make preliminary schedules in her mind for her retirement. Only a few more months to go, and she'd never again suffer through boredom at a fashionable party of any kind.

"I shall arrange for delivery of the *Irish Times*

every day," she said to Scarlett, "and you must study every word in it. Everyone you will meet in Dublin will expect you to be familiar with the news it reports."

"Dublin? You didn't tell me we were going to Dublin."

"Didn't I? I thought surely I had. I do apologize, Scarlett. Dublin is the center of everything, you will love it. It's a real city, not an overgrown country town like Drogheda or Galway. And the Castle is the most thrilling thing you will ever experience in your entire life."

"A Castle? Not a ruin? I didn't know there was such a thing. Does the Queen live there?"

"No, thank heaven. The Queen is a fine ruler but an extremely dull woman. No, the Castle in Dublin is ruled by Her Majesty's representative, the Viceroy. You will be presented to him and to the Vicereine in the Throne Room . . ." Mrs. Montague painted a word picture for Scarlett of pomp and splendor beyond anything she'd ever heard of. It made Charleston's Saint Cecilia sound like nothing at all. And it made Scarlett want success in Dublin society with all her heart. That would put Rhett Butler in his place. He wouldn't be important to her at all.

It was safe to tell her now, Charlotte thought. After this week's success the invitation will surely come. There's no longer a chance that I'll lose the deposit on the suite at the Shelbourne that I booked for the Season when I got Scarlett's note last year.

"Where's my precious Cat?" Scarlett called when

she ran into the house. "Momma's home, sweetheart." She found Cat, after a half hour's search, in the stables sitting atop Half Moon. She looked frighteningly small on the big horse. Scarlett muted her voice, so that she wouldn't spook Half Moon. "Come to Momma, darling, and give me a hug." Her heart thumped out of rhythm while she watched her child jump down into the straw near the powerful, metal-shod hooves. Cat was out of Scarlett's sight until her small dark face popped up over the half door to the stall. She was climbing it, not opening it. Scarlett knelt to catch her in an embrace. "Oh, I'm so happy to see you, angel. I missed you a lot. Did you miss me?"

"Yes." Cat wriggled out of her arms. Well, at least she missed me, she's never said that before. Scarlett stood up when the warm surge of love for Cat subsided into the total devotion that was her habitual emotion.

"I didn't know you liked horses, Kitty Cat."

"I do. I like animals."

Scarlett forced herself to sound cheerful. "Would you like to have a pony of your own? The right size for a little girl?" I won't let myself think of Bonnie, I won't. I promised that I wouldn't hobble Cat or wrap her in cottonwool because I lost Bonnie in the accident. I promised Cat when she was fresh born that I'd let her be whoever she turned out to be, that I'd give her all the freedom a free spirit needs to have. I didn't know it would be so hard, that I'd want to protect her every single minute. But I've got to keep my promise. I know it was right. She'll have a pony if she wants one, and she'll learn to jump, and I'll make myself watch if it kills me. I love Cat too much to hem her in.

Scarlett had no way of knowing that Cat had walked down to Ballyhara town while she was away. Three now, Cat was becoming interested in other children and games. She went looking for some of the playmates who'd been at her birthday party. A group of four or five little boys were playing in the wide street. When she walked toward them, they ran away. Two stopped long enough to scoop up rocks and throw them at her. *"Cailleach! Cailleach!"* they screamed in terror. They'd learned the word from their mothers, the Gaelic for witch.

Cat looked up at her mother. "Yes, I'd like a pony," she said. Ponies didn't throw things. She considered telling her mother about the boys, asking her about the word. Cat liked to learn new words. But she didn't like that word. She wouldn't ask. "I'd like a pony today."

"I can't find a pony today, baby. I'll start looking tomorrow. I promise. Let's go home now and have tea."

"With cakes?"

"Definitely with cakes."

Up in their rooms Scarlett got out of her beautiful travelling suit as quickly as she could. She felt an undefined need to wear her shirt and skirt and bright peasant stockings.

By mid-December Scarlett was pacing the long hallways of the Big House like a caged animal. She had forgotten how much she hated the dark, short, wet days of winter. She thought about going down to Kennedy's several times, but ever since her unfortunate party for all the townspeople, she no longer felt as easy with them as once she had. She rode a little bit. It wasn't necessary, the grooms kept all the horses exercised. But she needed to be out, even in the ice-filled rain. When there were a few hours of sun she watched while Cat rode her Shetland pony in great joyful loops across the frozen meadow. Scarlett knew it was bad for next summer's grass, but Cat was as restless as she was. It was all Scarlett could do to persuade her to stay indoors, even in the kitchen or the stables.

On Christmas Eve Cat lit the Christ Child candle and then all the candles she could reach on the Christmas tree. Colum held her up to reach the higher ones. "Outlandish English custom," he said. "You'll probably burn your house to the ground."

Scarlett looked at the bright decorations and glowing candles on the tree. "I think it's very pretty even if the Queen of England did start the fashion," she said. "Besides, I've got holly over all the windows and doors, too, Colum, so it's Irish everywhere in Ballyhara except this room. Don't be such a grumpy."

Colum laughed. "Cat O'Hara, did you know your godfather was a grumpy?"

"Today yes," said Cat.

This time Colum's laugh wasn't forced. "Out of the mouths of babes," he said. "It's my fault for asking."

He helped Scarlett bring out Cat's present after

she fell asleep. It was a full-size stuffed toy pony on rockers.

On Christmas morning Cat looked at it with scorn. "It's not real."

"It's a toy, darling, for indoors in this nasty weather."

Cat climbed on it and rocked. She conceded that for a pony that wasn't real it was not a bad toy.

Scarlett breathed a sigh of relief. She wouldn't feel quite so guilty now when she went to Dublin. She was to meet Charlotte at the Gresham Hotel there the day after New Year's barm brack and tea.

77

Scarlett had no idea Dublin was so near. It seemed she was barely settled in the train at Trim before Dublin was announced. Evans, Charlotte Montague's maid, met her and directed a porter to take her cases. Then, "Follow me, if you please, Mrs. O'Hara," Evans said, and walked off. Scarlett had trouble keeping up with her because of the hurrying crowds in the station. It was the biggest building Scarlett had ever seen, and the busiest.

But nothing like as busy as Dublin's streets. Scarlett pressed her nose to the window of the hackney in her excitement. Charlotte was right, she was going to love Dublin.

All too soon the hackney stopped. Scarlett stepped down, helped by a lavishly uniformed attendant. She was staring at a passing horse-drawn tram when Evans touched her arm. "This way, please."

Charlotte was waiting for her behind a tea table in the sitting room of their suite of rooms. "Charlotte!" Scarlett exclaimed, "I saw a streetcar with an upstairs and a downstairs, and both of them packed full."

"Good afternoon to you, too, Scarlett. I'm pleased that Dublin pleases you. Give Evans your wraps and come and have tea. We have a great deal to do."

That evening Mrs. Sims arrived with three assistants carrying muslin-wrapped gowns and dresses. Scarlett stood and moved as ordered while Mrs. Sims and Mrs. Montague discussed every detail of every garment. Each evening gown was more elegant than the one that preceded it. Scarlett preened before the pier glass when she wasn't being prodded and pinched by Mrs. Sims.

When the dressmaker and her woman left Scarlett discovered suddenly that she was exhausted. She was happy to agree when Charlotte suggested they dine in the suite, and she ate ravenously.

"Do not gain so much as a millimeter around the middle, Scarlett, or you'll have to be fitted all over again," Charlotte warned.

"I'll run it all off shopping," Scarlett said. She buttered another piece of bread. "I saw at least eight shop windows that looked wonderful on the drive from the station."

Charlotte smiled indulgently. She'd receive a very welcome commission from every shop Scarlett patronized. "You'll have all the shopping your heart desires, I can promise you that. But only in the afternoons. In the mornings, you'll be sitting for your portrait."

"That's nonsense, Charlotte. What do I want with a portrait of myself! I had one done once, and I hated it. I looked mean as a snake."

"You will not look mean in this one, take my word. Monsieur Hervé is an expert at ladies. And the portrait is important. It must be done."

"I'll do it, because I do everything you say, but I won't like it, take my word."

The next morning Scarlett was awakened by the sound of traffic. It was still dark, but street lamps showed her four lines of wagons and drays and carriages of every description moving along the street below her bedroom window. No wonder Dublin has such wide streets, she thought happily, almost everything in Ireland with wheels on it is here. She sniffed, sniffed again. I must be going crazy. I could swear I smell coffee.

Fingers tapped gently on her door. "Breakfast is in the sitting room when you're ready," said Charlotte. "I've sent the waiter away, all you need is a wrapper."

Scarlett nearly knocked Mrs. Montague down opening the door. "Coffee! If you knew how much I've missed coffee. Oh, Charlotte, why didn't you tell me they drink coffee in Dublin? I'd have taken the train every morning just for breakfast."

The coffee tasted even better than it smelled. Luckily Charlotte preferred tea, because Scarlett drank the entire pot.

Then she obediently put on the silk stockings and combinations Charlotte unpacked from a box. She felt quite wicked. The light slippery undergarments were altogether different from the batiste or muslin she'd worn all her life. She tied her wool dressing gown tightly around her when Evans came in with a woman she'd never seen before. "This is Serafina," said Charlotte. "She's Italian, so don't be concerned if you don't understand a word she says. She's going to do your hair. All you have to do is sit still and let her talk to herself."

She's having a one-way conversation with every hair on my head, thought Scarlett after nearly an hour. Her neck was getting stiff, and she hadn't the faintest idea what the woman was doing to her. Charlotte had seated her near the window in the sitting room where the morning light was strongest.

Mrs. Sims and one assistant looked as impatient as Scarlett felt. They'd arrived twenty minutes earlier.

"*Ecco!*" said Serafina.

"*Benissimo,*" said Mrs. Montague.

"Now," said Mrs. Sims.

Her assistant lifted the muslin wrap from the gown Mrs. Sims was holding. Scarlett drew in her breath. The white satin glistened in the light, and the light made the silver embroidery shine as if it were a living thing. It was a fantasy of a gown. Scarlett stood, her hands reached out to touch it.

"Gloves first," Mrs. Sims commanded. "Every finger would leave a mark." Scarlett saw that the dressmaker was wearing white kid gloves. She took the pristine long gloves Charlotte was holding out to her. They were already folded back and powdered for her to get them on without stretching.

When she had smoothed them all the way up, Charlotte used a small silver buttonhook with rapid competence, Serafina dropped a silk handkerchief over her head and removed her wrapper, and then Mrs. Sims lowered the dress onto Scarlett's upraised arms and onto her body. While she fastened the back, Serafina deftly removed the handkerchief and made a few delicate touches to Scarlett's hair.

There was a knock at the door. "Well timed," said Mrs. Montague. "That will be Monsieur Hervé. We'll want Mrs. O'Hara over here, Mrs. Sims." Charlotte led Scarlett to the center of the room. Scarlett could hear her opening the door and speaking in a low voice. *I suppose she's talking French and expects me to. No, Charlotte must know me better than that by now. I wish I had a looking glass, I want to see the gown on me.*

She lifted one foot, then the other when Mrs. Sims' assistant tapped her toes. She couldn't see the slippers the woman slipped onto her feet, Mrs. Sims was poking her in the shoulder blades and hissing at her about standing up straight. The assistant fiddled with the bottom of her skirt.

"Mrs. O'Hara," said Charlotte Montague, "please allow me to present Monsieur François Hervé."

Scarlett looked at the rotund bald man who walked in front of her and bowed. "How do you do," she said. Was she supposed to shake hands with a painter?

"*Fantastique,*" said the painter. He snapped his fingers. Two men carried the enormous pier glass to a spot between the windows. When they stepped away Scarlett saw herself.

The white satin gown was more decolleté than she'd realized. She stared at the daring expanse of bosom and shoulder. Then at the reflection of a woman she hardly recognized. Her hair was piled high on her head in a mass of curls and tendrils so artful that they looked almost happenstance. The white satin glimmered the narrow length of her body, and a silver-encrusted white satin train spread in a sinuous semicircle around the white satin slippers, with silver heels.

Why, I look like Grandma Robillard's portrait more than I look like me.

The years of habitual girlishness fell away. She was looking at a woman, not the flirtatious belle of Clayton County. And she liked what she saw very much. She was mystified and excited by this stranger. Her soft lips quivered faintly at the corners, and her tilted eyes took on a deeper, more mysterious sheen. Her chin lifted in supreme self-confidence, and she looked directly into her own eyes with challenge and approval.

"That's it," whispered Charlotte Montague to herself. "That's the woman to take all Ireland by storm. The whole world, if she wants it."

"Easel," murmured the artist. "Quickly, you

cretins. I shall do a portrait that will make me famous."

"I don't understand it," Scarlett said to Charlotte after the sitting. "It's like I never saw that person before in my life, yet I knew her . . . I'm confused, Charlotte."

"My dear child, that is the beginning of wisdom."

"Charlotte, do let's ride one of those darling trams," Scarlett begged. "I deserve a reward after standing like a statue for hours on end."

It had been a long sitting, Charlotte agreed; future ones would probably be shorter. For one thing it would likely rain, and without good light M. Hervé wouldn't be able to paint.

"Then you agree? We'll take the tram?" Charlotte nodded. Scarlett felt like hugging her, but Charlotte Montague wasn't that kind of person. And, in an undefined way, neither was she any longer, Scarlett felt. The view of herself as a woman, no longer a girl, had thrilled her but unsettled her, too. It was going to take some getting used to.

They climbed the iron spiral to the upper level of the tram. It was exposed and very cold, but the view was superb. Scarlett looked on all sides at the city, the crowded wide streets, the swarming wide sidewalks. Dublin was the first real city she'd ever seen. It had a population of more than a quarter million people. Atlanta was a boomtown of twenty thousand.

The tram moved on its tracks through the traffic with inexorable right of way. Pedestrians and vehicles scattered hastily at the last minute as it approached. Frenzied and noisy, the narrow escapes delighted Scarlett.

Then she saw the river. The tram stopped on the bridge and she could see along the Liffey. Bridge after bridge after bridge, all different, all teeming with traffic. The quays enticing with shop fronts and crowds. The water bright in the sunlight.

The Liffey was left behind, the tram was suddenly in shadow, tall buildings were near on both sides. Scarlett felt the chill.

"We'd better go down at the next stop," said Charlotte. "We get off at the following one." She led the way. After they crossed a bedlam intersection Charlotte gestured toward the street that curved ahead of them. "Grafton Street," she said, as if she were making an introduction. "We'll want to take a hackney back to the Gresham, but on foot is the only way to see the shops. Would you like coffee before we begin? You should become acquainted with Bewley's."

"I don't know, Charlotte. I might just take a look inside this shop first. That fan in the window—see the one in that back corner, with the pink tassels—it's the most adorable thing. Oh, and that Chinesey one, I didn't see that at first. And that precious pomander! Look Charlotte, at the embroidery on those gloves. Have you ever? Oh, my goodness."

Charlotte nodded at the liveried door attendant. He pulled the door wide and bowed.

She didn't mention that there were at least four more shops on Grafton Street with hundreds of fans and gloves. Charlotte was quite sure that Scarlett would discover for herself that a major attribute of a major city is an infinite spectrum of temptation.

After ten days of sittings and fittings and shopping Scarlett went home to Ballyhara with dozens of presents for Cat, several gifts for Mrs. Fitz and Colum, ten pounds of coffee and a coffee maker for herself. She was in love with Dublin and could hardly wait to return.

At Ballyhara her Cat was waiting. As soon as the train left the city, Scarlett was in a fever to get home. She had so many things to tell Cat, so many plans for the time when she'd take her funny little monkey of a country child to the city. She had to hold her after-Mass office hours, too. She'd delayed them for a week already. And soon it would be Saint Brigid's Day. Scarlett thought that was the best of all, the moment when the year really began with the turning of the first sod. How very, very lucky she was. She had both—country and city, The O'Hara and that still unknown woman in the pier glass.

Scarlett left Cat engrossed in a picture book of animals, her other presents still unwrapped. She ran down the drive to Colum's gatehouse with the cashmere muffler she'd brought him and all her impressions of Dublin to share.

"Oh, I'm sorry," she said when she saw that he had a guest. The well-dressed man was a stranger to her.

"Not at all, not at all," said Colum. "Come meet John Devoy. He's just in from America."

Devoy was polite but clearly not pleased to be interrupted. Scarlett made her excuses, left Colum's gift, and walked home briskly. Now what kind of American comes to an out-of-the-way place like Ballyhara and isn't pleased to meet another American? He must be one of Colum's Fenians, that's it! And he's annoyed because Colum isn't part of that crazy revolution thing any more.

The reverse was the truth. John Devoy was seriously leaning towards support for Parnell, and he was one of the most influential American Fenians. If he abandoned support for the revolution, the blow would be nearly mortal. Colum argued passionately against Home Rule long into the night.

"The man wants power and will use any treachery to get it," he said about Parnell.

"What about you, Colum?" Devoy retorted. "Sounds to me like you can't stand a better man getting your job done, and done better."

Colum's reply was immediate. "He'll make speeches in London till Hell freezes, and he'll win headlines in all the newspapers, but we'll still be left with starving Irish under the boots of the English. The Irish people will win nothing at all. And when they tire of Mr. Parnell's headlines they'll revolt. With no organization and no hope of success. I tell you, Devoy, we're waiting too long. Parnell talks, you talk, I talk—and all the while the Irish suffer."

After Devoy went to Kennedy's Inn for the night Colum paced his small sitting room until the oil in the lamp burned out. Then he sat in the cold darkness on a stool by the dying embers on the hearth. Brooding on Devoy's angry outburst. Could the man be right? Was power the motive, and not love for Ireland? How could a man know the truth of his own soul?

Thin watery sunlight shone briefly as Scarlett drove a spade into the earth on Saint Brigid's Day. It was a good omen for the year to come. To celebrate, she treated everyone in Ballyhara town to porter and meat pies at Kennedy's. It was going to be the best year of all, she was sure of it. The next day she went to Dublin for the six weeks known as the Castle Season.

78

She and Charlotte had a suite of rooms at the Shelbourne Hotel this time, not the Gresham. The Shelbourne was THE place to stay in Dublin for the Season. Scarlett hadn't gone inside the imposing brick building on her previous visit to Dublin. "We choose the occasion to be seen," Charlotte told her. Now she gazed around the huge hall inside the entrance and understood why Charlotte wanted them to be here. Everything was imposingly grand—the space, the staff, the guests, the controlled hushed busyness. She lifted her chin, then followed the porter up the half-flight to the first floor, the most desirable of desirables. Though Scarlett did not know it, she looked exactly like Charlotte's description to the doorman. "You will know her at once. She is extremely beautiful, and she carries her head like an empress."

In addition to the suite, a private drawing room was reserved for Scarlett's use. Charlotte showed it to her before they went down for tea. The finished portrait stood on a brass easel in a corner of the green brocaded room. Scarlett looked at it with wonder. Did she really look like that? That woman wasn't afraid of anything, and she felt as nervous as a cat. She followed Charlotte downstairs in a daze.

Charlotte identified some of the people at other tables in the sumptuous lounge. "You'll meet them all eventually. After you're presented, you'll serve tea and coffee in your drawing room every afternoon. People will bring people to meet you."

Who? Scarlett wanted to ask. Who will bring people, and who are the people they'll bring? But she didn't bother. Charlotte always knew what she was doing. The only thing Scarlett needed to be responsible for was not getting tangled up in her train when she backed away after her presentation. Charlotte and Mrs. Sims were going to coach her with a practice presentation gown every day until The Day.

The heavy white envelope bearing the Chamberlain's seal was delivered to the hotel the day after Scarlett arrived. Charlotte's expression gave no hint of how relieved she was. One never knew for sure about best-laid plans. She opened it with steady fingers. "First Drawing Room," she said, "as expected. Day after tomorrow."

Scarlett waited in a group of white-gowned girls and women on the landing outside the closed double doors to the Throne Room. It seemed to her she'd been doing nothing but waiting for a hundred years. Why on earth had she agreed to do this? Scarlett couldn't answer her own question, it was too complex. In part she was The O'Hara, determined to conquer the English. In part she was an American girl dazzled by the grandeur of the British Empire's royal panoply. At bottom, Scarlett had never in her life backed down from a challenge and never would.

Another name was called. Not hers. God's nightgown! Were they going to make her be last? Charlotte hadn't warned her about that. Charlotte hadn't even told her until the last minute that she'd be alone all the way. "I'll find you in the supper room after the Drawing Room is over." That was a fine way to treat her, throwing her to the wolves like that. She stole another glance down her front. She was terrified that she might just fall right out of the scandalously low-cut gown. That would really make this—what had Charlotte said? "An experience to remember."

"Madam The O'Hara of Ballyhara."

Oh, Lord, that's me. She repeated Charlotte Montague's coaching litany to herself. Walk forward, stop outside the door. A footman will lift the train you have looped over your left arm and arrange it behind you. The Gentleman Usher will open the doors. Wait for him to announce you.

"Madam The O'Hara of Ballyhara."

Scarlett looked at the Throne Room. Well, Pa,

what do you think of your Katie Scarlett now? she thought. I'm going to stroll along that fifty miles or so of red carpet runner and kiss the Viceroy of Ireland, cousin of the Queen of England. She glanced at the majestically dressed Gentleman Usher, and her right eyelid quivered in what might almost have been a conspiratorial wink.

The O'Hara walked like an empress to face the Viceroy's red-bearded magnificence and present her cheek for the ceremonial kiss of welcome.

Turn to the Vicereine now and curtsey. Back straight. Not too low. Stand up. Now back, back, back, three steps, don't worry, the weight of the train holds it away from your body. Now extend your left arm. Wait. Let the footman have plenty of time to arrange the train over your arm. Now turn. Walk out.

Scarlett's knees obligingly waited until she was seated at one of the supper tables before they started trembling.

Charlotte made no attempt to hide her satisfaction. She entered Scarlett's bedroom with the stiff squares of white cardboard fanned in her hand. "My dear Scarlett, you were a dazzling success. These invitations arrived before even I was up and dressed. State Ball, that's quite special. Saint Patrick's Ball, that was to be expected. Second Drawing Room, you'll be able to watch other people running the gauntlet. And a small dance in the Throne Room. Three-fourths of the peers in Ireland have never been invited to one of the small dances."

Scarlett giggled. The terror of being presented

was behind her, and she was a success! "I guess I won't mind now that I spent last year's wheat crop on all those new clothes. Let's go shopping today and spend this year's crop."

"You won't have time. Eleven gentlemen, including the Gentleman Usher, have written to ask permission to call on you. Plus fourteen ladies, with their daughters. Tea time won't be long enough. You'll have to serve coffee and tea in the mornings, too. The maids are opening your drawing room right now. I ordered pink flowers, so wear your brown and rose plaid taffeta for the morning and the green velvet faced in pink for the afternoon. Evans will be here to do your hair as soon as you're up."

Scarlett was the Season's hit. Gentlemen flocked to meet the rich widow who was also—*mirabile dictu*—fantastically beautiful. Mothers swarmed her private reception room with daughters in tow to meet the gentlemen. After the first day, Charlotte never ordered flowers again. Admirers sent so many that there wasn't room for all of them. Many of the bouquets contained leather cases from Dublin's finest jeweler, but Scarlett reluctantly returned all the brooches, bracelets, rings, earrings. "Even an American from Clayton County, Georgia, knows that you're expected to pay back favors," she told Charlotte. "I won't be obligated to anybody, not that way."

Her goings and comings were reported faithfully and sometimes even accurately in the gossip column of the daily *Irish Times*. Shop owners in morning coats came themselves to show her choice items they hoped she might like, and she defiantly bought herself many of the jewelry pieces she had refused to accept. The Viceroy danced with her twice at the State Ball.

All the guests at her coffees and teas admired her portrait. Scarlett looked at it every morning and every afternoon before the first visitors arrived. She was learning herself. Charlotte Montague observed the metamorphosis with interest. The practiced flirt vanished, replaced by a serene, somewhat amused woman who had only to turn her smoky green eyes on man, woman, or child to draw them, mesmerized, to her side.

I used to work like a mule to be charming, Scarlett thought, now I don't do anything at all. She couldn't understand it at all, but she accepted the gift of it with simple gratitude.

"Did you say two hundred people, Charlotte? That's what you call a small dance?"

"Relatively. There are always five or six hundred at the State and Saint Patrick's balls and more than a thousand at the Drawing Rooms. You certainly already know at least half the people who'll be there, probably many more than half."

"I still think it's tacky that you weren't invited."

"It's the way things are. I'm not offended." Charlotte was anticipating the evening with pleasure. She planned to go over her account book. Scarlett's success and Scarlett's extravagance had greatly exceeded even Charlotte's most optimistic expectations. She felt like a nabob, and she liked to gloat over her wealth. Admission to the coffee hour alone was bringing in "gifts" of almost a hundred pounds a week. And there were still two weeks left in the Season. She would see Scarlett off to her privileged evening with a light heart.

Scarlett paused in the doorway of the Throne Room to enjoy the spectacle. "You know, Jeffrey, I never get used to this place," she said to the Gentleman Usher. "I'm like Cinderella at the ball."

"I'd never associate you with Cinderella, Scarlett," he said adoringly. Scarlett's wink had put his heart in her pocket when she entered the First Drawing Room.

"You'd be surprised," Scarlett said. She nodded absentmindedly in response to bows and smiles from familiar faces nearby. How lovely it was. It couldn't be real, she couldn't really be here. Everything had happened so fast; she needed time to absorb it.

The great room shimmered gold. Gilded columns supported the ceiling, gilded flat column pilasters filled the walls between the tall windows draped in gold-fringed crimson velvet. Gilt armchairs upholstered in crimson surrounded the supper tables along the walls, each table centered with a gold candelabrum. Gilt covered the intricately carved gaslit chandeliers and the massive canopy above the gold and red thrones. Gold lace trimmed men's court dress of brocaded silk skirted coats and white satin knee breeches. Gold buckles decorated their satin dancing pumps. Gold buttons, gold epaulets, gold frogging, gold braid gleamed on the dress uniforms of regimental officers and the court uniforms of Viceregal officials.

Many of the men wore bright sashes slashed across their chests, pinned with jewelled orders; the Viceroy's knee breeches touched the Garter around his leg. The men were almost more splendid than the women.

Almost, but not quite, for the women were jewelled at neck, breast, ears, and wrists; many wore tiaras as well. Their gowns were made of rich materials—satin, velvet, brocade, silk—embroidered often in glowing silks or gold and silver threads.

A body could get blinded just looking, I'd better go on in and make my manners. Scarlett made her way across the room to curtsey to the Viceregal host and hostess. The music started as she finished.

"May I?" A gold-braided red arm crooked to offer support for her hand. Scarlett smiled. It was Charles Ragland. She'd met him at a house party, and he had called on her every day since her arrival in Dublin. He made no secret of his admiration. Charles' handsome face blushed every time she spoke to him. He was awfully sweet and attractive, even though he was an English soldier. They weren't at all like Yankees, no matter what Colum said. For one thing, they were infinitely better dressed. She rested her hand lightly on Ragland's arm, and he escorted her into the pattern of the quadrille.

"You are very beautiful tonight, Scarlett."

"So are you, Charles. I was just thinking that the men are more dressed up than the ladies."

"Thank heaven for uniforms. Knee breeches are the devil to wear. A man feels a perfect fool in satin shoes."

"Serves them right. They've been peeking at ladies' ankles for ages, let them see what it feels like when we ogle their legs."

"Scarlett, you shock me." The pattern shifted and he was gone.

I probably do, Scarlett thought. Charles was as innocent as a schoolboy sometimes. She looked up at her new partner.

"My God!" she said aloud. It was Rhett.

"How flattering," he said with his twisty half smile. No one else smiled like that. Scarlett was filled with light, with lightness. She felt as if she were floating above the polished floor, buoyant with happiness.

And then, before she could speak again, the quadrille took him away. She smiled automatically at her new partner. The love burning in her eyes took his breath away. Her mind was racing: Why is Rhett here? Could it be because he wanted to see me? Because he had to see me, because he couldn't keep away?

The quadrille moved at its stately tempo, making Scarlett frantic with impatience. When it ended, she was facing Charles Ragland. It took all her self-control to smile and thank him and murmur a hasty excuse before she turned to search for Rhett.

Her eyes met his almost immediately. He was standing only an arm's length away.

Scarlett's pride kept her from reaching out to him. He knew I'd be looking for him, she thought

1024

angrily. Who does he think he is, anyhow, to come strolling into my world and just stand there and expect me to fall into his arms? There are plenty of men in Dublin—in this room, even—who've been smothering me with attention, hanging around my drawing room, sending flowers every day, and notes, and even jewelry. What makes Mister High and Mighty Rhett Butler think that all he has to do is lift his little finger and I'll come running?

"What a pleasant surprise," she said, and the cool tone of her voice pleased her.

Rhett held out his hand, and she put hers in it without thinking. "May I have this dance, Mrs. . . . er . . . O'Hara?"

Scarlett caught her breath in alarm. "Rhett, you're not going to tell on me? Everybody believes I'm a widow!"

He smiled and took her into his arms as the music began. "Your secret is safe with me, Scarlett." She could feel the rasp of his voice on her skin, and his warm breath. It made her weak.

"What the devil are you doing here?" she asked. She had to know. His hand was warm at her waist, strong, supporting, directing her body as they turned. Unconsciously Scarlett revelled in his strength and rebelled against his control over her even as she remembered the joy of following his steps in the giddying swirling motion of the waltz.

Rhett chuckled. "I couldn't resist my curiosity," he said. "I was in London on business, and everyone was talking about an American who was taking Dublin Castle by storm. 'Could that be Scarlett of the striped stockings?' I asked myself.

I had to find out. Bart Morland confirmed my suspicions. Then I couldn't get him to stop talking about you. He even made me ride with him through your town. According to him, you rebuilt it with your own hands."

His eyes raked over her from head to toe. "You've changed, Scarlett," he said quietly. "The charming girl has become an elegant, grown-up woman. I salute you, I really do."

The unvarnished honesty and warmth of his voice made Scarlett forget her resentments. "Thank you, Rhett," she said.

"Are you happy in Ireland, Scarlett?"

"Yes, I am."

"I'm glad." His words were rich with deeper meaning.

For the first time in all the years she'd known him, Scarlett understood Rhett, at least in part. He did come to see me, she understood, he's been thinking about me all this time, worrying about where I'd gone and how I was. He never stopped caring, no matter what he said. He loves me and always will, just as I'll always love him.

The realization filled her with happiness, and she tasted it, like champagne; sipped it, to make it last. Rhett was here, with her, and they were, in this moment, closer than they had ever been.

An aide-de-camp approached them when the waltz ended. "His Excellency requests the honor of the next dance, Mrs. O'Hara."

Rhett raised his eyebrows in the quizzical mockery Scarlett remembered so well. Her lips curved in a smile for him alone. "Tell His Excellency that I will be delighted," she said. She looked at Rhett before she took the aide's arm. "In Clayton County," she murmured to Rhett, "we'd say that I was in high cotton." She heard his laughter follow her as she walked away.

I'm allowed, she told herself, and she looked back over her shoulder to see him laughing. It's really too much, she thought, it's not fair at all. He even looks good in those silly satin britches and shoes. Her green eyes sparkled with laughter when she curtseyed to the Viceroy before they began to dance.

Scarlett felt no real surprise that Rhett was no longer there when she looked for him again. For as long as she had known him, Rhett had appeared and disappeared without explanation. I shouldn't have been surprised to see him here tonight, she thought. I was feeling like Cinderella, why shouldn't the only Prince Charming I want be here? She could feel his arms around her as if he had left a mark; otherwise it would be easy to believe that she had made it all up— the gilded room, the music, his presence, even hers.

When she returned to her rooms at the Shelbourne, Scarlett turned up the gas and stood before a long looking glass in the bright light to look at herself and see what Rhett had seen. She looked beautiful and sure of herself, like her portrait, like the portrait of her grandmother.

Her heart began to ache. Why couldn't she be like the other portrait of Grandma Robillard? The one in which she was soft and flushed with love given and received.

For in Rhett's caring words, she knew, there had also been sadness and farewell.

In the middle of the night Scarlett O'Hara woke in her luxurious scented room on the best floor of the best hotel in Dublin and wept with racking convulsive sobs. "If only . . ." repeated again and again in her head like a battering ram.

79

The night's anguish left no visible marks on Scarlett. Her face was smoothly serene the next morning, and her smiles were as lovely as ever when she poured out coffee and tea for the men and women who crowded her drawing room. Sometime during the dark hours of the night she had found the courage to let Rhett go.

If I love him, she understood, I must not try to hold on to him. I have to learn to give him his freedom, just the way I try to give Cat hers because I love her.

I wish I could have told Rhett about her, he'd be so proud of her.

I wish the Castle Season was over. I miss Cat dreadfully. I wonder what she's up to.

Cat was running with the strength of desperation through the woods at Ballyhara. The ground mists of morning still clung in places, and she couldn't see where she was going. She stumbled and fell, but she got up right away. She had to keep running, even though she was short of breath from running so much already. She sensed another stone coming and ducked behind the protection of a tree trunk. The boys chasing her shouted and jeered. They had almost caught up with her, even though they'd never ventured into the woods near the Big House before. It was safe now. They knew The O'Hara was in Dublin with the English. Their parents talked about nothing else.

"There she is!" one shouted, and the others lifted their hands to throw.

But the figure stepping from behind a tree was not Cat. It was the *cailleach*, with a gnarled finger pointing. The boys howled with fear and ran.

"Come with me," said Grainne. "I will give you some tea."

Cat put her hand in the old woman's. Grainne came out from hiding and walked very slowly, and Cat had no trouble keeping pace with her. "Will there be cakes?" Cat asked.

"There will," said the *cailleach*.

Although Scarlett grew homesick for Ballyhara, she lasted the Castle Season out. She'd given Charlotte Montague her word. It's exactly like the Season in Charleston, she thought. Why is it, I wonder, that fashionable people work so hard at having fun for so long at a time? She soared from success to even greater success, and Mrs. Fitz shrewdly took advantage of the rapturous paragraphs in the *Irish Times* that described them. Every evening she took the newspaper down to Kennedy's bar to show the people of Ballyhara how famous The O'Hara was. Day by day, grumbling about Scarlett's fondness for the English gave way to pride that The O'Hara was more admired than any of the Anglo women.

Colum did not applaud Rosaleen Fitzpatrick's cleverness. His mood was too somber for him to see the humor in it. "The Anglos will seduce her just as they're doing John Devoy," he said.

Colum was both wrong and right. No one in Dublin wanted Scarlett to be less Irish. It was a large part of her attractiveness. The O'Hara was an original. But Scarlett had discovered an unsettling truth. The Anglo-Irish thought of themselves as being just as Irish as the O'Haras of Adamstown. "These families were living in Ireland before America was even settled," Charlotte Montague said one day in irritation. "How can you call them anything but Irish?"

Scarlett couldn't unravel the complexities, so she stopped trying. She didn't really have to, she decided. She could have both worlds—the Ireland of Ballyhara's farms and the Ireland of Dublin Castle. Cat would have them, too, when she grew up. And that's much better than she would have had if I'd stayed in Charleston, Scarlett told herself firmly.

When the Saint Patrick's Ball ended at four in the morning, the Castle Season was over. The next event was some miles away in County Kildare. Everyone would be at the Punchestown Races, Charlotte told her. She'd be expected to be there.

Scarlett declined. "I love racing and horses, Charlotte, but I'm ready to go home now. I'm late already with this month's office hours. I'll pay for the hotel reservations you made."

No need, said Charlotte. She could sell them for four times their cost. And she herself had no interest in horses.

She thanked Scarlett for making her an independent woman. "You are independent now as well, Scarlett. You don't need me any more. Stay on Mrs. Sims' good side and let her dress you. The Shelbourne has reserved your rooms for next year's Season. Your house will accommodate all the guests you ever want to have, and your housekeeper is the most professional woman I've ever met in that position. You are in the world now. Do with it what you will."

"What will you do, Charlotte?"

"I will have what I always wanted. A small apartment in a Roman palazzo. Good food, good wine, and day after day of sunlight. I abhor rain."

Even Charlotte couldn't complain about this weather, Scarlett thought. The spring was sunnier than anyone could remember a spring ever being. The grass was tall and rich, and the wheat planted three weeks before on Saint Patrick's Day had already hazed the fields with tender fresh green. The harvest this year should make up for last year's disappointment and then some. It was wonderful to be home.

"How is Ree doing?" she asked Cat. It was just like her daughter to name the small Shetland pony "King," Scarlett thought indulgently. Cat valued her loves high. It was nice, too, that Cat used the Gaelic word. She liked to think of Cat as a true Irish child. Even though she did look like a gypsy. Her black hair would not stay neatly in its braids, and the sunny weather had browned her even more. Cat took off hat and shoes the moment she got outside.

"He doesn't like it when I ride him with a saddle. I don't like it either. Bareback is better."

"No you don't, my precious. You've got to learn to ride with a saddle and so does Ree. Be thankful it's not a sidesaddle."

"The one you have for hunting?"

"Yes. You'll have one some day, but not for a long, long time." Cat would be four in October, not all that much younger than Bonnie was when she had her fall. The sidesaddle could wait for a very long time. If only Bonnie had been astride instead of still learning to ride sidesaddle—no, she mustn't think like that. "If only" could break your heart.

"Let's ride down to the town, Cat, would you like that? We could go see Colum." Scarlett was worried about him, he was so moody these days.

"Cat doesn't like town. Can we ride to the river?"

"All right. I haven't been to the river in a long time, that's a good idea."

"May I climb up in the tower?"

"You may not. The door's too high, and it's more than likely full of bats."

"Will we go see Grainne?"

Scarlett's hands tightened on her reins. "How do you know Grainne?" The wise woman had told her to keep Cat away, to guard her close to home. Who had taken Cat there? And why?

"She gave Cat some milk."

Scarlett didn't care for the sound of it. Cat only referred to herself in the third person when something made her nervous or angry. "What didn't you like about Grainne, Cat?"

"She thinks Cat is another little girl named Dara. Cat told her, but she didn't hear."

"Oh, honey, she knows it's you. That's a very special name she gave you when you were just a little baby. It's Gaelic, like the names you gave Ree and Ocras. Dara means oak tree, the best and strongest tree of all."

"That's silly. A girl can't be a tree. She doesn't have leaves."

Scarlett sighed. She was overjoyed when Cat wanted to talk, the child was so often quiet, but it wasn't always easy to talk to her. She's such an opinionated little thing, and she always can tell when you're fudging a little. The truth, the whole truth, or she gives you a look that could kill.

"Look, Cat, there's the tower. Did I tell you the story about how old it is?"

"Yes."

Scarlett wanted to laugh. It would be wrong to tell a child to lie, but sometimes a polite fib would be welcome.

"I like the tower," said Cat.

"I do too, sweetheart." Scarlett wondered why she hadn't come here for so long. She'd almost forgotten how strange the old stones made her feel. It was eerie and peaceful at the same time.

She made a promise to herself not to let so many months slip away before her next visit. This was, after all, the real heart of Ballyhara, where it had begun.

The blackthorn was already blooming in the hedges and it was still April. What a season they were having! Scarlett slowed the buggy for a long sniff. There was no real need to hurry, the dresses would wait. She was driving into Trim for a package of summer clothes Mrs. Sims had sent. There were six invitations to June house parties on her desk. She wasn't sure she was ready to start partying so soon, but she was ready to see some grown-ups. Cat was her heart of hearts, but . . . And Mrs. Fitz was so busy running the big household that she never had time for a friendly cup of tea. Colum had gone to Galway to meet Stephen. She didn't know how she felt about Stephen coming to Ballyhara. Spooky Stephen. Maybe he wouldn't be so spooky in Ireland. Maybe he'd just been so strange and silent in Savannah because he was mixed up in the gun business. At least that was over! The extra income she was getting now from the little houses in Atlanta was pleasant, too. She must have given the Fenians a fortune. Much better spent on frocks; frocks didn't hurt anyone.

Stephen would have all the news from Savannah, too. She was longing to know how everyone was. Maureen was just as bad about writing letters as she was. She hadn't heard anything about the Savannah O'Haras in months. Or about anyone else. It made sense that when she'd made the decision to sell up in Atlanta she'd decided to put everything in America behind her and never look back.

Still, it would be nice to hear about Atlanta folks. She knew, from the profits she was making, that the little houses were selling, so Ashley's business must be good. What about Aunt Pittypat, though? And India? Had she dried up so much she was dust? And all those people who had once been so important to her so long ago? I wish I'd kept in touch with the aunts myself instead of leaving money with my lawyer to send them their allowance from. I was right not letting them know where I was, I was right to protect Cat from Rhett. But maybe he wouldn't do anything now; look at the way he was at the Castle. If I write to Eulalie, I'll get all the Charleston news from her. I'll hear about Rhett. Could I bear it to hear that he and Anne are blissfully happy, raising racehorses and Butler babies? I don't believe I want to know. I'll let the aunts stay like they are.

All I'd get anyhow is a million crossed pages of lecturing, and I get enough lecturing from Mrs. Fitz to fill that hole. Maybe she's right about giving some parties; it is a shame to have that house and all those servants standing idle. But she's dead wrong about Cat. I don't give a fig what Anglo mothers do, I'm not going to have a nanny running Cat's life. I see little enough of her now, the way she's always off at the stables or in the kitchen or wandering over the place or up a tree somewhere. And the idea of sending her away to some convent school is just plain crazy! When she's old enough, the school in Ballyhara will do just fine. She'll have friends there, too. It's worrisome to me sometimes that she never wants to play with any other children . . . What on earth is going on? It's not Market Day. Why's the bridge all jammed up with people like this?

Scarlett leaned down from the buggy and touched a hurrying woman on the shoulder. "What's happening?" The woman looked up. Her eyes were bright, her whole face excited.

"It's a flogging. Better hurry, or you'll miss it."

A flogging. Scarlett didn't want to see some poor devil of a soldier being whipped. She had an idea that flogging was punishment in the military. She tried to turn the buggy around, but the pushing, hurrying mass of people avid to see the spectacle caught her up in their press. Her horse was buffeted, her buggy rocked and pushed. The only thing she could do was get down and hold the bridle, soothe the horse with strokes and soft sounds, walking at the pace of the people around her.

When forward motion stopped, Scarlett could hear the whistling of the lash and the dreadful liquid sound it made when it landed. She wanted to cover her ears, but she needed her hands to gentle the frightened horse. It seemed to her that the ghastly noises went on forever.

". . . one hundred. That's it," she heard, then the groaning disappointment of the mob. She held tightly on to the bridle; the pushing and shoving was worse than before as the crowd dispersed.

She didn't shut her eyes until too late. She'd already seen the mutilated body, and the picture was burned on her brain. He was tied onto an upright spoked wheel, his wrists and ankles bound with leather thongs. A purple-stained blue shirt hung over his rough woolen pants from the waist, baring what must have once been a broad back. Now it was a giant red wound with loose red strips of flesh and skin hanging from it.

Scarlett turned her head into the horse's mane. She felt sick. Her horse tossed his head nervously, throwing her away. There was a terrible sweet smell in the air.

She heard someone vomiting, and her stomach heaved. She leaned over as best she could without releasing the bridle and was sick onto the cobbles.

"All right then, lad, there's no shame to losing your breakfast after a flogging. Go along to the pub and have a large whiskey. Marbury'll help me cut him down." Scarlett raised her head to look at the speaker, a British soldier in the uniform of a sergeant in the Guards. He was talking to an ashen-faced private. The private stumbled away. Another came forward to assist the sergeant. They cut the leather from behind the wheel, and the body fell into the blood-soaked mud beneath it.

That was green grass last week, Scarlett thought. This can't be. That's meant to be soft green grass.

"What about the wife, Sergeant?" A pair of soldiers were holding the arms of a silent, straining woman in a hooded black cloak.

"Let her go. It's over. Let's go. The cart will come later to take him away."

The woman ran after the men. She caught the sergeant's gold-striped sleeve. "Your officer promised I could bury him," she cried. "He gave me his word."

The sergeant shoved her away. "I only had orders for the flogging, the rest is none of my business. Leave me be, woman."

The black-cloaked figure stood alone on the street, watching the soldiers walk into the bar. She made one sound, a shuddering sob. Then she turned and ran to the wheel, the blood-covered body. "Danny, oh Danny, oh my dear." She crouched, then kneeled in the ghastly mud, trying to lift torn shoulders and lolling head into her lap. Her hood fell away, revealing a pale fine-boned face, neatly chignoned golden hair, blue eyes in shadowed circles of grief. Scarlett was frozen in place. To move, to clatter wheels over cobbles would be an obscene intrusion on the woman's tragedy.

A dirty little boy ran barefoot across the square. "Can I have a button or something, lady? My ma wants a keepsake." He shook the woman's shoulder.

Scarlett raced over the cobbles, the blood-spattered grass, the edge of the churned mud. She grabbed the boy's arm. He looked up, startled, mouth gaping. Scarlett slapped his face with all the strength in her arm. The sound of it was like the crack of a rifle shot. "Get out of here, you filthy little devil! Get out of here." The boy ran, bawling with fear.

"Thank you," said the wife of the man who had been beaten to death.

She was in it now, Scarlett knew. She had to do what little could be done. "I know a doctor in Trim," she said. "I'll go get him."

"A doctor? Will he want to bleed him, do you think?" Her bitter, desperate words were English-accented, like the voices at the Castle balls.

"He'll prepare your husband for burial," said Scarlett quietly.

The woman's bloody hand seized the hem of Scarlett's skirt. She lifted it to her lips, an abject kiss of gratitude. Scarlett's eyes clouded with tears. My God, I don't deserve this. I would have turned the buggy if I could. "Don't," she said, "please don't."

The woman's name was Harriet Stewart, her husband's Daniel Kelly. That was all Scarlett knew until Daniel Kelly was in the closed coffin inside the Catholic Chapel. Then the widow, who had spoken only to answer the priest's questions, looked around her with wild, darting eyes. "Billy, where's Billy? He should be here." The priest found out that there was a son, locked in a room at the hotel to keep him away from the flogging. "They were very kind," said the woman, "they let me pay with my wedding ring, though it's not gold."

"I'll bring him," Scarlett said. "Father? You'll take care of Mrs. Kelly?"

"That I will. Bring a bottle of brandy, too, Mrs. O'Hara. The poor lady's near breaking."

"I will not break down," Harriet Kelly said.

"I cannot. I must take care of my boy. He's such a little boy, only eight." Her voice was thin and brittle as new ice.

Scarlett hurried. Billy Kelly was a sturdy blond boy, big for his age, loud with anger. At his captivity behind the thick locked door. At the British soldiers. "I'll get a rod of iron from a smithy and smash their heads till they shoot me," he shouted. The innkeeper needed all his burly strength to hold the boy.

"Don't be a fool, Billy Kelly!" Scarlett's sharp words were like cold water thrown in the child's face. "Your mother needs you, and you want to add to her grief. What kind of man are you?"

The innkeeper could release him then. The boy was still. "Where is my mother?" he said, and he sounded as young and frightened as he was.

"Come with me," said Scarlett.

80

Harriet Stewart Kelly's story was revealed slowly. She and her son had been at Ballyhara for more than a week before Scarlett learned even the bare bones of it. Daughter of an English clergyman, Harriet had taken a post as assistant governess in the family of Lord Witley. She was well educated, for a woman, nineteen, and completely ignorant of the world.

One of her duties was to accompany the children of the house on their rides before breakfast. She fell in love with the white smile and playful lilting voice of the groom who also accompanied them. When he asked her to run away with him, she thought it the most romantic adventure in the world.

The adventure ended on the small farm of Daniel Kelly's father. There were no references and so no jobs for a runaway groom or governess. Danny worked the stony fields with his father and brothers, Harriet did what his mother told her to do, for the most part scrubbing and darning. She had mastered fine embroidery as one of the accomplishments necessary to a lady. That Billy was her only child was testimony to the death of the romance. Danny Kelly missed the world of fine horses in grand stables and the dashing striped waistcoat, top hat, and tall leather boots that were a groom's dress livery. He blamed Harriet for his fall from grace, consoled himself with whiskey. His family hated her because she was English, and Protestant.

Danny was arrested when he attacked an English officer in a bar. His family gave him up for dead when he was sentenced to a hundred stripes of the whip. They were already holding the wake when Harriet took Billy's hand and a loaf of bread and set out to walk the twenty miles to Trim, the site of the insulted officer's regimental barracks. She pled for her husband's life. She was granted his body for burial.

"I'll take my son to England, Mrs. O'Hara, if you will lend me the fare. My parents are dead, but I have cousins who might give us a home. I'll repay you from my wages. I'll find some kind of work."

"What nonsense," said Scarlett. "Haven't you

noticed that I have a little girl running wild as a woods colt? Cat needs a governess. Besides, she's already attached herself to Billy like a shadow. She needs a friend even more. You'd be doing me a mighty big favor if you'd stay, Mrs. Kelly."

It was true, as far as it went. What Scarlett didn't say was that she had no confidence at all in Harriet's ability to get herself on the right boat to England, much less earn a living once she got there. She's got plenty of spine but no smarts, was Scarlett's summing-up. The only things she knows are things she learned out of books. Scarlett's opinion of bookish people had never been very high.

Despite her scorn for Harriet's lack of practical sense, Scarlett was pleased to have her in the house. Ever since she'd returned from Dublin, Scarlett had found the big house disturbingly empty. She hadn't expected to miss Charlotte Montague, but she had. Harriet filled the gap nicely. In many ways she was even better company than Charlotte, because Harriet was fascinated by even the smallest thing the children did, and Scarlett heard about small adventures that Cat would not have thought worth reporting.

Billy Kelly was company for Cat, too, and Scarlett's uneasiness about Cat's isolation was laid to rest. The only drawback to Harriet's presence was Mrs. Fitzpatrick's hostility. "We don't want English at Ballyhara, Mrs. O," she had said when Scarlett brought Harriet and her son from Trim. "It was bad enough having the Montague woman here but at least she did something useful to you."

"Well, maybe you don't want Mrs. Kelly, but I do, and it's my house!" Scarlett was tired of being told what she should and shouldn't do. Charlotte had done it, and now Mrs. Fitz. Harriet never criticized her at all. On the contrary. She was so grateful for the roof over her head and Scarlett's hand-me-down clothes that sometimes Scarlett felt like shouting at her not to be so all-fired meek and mild.

Scarlett felt like shouting at everybody, and she was ashamed of herself, because there was absolutely no reason for her ill temper. Never in memory had there been such a growing season, everyone said. The grain was already half again as tall as normal, and the potato fields were thick with strong green growth. One glorious sunny day followed another, and the celebrations at weekly Market Day in Trim lasted long into the soft warm night. Scarlett danced until her shoes and stockings had holes in them, but the music and laughter failed to raise her spirits for long. When Harriet sighed romantically about the young couples walking along the river with their arms entwined, Scarlett turned away from her with an impatient shrug of the shoulders. Thank goodness for the invitations that were coming daily in the mail, she thought. The house parties were beginning soon. It seemed that the elegant festivities in Dublin and the temptations of the shops had made Trim Market Day lose most of its appeal.

By the end of May the waters of the Boyne were so low that one could see the stones laid centuries before as footing for the ford. The farmers were looking anxiously at the clouds blown by the west wind across the beautiful low sky. The fields needed rain. The brief showers that refreshed the air wet the soil only enough to draw the roots of wheat and timothy grass toward the surface, weakening the stalks.

Cat reported that the north track to Grainne's cottage was turning into a beaten path. "She has more butter than she can eat," Cat said, spreading her own butter on a muffin. "People are buying spells for rain."

"You've decided to be friends with Grainne?"

"Yes. Billy likes her."

Scarlett smiled. Whatever Billy said was law to Cat. It was lucky the boy was so good natured; Cat's adoration could have been a terrible trial. Instead he was as patient as a saint. Billy had inherited his father's "way with horses." He was teaching Cat to be an expert rider, far beyond anything that Scarlett could have done. As soon as Cat was a few years older, she'd be on a horse, not a pony. She mentioned at least twice a day that ponies were for little girls and Cat was a big girl. Fortunately it was Billy who said "not big enough." Cat would never have accepted it from Scarlett.

Scarlett went to a house party in Roscommon in early June, confident that she was in no way deserting her daughter. She probably won't even notice that I'm not there. How humbling.

"Isn't the weather splendid?" said everyone at the party. They played tennis on the lawn after dinner in the soft clear light that lasted until after ten o'clock.

Scarlett was pleased to be with so many of the people she'd liked most in Dublin. The only one she didn't greet with real enthusiasm was Charles Ragland. "It was your regiment that flogged that pitiful man to death, Charles. I'll never forget, and I'll never forgive. Wearing regular clothes doesn't change the fact that you're an English soldier, and that the military are monsters."

Charles was surprisingly unapologetic. "I'm truly sorry that you saw it, Scarlett. Flogging's a filthy business. But we're seeing things that are even worse, and they must be stopped."

He declined to give examples, but Scarlett heard from general conversation about the violence against landlords that was cropping up all over Ireland. Fields were torched, cows had their throats cut, an agent for a big estate near Galway was ambushed and hacked to pieces. There was hushed, anxious talk about a resurgence of the Whiteboys, organized bands of marauders that had terrified landowners more than a hundred years before. It couldn't be, said wiser heads. These latest incidents were scattered and sporadic and usually the work of known troublemakers. But they did tend to make one a bit uncomfortable when the tenants stared in the carriage as one drove past.

Scarlett forgave Charles. But, she said, he mustn't expect her to forget. "I'll even take the blame for the flogging if it will make you remember me," he said ardently. Then he blushed like a boy. "Dammit, I invent speeches worthy of

Lord Byron when I'm in the barracks thinking of you, then I blurt out some rubbish when I'm in your presence. You know, don't you, that I'm most abominably in love with you?"

"Yes, I know. It's all right, Charles. I don't believe I would have liked Lord Byron, and I like you very much."

"Do you, my angel? Might I hope that—"

"I don't think so, Charles. Don't look so desperate. It's not you. I don't think so with anybody." The sandwiches in Scarlett's room slowly curled up their edges during the night.

"It's so good to be home! I'm afraid I'm an awful kind of person, Harriet. When I'm away I always get an itch to be home, no matter how much fun I'm having. But I'll bet you I start thinking about the next party I've accepted before this week's out. Tell me all about what happened while I was gone. Did Cat pester Billy half to death?"

"Not too much. They've invented a new game they call 'sink the Vikings.' I don't know where the name comes from. Cat said you could explain, she only remembered enough to make up the name. They've put a rope ladder on the tower. Billy hauls rocks up it, then they throw them through the slits into the river."

Scarlett laughed. "That minx. She's been nagging me about getting up in the tower for ages. And I notice she's got Billy doing the heavy work. Before she's even four years old. She's going to be a terror by the time she's six. You'll have to beat her with a stick to make her learn her letters."

"Probably not. She's already curious about the animal alphabet in her room."

Scarlett smiled at the implied suggestion that her daughter was probably a near-genius. She was willing to believe that Cat could do everything earlier and better than any child in the history of mankind.

"Will you tell me about the house party, Scarlett?" Harriet asked wistfully. Experience hadn't caused her to lose her romantic dreaminess.

"It was lovely," said Scarlett. "We were—oh, about two dozen, I guess—and for once there was no boring old retired general to talk about what he'd learned from the Duke of Wellington. We had a knock-down-drag-out croquet tournament with someone taking bets and giving odds like a horse race. I was on a team with—"

"Mrs. O'Hara!" The words were screamed, not spoken. Scarlett jumped up from her chair. A maid ran in, panting and red-faced. "Kitchen . . . " she gasped. "Cat . . . burned . . . " Scarlett almost knocked her down when she tore past her.

She could hear Cat wailing when she was only halfway through the colonnade from house to kitchen wing. Scarlett ran even faster. Cat never cried.

"She didn't know the pan was hot" . . . "already buttered her hand" . . . "dropped it soon as she picked it up" . . . "Momma . . . Momma . . ." The voices were all around her. Scarlett heard only Cat's.

"Momma's here, darling. We'll fix Cat up quick as a wink." She scooped the crying child up in her arms and hastened to the door. She'd seen the furious red weal across Cat's palm. It was so swollen her little fingers were spread wide.

The drive had doubled its length, she'd swear it. She was running as fast as she could without risking a fall. If Dr. Devlin's not at his house, he won't have a roof over his head when he comes back. I'll throw out every stick of furniture he owns, and his family with it.

But the doctor was there. "Now, now, there's no need to be in such a state, Mrs. O'Hara. Aren't children having accidents all the time? Let me take a look at it."

Cat screamed when he pressed her hand. It tore Scarlett like a knife.

"It's a bad burn, and that's a fact," said Dr. Devlin. "We'll keep it greased till the blister fills, then cut and drain the liquid."

"She's hurting now, Doctor. Can't you do something?" Cat's tears were soaking Scarlett's shoulder.

"Butter's best. It will cool it in time."

"In time?" Scarlett turned and ran. She thought of the liquid on her tongue when Cat was born, the blessed quick release from pain. She'd take her baby to the wise woman.

So far—she'd forgotten the river and the tower were so far. Her legs were getting tired, that mustn't be. Scarlett ran as if the hounds of Hell were in pursuit. "Grainne!" she cried when she reached the hollies. "Help! For God's sake, help."

The wise woman stepped out from a shadow.

"We'll sit here," she said quietly. "There's no more running needed." She sat on the ground and held up her arms. "Come to Grainne, Dara. I'll make the hurt go away."

Scarlett put Cat into the wise woman's lap. Then she crouched on the ground, poised to snatch her child and run again. To wherever there might be help. If she could think of any place or anyone.

"I want you to put your hand in mine, Dara. I won't touch it. Lay it in my hand yourself. I will talk to the burn and it will heed me. It will go away." Grainne's voice was calm, certain. Cat's green eyes looked into Grainne's placid wrinkled face. She placed the back of her injured small hand against Grainne's herb-stained leathery palm.

"You have a big, strong burn, Dara. I will have to persuade it. It will take a long time, but it will begin to feel better soon." Grainne blew gently on the burned flesh. Once, twice, three times. She put her lips close to their two hands and began to whisper into Cat's palm.

Her words were inaudible, her voice like the whisper of soft young leaves or clear shallow water running over pebbles in sunlight. After a few minutes, no more than three, Cat's crying stopped, and Scarlett sank onto the ground, slack-muscled from relief. The whispering continued, low, monotonous, relaxing. Cat's head nodded, then dropped onto Grainne's breast. The whispers went on. Scarlett leaned back on her elbows. Later her head drooped and she slid onto the ground, supine and soon sleeping. And still Grainne whispered to the burn, on and on, while Cat slept and Scarlett slept, and slowly, slowly the swelling subsided and the red receded until Cat's skin was as if she had never burned it at all. Grainne lifted her head then and licked her cracked lips. She laid Cat's hand over the other, then folded her two arms around the sleeping child and rocked gently forth and back, humming under her breath. After a long while she stopped.

"Dara." Cat opened her eyes. "It's time to go. You tell your mother. Grainne is tired and will sleep now. You must take your mother home." The wise woman stood Cat on her feet. Then she turned and went into the holly thicket on her hands and knees.

"Momma. It's time to go."

"Cat? How could I fall asleep like that? Oh, my angel, I'm so sorry. What happened? How do you feel, baby?"

"I had my nap. My hand is well. May I go up in the tower?"

Scarlett looked at her little girl's unblemished palm. "Oh, Kitty Cat, your Momma really needs a hug and a kiss, please." She held Cat to her for a moment, then let her go. It was her gift to Cat.

Cat pressed her lips to Scarlett's cheek. "I think I'd rather have tea and cakes than go in the tower right now," she said. It was her gift to her mother. "Let's go home."

"The O'Hara was under a spell and the witch and her changeling were talking in a tongue

1050

known to no man." Nell Garrity had seen it with her own eyes, she said, and that frightened she was she turned on her heel into the Boyne, forgetting altogether she needed to go back to the ford. She would have drowned for certain sure had the river been its usual deep self.

"Casting spells on the clouds to make them pass us by they were."

"And didn't Annie McGinty's cow go dry that very day and her one of the best milkers in all Trim?"

"Dan Houlihan in Navan has the affliction of warts on his feet so bad he can't put them to the floor."

"The changeling rides a wolf disguised as a pony by day."

"Her shadow fell on my churn and the butter never cameo."

"Those who know say she sees in the dark, her eyes glowing like fire for her prowling."

"And did you never hear the tale of her birthing, Mr. Reilly? It was on All Hallows' Eve, and the sky fairly torn to shreddings with comets . . ."

The stories were carried from hearth to hearth throughout the district.

It was Mrs. Fitzpatrick who found Cat's tabby on the doorstep of the Big House. Ocras had been strangled, then disembowelled. She rolled the remains into a cloth and hid it in her room until she could go unobserved to the river to dispose of it.

Rosaleen Fitzpatrick burst into Colum's house

without knocking. He looked up at her, but he remained seated in his chair.

"Just what I thought I'd be finding!" she exclaimed. "You can't do your drinking in the bar like an honest man, you've got to hide your weakness here with that sorry excuse for a man." Her voice was rich with contempt, as was her gesture when she prodded Stephen O'Hara's limp legs with her booted foot. He was snoring unevenly through his slack open mouth. The smell of whiskey clung to his clothes, saturated his breath.

"Leave me be, Rosaleen," Colum said wearily. "My cousin and myself are mourning the death of Ireland's hopes."

Mrs. Fitzpatrick put her hands on her hips. "And what about the hopes of your other cousin, then, Colum O'Hara? Will you drown yourself in another bottle when Scarlett is mourning the death of her darling babe? Will you sorrow with her when your godchild is dead? Because I tell you, Colum, the child is in mortal danger."

Rosaleen fell on her knees before his chair. She shook his arm. "For the love of Christ and His Blessed Mother, Colum, you've got to do something! I've tried every way I know how, but the people won't listen to me. Mayhap its even too late for them to listen to you, but you've got to make the try. You cannot hide away from the world like this. The people feel your desertion, and so does your cousin Scarlett."

"Katie Colum O'Hara," mumbled Colum.

"Her blood will be on your hands," said Rosaleen with cold clarity.

Colum made a leisurely round of visits to every house, cottage, and bar in Ballyhara and Adamstown the following day and night. The first visit was to Scarlett's office, where he found her studying the estate ledgers. Her frown smoothed out when she saw him at the door, reappeared when he suggested she give a party to welcome her cousin Stephen back to Ireland.

She capitulated at last, as he'd known she would, and then Colum was able to use the invitation to the party as his reason for all the other visits. He listened keenly for indications that Rosaleen's warning had a basis, but he heard nothing, to his great relief.

After Sunday Mass, all the villagers and O'Haras from all County Meath came to Ballyhara to welcome Stephen home and to hear about America. There were long trestle tables on the lawn with steaming platters of boiled salt beef and cabbage, baskets piled with hot boiled potatoes, and foamy pitchers of porter. The French doors were open to the drawing room with its ceiling of Irish heroes, as invitation into the Big House for any who cared to enter.

It was almost a good party.

Scarlett consoled herself afterwards with the thought that she'd done her best, and she'd had a long time with Kathleen. "I've missed you so, Kathleen," she'd told her cousin. "Nothing's the same since you left. The ford might be under ten feet of water for all the good it does me, I can't stand to go to Pegeen's house."

"And if things always stayed the same, Scarlett, what would be the reason for bothering to draw breath?" Kathleen replied. She was mother to a healthy boy and expecting a brother for him, she hoped, in six months.

She hasn't missed me at all, Scarlett realized sadly.

Stephen talked no more in Ireland than he had in America, but the family didn't seem to mind. "He's a silent man, and that's the all of it." Scarlett avoided him. He was still Spooky Stephen to her. He had brought back one delicious piece of news. Grandfather Robillard had died and left his estate to Pauline and Eulalie. They were in the pink house together, took their constitutionals every day, and were reputed to be even richer than the Telfair sisters.

They heard thunder in the distance at the O'Hara party. Everyone stopped talking, stopped eating, stopped laughing to look up in hope at the mocking bright blue sky. Father Flynn added a special Mass every day and people lit candles with private prayers for rain.

On Midsummer Day the clouds borne on the west wind began to pile together instead of scudding past. By late afternoon they filled the horizon, half-black and heavy. The men and women who were building the bonfire for the night's celebration lifted their heads into the staccato gusts of wind, smelling rain. It would be a celebration indeed if the rains returned and the crops were saved.

The storm broke at first dark, in a cannonade

of deafening cracks of lightning that lit up the sky brighter than day, and a deluge of rain. People fell to the ground and covered their heads. Hail peppered them with stones of ice as big as walnuts. Cries of pain and fear filled the moments of silence between lightning cracks.

Scarlett was leaving the Big House for the music and dancing at the bonfire. She ducked back inside, soaked to the skin in only seconds, and ran upstairs to find Cat. She was looking out the window, her green eyes wide, her ears covered by her hands. Harriet Kelly huddled in a corner holding Billy close for protection. Scarlett kneeled beside Cat to watch the rampage of nature.

It lasted a half hour, then the sky was clear, star-studded, with a gleaming three-quarter moon. The bonfire was sodden and scattered; it would not be lighted this night. And the fields of grass and wheat were flattened by the hail that covered them in gray-white misshapen balls. A keening rose from the throats of the Irish of Ballyhara. Its piercing sound cut through the stone walls and glass panes into Cat's room. Scarlett shuddered and drew her dark child close. Cat whimpered softly. Her hands were not enough to hold back the sound.

"We've lost our harvest," Scarlett said. She was standing on a table in the middle of Ballyhara's wide street, facing the people of the town. "But there's plenty to be saved. The grass will still dry to hay, and we'll have straw from the wheat stalks even though there'll be no kernels to grind for flour. I'm going now to Trim and Navan and Drogheda to buy supplies for the winter. There'll be no hunger in Ballyhara. That I promise you, my word as The O'Hara."

They cheered her then.

But at night by their hearths they talked about the witch and the changeling and the tower where the changeling had stirred the ghost of the hanged lord to vengeance.

81

The clear skies and relentless heat returned, and lasted. The front page of the *Times* was made up entirely of reports and speculations on the weather. Pages two and three had more and more items about outrages against landlords' property and agents.

Scarlett glanced at the newspaper every day, then threw it aside. At least she didn't have to worry about her tenants, thank God for that. They knew she'd take care of them.

But it wasn't easy. Too often, when she arrived in a town or city that was supposed to have stock-piles of flour and meal, she discovered that the supplies were only rumors, or were all gone. In the beginning she haggled with vigor about the inflated prices, but as supplies became more scarce, she was so happy to find anything at all that she paid whatever was asked, often for inferior goods.

It's as bad as it was in Georgia after the War, she thought. No, it's worse. Because then we were fighting the Yankees, who stole or burned everything. Now I'm fighting for the lives of more people than I ever had depending on me at Tara. And I don't even know who the enemy is. I can't believe God's put a curse on Ireland.

But she bought a hundred dollars' worth of candles for the people of Ballyhara to light in supplication when they prayed in the chapel. And she rode her horse or drove her wagon carefully around the piles of stones that had begun to appear beside roads or in fields. She didn't know what older deities were being appeased, but if they'd bring rain she was willing to give them every stone in County Meath. She'd carry them with her own hands if she had to.

Scarlett felt helpless, and it was a new and frightening experience. She had thought she understood farming because she'd grown up on a plantation. The good years at Ballyhara had, in fact, been no more than she expected, because she had worked hard and demanded hard work from others. But what was she to do, now that willingness to work wasn't enough?

She continued to go to the parties she had accepted in such high spirits. Now she was looking for information from other landowners, not for entertainment.

Scarlett arrived a day late at Kilbawney Abbey for the Giffords' house party. "I'm terribly sorry, Florence," she said to Lady Gifford, "if I had any manners at all I would have thought to send a telegram. But the truth is, I was going from pillar to post looking for flour and meal contracts and I completely lost track of what day it was."

Lady Gifford was so relieved that Scarlett was there that she forgot to be offended. Everyone else at the house party had accepted her invitation instead of another because she'd held out the bait that Scarlett was coming.

"I've been waiting for the opportunity to shake your hand, young woman." The knickerbockered gentleman pumped Scarlett's hand vigorously. He was a vigorous old man, the Marquess of Trevanne, with an undisciplined white beard and an alarmingly purple-veined beak of a nose.

"Thank you, sir," said Scarlett. What for? she wondered.

The marquess told her, in the loud voice of the deaf. He told the entire house party, whether they wanted to listen or not. His bellows reached all the way out to the croquet lawn.

She deserved congratulations, he roared, for rescuing Ballyhara. He'd told Arthur not to be such a fool, not to waste his money buying ships from the thieves who robbed him, claiming the timbers were sound. But Arthur wouldn't listen, he was determined to ruin himself. Eighty thousand pounds he'd paid, more than half his patrimony, enough to buy all the land in County Meath. He was a fool, he'd always been a fool, the man never had any sense at all, even when they were boys together he'd known it. But demme, he'd loved Arthur like a brother even if he was a fool. No man ever had a truer friend than Arthur was to him. He had wept, yes, ma'am, actually wept when Arthur hanged

1058

himself. He'd always known he was a fool, but who could have dreamed he'd be such a fool as that? Arthur loved that place, he gave his heart to it, and in the end his life. It was criminal that Constance abandoned it the way she did. She should have preserved it as a memorial to Arthur.

The marquess was grateful to Scarlett for doing what Arthur's own widow didn't have the decency to do.

"I'd like to shake your hand again, Mistress O'Hara."

Scarlett surrendered it to him. What was this old man telling her? The young lord of Ballyhara hadn't hanged himself, a man from the town had dragged him to the tower and hung him. Colum said so. The marquess must be wrong. Old people got things mixed up in their memories . . . Or Colum was wrong. He'd only been a child, he only knew what people said, he wasn't even in Ballyhara then, the family was at Adamstown . . . The marquess wasn't in Ballyhara either, he only knew what people said. It's all too complicated.

"Scarlett, hello." It was John Morland. Scarlett smiled sweetly at the marquess and retrieved her hand. She tucked it in Morland's elbow.

"Bart, I'm so glad to see you. I looked for you at every single party of the Season and never found you."

"I passed this year. Two mares in foal outrank a viceroy every time. How have you been?"

It had been an aeon since she'd last seen him, and so much had happened. Scarlett hardly knew where to begin. "I know what interests you, Bart," she said. "One of the hunters you helped me buy is outjumping Half Moon. Her name is Comet. It's as if one day she looked up and decided it was fun instead of work . . ." They strolled off to a quiet corner to talk. In due time Scarlett learned that Bart had no news of Rhett at all. She also learned more than she wanted to know about delivering a foal when it was turned in the mare's womb. It didn't matter. Bart was one of her favorite people and always would be.

All the talk was of the weather. Ireland had never before in its history had a drought, and what else could this succession of sunny days be called? There was almost no corner of the country that didn't need rain. There'd be trouble for sure when rents were due in September.

She hadn't thought of that. Scarlett's heart felt like lead. Of course the farmers wouldn't be able to pay their rents. And if she didn't make them pay, how could she expect the town tenants to pay? The shops and bars, even the doctor, depended on the money the farmers spent with them. She was going to have no income at all.

It was horribly difficult to keep up the appearance of cheerfulness, but she had to. Oh, she'd be glad when the weekend was over.

The final night of the party was July 14, Bastille Day. Guests had been told to bring fancy dress. Scarlett wore her best and brightest Galway clothes, with four petticoats of different colors beneath a red skirt. Her striped stockings were scratchy in the heat, but they caused such a sensation that it was worth the discomfort.

"I never dreamed the peasants were so charmingly dressed under their dirt," Lady Gifford exclaimed. "I'm going to buy some of everything to take to London next year. People will be begging for the name of my dressmaker."

What a stupid woman, thought Scarlett. Thank goodness this is the last night.

Charles Ragland came in for the dancing after dinner. The party he'd been to had broken up that morning. "I would have left anyhow," he told Scarlett later. "When I heard that you were so near, I had to come."

"So near? You were fifty miles away."

"A hundred would be the same."

Scarlett let Charles kiss her in the shadow of the great oak tree. It had been so terribly long since she'd been kissed, or felt a man's strong arms tighten protectively around her. She felt herself melting in his embrace. It felt wonderful.

"Beloved," Charles said hoarsely.

"Shhh. Just kiss me till I'm dizzy, Charles."

Dizzy she became. She held on to his broad muscular shoulders to keep from falling. But when he said he'd come to her room, Scarlett drew away from him, her head clear. Kisses were one thing, sharing her bed was out of the question.

She burned the contrite note he slid under her door during the night, and she left too early in the morning to need to say goodbye.

When she got home, she went at once to find Cat. It came as no surprise to learn that she and Billy had gone to the tower. It was the only cool place on Ballyhara. What was a surprise was to find Colum and Mrs. Fitzpatrick waiting for her under a big tree at the rear of the house, with a lavish tea spread on a shadowed table.

Scarlett was delighted. Colum had been such a stranger for so long, so stand-offish about coming up to the Big House. It was wonderful to have her almost-brother back.

"I've got the strangest story to tell you," she said. "It drove me half-crazy with curiosity when I heard it. What do you think, Colum? Is it possible that the young lord really hanged himself in the tower?" Scarlett described the Marquess of Trevanne with laughing, wicked accuracy and mimicked his speech as she repeated it.

Colum set down his teacup with tightly controlled precision. "I have no opinion, Scarlett darling," he said, and his voice was as light and laughing as Scarlett liked to remember it. "Anything is possible in Ireland, else we would be plagued with snakes like the rest of the world." He smiled as he stood up. "And now I must go. I tarried from my day's duties only to see your beautiful self. Disregard anything this woman may tell you about my fondness for the cakes I ate with my tea."

He walked away so rapidly that Scarlett had no time to wrap some cakes in a napkin for him to take along.

"I'll return shortly," said Mrs. Fitz, and she hurried after Colum.

"Well!" said Scarlett. She saw Harriet Kelly in the distance, at the end of the browned lawn, and waved at her. "Come have tea," Scarlett shouted. There was plenty left.

Rosaleen Fitzpatrick had to lift up her skirt and run to catch up with Colum halfway down the long drive. She walked silently at his side until she caught her breath sufficiently so that she could speak. "And what happens now?" she asked. "You're rushing to your bottle, is that the truth of it?"

Colum stopped, turned to face her. "There is no truth of anything, and that is what scours my heart. Did you hear her, then? Quoting the Englishman's lies, believing them. Just as Devoy and the others believe the shining English lies of Parnell. I could stay no longer, Rosaleen, for fear of smashing her English teacups and howling protest like a chained dog."

Rosaleen looked at the anguish in Colum's eyes and hardened her expression. Too long had she poured sympathy on his wounded spirit; it had not helped. He was tortured by his sense of failure and betrayal. After more than twenty years of working for Ireland's freedom, after success at his assigned task, after filling the arsenal in the Protestant church at Ballyhara, Colum had been told it was all valueless. Parnell's political actions had more meaning. Colum had always been willing to die for his country; he could not bear to live without believing that he was helping her.

Rosaleen Fitzpatrick shared Colum's distrust of Parnell; she shared his frustration that his work, and hers, had been discarded by the Fenian leaders. But she could put her own feelings aside to follow orders. Her commitment was as great as his, perhaps greater, for she lusted for personal revenge even more than justice.

Now, however, Rosaleen put aside her allegiance to Fenianism. Colum's suffering meant more to her than Ireland's, for she loved him in a way that no woman should permit herself to love a priest, and she could not let him destroy himself through doubt and anger.

"What kind of Irishman are you then, Colum O'Hara?" she said harshly. "Will you let Devoy and the others rule alone and wrongly? You hear what's happening. The people are fighting on their own, and paying a fearful price for lack of a leader. They do not want Parnell, no more than you. You created the means for an army. Why don't you go now and build the army to use the means instead of drinking yourself to blindness like any bravery-spouting layabout in a corner bar?"

Colum looked at her, then beyond her, and his eyes slowly filled with hope.

Rosaleen dropped her gaze to the ground. She couldn't chance letting him see the emotion burning in her eyes.

"I don't know how you can bear this heat," said Harriet Kelly. Under her parasol, there was a sheen of perspiration on her delicate face.

"I love it," Scarlett said. "It's just like home. Have I ever told you about the South, Harriet?"

She had not, Harriet said.

"Summer was my favorite time," said Scarlett. "The heat and the dry days were just what was wanted. It was so beautiful, the cotton plants green and fixing to bust open, all in row after row, stretching as far as your eye could see. The field hands would sing when they hoed, you could hear the music in the distance, kind of hanging there in the air." She heard her own words and was horrified. What was she saying? "Home?" This was her home now. Ireland.

Harriet's eyes were dreamy. "How lovely," she sighed.

Scarlett looked at her with disgust, then turned it on herself. Romantic dreaminess had gotten Harriet Kelly into more trouble than she knew what to do with, and she still didn't know any better.

But I do. I didn't have to put the South behind me, General Sherman did it for me, and I'm too old to pretend it never happened.

I don't know what's wrong with me, I'm all at sixes and sevens. Maybe it's the heat, maybe I've lost the knack of it.

"I'm going to go work on the accounts, Harriet," said Scarlett.

The neat rows of numbers were always calming for her, and she felt like she was about to jump out of her skin.

The account books were terribly depressing. The only money she had coming in was the profit from the little houses she was building on the edge of Atlanta. Well, at least that money was no longer going to that revolutionary movement Colum used to belong to. It would help some—a lot, really. But not nearly enough. She'd spent incredible sums on the house and the village. And Dublin. She couldn't believe how extravagant she'd been in Dublin, although the orderly columns of numbers proved it beyond question.

If only Joe Colleton would shave a little in building those houses. They'd still sell like hotcakes, but the profit would be much bigger. She wouldn't let him buy cheaper lumber—the whole reason for building them in the first place was to keep Ashley in business. There were plenty of other ways to cut expenses. Foundations . . . chimneys . . . brick didn't have to be top quality.

Scarlett shook her head impatiently. Joe Colleton would never do it on his own. He was just like Ashley, bone honest and full of unbusinesslike ideals. She remembered them talking together at the site. If ever there were birds of a feather, it was those two. She wouldn't be surprised if they stopped in the middle of talking lumber prices to start talking about some fool book they'd read.

Scarlett's eyes grew thoughtful.

She ought to send Harriet Kelly to Atlanta.

She'd be a perfect wife for Ashley. They were another two of a kind, living out of books, hopeless in the real world. Harriet was a ninny in lots of ways, but she stuck by her obligations—she'd stayed with her no-good husband for nearly ten years—and she had her own kind of gumption. It took a lot of sand to walk in to the commanding officer in broken shoes and beg for Danny Kelly's life. Ashley needed that kind of steel behind him. He needed somebody to take care of, too. It couldn't be doing him any good having India and Aunt Pitty fussing over him all the time. What it was likely doing to Beau was too awful to think about. Billy Kelly would teach him a thing or three. Scarlett grinned. She'd better send a box of smelling salts for Aunt Pitty along with Billy Kelly.

Her grin faded. No, it wouldn't do. Cat would be heartbroken without Billy. She'd drooped for a week when Ocras ran away, and the tabby hadn't been one-tenth of what Billy was in her life.

Besides, Harriet couldn't stand the heat.

No, it wouldn't do at all. Not at all.

Scarlett bent her head to the account books again.

82

"We've got to stop spending so much money," Scarlett said angrily. She shook the account book at Mrs. Fitzpatrick. "There's no reason on earth for feeding this army of servants when flour for bread costs a fortune. At least half of them will have to be let go. What good do they do, anyhow? And don't sing me that old song about having to churn the cream to make the butter, because if there's one thing that there's too much of these days, it's butter. You can't sell it for hapenny a pound."

Mrs. Fitzpatrick waited for Scarlett's tirade to end. Then she calmly took the book from her and put it on a table. "You'd turn them out onto the road, then?" she said. "They'll find plenty of company, for many of the Big Houses in Ireland are doing just what you're proposing. Not a day goes by we don't have a dozen or more poor souls begging a bowl of soup at the kitchen door. Will you add to their number?"

Scarlett strode impatiently to the window. "No, of course not, don't be ridiculous. But there must be some way we can cut expenses."

"It's more costly to feed your fine horses than your servants." Mrs. Fitzpatrick's voice was cold.

Scarlett turned on her. "That will be all," she said furiously. "Leave me alone." She picked up the book and went to her desk. But she was too upset to concentrate on the accounts. How could Mrs. Fitz be so mean? She must know that I enjoy hunting more than anything else in my life. The only thing that's getting me through this horrible summer is knowing that come fall, the hunting will begin again.

Scarlett closed her eyes and tried to remember the crisp cold mornings, with the night's light frost turned to trailing mist, and the sound of the horn signalling the beginning of the chase. A tiny muscle jumped involuntarily in the soft flesh over her clenched jaw. She wasn't good at imagining, she was good at doing.

She opened her eyes and worked doggedly on the accounts. With no grain to sell and no rents to collect, she was going to lose money this year. The knowledge bothered her, because she had always made money in business and losing it was a highly disagreeable change.

But Scarlett had grown up in a world where it was accepted that sometimes a crop failed or a storm wrought havoc. She knew that next year would be different, and certainly better. She was not a failure because of the disaster of the drought and the hail. It wasn't like the lumber business or the store where she would have been responsible if there had been no profit.

Besides, the losses would barely make a dent in her fortune. She could be extravagant for the rest of her life, and the crops at Ballyhara could fail every year, and she would still have plenty of money.

Scarlett sighed unconsciously. For so many years she had worked and scrimped and saved, thinking that if only she could have enough money, she would be happy. Now she had it, thanks to Rhett, and somehow it didn't mean anything at all. Except that there was no longer anything to work for, to scheme and strive for.

She wasn't foolish enough to want to be poor and desperate again, but she needed to be challenged, to use her quick intelligence, to conquer obstacles. And so she thought with longing about jumping fences and ditches and taking chances on a powerful horse that she controlled by force of will.

When the accounts were done, Scarlett turned to the pile of personal mail with a silent groan. She hated writing letters. She already knew what was in the mail. Many were invitations. She put them in a stack. Harriet could pen the polite refusals for her, no one would know she hadn't written them herself, and Harriet loved being useful.

There were two more proposals. Scarlett received at least one a week. They pretended to be love letters, but she knew very well that they wouldn't be there if she wasn't a rich widow. Most of them, anyhow.

She replied to the first one with the convenient phrases about "honored by your regard" and "unable to return your affection to the degree you merit" and "place incalculable value on your friendship" that protocol demanded and supplied.

The second was not so easy. It was from Charles Ragland. Of all the men she had met in Ireland, Charles was the most truly eligible to her. His adoration was convincing, not at all like the elaborate fawning over her that so many men did. He wasn't after her money, she was sure of that. He came from money himself, his people were big landowners in England. He was a younger son, and he'd chosen the army instead of the Church. But he must have some money of his own. His dress uniform cost more than all her ball gowns put together, she was sure.

What else? Charles was handsome. He was as big as Rhett, only blond instead of dark. Not washed-out blond, though, like so many fair people. His hair was gold, with just a touch of red in it, startling against his tanned skin. He was really very good looking. Women looked at him like they could eat him with a spoon.

So why didn't she love him? She had thought about it, she'd thought often and long. But she couldn't, she didn't care enough.

I want to love somebody. I know how it feels to love, it's the best feeling in the world. I can't bear the unfairness, that I learned about loving too late. Charles loves me, and I want to be loved, I need it. I'm lonely by myself without it. Why can't I love him?

Because I love Rhett, that's why. That's why for Charles and for every other man in the world. They're none of them Rhett.

You will never have Rhett, her mind told her.

And her heart cried out in anguish: Do you think I don't know that? Do you think I can ever completely forget it? Do you think that it doesn't haunt me every time I see him in Cat? Do you think it doesn't spring on me from nowhere just when I believe that my life is my own?

Scarlett wrote carefully, looking for the kindest words she knew to say no to Charles Ragland. He would never understand if she told him that she truly liked him, that in a very small way perhaps she even loved him because he loved her, and that her affection for him made it impossible for her to marry him. She wished better for him than a wife who would forever belong to another man.

The year's final house party was not far from Kilbride, which was not far from Trim. Scarlett could drive herself instead of all the complications of taking the train. She left very early in the morning when it was still cool. Her horses were suffering from the heat, despite being sponged down four times a day. Even she had started to feel it; she felt twitchy and sweaty almost all night when she was trying to sleep. Thank heaven it was August. The summer was almost done, if it would only admit it.

The sky was still tinged with pink, but there was already a haze of heat in the distance. Scarlett hoped she'd calculated the time right for the trip. She'd like to have her horse and herself in the shade when the sun was full up.

I wonder if Nan Sutcliffe will be up? She never looked like an early riser to me. No matter. I wouldn't mind having a cool bath and changing my clothes before I see anybody. I do hope there's a decent maid for me here, not like that ham-handed idiot at the Giffords'. She practically tore the sleeves off my frocks hanging them up. Maybe Mrs. Fitz is right, she usually is. But I don't want a personal maid hanging around me every minute of my life. Peggy Quinn does all I need at home, and if people want me to come visit they'll just have to put up with me not bringing my maid. I really should give a house party myself, to pay back all the hospitality I owe. Everyone has been so kind . . . But not yet. Next summer will do. I can say this year was just too hot, plus I was worried about the farms . . .

Two men stepped from shadows on each side of the road. One caught the horse's bridle; the other was pointing a rifle. Scarlett's mind raced, her heart did too. Why hadn't she thought to bring the revolver with her? Maybe they'd just take her rig and her cases and let her walk back to Trim if she swore not to tell what they looked like. Idiots! Why couldn't they at least be wearing those masks, like she'd read about in the newspaper?

For the love of God! They were in uniform, they weren't Whiteboys at all.

"Damn your eyes, you scared me half to death!" She could still barely see the men. The green uniforms of the Royal Irish Constabulary blended into the shadowy hedgerows.

"I'll have to ask you for some identification, madam," said the man holding her horse. "Kevin, you look in the back there."

"Don't you dare touch my things. Who do you think you are? I am Mrs. O'Hara of Ballyhara, on my way to the Sutcliffes' at Kilbride. Mr. Sutcliffe is a magistrate, and he'll see to it that both of you end up in the dock!" She didn't really know that Ernest Sutcliff was a magistrate, but he looked like one with his bushy ginger mustache.

"Mrs. O'Hara is it?" The Kevin who'd been told to search her buggy came forward beside her. He took off his hat. "We heard tell of you in barracks, ma'am. I was asking Johnny here only a couple of weeks ago should we go over and make ourselves known to you?"

Scarlett stared incredulously. "Whatever for?" she said.

"They're saying you're from America, Mrs. O'Hara, a fact I can tell the truth of myself after hearing you speak. They're also saying you come from the grand state called Georgia. It's a place we two hold a fondness for in our hearts, seeing we both fought in the army there back in 'sixty-three and more."

Scarlett smiled. "You did?" Think of meeting someone from home on the road to Kilbride. "Where were you? What part of Georgia? Were you with General Hood?"

1073

"No, ma'am, I was one of Sherman's boys. Johnny there, he was with the Confederates, that's where he got the name, for Johnny Reb and all that."

Scarlett shook her head to clear it. She couldn't be hearing right. But more questions and more answers confirmed it. The two men, both Irish, were now the best of friends. With happy shared memories of being on opposite sides in a savage war.

"I don't understand," she admitted at last. "You were trying to kill each other fifteen years ago, and you're friends now. Don't you even argue about the North and the South and who was right?"

"Johnny Reb" laughed. "What's it to a soldier the right and the wrong of it all? He's there for the fighting, that's what he likes. Doesn't matter who you're fighting, long as he gives you a good fight."

When Scarlett reached the Sutcliffes' house she shocked their butler almost out of his professional composure by asking for a brandy with her coffee. She was more confused than she could handle.

Afterwards she bathed and put on a fresh frock and came downstairs, her composure restored. Until she saw Charles Ragland. He shouldn't be at this party! She acted as if she hadn't noticed him.

"Nan, how lovely you look. And I just love your house. My room's so pretty I might stay forever."

"Nothing would please me more, Scarlett. You know John Graham, don't you?"

"Only by reputation. I've been angling for a n introduction. How, do you do, Mr. Graham?"

"Mrs. O'Hara." John Graham was a tall slender man with the loose-limbed ease of the natural athlete. He was the Master of the Hounds of the Galway Blazers, perhaps the most famous hunt in all Ireland. Every fox hunter in Great Britain hoped to be invited to join one of the Blazers' hunts. Graham knew it, and Scarlett knew that he knew it. There was no point in being coy.

"Mr. Graham, are you open to bribery?" Why didn't Charles quit staring at her like that? What was he doing here anyhow?

John Graham threw back his silvered head in laughter. His eyes were lively with it when he looked back down at Scarlett. "I have always heard that you Americans come straight to the point, Mrs. O'Hara. Now I see it's true. Tell me, what precisely did you have in mind?"

"Would an arm and a leg do? I can stay on a sidesaddle with one leg—it's the only good thing about a sidesaddle that I can think of—and I only need one hand for the reins."

The Master smiled. "Such an extravagant offer. I've heard that about Americans, too, that they tend to extravagance."

Scarlett was tiring of banter. And Charles' presence made her edgy. "What you may not have heard, Mr. Graham, is that Americans take fences where the Irish go through gates and the

English go back home. If you'll let me ride with the Blazers, I'll take at least a pad or I'll eat a flock of crows in front of you all—without salt."

"By God, madam, with style like yours, you'll be welcome any time you say."

Scarlett smiled. "I'll take you up on that." She spit in her hand. Graham smiled broadly and spit in his. The slap they gave each other's palm resounded throughout the long gallery.

Then Scarlett strode over to Charles Ragland. "I told you in my letter, Charles, that this was the one house party in the whole country you should stay away from. It's mean of you to come."

"I'm not here to embarrass you, Scarlett. I wanted to tell you myself, not in a letter. You needn't worry about my pressing you or importuning you. I understand that no means no. The regiment's going to Donegal next week; it was my last chance to say what I wanted to say. And, I confess, to see you again. I promise not to lurk or gaze with soulful eyes." He smiled with rueful humor. "I practiced that speech, too. How did it sound?"

"Pretty fair. What's in Donegal?"

"Whiteboy trouble. It seems to be more concentrated there than any other county."

"Two constables stopped me to search my buggy."

"All the patrols are out now. With rents coming due soon—but I don't want to talk military. What did you say to John Graham? I haven't seen him laugh like that in years."

"Do you know him?"

"Very well. He's my uncle."

Scarlett laughed until her sides ached. "You English. Is that what 'diffident' means? If you'd only brag a little, Charles, you could have saved me a lot of trouble. I've been trying to get with the Blazers for a year, but I didn't know anybody."

"The one you'll really like is my Aunt Letitia. She can ride Uncle John into the ground and never look back. Come on, I'll introduce you."

There were promising rumbles of thunder, but no rain. By midday the air was stifling. Ernest Sutcliffe rang the dinner gong to get everyone's attention. He and his wife had planned something different for the afternoon, he said nervously. "There is the usual croquet and archery, what? Or the library and billiards in the house, what? Or whatever one does customarily. What?"

"Do get on with it Ernest," said his wife.

With many starts and stops and sputters Ernest got on with it. There were bathing costumes for anyone who wanted one and ropes strung across the river for the adventurous to hold on to while cooling off in the rushing water.

"Hardly 'rushing,' " amended Nan Sutcliffe, "but a decent little current. Footmen will be there with iced champagne."

Scarlett was one of the first to accept. It sounded like being in a cool tub all afternoon.

It was immensely more enjoyable than a cool tub, even though the water was warmer than she'd hoped it would be. Scarlett moved along the rope hand over hand towards the center and deeper water. Suddenly she found herself in the grip of the current. It was colder, so much colder that gooseflesh rose on her arms, and very swift. It pushed her up against the rope then knocked her feet out from under her. She was holding on for her life. Her legs gyrated out of control and the current twisted her body in half circles. She felt a dangerous temptation to let go of the rope and ride swirling in the current wherever it would take her. Free of the earth under her feet, free of walls or roads or anything controlled and controlling. For long heart-racing moments she imagined herself letting go, just letting go.

She was shaking from the effort she had to make to keep her grip fast on the rope. Slowly, with intense concentration and determination, she moved on, hand over hand, until she was free of the current's pull. She turned her head away from the others splashing and shouting in the water, and she cried, she didn't know why.

There were slow eddies, like fingers from the current, in the warmer water outside it. Scarlett slowly became aware of their caresses, then she let herself float among them. Warm tendrils of movement stroked her legs, her thighs, her body, her breasts, twined around her waist and her knees beneath the wool tunic and bloomers. She felt longings she could not name, an emptiness that cried out to be filled within her. "Rhett," she whispered against the rope, bruising her lips, inviting the roughness and the hurt.

"Isn't this splendid fun?" cried Nan Sutcliffe. "Who wants champagne?"

Scarlett forced herself to look around. "Scarlett, you brave thing, you went right through the frightening part. You'll have to come back. None of us has the nerve to bring your champagne to you."

Yes, thought Scarlett, I have to go back.

After dinner she made her way to Charles Ragland's side. Her cheeks were very pale, her eyes very bright.

"May I offer you a sandwich tonight?" she asked quietly.

Charles was an experienced, skillful lover. His hands were gentle, his lips firm and warm. Scarlett closed her eyes and let her skin receive his touch the way it had received the caresses of the river. Then he spoke her name, and she felt the ecstatic sensations slipping away. No, she thought, no, I don't want to lose it, I mustn't. She closed her eyes tighter, thought of Rhett, pretended that the hands were Rhett's hands, the lips Rhett's lips, that the warm, strong thrusting filling her aching emptiness was Rhett's.

It was no good. It was not Rhett. The sorrow of it made her want to die. She turned her face away from Charles' questing mouth and wept until he was at rest.

"My darling," he said, "I love you so."

"Please," Scarlett sobbed, "oh, please go away."

"What is it, darling, what's wrong?"

"Me. Me. I was wrong. Please leave me alone." Her voice was so small, so poignant with despair that Charles reached out to comfort her, then drew back in full knowledge that there was only one comfort he could give. He moved quietly as he gathered his clothes, and he shut the door behind him with only the slightest sound.

83

I have gone to join my regiment. I will love you forever.

Yours, Charles.

Scarlett folded the note carefully, tucked it beneath the pearls in her jewel case. If only . . .

But there was little room in her heart for anyone. Rhett was there. Laughing at her, outwitting her, challenging her, surpassing her, dominating her, sheltering her.

She went down to breakfast with bruise-like dark shadows under her eyes, imprint of the desolate weeping that had replaced sleep for her. She looked cool in her mint-green linen frock. She felt encased in ice.

She was obliged to smile, talk, listen, laugh. Guests had a duty to make a house party a success. She looked at the people seated along the sides of the long table. Smiling, talking, listening, laughing. How many of them, she wondered, have wounds inside them, too? How many feel dead, and grateful for it? How brave people are.

She nodded at the footman who was holding a plate for her at the long sideboard. At her signal he opened the big silver serving dishes one after another for her approval. Scarlett accepted some rashers of bacon and a spoonful of salt and scrambled eggs. "Yes, a grilled tomato," she said, "no, nothing cold." Ham, preserved goose, jellied quail eggs, spiced beef, salted fish, aspics, ices, fruits, cheeses, breads, relishes, jams, sauces, wines, ale, cider, coffee—all no. "I'll have tea," she said.

She was sure she could swallow some tea. Then she'd be able to go back to her room. Luckily this was a big party, and mostly for shooting. Most of the men would already be out with their guns. There would be luncheon in the house and somewhere on the grounds, wherever the shoot was. There would be tea served indoors and out. Everyone could choose amusements. No one was required to be any special place at any special time until dinner was served. The guest card in her room said to gather in the drawing room after the first dinner gong at seven forty-five. Processing into dinner at eight.

She indicated a chair beside a woman she hadn't met before. The footman deposited her plate and the small tray with individual tea service. Then he pulled out the chair, seated her, shook out the folds of her napkin, and draped it across her lap. Scarlett nodded to the woman. "Good morning," she said, "my name is Scarlett O'Hara."

The woman had a lovely smile. "Good morning. I've been looking forward to meeting you. My cousin Lucy Fane told me that she'd met you at Bart Morland's. When Parnell was there. Tell me, don't you find it delectably seditious to admit that one supports Home Rule? My name's May Taplow, by the way."

"A cousin of mine said he was sure I wouldn't be for Home Rule at all if Parnell was short and fat and had warts," Scarlett said. She poured her tea while May Taplow laughed. "Lady May Taplow" to be exact, Scarlett knew. May's father was a duke, her husband the son of a viscount. Funny how one picked up these things as time and parties went by. Funnier still how a country girl from Georgia got used to thinking about "one" doing this and that. Next thing you know, I'll be saying "toe-mah-toe" so that the footmen will know what it is I want. Guess it's no different really from telling a darky you want goobers so he'll know you'd like a handful of peanuts.

"I'm afraid your cousin would be dead on the nose if he accused me of the same thing," May confided. "I lost all interest in the succession when Bertie started to put on weight."

It was Scarlett's turn to confess. "I don't know who Bertie is."

"Stupid of me," said May, "of course you don't. You don't do the London Season, do you? Lucy said you run your own estate all alone. I do think that's wonderful. Makes the men who can't cope without a bailiff look as pouffish as they are, half of them. Bertie's the Prince of Wales. A dear, really, so enjoys being naughty, but it's beginning to show. You would adore his wife, Alexandra. Deaf as a post, you can't possibly tell her a secret unless you write it down, but beautiful past measuring and as sweet as she is pretty."

Scarlett laughed. "If you had any idea, May, what I feel like, you'd die laughing. Back home when I was growing up, the most high-toned gossip going was about the man who owned the new railroad. Everybody wondered when he'd started wearing shoes. I can hardly believe I'm chatting about the King of England to be."

"Lucy told me I'd be mad about you, and she was dead on the nose. Promise me you'll stay with us if you ever decide to do London. What did you decide about the railway man? What kind of shoes did he have? Did he limp when he walked? I'm sure I would adore America."

Scarlett discovered with surprise that she'd eaten all her breakfast. And that she was still hungry. She lifted her hand and the footman behind her chair stepped forward. "Excuse me, May, I'm going to ask for seconds," she said. "Some kedgeree, please, and some coffee, lots of cream."

Life goes on. A mighty good life, too. I made up my mind I was going to be happy and I guess I am. I've just got to notice it.

She smiled at her new friend. "The railroad man was as Cracker as they come."

May looked confused.

"Oh. Well, Cracker is what we call a white man who likely never wore shoes. That's not the same as poor white . . ." She enthralled the Duke's daughter.

It rained that evening during dinner. All the house party ran outside and capered for joy. The impossible summer would soon be over.

Scarlett drove home at midday. It was cool,

the dusty hedgerows had been washed clean, and soon the hunting season would begin. The Galway Blazers! I'll definitely want my own horses. I'll have to see about sending them ahead by rail. The best thing, I suppose, would be to load them at Trim, then to Dublin, then back across to Galway. Otherwise it's the long road to Mullingar, then rest them, then train to Galway. I wonder if I should send feed, too? I'll have to find out about stabling. I'll write to John Graham tomorrows. . . .

She was home before she knew it.

"Such good news, Scarlett!" She'd never seen Harriet looking so excited. Why, she's much prettier than I thought. With the right clothes—

"While you were gone a letter came from one of my cousins in England. I told you, did I not, that I'd written of my good fortune and your kindness? This cousin, his name is Reginald Parsons but the family always called him Reggie, has arranged for Billy to be admitted to the school his son attends, Reggie's son, that is. His name is—"

"Wait a minute, Harriet. What are you talking about? Billy's going to the school in Ballyhara, I thought."

"Naturally he'd have had to if there was no alternative. That's what I wrote to Reggie."

Scarlett's jaw set. "What's wrong with the school here, I'd like to know."

"Nothing is wrong with it, Scarlett. It's a good Irish village school. I want something better for Billy, surely you understand that."

"Surely I do no such thing." She was prepared to defend Ballyhara's school, Irish schools, Ireland itself, at the top of her lungs if need be. Then she took a good look at Harriet Kelly's soft, defenseless face. It was no longer soft, there was no weakness. Harriet's gray eyes were normally hazy with dreams; now they looked like steel. She was ready to fight anyone, anything for her son. Scarlett had seen the same kind of thing before, the lamb turned lion, when Melanie Wilkes took a stand about something she believed in.

"What about Cat? She'll be so lonely without Billy."

"I'm sorry, Scarlett, but I have to think of what's best for Billy."

Scarlett sighed. "I'd like to suggest a different alternative, Harriet. You and I both know that in England Billy will always be branded the Irish son of an Irish stable groom. In America he can become anything you want him to be . . ."

Early in September Scarlett held a stoically silent Cat in her arms to wave goodbye to Billy and his mother as their ship left Kingstown Harbor for America. Billy was crying; Harriet's face had the radiance of resolve and hope. Her eyes were cloudy with dreams. Scarlett hoped at least part of the dreams would come true. She had written to Ashley and Uncle Henry Hamilton, telling them about Harriet and asking them to watch out for her and help her find a place to stay and work as a teacher. She was sure they'd do that much at least. The rest was up to Harriet and circumstances.

"Let's go to the zoo, Kitty Cat. There are giraffes and lions and bears and a big, big elephant."

"Cat likes lions best."

"You might change your mind when you see the baby bears."

They stayed in Dublin for a week, going to the zoo every day, eating cream buns in Bewley's coffee shop afterwards, then the puppet theater followed by high tea at the Shelbourne with silver tiers of sandwiches and scones, silver bowls of whipped cream, silver trays of éclairs. Scarlett learned that her daughter was indefatigable and had a digestive system of cast iron.

Back at Ballyhara she helped Cat turn the tower into Cat's private place, to be visited only by invitation. Cat swept the dried cobwebs and droppings of centuries out of the high doorway, then Scarlett pulled up bucket after bucket of water from the river and the two of them scrubbed the walls and floor of the room. Cat laughed and splashed and blew soap bubbles while she scrubbed. It reminded Scarlett of the baths when Cat was a baby. She didn't mind at all that it took them over a week to get the place clean. Nor did she mind that the stone steps to upper levels were missing. Cat would have liked to wash the tower all the way to the top.

They finished just in time for what would have been Harvest Home in a normal year. Colum had advised her not to try and make a celebration when there was nothing to celebrate. He helped her distribute the sacks of flour and meal, salt and sugar, potatoes and cabbages that came to the town on wide wagons from all the suppliers Scarlett had found.

"They didn't even say 'thank you,' " she said bitterly when the ordeal was over. "Or if they did, they sure didn't act like they meant it. You'd think it might just dawn on a few people that I'm hurting from the drought, too. My wheat and grass were ruined the same as theirs, and I'm losing all my rents, and I bought all that stuff."

She couldn't verbalize the deepest hurt of all. The land, the O'Hara land, had turned against her, and the people, her people, of Ballyhara.

She poured all of her energies into Cat's tower. The same woman who hadn't so much as peered through a window to see what was happening to her house now spent hours going through all the rooms, scrutinizing each piece of furniture, each rug, every blanket, quilt, pillow, selecting the best. Cat was the final arbiter. She looked over her mother's choices and picked a bright flowered bathmat, three patchwork quilts, and a Sevres vase, the vase for her paintbrushes. The mat and quilts went into a deep wide indentation in the massively thick wall of the tower. For her nap, said Cat. Then she patiently went back and forth, house to tower, with her favorite picture books, her paint box, her leaf collection, and a box containing stale crumbs saved from cakes that she had especially liked. She was planning to lure birds and animals to her room. Then she'd paint their pictures on her wall.

Scarlett listened to Cat's plans and watched

her laborious preparations with pride in Cat's determination to create a world that would satisfy her even without Billy in it. She could learn from her four-year-old daughter, she thought sadly. On Halloween she gave Cat the birthday party that the little girl designed for herself. There were four small cakes, each with four candles. They ate one of the cakes themselves, sitting on the clean floor of Cat's tower sanctuary. They gave the second one to Grainne, eating it with her. Then they went home, leaving the other two cakes for the birds and animals.

The next day not a crumb was left, Cat reported with excitement. She didn't invite her mother to come see. The tower was all hers now.

Like everyone else in Ireland, Scarlett read the newspapers that autumn with alarm that grew into outrage. For her, the alarm was caused by the number of evictions reported. The farmers' efforts to fight back were perfectly understandable as far as she was concerned. Attacking a bailiff or a pair of constables with fists or pitchfork was only a normal human reaction, and she was sorry that it stopped none of the evictions. It wasn't the fault of the farmer that crops had failed and there was no money from sale of the grain. She knew all about that herself.

At nearby hunts the talk was always about the same thing, and the landowners were much less tolerant than Scarlett. They were worried by the instances of resistance by farmers. "Dammit, what do they expect? If they don't pay their rents, they don't keep their houses. They know that, it's always been like that. Bloody insurgence, that's what's going on . . ."

But Scarlett's reactions became the same as her neighboring estate owners' when the Whiteboys entered in. There had been scattered incidents during the summer. The Whiteboys were more organized now, and more brutal. Night after night barns and hayricks were torched. Cattle and sheep were killed, pigs slaughtered, donkeys and plow horses had legs broken or tendons cut. Shop windows were smashed, and manure or burning torches thrown inside. And more and more as autumn turned to winter there were attacks from concealment against military men, English soldiers and Irish constables, and gentry in carriages or on horseback. Scarlett took two grooms along on the roads to the meets.

And she worried constantly about Cat. Losing Billy seemed to have upset Cat much less than she had feared. Cat never moped, and she never whined. She was always occupied with some project or some game she invented for herself. But she was only four, it made Scarlett nervous now that Cat went off by herself so much. Scarlett was determined not to cage her child, but she began to wish that Cat were less agile, less independent, less fearless. Cat visited stables and barns, stillroom and dairy, garden and gardensheds. She wandered through woods and fields like a wild creature at home there, and the house was a land of opportunity for play in rooms that were cleaned but not used, attics full of boxes and trunks, basements with wine racks, barrels of foodstuffs, rooms for servants, for silver, for milk, butter, cheese, ice, ironing, washing, sewing; carpenter's repairs, bootblacking, the myriad activities that maintained the Big House.

There was never any point in looking for Cat. She might be anywhere. She always came home for her meals and bath time. Scarlett couldn't figure out how the child knew what time it was, but Cat was never late.

Mother and daughter went riding together every day after breakfast. But Scarlett grew afraid to go out on the roads because of the Whiteboys, and she didn't want to spoil the intimacy of their rides by taking grooms along, so their route became the path she had first used, past the tower and through the ford and into the boreen that led to Daniel's cottage. Pegeen O'Hara might not like it, she thought, but she'll have to put up with Cat and me if she wants me to keep on paying Seamus' rent. She wished Daniel's youngest son, Timothy, wasn't taking such a long time about finding a bride. He would have the little cottage when he did, and the girl could only be an improvement on Pegeen. Scarlett missed the easy intimacy she had known with her family before Pegeen joined it.

Every time she left for a hunt Scarlett asked Cat if she minded being left. The little brown forehead wrinkled with perplexity above Cat's clear green eyes. "Why do people mind?" she asked. It made Scarlett feel better. In December she explained to Cat that she'd be gone for a longer time because she was going a long way, on the train. Cat's response was the same.

Scarlett set off for the long-awaited hunt with the Galway Blazers on a Tuesday. She wanted a day of rest for herself as well as her horses before Thursday's hunt. She wasn't tired; on the contrary, she was almost too excited to sit still. But she wasn't about to take any chances. She had to be better than her best. If Thursday was a triumph, she'd stay for Friday and Saturday as well. Her best would be good enough then.

At the end of the first day's hunting, John Graham presented Scarlett with the gore-gummed pad that she had won. She accepted it with a court curtsey. "Thank you, Your Excellency." Everyone applauded.

The applause was even louder when two stewards came in bearing a huge platter that held a steaming pie. "I've been telling everyone about your sporting bet, Mrs. O'Hara," said Graham, "and we'd devised a small joke for you. This is a pie of minced crow meat. I will now take the first bite. The rest of the Blazers will follow. I had expected you to be doing it unaccompanied."

Scarlett smiled her sweetest smile. "I'll sprinkle some salt on it for you, sir."

She first noticed the hawk-faced man on the black horse on Friday when he made an impossible jump ahead of her and she reined in abruptly to watch, nearly losing her seat. He rode with an arrogant fearlessness that made her own recklessness seem tame.

Afterwards, people surrounded him at the hunt

breakfast, all of them talking, the man saying little. He was tall enough for her to see his aquiline face and dark eyes and hair almost blue it was so black.

"Who is that bored-looking tall man?" she asked a woman she knew.

"My dear!" The woman said with excitement. "Isn't he too fascinating for words?" She sighed happily. "Everyone says he's the most wicked man in Britain. His name is Fenton."

"Fenton what?"

"Just Fenton. He's the Earl of Fenton."

"You mean he doesn't have any name of his own at all?" She'd never understand all this English title rigmarole, Scarlett thought. It made no sense at all.

Her companion smiled. A superior smile, it seemed to Scarlett, and she became angry. But the woman quickly disarmed her. "Isn't it silly?" she said. "His Christian name is Luke; I don't know what the family name is. I just think of him as Lord Fenton. No one in my circle of friends is important enough to address him any other way, except 'Milord' or 'Lord Fenton' or 'Fenton.' " She sighed again. "He's terribly grand. And so outrageously attractive."

Scarlett made no comment aloud. Privately she thought he looked like he needed taking down a peg or two.

Returning from the kill on Saturday, Fenton walked his horse alongside Scarlett's. She was glad she was on Half Moon; it put her almost at eye level. "Good morning," said Fenton, touching the brim of his top hat. "I understand we're neighbors, Mistress O'Hara. I'd like to call and pay my respects, if I may."

"That would be very pleasant. Where is your place?"

Fenton raised his thick black eyebrows. "Don't you know? I'm on the opposite side of the Boyne, Adamstown."

Scarlett was glad she hadn't known. Obviously he'd expected her to. What conceit.

"I know Adamstown well," she said, "I have some O'Hara cousins who are tenants of yours."

"Indeed? I've never known my tenants' names." He smiled. His teeth were brilliantly white. "It is quite charming, that American candor about your humble origins. It was mentioned in London, even, so you see it's serving your purposes very well." He touched his crop to his hat and moved off.

The nerve of the man! And the bad manners—he didn't even tell me his name. As if he was sure I must have asked someone. Oh, I do wish I hadn't!

When she got home she told Mrs. Fitz to give instructions to the butler: she was not at home to the Earl of Fenton the first two times he called.

Then she concentrated on decorating the house for Christmas. She decided they really should have a bigger tree this year.

Scarlett opened the parcel from Atlanta as soon as it was delivered to her office. Harriet Kelly had sent her some cornmeal, bless her heart. I guess I talk about missing corn bread more than I know I do. And a present for Cat from Billy.

I'll let her have it when she comes home for tea. Ah, here it is, a nice fat letter. Scarlett settled herself comfortably with a pot of coffee to read it. Harriet's letters were always full of surprises.

The first one she wrote when she arrived in Atlanta had brought—among eight tightly written pages of rhapsodic thanks—the unbelievable story that India Wilkes had a serious beau. A Yankee, no less, who was the new minister at the Methodist church. Scarlett relished the idea. India Wilkes—Miss Confederacy Noble Cause herself. Let a Yankee in britches come along and give her the time of day and she'll forget there ever was a war.

Scarlett skimmed the pages about Billy's accomplishments. Cat might be interested, she'd read them aloud later. Then she found what she was looking for. Ashley had asked Harriet to marry him.

It's what I wanted, isn't it? It's silly for me to feel a twinge of jealousy. When's the wedding? I'll send a magnificent present. Oh, for heaven's sake! Aunt Pitty can't live alone in the house with Ashley after India's wedding because it wouldn't be proper. I do not believe it. Yes, I do. It's just what Aunt Pitty would swoon over, worrying about how it would look for her, the oldest spinster in the world, to be living with a single man. At least that gets Harriet married pretty soon. Not exactly the most passionate proposal in the world, but I'm sure Harriet can do it up with lace and rosebuds in her mind. Too bad the wedding's in February. I'd have been tempted to go, but not tempted enough to miss the Castle

Season. It hardly seems possible that I once thought Atlanta was a big city. I'll see if Cat would like to go to Dublin with me after New Year's. Mrs. Sims said the fittings would only take a few hours in the mornings. I wonder what they do with those poor zoo animals in the winter?

"Have you another cup in that pot, Mistress O'Hara? It was a chilly ride over here."

Scarlett stared up at the Earl of Fenton, her mouth gaping surprise. Oh, Lord, I must look a sight, I hardly even brushed my hair this morning. "I told my butler to say I'm not at home," she blurted.

Fenton smiled. "But I came the back way. May I sit down?"

"I'm amazed you wait to be asked. Please do. Ring the bell first, though. I've only got one cup, seeing I wasn't at home to visitors."

Fenton tugged the bellpull, took a chair close to hers. "I'll use your cup if you don't mind. It will take a week for another to get here."

"I do mind. So there!" Scarlett blurted. Then she burst out laughing. "I haven't said 'so there' in twenty years. I'm surprised I didn't stick out my tongue, too. You're a very irritating man, Milord."

"Luke."

"Scarlett."

"May I have some coffee?"

"The pot's empty . . . so there."

Fenton looked a little less overbearing when he laughed as he did then.

84

Scarlett visited her cousin Molly that afternoon, throwing that socially ambitious creature into such a frenzy of gentility that Scarlett's offhand questions about the Earl of Fenton were barely noticed. The visit was very short. Molly didn't know anything at all, save that the Earl's decision to spend some time at his Adamstown estate had shocked his servants and his agent. They kept the house and stables ready at all times, just in case he might choose to come there, but this was the first time in nearly five years that he had arrived.

The staff were now all preparing for a house party, said Molly. There had been forty guests when the Earl last came, all with servants of their own, and horses. The Earl's hounds and their attendants had come, too. There had been two weeks of hunting, and a Hunt Ball.

At Daniel's cottage, the O'Hara men commented on the Earl's arrival with bitter humor. Fenton had picked his time badly, they said. The fields were too dry and hard to be ruined by the hunters, like last time. The drought had been there before him and his friends.

Scarlett returned to Ballyhara no wiser than she'd left it. Fenton had said nothing to her about a hunt, or about a house party. If he gave one, and she wasn't invited, it would be a terrible slap in the face. After dinner she wrote a half dozen notes to friends she'd made during the Season.

"Such a fuss in these parts," she scribbled, "about Lord Fenton popping up at his place near here. He's been absentee for so many years that even the shopkeepers don't have any good gossip about him."

She smiled as she sealed the notes. *If that doesn't bring out the skeletons in his closet, I don't know what will.*

The next morning she dressed with care in one of the gowns she'd worn at her drawing rooms in Dublin. *I don't care a fig about looking attractive for that irritating man,* she told herself, *but I will not let him sneak up on me again when I'm not ready for guests.*

The coffee grew cold in the pot.

Fenton found her in the fields exercising Comet that afternoon. Scarlett was wearing her Irish clothes and cloak, riding astride.

"How sensible you are, Scarlett," he said. "I've always been convinced that sidesaddles are ruinous to a good horse, and that looks like a fine one. Would you care to match him against mine in a short race?"

"I'd be delighted," Scarlett said, with honeyed sweetness. "But the drought left everything so parched that the dust behind me will probably choke you half to death."

Fenton raised his eyebrows. "Loser provides champagne to lay the dust in the throat of both," he challenged.

"Done. To Trim?"

"To Trim." Fenton wheeled his horse and began the race before Scarlett knew what was happening. She was coated with dust before she caught up with him on the road, choking as she urged Comet alongside, coughing when they thundered across the bridge into town in a tie.

They reined in on the green beside the castle walls. "You owe me a drink," said Fenton.

"The devil you say! It was a tie."

"Then I owe you one as well. Shall we have two bottles, or would you prefer to break the tie by racing back?"

Scarlett kicked Comet sharply and took a head start. She could hear Luke laughing behind her.

The race ended in the forecourt of Ballyhara. Scarlett won, but barely. She grinned happily, pleased with herself, pleased with Comet, pleased with Luke for the fun she'd had.

He touched the brim of his dusty hat with his crop. "I'll bring the champagne for dinner," he said. "Expect me at eight." Then he galloped off.

Scarlett stared after him. The nerve of the man! Comet sidestepped skittishly, and she realized that she had let the reins go slack. She gathered them up and patted Comet's lathered neck. "You're right," she said aloud. "You need a cool-down and a good grooming. So do I. I think I've just been tricked good and proper." She began to laugh.

"What's that for?" asked Cat. She watched her mother inserting the diamonds in her earlobes with fascination.

"For decoration," said Scarlett. She tossed her head and the diamonds swayed and sparkled beside her face.

"Like the Christmas tree," said Cat.

Scarlett laughed. "Sort of, I guess. I never thought of that."

"Will you decorate me for Christmas, too?"

"Not until you're much, much older, Kitty Cat. Little girls can have tiny pearl necklaces or plain gold bracelets, but diamonds are for grown-up ladies. Would you like to have some jewelry for Christmas?"

"No. Not if it's for little girls. Why are you decorating you? It's not Christmas yet for days and days."

Scarlett was startled to realize that Cat had never seen her in evening dress before. When they had been in Dublin, they'd always dined in their rooms at the hotel. "There's a guest coming for dinner," she said, "a dress-up guest." The first one at Ballyhara, she thought. Mrs. Fitz was right all along, I should have done this sooner. It's fun to have company and get dressed up.

The Earl of Fenton was an entertaining and polished dinner companion. Scarlett found herself talking much more than she had intended—about hunting, about learning to ride as a child, about Gerald O'Hara and his Irish love of horses. Fenton was very easy to talk to.

So easy that she forgot what she wanted to ask him until the end of the meal. "I suppose your guests will be arriving any minute," she said as the dessert was served.

"What guests?" Luke held his glass of champagne up to examine the color.

"Why, for your hunting party," said Scarlett.

Fenton tasted the wine and nodded approval to the butler. "Where did you get that idea? I'm not having a hunt, nor any guests.

"Then what are you doing in Adamstown? They say you never come here."

The glasses were both filled. Luke lifted his in a toast to Scarlett., "Shall we drink to amusing ourselves?" he said.

Scarlett could feel herself blushing. She was almost certain she had just been propositioned. She raised her glass in response. "Let's drink to you being a good loser of very good champagne," she said with a smile, looking at him through lowered lashes.

Later, when she was getting ready for bed, she turned Luke's words over and over in her mind. Had he come to Adamstown just to see her? And did he intend to seduce her? If he did, he was in for the surprise of his life. She'd beat him at that game just like she had beat him in the race.

It would be fun, too, to make such an arrogant self-satisfied man fall hopelessly in love with her. Men shouldn't be that handsome and that rich; it made them think they could have everything their own way.

Scarlett climbed into bed and nestled under the covers. She was looking forward to going riding with Fenton in the morning as she'd promised.

They raced again, this time to Pike Corner, and Fenton won. Then back to Adamstown, and Fenton won again. Scarlett wanted to get fresh horses and try again, but Luke declined with a laugh. "You might break your neck in your determination, and I'd never collect my winnings."

"What winnings? We had no bet on this race."

He smiled and said nothing more, but his glance roved over her body.

"You're insufferable, Lord Fenton!"

"So I've been told, more than once. But never with quite so much vehemence. Do all American women have such passionate natures?"

You'll never find out from me, Scarlett thought, but she curbed her tongue as she curbed her horse. It had been a mistake to let him goad her into losing her temper, and she was even more annoyed with herself than she was with him. I know better than that. Rhett always used to make me fly off the handle, and it gave him the upper hand every time.

. . . Rhett . . . Scarlett looked at Fenton's black hair and dark mocking eyes and superbly tailored clothes. No wonder her eyes had sought him out in the crowded field at the Galway Blazers. He did have a look of Rhett about him. But only at first. There was something very different, she didn't know exactly what.

"I thank you for the race, Luke, even if I didn't win," she said. "Now I've got to be going, I have work to do."

A momentary look of surprise showed on his face, then he smiled. "I expected you to have breakfast with me."

Scarlett returned his smile. "I expect you did." She could feel his eyes on her as she rode away.

When a groom rode over to Ballyhara in the afternoon with a bouquet of hothouse flowers and Luke's invitation to dinner at Adamstown, she wasn't surprised. She wrote a note of refusal for the groom to take back.

Then she ran upstairs, giggling, to put on her riding habit again. She was arranging his flowers in a vase when Luke strode through the door into the long drawing room.

"You wanted another race to Pike Corner, if I'm not mistaken," he said.

Scarlett's laughter was in her eyes only. "You're not mistaken about that," she said.

Colum climbed up onto the bar in Kennedy's. "Now stop your yawping, all of you. What more could the poor woman do, I ask you? Did she forgive your rents or did she not? And did she not give you food for the winter? And more grain and meal in the storehouse waiting for when you run out of what you've got. It's ashamed I am to see grown men pulling their mouths into a baby's pout and inventing grievances as excuse for having another pint. Drink yourselves into the floor if you want to—it's a man's right to poison his stomach and addle his head—but don't be blaming your weakness on The O'Hara."

"She's gone over to the landlords" . . . "prancing off to the lords and ladies all summer" . . . "hardly a day goes by she's not tearing down the road racing the black devil lord of Adamstown" . . . The bar was aroar with angry shouts.

Colum shouted them all down. "What kind of men are they that gossip like a bunch of women about another woman's clothes and parties and romances? You make me sick, the lot of you." He spit on the top of the bar. "Who wants to lick that up? You're not men, it should suit you fine."

The sudden silence could have produced any kind of reaction. Colum spread his feet apart and held his hands loosely in front of him ready to form fists.

"Ach, Colum, it's that restless we are with no reason to do a little burning and shooting like the lads we hear about in other towns," said the oldest of the farmers. "Get down from there and get out your *bodhran* and I'll be the whistle and Kennedy the fiddle with you. Let's sing some songs about the rising and get drunk together like good Fenian men."

Colum literally jumped at the chance to calm things down. He was already singing when his boots hit the floor.

> *There beside the singing river,*
> *that dark mass of men were seen*
> *Far above the shining weapons*
> *hung their own beloved green.*
> *"Death to every foe and traitor!*
> *Forward! strike the marching tune*
> *And hurrah my boys, for freedom,*
> *'tis the risin' of the moon!"*

It was true that Scarlett and Luke raced their horses on the roads around Ballyhara and Adamstown. Also over fences, ditches, hedges, and the Boyne. Almost every morning for a week he forded the cold river and strode into the morning room with a demand for coffee and challenge to a race. Scarlett was always waiting for him with seeming composure, but in fact Fenton kept her constantly on edge. His mind was quick, his conversation unpredictable, and she could not relax her attention or her defenses for a minute. Luke made her laugh, made her angry, made her feel alive to the ends of her fingertips and toes.

The all-out racing across the countryside released some of the tension she felt when he was around. The battle between them was clearer, their common ruthlessness undisguised. But the excitement she always felt when she forced her courage to its reckless limits was threatening as well as thrilling. Scarlett sensed something powerful and unknown, hidden deep within her, that was in danger of breaking free of her control.

Mrs. Fitz warned her that the townspeople were disturbed by her behavior. "The O'Hara is losing their respect," she said sternly. "Your social life with the Anglos is different, it's distant. This racketing around with the Earl of Fenton rubs their noses in your preference for the enemy."

"I don't care if their damn noses are rubbed bloody. My life is my own business."

Scarlett's vehemence startled Mrs. Fitzpatrick. "Is it like that, then?" she said, and her tone wasn't stern at all. "Are you in love with him?"

"No, I'm not. And I'm not going to be. So leave me alone, and tell all of them to leave me alone, too."

Rosaleen Fitzpatrick kept her thoughts to herself after that. But her instincts as a woman saw trouble in the feverish brightness of Scarlett's eye

Am I in love with Luke? Mrs. Fitzpatrick's question forced Scarlett to question herself. No, she answered at once.

Then why am I out of sorts all day on the mornings he doesn't show up?

She could find no convincing answer.

She thought about what she'd learned from the letters of friends responding to her mention of him. The Earl of Fenton was notorious, they all said. He possessed one of the greatest fortunes in Britain, owned properties in England and Scotland as well as his estate in Ireland. He was an intimate of the Prince of Wales, maintained a huge town house in London where rumored bacchanals alternated with famously elaborate entertainments to which all Society schemed for invitations. He had been the favored target of matchmaking parents for over twenty years, ever since he had inherited his title and wealth at the age of eighteen, but he had escaped capture by anyone, even several noted beauties with fortunes of their own. There were whispered stories about broken hearts, shattered reputations, even suicides. And more than one husband had met him on the duelling field. He was immoral, cruel, dangerous, some said evil. Therefore, of course, the most mysterious and fascinating man in the world.

Scarlett imagined the sensation it would cause if an Irish-American widow in her thirties succeeded where all the titled English beauties had failed, and her lips curved in a small, secret smile that faded at once.

Fenton showed none of the signs of a man desperately in love. He intended to possess her, not marry her.

Her eyes narrowed. I'm not about to let him add my name to the long list of his conquests.

But she couldn't help wondering what it would be like to be kissed by him.

85

Fenton whipped his horse into a burst of speed and passed Scarlett, laughing aloud. She bent forward, crying aloud to Half Moon to go faster. Almost immediately she had to pull back on the reins. The road curved between high stone walls, and Luke had stopped up ahead, with his horse turned to block the way.

"What are you playing at?" she demanded. "I could have crashed right into you."

"Exactly what I had in mind," said Fenton. Before Scarlett understood what was happening, he had caught hold of Half Moon's mane and drawn the two horses close. His other hand closed over the back of Scarlett's neck and held her head immobile while his mouth fastened over hers. His kiss was bruising, commanding her lips to open, drawing her tongue between his teeth. His hand forced her to succumb. Scarlett's heart pounded with surprise, fear, and—as the kiss lasted on and on—a thrill of surrender to his strength. When he released her she was shaken and weak.

"Now you'll stop refusing my invitations to dinner," said Luke. His dark eyes glittered with satisfaction.

Scarlett gathered her wits. "You presume too much," she said, hating her breathlessness.

"Do I? I doubt it." Luke's arm curved along her back and held her against his chest while he kissed her again. His hand found her breast and squeezed it to the border of pain. Scarlett felt a surging response, a longing for his hands on all her body, and his brutal lips against her skin.

The nervous horses moved, breaking the embrace, and Scarlett was nearly unseated. She fought for balance on the saddle and in her thoughts. She mustn't do this, she mustn't give herself to him, give in to him. If she did, he'd lose interest as soon as he conquered her, she knew it.

And she didn't want to lose him. She wanted him. This was no lovesick boy like Charles Ragland, this was a man. She could even fall in love with a man like this.

Scarlett stroked Half Moon, calming him, thanking him in her heart for saving her from folly. When she turned to face Fenton, her swollen lips were stretched in a smile.

"Why don't you put on an animal's pelt and drag me to your house by my hair?" she said. There was precisely the right blend of humor and contempt in her voice. "Then you wouldn't frighten the horses." She urged Half Moon into a walk, then a trot, heading back the way they had come.

She turned her head and spoke over her shoulder. "I won't come to dinner, Luke, but you may follow me to Ballyhara for coffee. If you want more than that, I can offer you early luncheon or late breakfast."

Scarlett murmured softly to Half Moon, urging hurry. She couldn't read the meaning of the scowl on Fenton's face, and she felt something very like fear.

She had already dismounted when Luke rode into the stableyard. He swung a leg over and slid down from his horse, throwing the reins to a groom.

Scarlett pretended not to notice that Luke had commandeered the only groom in sight. She led Half Moon inside the stable herself to find another boy.

When her eyes adjusted to the dim light, she stopped in her tracks, afraid to move. Cat was in the stall directly in front of her, standing barefoot and bare-legged atop Comet, with her small arms outstretched for balance. She had on a heavy Aran jersey, borrowed from one of the stableboys. It bunched over her tucked-up skirts, and the sleeves hung past the ends of her fingers. As usual her black hair had escaped its braids and was a mass of tangles. She looked like an urchin, or a gypsy child.

"What are you doing, Cat?" said Scarlett quietly. She knew the big horse's edgy disposition. A loud noise could spook him.

"I'm starting to practice circus," said Cat. "Like the picture in my book of the lady on the horse. When I go in the ring I'll need a parasol please."

Scarlett kept her voice even. This was more frightening even than Bonnie. Comet could shy Cat off, then crush her. "It would be more fair if you waited to start next summer. Your feet must feel very cold on Comet's back."

"Oh." Cat slid onto the floor at once, next to the metal-shod hooves. "I didn't think of that." Her voice came from deep in the gated stall. Scarlett held her breath. Then Cat climbed over the gate with her boots and wool stockings in her hand. "I knew the boots would hurt."

Scarlett willed herself not to grab her child in her arms and hold her safe. Cat would resent her relief. She looked to her right for a groom to take Half Moon. She saw Luke, standing quietly and staring at Cat.

"This is my daughter, Katie Colum O'Hara," she said. And make of it what you will, Fenton, she thought.

Cat looked up from her concentration on tying her boot laces. She studied Fenton's face before she spoke. "My name is Cat," she said. "What is your name?"

"Luke," said the Earl of Fenton.

"Good morning, Luke. Would you like the yellow of my egg? I'm going to eat my breakfast now."

"I would like that very much," he said.

They made a strange procession; Cat led the way to the house, with Fenton walking beside her, adjusting his long stride to her short legs.

"I had my breakfast before," Cat told him, "but I'm hungry again, so I will have breakfast again."

"That strikes me as eminently sensible," he said. There was no mockery in his thoughtful tone of voice.

Scarlett followed the two of them. She was still unsettled by the fright Cat had given her, and she had not yet quite recovered from the moments of passionate emotion when Luke kissed her. She felt dazed and confused. Fenton was the last man on earth she would have expected to love children, and yet he seemed to be fascinated by Cat. He was treating her exactly right, too, taking her seriously, not condescending to her because she was so small. Cat had no patience with people who tried to baby her. Somehow Luke seemed to sense that and respect it.

Scarlett felt tears fill her eyes. Oh, yes, she could love this man. What a father he could be to her beloved child. She blinked rapidly. This was not the time for sentimentality. For Cat's sake as well as for her own, she had to be strong and clear headed.

She looked at Fenton's sleek dark head, inclined toward Cat. He looked very tall and broad and powerful. Invincible.

She shivered inwardly, then rejected her cowardice. She would win. She had to, now. She wanted him for herself and for Cat.

Scarlett nearly laughed at the scene Luke and Cat presented. Cat was totally absorbed in the delicate business of cutting off the top of her boiled egg without shattering it; Fenton was watching Cat with equal concentration.

Suddenly, without warning, desperate grief drove Scarlett's amusement away. Those dark eyes watching Cat should be Rhett's, not Luke's! Rhett should be the one fascinated by his daughter, Rhett the one to share her breakfast egg, Rhett the one to walk beside her, matching his pace to her small steps.

Painful longing carved a hollow in Scarlett's breast where her heart should be, and anguish— so long held at bay—flooded in to fill it. She ached for Rhett's presence, for his voice, for his love.

If only I'd told him about Cat before it was too late . . . If only I'd stayed in Charleston . . . If only . . .

Cat tugged at Scarlett's sleeve. "Are you going to eat your egg, Momma? I'll open it for you."

"Thank you, darling," said Scarlett to her child. Don't be a fool, she said to herself. She smiled at Cat, and at the Earl of Fenton. What was past was past, and she had to think about the future. "I have a suspicion you're going to have another yolk to eat, Luke," Scarlett laughed.

Cat said goodbye and ran outdoors after breakfast, but Fenton stayed. "Bring more coffee," he told the maid, without looking at her. "Tell me about your daughter," he said to Scarlett.

"She only likes the white of the egg," Scarlett answered, smiling to mask her worry. What should she tell him about Cat's father? Suppose Luke asked his name, how he died, who he was.

But Fenton asked only about Cat. "How old is this remarkable daughter of yours, Scarlett?"

He professed astonishment when told that Cat was barely four, asked if she was always so self-possessed, if she had always been precocious, if she was very high-strung . . . Scarlett warmed to his genuine interest and talked until her throat was raw about the marvels of Cat O'Hara. "You should see her on her pony, Luke, she rides better than I do—or you . . . And she climbs everything like a monkey. The painters had to pluck her off their ladders . . . She knows the woods as well as any fox, and she has a built-in compass, she never gets lost . . . 'High-strung'? There's not a nervous bone in her body. She's so fearless that it terrifies me sometimes. And she never carries on when she gets a bump or a bruise. Even when she was a baby she hardly ever cried, and when she started walking, she'd just look surprised when she fell, then got right back up again . . . Of course she's healthy! Didn't you see how straight and strong she is? She eats like a horse, too, and never gets sick. You wouldn't believe the number of éclairs and cream buns she can tuck away without turning a hair . . ."

When Scarlett heard the hoarseness in her voice, she looked at the clock and laughed. "My grief, I've been bragging for an age. It's all your fault, Luke, for egging me on so. You should have shut me up."

"Not at all. I'm interested."

"Watch out or you'll make me jealous. You act like you're falling in love with my daughter."

Fenton raised his eyebrows. "Love is for shop-keepers and penny romances. I'm interested in her." He stood and bowed, lifted Scarlett's hand from her lap and brushed it with a light kiss. "I leave for London in the morning, so I'll take leave of you now."

Scarlett stood up, close to him. "I'll miss our races," she said, meaning every word. "Will you be back soon?"

"I'll call on you and Cat when I return."

Well! thought Scarlett after he was gone. He didn't even try to kiss me goodbye. She didn't know whether it was a compliment or an insult. He must regret the way he acted when he kissed me before, she decided. I guess he lost control of himself. And he sure is scared of the word "love."

She concluded that Luke showed all the symptoms of a man who was falling in love against his will. It made her very happy. He'd be a wonderful father for Cat . . . Scarlett touched her bruised lips gently with the tip of a finger. And he was a very exciting man.

86

Luke was very much on Scarlett's mind during the following weeks. She was restless, and on bright mornings she raced alone over the routes they'd followed together. When she and Cat decorated the tree, she remembered the pleasure of dressing up for dinner the night he first came to Ballyhara. And when she pulled the wishbone of the Christmas goose with Cat, she wished that he would return from London soon.

Sometimes she closed her eyes and tried to remember the way it felt to have his arms around her, but every attempt made her tearfully angry, because Rhett's face and Rhett's embrace and Rhett's laughter always filled her memory instead. That was because she'd known Luke such a short time, she told herself. In time his presence would blot out the memories of Rhett, that was only logical.

On New Year's Eve there was a great racket, and Colum marched in beating the *bodhran* followed by two fiddlers and Rosaleen Fitzpatrick playing the bones. Scarlett screeched with joyful surprise and ran to hug him. "I'd given up hope that you'd ever come home, Colum. Now it's bound to be a good year, with a beginning like this." She got Cat up from her sleep, and they saw in the first moments of 1880 with music and love all around them.

New Year's Day began with laughter as the barm brack shattered against the wall, showering crumbs and currants all over Cat's dancing body and upturned, open-mouthed face. But afterwards the sky darkened with clouds, and an icy wind tore at Scarlett's shawl when she made the rounds of New Year's visits in her town. Colum took a drink in every house, liquor, not tea, and talked politics with the men until Scarlett thought she would scream.

"Will you not come to the bar, then, Scarlett darling, and raise a glass to a brave New Year and new hope for the Irish?" said Colum after the last cottage had been visited.

Scarlett's nostrils flared at the smell of whiskey on him. "No, I'm tired and cold and I'm going home. Come with me and we'll have a quiet time by the fire."

"A quiet time is what I dread most, Scarlett *aroon.* Quiet lets the darkness creep into a man's soul." Colum walked unsteadily through the door of Kennedy's bar, and Scarlett trudged slowly up the drive to the Big House, holding her shawl close around her. Her red skirt and the blue and yellow stripes on her stockings looked drab in the cold gray light.

Hot coffee and a hot bath, she promised herself as she pushed open the heavy front door. She heard a stifled giggle when she entered the hall, and her heart tightened. Cat must be playing hide and seek. Scarlett pretended to suspect nothing. She closed the door behind her, dropped her shawl on a chair, then looked around.

"Happy New Year, The O'Hara," said the Earl of Fenton. "Or is it Marie Antoinette? Is this the peasant costume all the best dressmakers in London are creating for costume balls this year?" He was on the landing of the staircase.

Scarlett stared up at him. He was back. Oh, why had he caught her looking this way? It wasn't what she'd planned at all. But it didn't matter. Luke was back, and so soon, and she no longer felt tired at all. "Happy New Year," she said. And it was.

Fenton stepped to one side, and Scarlett saw

Cat on the stairs behind him. Both Cat's arms were held up for her two hands to steady the gleaming jewelled tiara on her tousled head. She walked down the steps to Scarlett, her green eyes laughing, her mouth twitching to keep from grinning. Behind her trailed a long, wide slash of color, a crimson velvet robe bordered with a wide band of ermine.

"Cat's wearing your regalia, Countess," Luke said. "I've come to arrange our marriage."

Scarlett's knees gave way and she sat on the marble floor in a circle of red, with green and blue petticoats spilling from beneath. A flicker of anger mixed with her shocked thrill of triumph. This couldn't be true. It was too easy. It took all the fun out of everything.

"It seems our surprise was a success, Cat," said Luke. He untied the heavy silk cords at her neck and took the tiara from her hands. "You may go now. I have to talk to your mother."

"Can I open my box?"

"Yes. It's in your room."

Cat looked at Scarlett, smiled, then ran giggling up the stairs. Luke gathered the robe over his left arm, held the tiara in his left hand, and walked down to stand near Scarlett with his right hand reaching down to her. He looked very tall, very big, his eyes very dark. She gave him her hand, and he lifted her to her feet.

"We'll go into the library," said Fenton. "There's a fire, and a bottle of champagne for a toast to seal the bargain."

Scarlett allowed him to lead the way. He

wanted to marry her. She couldn't believe it. She was numb, speechless with shock. While Luke poured the wine she warmed herself at the fire.

Luke held a glass out to her. Scarlett took it. Her mind was beginning to register what was happening, and she found her voice.

"Why did you say 'bargain,' Luke?" Why hadn't he said he loved her and wanted her to be his wife?

Fenton touched the rim of his glass to hers. "What else is marriage but a bargain, Scarlett? Our respective solicitors will draw up the contracts, but that's just a matter of form. You know, surely, what to expect. You're not a girl or an innocent."

Scarlett set her glass carefully on a table. Then she lowered herself carefully into a chair. Something was horribly wrong. There was no warmth in his face, in his words. He wasn't even looking at her. "I would like for you to tell me, please," she said slowly, "what to expect."

Fenton shrugged impatiently. "Very well. You'll find me quite generous. I assume that is your chief concern." He was, he said, one of the wealthiest men in England, although he expected she had found that out for herself. He genuinely admired her astuteness at social climbing. She could keep her own money. He would naturally provide her with all her clothing, carriages, jewels, servants, et cetera. He expected her to be a credit to him. He had observed that she had the ability.

She could also keep Ballyhara for her lifetime.

It seemed to amuse her. For that matter, she could play with Adamstown, too, when she wanted to muddy her boots. After her death Ballyhara would go to their son, even as Adamstown would be his upon Luke's death. The joining of contiguous lands had always been one of the chief causes for marriage.

"For, of course, the essential feature of the bargain is that you provide me with an heir. I'm the last of my line, and it's my duty to continue it. Once I get a son on you, your life is your own, with the usual attention to maintaining a semblance of discretion."

He refilled his glass, then drained it. Scarlett could thank Cat for her tiara, said Luke. "I had, needless to say, no thought of making you the Countess of Fenton. You're the kind of woman I enjoy playing with. The stronger the spirit, the greater the pleasure in breaking it to my will. It would have been interesting. But not as interesting as that child of yours. I want my son to be like her—fearless, with indestructible rude health. The Fenton blood has been thinned by inbreeding. Infusing your peasant vitality will remedy that. I note that my tenant O'Haras, your family, live to a great age. You are a valuable possession, Scarlett. You will give me an heir to be proud of, and you won't disgrace him or me in society."

Scarlett had been staring at him like an animal mesmerized by a serpent. But now she broke the spell. She took her glass from the table. "I will when Hell freezes over!" she cried, then she threw the glass into the fire. The alcohol flared in an explosion of flame. "There's your toast to seal your bargain, Lord Fenton. Get out of my house. You make my flesh crawl."

Fenton laughed. Scarlett tensed, poised to spring at him, to batter his laughing face. "I thought you cared for your child," he said with a sneer. "I must have been mistaken." The words kept Scarlett from moving.

"You disappoint me, Scarlett," he said, "you really do. I attributed more shrewdness to you than you are demonstrating. Forget your injured vanity and consider what you have in your grasp. An impregnable position in the world for yourself and your daughter. It's unprecedented but I have the power to overthrow precedent, even law, if I choose. I shall arrange an adoption, and Cat will become the Lady Catherine. 'Katie' is, of course, out of the question, it's a kitchen maid's name. As my daughter she will have immediate and unquestioned access to the best of everything she will ever need, or want. Friends, ultimately marriage—she will have only to choose. I will never harm her; she's too valuable to me as a model for my son to follow. Can you deny all that to her because your lower-class yearning for romance is unfulfilled? I don't think so."

"Cat doesn't need your precious titles and 'best of everything,' Milord, and neither do I. We've done very well without you, and we'll keep on the way we are."

"For how long, Scarlett? Don't rely on your success in Dublin too much. You were a novelty, and novelties have short spans of life. An orang-utan could be the toast of a provincial setting

1119

like Dublin if it were well dressed. You have one more Season, two at the most, and then you will be forgotten. Cat needs the protection of a name and a father. I'm one of a very few men with the power to remove the taint from a bastard child—no, save your protests, I don't care what tale you concoct. You would not be in this godforsaken corner of Ireland if you and your child were welcome in America.

"Enough of this. It's beginning to bore me, and I detest being bored. Send word when you've come to your senses, Scarlett. You'll agree to my bargain. I always get what I want." Fenton began to walk to the door.

Scarlett called to him to stop. There was one thing she had to know. "You can't force everything in the world to do what you want, Fenton. Did it ever cross your mind that your brood mare wife might give birth to a girl-child and not a boy?"

Fenton turned to face her. "You're a strong, healthy woman. I should get a male child eventually. But even at the worst, if you give me only girls, I'll arrange that one of them marry a man willing to give up his name and take hers. Then my blood will still inherit the title and continue the line. My obligation will be satisfied."

Scarlett's coldness was the equal of his. "You think of everything, don't you? Suppose I was barren? Or you couldn't father a child?"

Fenton smiled. "My manhood is proven by the bastards I've scattered through all the cities of Europe, so your attempted insult doesn't touch me. As for you, there's Cat." A look of surprise crossed his face, and he strode back toward Scarlett, making her shrink from his sudden approach.

"Come now, Scarlett, don't be dramatic. Haven't I just told you I only break mistresses, not wives? I have no desire to touch you now. I was forgetting the tiara, and I must put it in safekeeping until the wedding. It's a family treasure. You'll wear it in due time. Send word when you capitulate. I am going to Dublin to open my house there and prepare for the Season. A letter will find me on Merrion Square." He bowed to her with full courtly flourishes and left, laughing.

Scarlett held her head proudly high until she heard the front door close behind him. Then she ran to shut and lock the library doors. Safe from the eyes of the servants, she threw herself onto the thick carpet and sobbed wildly. How could she have been so wrong about everything? How could she have told herself that she could learn to love a man who had no love in him? And what was she going to do now? Her mind was filled with the picture of Cat on the stairs, crowned and laughing with delight. What should she do?

"Rhett," Scarlett cried brokenly, "Rhett, we need you so much."

87

Scarlett gave no outward sign of her shame, but she condemned herself savagely for the emotions she'd felt for Luke. When she was alone, she picked at the memory like a half-healed scab, punishing herself with the pain of it.

What a fool she'd been to imagine a happy life as a family, to build a future on that one breakfast when Cat divided the eggs on their three plates. And what laughable conceit, to think she could make him love her. The whole world would ridicule her if it was known.

She had fantasies of revenge: she would tell everyone in Ireland that he had asked her to marry him and been refused; she would write to Rhett and he would come kill Fenton for calling his child a bastard; she would laugh in Fenton's face before the altar and tell him that she could never bear another child, that he'd made a fool of himself by marrying her; she would invite him to dinner and poison his food . . .

Hatred burned in her heart. Scarlett extended it to all the English, and she threw herself passionately into renewed support of Colum's Fenian Brotherhood.

"But I have no use for your money, Scarlett darling," he told her. "The work now is in planning the moves of the Land League. You heard us talking on New Year's, do you not remember?"

"Tell me again, Colum. There must be something I can do to help."

There was nothing. Land League membership was open only to tenant farmers, and there would be no action until rents came due in the spring. One farmer on each estate would pay, all the others would refuse, and if the landlord evicted, all would go to live at the cottage where the rent was paid up.

Scarlett couldn't see the reason for that. The landlord would just rent to someone else.

Ah, no, said Colum, that's where the League came in. They'd force everyone else to stay away, and, without farmers, the landlord would lose his rents and also his newly planted crops because there'd be no one to tend them. It was the idea of a genius; he was only sorry he hadn't thought of it himself.

Scarlett went to her cousins and pressured them to join the Land League. They could come to Ballyhara if they were evicted, she promised. Without exception every O'Hara refused. Scarlett complained bitterly to Colum.

"Don't be blaming yourself for the blindness of others, Scarlett darling. You're doing all that's needed to make up for their failings. Aren't you The O'Hara and a credit to the name? Do you not know that every house in Ballyhara and half of them in Trim have cuttings from the Dublin papers about The O'Hara being the shining Irish star in the Castle of the English Viceroy? They keep them in the Bible, with the prayer cards and pictures of the saints."

On Saint Brigid's Day there was a light rain. Scarlett said the ritual prayers for a good farm year with a fervor no other prayer had ever held, and she had tears on her cheeks when she turned the first sod. Father Flynn blessed it with holy water, then the chalice of water was passed from hand to hand for everyone to drink and share.

The farmers left the field quietly, with bowed heads. Only God could save them. No one could stand another year like the last one.

Scarlett returned to the house and removed her muddy boots. Then she invited Cat to have cocoa in her room while she got her things organized to be packed for Dublin. She would be leaving in less than a week. She didn't want to go—Luke would be there, and how could she face him? With her head held high, it was the only way. Her people expected it of her.

Scarlett's second Season in Dublin was an even greater triumph than her first. Invitations awaited her at the Shelbourne for all the Castle events, plus five small dances and two late-night suppers in the Viceregal private apartments. She also found in a sealed envelope the most coveted invitation of all: her carriage would be admitted through the special entrance behind the Castle. There'd be no more waiting in line for hours on Dame Street while carriages were allowed into the Castle yard four at a time to put down guests.

There were also cards requesting her presence at parties and dinners in private houses. These were reputed to be much more entertaining than the Castle events with their hundreds of people. Scarlett laughed, deep in her throat. An orangutan in fine clothes, was she? No, she was not, and the pile of invitations proved it. She was The O'Hara of Ballyhara, Irish and proud of it. She was an original! It made no difference that Luke was in Dublin. Let him sneer all he liked. She could look him in the eye without fear or shame, and be damned to him.

She sorted through the pile, picking and choosing, and a tiny bubble of excitement rose in her heart. It was nice to be wanted, nice to wear pretty gowns and dance in pretty rooms. So what if the social world of Dublin was Anglo? She knew enough now to recognize that Society's smiles and frowns, rules and transgressions, honors and ostracisms, triumphs and losses, were all part of a game. None of it was important, none of it mattered to the world of reality outside the gilded ballrooms. But games were made to be played, and she was a good player. She was glad, after all, that she'd come to Dublin. She liked to win.

Scarlett learned immediately that the Earl of Fenton's presence in Dublin had set off a frenzy of excitement and speculation.

"My dear," said May Taplow, "even in London people can talk of nothing else. Everyone knows Fenton considers Dublin a third-rate provincial outpost. His house hasn't been opened for decades. Why in the world is he here?"

"I can't imagine," Scarlett replied, relishing the thought of May's reaction if she told her.

Fenton seemed to turn up every place she went. Scarlett greeted him with cool good manners and ignored the expression of contemptuous confidence in his eyes. After the first encounter she didn't even fill with anger when she chanced to meet his gaze. He had no power to hurt her any more.

Not as himself. But she was pierced by pain again and again when she glimpsed the back of a tall dark-haired man clad in velvet or brocade, and it turned out to be Fenton. For Scarlett looked for Rhett in every crowd. He'd been at the Castle the year before, why not this year . . . this night . . . this room?

But it was always Fenton. Everywhere she looked, in the talk of everyone around her, in the columns of every newspaper she read. She could at least be thankful that he paid no special attention to her; then the gossips would have pursued her as well. But she wished to heaven that his name was not on every tongue every day.

Rumors gradually coalesced into two theories: he had readied his neglected house for a surreptitious, unofficial visit from the Prince of Wales; or he had fallen under the spell of Lady Sophia Dudley, who had been the talk of London's Season in May and was repeating her success now in Dublin. It was the oldest story in the world—a man sows his wild oats and resists the snares of women for years and years until bang!—when he's forty, he loses his head and his heart to beauty and innocence.

Lady Sophia Dudley was seventeen. She had hair the gold of ripe hay and eyes as blue as the summer sky and a pink-and-white complexion that put porcelain to shame. At least so said the ballads that were written about her and sold on all the street corners for a penny.

She was, in fact, a beautiful, shy girl who was very much under her ambitious mother's control and who blushed often and attractively because of all the attention and gallantries paid her. Scarlett saw quite a bit of her. Sophia's private drawing room was next to Scarlett's. It was second best in terms of furnishings and the view of Saint Stephen's Green, but first in terms of people vying for admission. Not that Scarlett's was by any means unattended; a rich and well-received widow with fascinating green eyes would always be in demand.

Why should I be surprised, thought Scarlett. I'm twice her age, and I had my turn last year. But sometimes she had trouble holding her tongue when Sophia's name was linked with Luke's. It was common knowledge that a duke had asked for Sophia's hand, but everyone agreed that she'd do better to take Fenton. A duke had precedence over an earl, but Fenton was forty times richer and a hundred times handsomer than the Duke. "And he's mine if I want him," Scarlett longed to say. Who'd they be writing ballads about then?

She scolded herself for her pettiness. She told herself she was a fool for thinking of Fenton's prediction that she would be forgotten after a year or two. And she tried not to worry about the little lines in the skin beside her eyes.

Scarlett returned to Ballyhara for her First Sunday office hours, thankful to get away from Dublin. The final weeks of the Season seemed endless.

It was good to be home, good to be thinking about something real, like Paddy O'Faolain's request for a bigger allocation of peat, instead of what to wear to the next party. And it was pure heaven to have Cat's strong little arms nearly strangle her with a fierce hug of welcome.

When the last dispute had been settled, the last request granted, Scarlett went to the morning room for tea with Cat.

"I saved your half," Cat said. Her mouth was smeared with chocolate from the éclairs Scarlett had brought from Dublin.

"It's a funny thing, Kitty Cat, but I'm not real hungry. Would you like some more?"

"Yes."

"Yes, thank you."

"Yes, thank you. May I eat them now?"

"Yes, you may, Miss Pig."

The éclairs were gone before Scarlett's cup was empty. Cat was dedicated when it came to éclairs.

"Where shall we go for our walk?" Scarlett asked her. Cat said she'd like to go visit Grainne.

"She likes you, Momma. She likes me more, but she likes you a lot."

"That would be nice," said Scarlett. She'd be glad to go to the tower. It gave her a feeling of serenity, and there was little serenity in her heart.

Scarlett closed her eyes and rested her cheek on the ancient smooth stones for a long moment. Cat fidgeted.

Then Scarlett pulled on the rope ladder to the high door to test it. It was weathered and stained. It felt strong enough. Still, she thought she'd better see about having a new one made. If it broke, and Cat fell—she couldn't bear to think of it.

She did so wish that Cat would invite her up into her room. She tugged at the ladder again, hinting.

"Grainne will be expecting us, Momma. We made a lot of noise."

"All right, honey, I'm coming."

The wise woman looked no older, no different from the first time Scarlett had seen her. *I'd even be willing to bet those are the same shawls she was wearing,* Scarlett thought. Cat busied herself in the small dark cottage, getting cups from their shelf, raking the ancient-smelling burning peat into a mound of glowing embers for the kettle. She was very much at home. "I'll fill the kettle at the spring," she said as she carried it outside. Grainne watched her lovingly.

"Dara visits me often," said the wise woman. "It's her kindness to a lonely soul. I haven't the heart to send her away, for she sees the right of it. Lonely knows lonely."

Scarlett bristled. "She likes to be alone, she doesn't have to be lonely. I've asked her time and again if she'd like to have children come play, and she always says no."

"It's a wise child. They try to stone her, but Dara is too quick for them."

Scarlett couldn't believe she'd heard right. "They do what?" The children from the town, Grainne said placidly, hunted through the woods for Dara, like a beast. She heard them, though, long before they got to her. Only the biggest ever came near enough to throw the stones they carried. And those came near only because they could run faster than Dara on longer, older legs.

She knew how to escape even them. They wouldn't dare chase her into her tower, they were afraid of it, haunted as it was by the ghost of the young hanged lord.

Scarlett was aghast. Her precious Cat tormented by the children of Ballyhara! She'd whip every single one of them with her own hands, she'd evict their parents and break every stick of their furniture into splinters! She started up out of her chair.

"You will burden the child with the ruin of Ballyhara?" said Grainne. "Sit you down, woman. Others would be the same. They fear anyone different to themselves. What they fear they try to drive away."

Scarlett sank back onto the chair. She knew the wise woman was right. She'd paid the price for being different herself, again and again. Her stones had been coldness, criticism, ostracism. But she had brought it on herself. Cat was only a little girl. She was innocent. And she was in danger! "I can't just do nothing!" Scarlett cried. "It's intolerable. I've got to make them stop."

"Ach, there's no stopping ignorance. Dara has found her own way, and it is enough for her. The stones do not wound her soul. She is safe in her tower room."

"It's not enough. Suppose a stone hit her? Suppose she got hurt? Why didn't she tell me she was lonely? I can't bear that she's unhappy."

"Listen to an old woman, The O'Hara. Listen from your heart. There is a land that men know of only from the songs of the *seachain.* Its name is Tir na nOg, and it lies beneath the hills. Men there are, and women too, who have found the way to that land and have never been seen again. There is no death in Tir na nOg, and no decay. There is no sorrow and no pain, nor hatred, nor hunger. All live in peace with one another, and there is plenty without labor.

"This is what you would give your child, you would say. But listen well. In Tir na nOg, because there is no sorrow, there is no joy.

"Do you hear the meaning of the *seachain*'s song?"

Scarlett shook her head.

Grainne sighed. "Then I cannot ease your heart. Dara has more wisdom. Leave her be." As if the old woman had called her, Cat came through the door. She was concentrating on the heavy, water-filled kettle, and she didn't look at her mother and Grainne. The two of them watched silently while Cat methodically set the kettle on the iron hook over the coals, then raked more coals into a heap below it.

Scarlett had to turn her head. If she continued to look at her child, she knew she wouldn't be able to stop herself from grabbing Cat in her arms and holding her tightly in a protective embrace. Cat would hate that. I mustn't cry, either, Scarlett told herself. It might frighten her. She'd sense how frightened I am.

"Watch me, Momma," said Cat. She was carefully pouring steaming water into an old brown china teapot. A sweet smell rose from the steam, and Cat smiled. "I put in all the right leaves, Grainne," she chortled. She looked proud and happy.

Scarlett caught hold of the wise woman's shawl. "Tell me what to do," she begged.

"You must do what's given you to do. God will guard Dara."

I don't understand anything she says, thought Scarlett. But somehow her terror was relieved. She drank Cat's brew in the companionable silence and warmth of the herb-scented shadowy room, glad that Cat had this place to come to. And the tower. Before she returned to Dublin, Scarlett gave orders for a new, stronger rope ladder.

88

Scarlett went to Punchestown for the races this year. She'd been invited to Bishopscourt, the seat of the Earl of Clonmel, who was known as Earlie. To her delight, Sir John Morland was also a guest. To her dismay, the Earl of Fenton was there.

Scarlett rushed over to Morland as soon as she could. "Bart! How are you? You're the biggest stay-at-home I've ever heard of in my life. I look for you all the time, but you're never anywhere."

Morland was gleaming with happiness and cracking his knuckles loudly. "I've been busy, the most splendid kind of busy, Scarlett. I've got a winner, I'm sure of it, after all these years."

He'd talked like this before. Bart so loved his horses that he was always "sure" each foal was the next Grand National champion. Scarlett felt like hugging him. She'd have loved John Morland even if he had no connection at all to Rhett.

". . . named her Diana, fleet of foot and all that sort of thing, you know, plus John for me. Hang it all, I'm practically her father except for the biology part. It came out Dijon when I put it together. Mustard, I thought, that won't do at all. Too damn French for an Irish horse. But then I thought again. Hot and peppery, so strong it makes your eyes water. That's not a bad profile. Sort of 'get out of my way, I'm coming through' and all that. So Dijon it is. She's going to make my fortune. Better lay a fiver on her, Scarlett, she's a sure thing."

"I'll make it ten pounds, Bart." Scarlett was trying to think of some way to mention Rhett. What John Morland was saying didn't register at first.

". . . be really sunk if I'm wrong. My tenants are doing that rent strike thing the Land League dreamed up. Leaves me without money for oats. I wonder now how I could have thought so highly of Charles Parnell. Never thought the fellow would end up hand in glove with those barbarian Fenians."

Scarlett was horrified. She'd never dreamed the Land League would be used against anyone like Bart.

"I can't believe it, Bart. What are you going to do?"

"If she wins here, even places, then I suppose the next big one is Galway and after that Phoenix Park, but maybe I'll sort of tuck in one or two smaller races in May and June, to keep her mind on what's expected of her, so to speak."

"No, no, Bart, not about Dijon. What are you going to do about the rent strike?"

Morland's face lost some of its glow. "I don't know," he said. "All I've got are my rents. I've never evicted, never even thought of it. But now I'm up against it, I might have to. Be a bloody shame."

Scarlett was thinking about Ballyhara. At least she was safe from any trouble. She'd forgiven all rents until the harvest was in.

"I say, Scarlett, I forgot to mention it. I received some very good news from our American friend Rhett Butler."

Scarlett's heart leapt. "Is he coming over?"

"No. I was expecting him. Wrote to him about Dijon, you see. But he wrote back that he couldn't come. He's to be a father in June. They took extra care this time, kept the wife in bed for months until there wasn't any danger of what happened last time. But everything's splendid now. She's up and happy as a lark, he says. He is too, of course. Never saw a man in my life cared as much about being a proud father as Rhett."

Scarlett caught hold of a chair for support. Whatever unrealistic daydreams and hidden hopes she might have had were over.

Earlie had reserved a complete section of the white iron grillework stands for his party. Scarlett stood with the others, scanning the course through mother-of-pearl opera glasses. The turf track was brilliant green, the infield of the long oval was a mass of movement and color. People stood on wagons, on the seats and roofs of their carriages, walked around singly and in groups, massed at the interior rail.

It began to rain and Scarlett was grateful for the second tier of grandstand overhead. It made a roof for the privileged seat-holders below.

"Good show," Bart Morland chortled. "Dijon is a great little mudder."

"Do you fancy anything, Scarlett?" said a smooth voice in her ear. It was Fenton.

"I haven't decided yet, Luke."

When the riders came onto the track, Scarlett cheered and applauded with the rest. She agreed twenty times with John Morland that even the naked eye could pick out Dijon as the handsomest horse there. All the time she was talking and smiling her mind was methodically making its way through the options, the plusses and the minuses of her life. It would be highly dishonorable to marry Luke. He wanted a child, and she could not give him one. Except Cat, who would be safe and secure. No one would ever question who her real father was. Not quite true, they would wonder but it would make no difference. She would eventually be The O'Hara of Ballyhara, and the Countess of Fenton.

What kind of honor do I owe Luke? He has none himself, why should I feel he's entitled to it from me?

Dijon won. John Morland was in transports. Everyone crowded around him, shouting and pounding on his back.

Under cover of the happy rowdiness, Scarlett turned to Luke Fenton. "Tell your solicitor to see mine about the contracts," she said. "I choose late September for the wedding date. After Harvest Home."

"Colum, I'm going to marry the Earl of Fenton," said Scarlett.

He laughed. "And I'll take Lilith for a bride. Such merrymaking there'll be, with the legions of Satan for guests at the wedding feast."

"It's not a joke, Colum."

His laughter stopped as if severed by a blade, and he stared at Scarlett's pale, determined face. "I'll not allow it," he shouted. "The man's a devil and an Anglo."

Patches of red blotched Scarlett's cheeks. "You . . . will . . . not . . . *allow?*" she said slowly. "You . . . will . . . not . . . allow? Who do you think you are, Colum? God?" She walked to him, eyes blazing, and thrust her face close to his. "Listen to me, Colum O'Hara, and listen good. Not you or anybody else on earth can talk to me like that. I won't take it!"

His stare matched hers, and his anger, and they stood in stony confrontation for a timeless moment. Then Colum tilted his head to one side and smiled. "Ah, Scarlett darling, if it isn't the O'Hara temper in the both of us, putting words we don't mean in our two mouths. I'm begging your forgiveness, now; let's talk this thing over."

Scarlett stepped back. "Don't charm me, Colum," she said sadly, "I don't believe it. I came to talk to my closest friend, and he's not here. Maybe he never was."

"Not so, Scarlett darling, not so!"

Her shoulders hunched in a brief, dejected shrug. "It doesn't matter. I've made up my mind. I'm going to marry Fenton and move to London in September."

"You're a disgrace to your people, Scarlett O'Hara." Colum's voice was like steel.

"That's a lie," said Scarlett wearily. "Say that to Daniel, who's buried in O'Hara land that was lost for hundreds of years. Or to your precious Fenians, who've been using me all this time. Don't worry, Colum, I'm not going to give you away. Ballyhara will stay just as it is, with the inn for the men on the run, and the bars for you all to talk against the English in. I'll make you bailiff for me, and Mrs. Fitz will keep the Big House going just the way it is. That's really what you care about, not me."

"No!" The cry burst from Colum's lips. "Ach, Scarlett, you're grievous wrong. You're my pride and my delight, and Katie Colum holds my heart in her tiny hands. 'Tis only that Ireland is my soul and must be first." He held out his hands to her in supplication. "Say you believe me, for I'm speaking the plain truth of it."

Scarlett tried to smile. "I do believe you. And you have to believe me. The wise woman said, 'You'll do what's given you to do.' That's what you're doing with your life, Colum, and it's what I'm doing with mine."

Scarlett's steps dragged as she walked to the Big

House. It was as if the heaviness of her heart had travelled to her feet. The scene with Colum had cut deep. She had gone to him before anyone else, expecting understanding and compassion, hoping against hope that he might tell her some way out of the path she had chosen. He had failed her, and she felt very alone. She dreaded telling Cat that she was going to be married, that they'd have to leave Ballyhara's woods that Cat so loved and the tower that was her special place.

Cat's reaction lifted her heart. "I like cities," said Cat. "That's where the zoo is." I am doing the right thing, thought Scarlett. Now I know it without a doubt. She sent to Dublin for picture books of London and wrote to Mrs. Sims asking for an appointment. She had to order a wedding gown.

A few days later a messenger from Fenton came with a letter and a package. In the letter he said that he would be in England until the week of the wedding. The announcement would not appear until after the London Season. And Scarlett should have her gown designed to complement the jewels sent by the same messenger as the letter. She still had three months to herself! No one would press her with questions or invitations until the news of the engagement was released.

Inside the package she found a square shallow box of oxblood leather, finely tooled in gold. The hinged top lifted and Scarlett gasped. The case was lined in padded gray velvet, shaped and compartmented to display a necklace, two bracelets, and a pair of earrings.

The settings were fashioned of heavy old

gold with a dull, almost bronze finish. The jewels were pigeon's blood rubies, matched stones, each as large as her thumb nail. The earrings were single oval ruby drops from an intricately shaped boss. Bracelets held a dozen stones each, and the necklace was made up of two rows of stones linked by swagged thick chains. For the first time Scarlett understood the difference between jewelry and jewels. No one would ever refer to these rubies as jewelry. They were too exceptional and too valuable. They were, without doubt, jewels. Her fingers were trembling when she clasped the bracelets on her wrists. She couldn't do the necklace by herself, she had to ring for Peggy Quinn. When she saw herself in the looking glass, Scarlett drew in a long breath. Her skin looked like alabaster with the dark richness of the rubies against it. Her hair was in some way darker and more lustrous. She tried to remember what the tiara looked like. It, too, was set with rubies. She would look like a queen when she was presented to the Queen. Her green eyes narrowed slightly. London was going to be a much more challenging game than Dublin. She might even learn to like London very much.

Peggy Quinn lost no time telling the news to the other servants and her family in Ballyhara town. The magnificent parure plus the ermine-trimmed robe plus the weeks of morning coffee could only mean one thing. The O'Hara was going to wed the rack-renting villain Earl of Fenton.

And what will become of us? The question and

apprehension spread from hearth to hearth like a brushfire.

Scarlett and Cat rode together through the wheat fields in April. The child wrinkled her nose at the strong smell of freshly spread manure. The stables and barns never reeked this way; they were mucked out daily. Scarlett laughed at her. "Don't you ever make faces at manured land, Cat O'Hara. It's sweet perfume to a farmer, and you've got farmers' blood in your veins. I don't want you ever to forget it." She looked over the plowed and planted and enriched acres with pride. This is mine. I brought it back to life. She knew she'd miss this part of her life most of all when they moved to London. But she'd always have the memory and the satisfaction. In her heart, she would forever be The O'Hara. And someday Cat could return, when she was grown and could protect herself. Then she would earn the name "The O'Hara" for herself. "Never, ever forget where you come from," Scarlett told her child. "Be proud."

"You'll have to swear on a stack of Bibles not to tell a soul," Scarlett warned Mrs. Sims.

Dublin's most exclusive dressmaker gave Scarlett her most freezing stare. "No one has ever had cause to question my discretion, Mrs. O'Hara."

"I'm to be married, Mrs. Sims, and I want you to create my gown." She held out the jewel case in front of her and opened it. "These will be worn with it."

Mrs. Sims' eyes and mouth made O's. Scarlett felt repaid for all the hours of torture she'd spent in the dressmaker's dictatorial fittings. She must have shocked ten years off the woman's life.

"There's a tiara also," Scarlett said in an off-handed manner, "and I'll want my train edged in ermine."

Mrs. Sims shook her head vigorously. "You cannot do that, Mrs. O'Hara. Tiaras and ermine are only for the grandest ceremonies at Court. Most particularly ermine. In all likelihood, it hasn't been worn since Her Majesty's wedding."

Scarlett's eyes glittered. "But I don't know all that, do I, Mrs. Sims? I'm only an ignorant American who will become a countess over-night. People are going to cluck-cluck and shake their heads no matter what I do. So I'm going to do what I want, the way I want it!" The misery in her heart became cutting imperiousness in her voice.

Mrs. Sims cringed inwardly. Her agile mind swiftly sorted through Society gossip to identify Scarlett's future husband. They'll be a well-matched pair, she thought. Trample all decent tradition and be admired the more for it. What was the world coming to? Still, a woman had to make her way in it, and people would be talking about the wedding for years to come. Her handiwork would be on display as never before. It must be magnificent.

Mrs. Sims' habitual haughty certainty returned. "There's only one gown that will do justice to ermine and these rubies," she said. "White silk velvet with overlaid lace, Galway would be best. How long do I have? The lace must be made, then sewn onto the velvet around each petal of each flower. It takes time."

"Will five months do?"

Mrs. Sims' well-kept hands dishevelled her well-groomed hair. "So short . . . Let me think . . . If I get two extra needlewomen . . . if the nuns will do only this . . . It will be the most talked-about wedding in Ireland, in Britain . . . It must be done, no matter what." She realized she was talking aloud, and her fingers covered her mouth. Too late.

Scarlett took pity on her. She stood and held out her hand. "I leave the gown in your care, Mrs. Sims. I have every confidence in you. Let me know when you need me to come to Dublin for the first fitting."

Mrs. Sims took her hand and squeezed it. "Oh, I'll come to you, Mrs. O'Hara. And it would please me if you called me Daisy."

In County Meath the sunny day made no one happy. Farmers worried about another year like the year before. At Ballyhara they shook their heads and predicted doom. Wasn't the change-ling seen coming from the witch's cottage by Molly Keenan? And another time by Paddy Con-roy, though what he was doing going there him-self he wouldn't say outside the confessional. They did say, too, that there'd been owls heard in daylight over to Pike Corner, and Mrs. Mac-Gruder's prize calf had died in the night for no cause at all. Rain, when it came the next day, did nothing to stop the rumors.

Colum went with Scarlett to the hiring fair in Drogheda in May. The wheat was well begun, the meadow grass very nearly ready for cutting, the rows of potatoes bright green with healthy foliage. Both of them were unusually quiet, each of them preoccupied with private concerns. For Colum the worry came from the increase in militia and constabulary troops all over County Meath. An entire regiment was coming to Navan, said his informants. The Land League's work was good; he'd be the last to deny the good of reduced rents. But the rent strikes had stirred up the landlords. Now evictions were done without prior warning and the thatch burned before the people could drag their furnishings out of the house. It was said two children had burned to death. Two soldiers were wounded the next day. Three Fenians had been arrested in Mullingar, including Jim Daly. Inciting violence was the charge although he'd been serving drinks in his bar day and night all the week.

Scarlett remembered the hiring fair for only one thing. Rhett had been with Bart Morland there. She avoided even looking in the direction of the horse sales; when Colum suggested they walk around and enjoy the fair, she all but shouted when she told him no, she wanted to get home. There'd been a distance between them ever since she told Colum she was going to marry Fenton. He didn't say anything harsh, but he didn't have to. Anger and accusation were hot in his eyes.

It was the same with Mrs. Fitz. Who did they

think they were anyhow, judging her like that? What did they know about her sorrows and her fears? Wasn't it enough that they'd have Ballyhara to themselves after she left? That was all they had ever really wanted. No, that wasn't fair. Colum was her almost-brother, Mrs. Fitz her friend. All the more reason they should be sympathetic. It wasn't fair. Scarlett began to think she saw disapproval everywhere, even on the faces of Ballyhara's shopkeepers when she made the special effort to think of things to buy from them in these lean months before the harvest. Don't be a fool, she told herself, you're imagining things because you're not really sure yourself about what you're going to do. It's the right thing, it is, for Cat and for me. And it's nobody else's business what I do. She was irritable with everyone except Cat, and she saw little of her. One time she even climbed several rungs of the new rope ladder, but then she backed down. I'm a grown woman, I can't go boohooing to a little child for comfort. She worked in the hayfields day after day, glad to be busy, grateful for the ache in her arms and legs after the labor. Grateful, most of all, for the rich crop. Her fears about another bad harvest gradually went away.

Midsummer Night, June 24, completed the cure. The bonfire was the biggest ever, the music and dancing were what she'd been needing to relax her tense nerves and restore her spirits. When, as timeless tradition demanded, the toast to The O'Hara was shouted over the fields of Ballyhara, Scarlett felt that all was right with the world.

Still, she was a little sorry she'd refused all the house party invitations for the summer. She had to, she was afraid to leave Cat. But she was lonely, and she had too much time on her hands, too much time to think and worry. She was almost happy when she received the semi-hysterical telegram from Mrs. Sims, saying that the lace had not arrived from the convent in Galway, nor had she had any reply to her letters and telegrams.

Scarlett was smiling when she drove her buggy to the train depot in Trim. She was an old hand at battling with Mother Superiors, and she was glad to have a clear-cut reason for a fight.

89

There was just time enough in the morning to dash to Mrs. Sims' workshop, calm her down, gather the specifics of yardage and pattern of lace ordered, and race to the station for the early train to Galway. Scarlett settled herself comfortably and opened the newspaper.

My grief, there it is. The Irish Times had printed the announcement of the wedding plans on the front page. Scarlett darted looks at the other passengers in the compartment to see if any of them were reading the paper. The tweed-suited sportsman was engrossed in a sporting magazine; the nicely dressed mother and son were playing cribbage. She read about herself again. The *Times* had added a great deal of its own commentary to the formal announcement. Scarlett smiled at the part about "The O'Hara of Ballyhara, a beautiful ornament to the innermost circles of Vice-regal society" and "exquisite and dashing equestrienne."

She had brought only a single small case with her for her stay in Dublin and Galway, so she needed only one porter to accompany her from the station to the nearby hotel.

The reception area was jammed with people. "What the devil?" said Scarlett.

"The races," said the porter. "You didn't do something so foolish as to come to Galway not knowing, did you? You'll find no room to sleep in here."

Impertinent, thought Scarlett, see if you get a tip. "Wait here," she said. She weaved her way to the reception desk. "I'd like to speak to the manager."

The harassed desk clerk looked her up and down, then said, "Yes, of course, madam, one moment," and vanished behind an etched-glass screen. He returned with a balding man in a black frock coat and striped trousers.

"Is there some complaint, madam? I'm afraid that the hotel's service does become less, ah, flawless, shall we say, when the races are in progress. Whatever inconvenience—"

Scarlett interrupted him. "I remember the service as flawless." She smiled winningly. "That's why I like to stay at the Railway. I'll need a room tonight. I am Mrs. O'Hara of Ballyhara."

The manager's unctuousness evaporated like August dew. "A room tonight? It's quite out of—" The desk clerk was pulling at his arm. The manager glared at him. The clerk murmured in his ear, jabbed his finger at a *Times* on the desk.

The hotel manager bowed to Scarlett. His smile was quivering with the will to please. "Such an honor for us, Mrs. O'Hara. I trust you'll accept a very particular suite, the finest in Galway, as the guest of the management. Do you have baggage? A man will take it up."

Scarlett gestured to the porter. There was really a lot to be said for marrying an earl. "Send this to my rooms. I'll be back later."

"At once, Mrs. O'Hara."

In truth Scarlett didn't expect to need the rooms at all. She hoped she'd be able to get the afternoon train back to Dublin, maybe even the early afternoon train, then she'd have time to connect for the evening journey back up to Trim. Thank heavens for the long days. I'll have until ten tonight if I need it. Now let's see if the nuns are as impressed by the Earl of Fenton as the hotel manager was. Too bad he's Protestant. I guess I shouldn't have made Daisy Sims swear to keep everything a secret.

Scarlett started toward the door to the square. Phew, what a smelly crowd. It must be raining on their tweeds at the track. Scarlett edged between two gesticulating, red-faced men. She bumped headlong into Sir John Morland and hardly recognized him. He looked as if he were extremely ill. There was no color in his normally ruddy face and no light in his usually warm, interested eyes. "Bart, my dear. Are you all right?"

He seemed to have trouble bringing her face into focus. "Oh, sorry Scarlett. Not quite myself. One too many and all that kind of thing."

At this hour of the day? It wasn't like John Morland to drink too much at any time, and certainly not before luncheon. She took firm hold of his arm. "Come along, Bart. You're going to have coffee with me and then something to eat." Scarlett walked him to the dining room. Morland's steps were unsteady. I guess I'll be needing my room after all, she thought, but Bart's a lot more important than rushing off after some lace. What on earth could have happened to him?

After a great deal of coffee she found out. John Morland broke down and cried when he told her.

"They burned my stables, Scarlett, they burned my stables. I'd taken Dijon to race at Balbriggan, not a big race at all, I thought she might like a run on the sands, and when we came home the stables were just black bins. My God, the smell! My God! I hear the horses screaming in my dreams, in my head even when I don't sleep."

Scarlett felt herself gagging. She put down her cup. It couldn't be. No one would do such a horrible thing. It had to be an accident.

"It was my tenants. Because of the rents, you see. How could they hate me so much? I tried to be a good landlord, I always tried. Why couldn't they burn the house? At Edmund Barrows' place they burned the house. They could have burned me in it, I wouldn't care. Not if they'd spared the horses. Name of God, Scarlett! What had my poor burned horses ever done to them?"

There was nothing she could say. All Bart's heart was in his stables . . . Wait, he'd been away with Dijon. His special pride and joy.

"You've got Dijon, Bart. You can start over, breed her. She's such a wonderful horse, the most beautiful I've ever seen. You can have the stables at Ballyhara. Don't you remember? You told me they were like a cathedral. We'll put in an organ. You can raise your new foals on Bach. You can't let things beat you, Bart, you've got to keep going on. I know, I've been down to the bottom myself. You can't give up, you just can't."

John Morland's eyes were like cold embers. "I'm going to England tonight on the eight o'clock boat. I never want to see an Irish face or hear an Irish voice again. I put Dijon in a safe place while I sold up. She's entered in the claiming race this afternoon, and when it's over, so is Ireland for me." His tragic eyes were at least steady. And dry. Scarlett almost wished he would begin to cry again. At least he'd felt something then. Now he looked as if he would never be able to feel anything ever again. He looked dead.

Then, as she watched, a transformation took place. Sir John Morland, Baronet, came back to life by effort of will. His shoulders firmed, and his mouth curved in a smile. His eyes even had a hint of laughter in them. "Poor Scarlett, I fear I rather put you through the wringer. It was beastly of me. Do forgive me. I'll soldier on. One does. Finish your coffee, there's a good girl, and come along to the track with me. I'll put a fiver on Dijon for you, and you can buy the champagne with your winnings when she shows her heels to the rest of the field."

Scarlett had never in her life respected anyone

as much as she did Bart Morland at that moment. She found a smile to meet his.

"I'll match your fiver with one of my own, Bart, and we'll have champagne, too. Done?" She spit in her palm, held it out. Morland spat, slapped, smiled.

"Good girl," he said.

On the way to the race course Scarlett tried to dredge up from her memory what she'd heard about "claiming races." All the horses running were for sale, their prices set by their owners. At the end of the race anyone could "claim" any one of the horses, and the owner was obliged to sell for the price he'd set. Unlike every other horse sale in Ireland, there was no bargaining. Unclaimed horses had to be reclaimed by their owners.

Scarlett didn't believe for a minute that horses couldn't be bought before the race began, no matter what the rules were. When they reached the race course, she asked Bart for the number of his box. She wanted, she said, to tidy up.

As soon as he was gone she found a steward and got directions to the officials' office where the claiming would take place. She hoped Bart had put a whopping big price on Dijon. She intended to buy her and send her to him later when he was settled in England.

"What do you mean Dijon's already been claimed? That's not supposed to happen until after the race.

The top-hatted official was careful not to smile. "You're not the only one with foresight, madam.

It must be an American trait. The gentleman who put in the claim was American, too."

"I'll double it."

"It cannot be done, Mrs. O'Hara."

"Suppose I bought Dijon from the Baronet before the race began?"

"Impossible."

Scarlett felt desperate. She had to have that horse for Bart.

"I might suggest one thing . . ."

"Oh, please. What can I do? It's really awfully important."

"You might ask the new owner if he would be willing to sell."

"Yes. I'll do that." She'd pay the man a king's ransom if need be. American, the official said. Good. Money talks in America. "Will you point him out to me?"

The top-hatted man consulted a sheet of paper. "You might find him at Jury's Hotel. He's listed that as his address. His name is Butler."

Scarlett had half-turned to leave. She stumbled to get her balance. Her voice was strangely thin when she spoke. "That wouldn't by any chance be Mr. Rhett Butler?"

It seemed to take an eternity for the man's eyes to return to the page in his hand, for him to read, for him to speak. "Yes, that is the name."

Rhett! Here! Bart must have written him about the stables, about selling up, about Dijon. He must be doing what I was going to do. He came all the way from America to help a friend.

Or to get a winner for the next Charleston races. It doesn't matter. Even poor, dear, tragic

1151

Bart doesn't matter, may God forgive me. I'm going to see Rhett. Scarlett realized that she was running, running, pushing people aside without apology. To the devil with everyone, everything. Rhett was here, only a few hundred yards away.

"Box eight," she gasped at a steward. He gestured. Scarlett forced herself to breathe slowly until she thought she must appear normal. No one could see her heart pounding, could they? She climbed the two steps into the bunting-trimmed box. Out on the great turfed oval twelve brightly shirted riders were whipping their horses towards the finish. All around Scarlett people were shouting, urging on the horses. She didn't hear a thing. Rhett was watching the race through field glasses. Even ten feet away she could smell the whiskey on him. He was rocking on his feet. Drunk? Not Rhett. He could always hold his liquor. Had Bart's disaster upset him that much?

Look at me, her heart begged. Put the glasses down and look at me. Say my name. Let me see your eyes when you say my name. Let me see something for me in your eyes. You loved me once.

Cheering and groans hailed the end of the race. Rhett lowered the glasses with a shaky hand. "Damn, Bart, that's my fourth loser in a row," he laughed.

"Hello, Rhett," she said.

His head snapped, and she saw his dark eyes. They held nothing for her, nothing but anger. "Why hello, Countess." His eyes raked her from her kidskin boots to her egret-plumed hat. "You are certainly looking—expensive." He turned abruptly towards John Morland. "You should have warned me, Bart, so I could stay in the bar. Let me by." And he sent Morland staggering as he pushed out of the box on the side away from Scarlett.

Her eyes followed him hopelessly as he plunged into the crowds. Then they filled with tears.

John Morland patted her shoulder clumsily. "I say, Scarlett, I apologize for Rhett. He's had too much to drink. That's two of us you've had to deal with today. Not much fun for you."

"Not much fun." Is that what Bart called it? "Not much fun" to be trampled on? I wasn't asking for much. Just to say hello, say my name. What gives Rhett the right to be angry and insulting? Can't I marry again after he threw me out like trash? Damn him. Damn him straight to Hell! Why is it fine and dandy for him to divorce me so he can marry a proper Charleston girl and have proper Charleston babies to grow up into more proper Charlestonians, but it's oh-so-disgraceful for me to marry again and give his child all the things that he should be the one to give her.

"I hope he falls over his own drunken feet and breaks his neck," she said to Bart Morland.

"Don't be too hard on Rhett, Scarlett. He had a real tragedy last spring. I'm ashamed to feel so sorry for myself about the stables when there are people like Rhett with troubles like his. I told you about the baby, didn't I? Beastly awful thing happened. His wife died having it, then the baby only lived for four days."

"What? What? Say that again." She shook his

arm so fiercely that Morland's hat fell off. He looked at her with confused dismay, almost fear. There was something so savage about her, something stronger than anything in his experience. He repeated that Rhett's wife and child were dead.

"Where did he go?" Scarlett cried. "Bart, you must know, you must have some idea, where would Rhett be likely to go?"

"I don't know, Scarlett. The bar—his hotel—any bar—anywhere."

"Is he going with you tonight to England?"

"No. He said he had some friends he wanted to look up. He's a really astonishing fellow, has friends everywhere. Did you know he was on safari with the Viceroy once? Some maharajah fellow was host. I must say I'm surprised he got so drunk. I don't remember him even keeping up with me. He took me to my hotel last night, put me to bed and all that. Was in fine fettle, a strong arm to lean on. I was counting on him, actually, to get me through the day. But when I came downstairs this morning, the porter fellow told me Rhett had ordered coffee and a newspaper while he waited for me, then suddenly bolted without even paying. I went in the bar to wait for him—Scarlett, what is it? I can't fathom you today. What are you crying for? Was it something I did? Did I say something wrong?"

Scarlett's eyes were flooded. "Oh, no, no, no, dearest, darlingest John Morland, Bart. You didn't say anything wrong at all. He loves me. He loves me. That's the rightest, most perfect thing I could ever hear."

Rhett came after me. That's why he came to Ireland. Not for Bart's horse, he could have bought her and all the rest of it by mail. He came for me as soon as he was free again. He must have been wanting me as much as I've been wanting him. I've got to go home. I don't know where to find him, but he can find me. The wedding announcement shocked him, and I'm glad. But it won't stop him. Nothing stops Rhett from going after what he wants. Rhett Butler's not impressed by titles and ermine and tiaras. He wants me and he'll come to get me. I know it. I knew he loved me, and I was right all the time. I know he'll come to Ballyhara. I've got to be there when he comes.

"Goodbye, Bart, I've got to go now," said Scarlett.

"Don't you want to see Dijon win? What about our fivers?" John Morland shook his head. She was gone. Americans! Fascinating types, but he'd never understand them.

She'd missed the through train to Dublin by ten minutes. The next one wouldn't leave until four. Scarlett bit her lip in frustration. "When is the next train east to anywhere?" The man behind the brass grille was maddeningly slow.

"You could go to Ennis, now, if you had a mind to. That's east to Athenry, then south. Two new carriages that train has, very nicely done they are too, say the ladies . . . or there's the Kildare train, but you'll not be able to take that one, the whistle's already sounded . . . Tuam, now, it's a short trip and more north than east, but the engine's the finest of all on the Great Western line . . . madam?"

Scarlett was shedding tears all over the uniform of the man at the barrier to the track. ". . . I only got the telegram two minutes ago, my husband's been run over by a milk dray, I've got to get that train to Kildare!" It would take her more than halfway to Trim and Ballyhara. She'd walk the rest of the way if she had to.

Every stop was torture. Why couldn't they hurry? Hurry, hurry, hurry, said her mind with the clack-clack of the wheels. Her case was in the best suite in Galway's Railway Hotel, in the convent sore-eyed nuns were putting the final tiny stitches into exquisite lace. None of it mattered. She must be home, waiting, when Rhett arrived. If only John Morland hadn't taken so long to tell her about everything, she could have been on the Dublin train. Rhett might even be on it, he could have been going anywhere when he left Bart's box.

It took nearly three and a half hours to get to Moate, where Scarlett got out of the train. It was after four, but at least she was on her way, instead of on the train that was just leaving Galway. "Where can I buy a good horse?" she asked the station master. "I don't care what it costs, as long as it has a saddle and bridle and speed." She had almost fifty miles still to go.

The owner of the horse wanted to bargain. Wasn't that half the pleasure of the selling? he asked his friends in the King's Coach bar after he bought a pint for every man there. The crazy woman had thrown gold sovereigns at him and

1156

gone off like the devil was on her trail. Astride! He didn't want to say how much lace she was showing nor how much leg with no decent covering to it at all, only a silk stocking and some boots not thick enough to walk on a floor with, never even to imagine resting in a stirrup.

Scarlett led the limping horse across the bridge into Mullingar just before seven o'clock. At the livery stable she handed the reins to a groom. "He's not lame, just winded and with a weakness," she said. "Cool him down slowly and he'll be as good as he ever was, not that he was ever much. I'll give him to you if you'll sell me one of the hunters you keep for the officers at the fort. Don't tell me you don't have any, I've hunted with some of the officers, and I know where they rented their mounts. Change over this saddle in under five minutes and there's an extra guinea for you." By ten after seven she was on her way, with twenty-six miles ahead and directions for a shortcut if she went cross-country instead of following the road.

She rode past Trim Castle and onto the road to Ballyhara at nine o'clock. Every muscle in her body ached, and her bones felt splintered. But she was only a little over three miles from home, and the misty twilight was gentle and soft on eyes and skin. A gentle rain began to fall. Scarlett leaned forward, patted the horse's neck. "A good walkaround and rubdown and the best hot mash in County Meath for you, whatever your name is. You took those jumps like a champion. Now we'll trot home easy, you deserve the rest." She half-closed her eyes and let her head loll. She'd sleep tonight like she'd never slept before. Hard to believe she'd been in Dublin this morning and crossed Ireland twice since breakfast.

There was the wooden bridge over the Knightsbrook. Once over the bridge I'm on Ballyhara. Only a mile to the town, a half-mile through it to the crossroad, then up the drive and I've made it. Five minutes, not much more than that. She sat up straight, clicked her tongue against her teeth, urged the horse with her heels.

Something's wrong. Ballyhara town's up ahead, and there are no lights in the windows. Usually the bars are glowing like moons by now. Scarlett kicked with the heels of her battered, delicate city boots. She had passed the first five dark houses before she saw the group of men at the crossroads in front of the Big House drive. Redcoats. Militia. What did they think they were doing in her town? She'd told them before, she didn't want them here. How bothersome, tonight of all nights, when she was about to drop from fatigue. Of course, that's why the windows are dark, they don't want to have to pull any pints for the English. I'll get rid of them and then things can get back to normal. I wish I didn't look so bedraggled. It's hard to order people around when your underclothes are hanging out all over the place. I'd better be walking. At least my skirts won't be up around my knees.

She reined in. It was hard not to groan when she swung her leg over the back of the horse. She could see a soldier—no, an officer—walking towards her from the group at the crossroad.

Well, good! She'd give him a piece of her mind, she was just in the mood to do it. His men were in her town, in her way, keeping her from getting home.

He stopped in front of the post office. He could, at the very least, have the manners to come all the way to her. Scarlett walked stiffly down the center of her town's wide street.

"You there, with the horse. Halt, or I'll fire." Scarlett stopped short. Not because of the officer's command; it was his voice. She knew that voice. God in heaven, that was the one voice in all the world she'd hoped never to hear again as long as she lived. She had to be wrong, she was so tired, that was it, she was imagining things, inventing nightmares.

"The rest of you, in your houses, there'll be no trouble if you send out the priest Colum O'Hara. I have a warrant for his arrest. No one will be hurt if he gives himself up."

Scarlett had a mad impulse to laugh. This couldn't be happening. She'd heard right, she did know the voice, she'd last heard it next to her ear speaking words of love. It was Charles Ragland. Once, only once in her entire life, she had gone to bed with a man who wasn't her husband, and now he had come from the far end of Ireland to her town to arrest her cousin. It was insane, absurd, impossible. Well, at least she could be sure of one thing—if she didn't die of shame when she looked at him, Charles Ragland was the one officer in the entire British army who would do what she wanted him to do. Go away and leave her and her cousin and her town alone.

She dropped the horse's reins and strode forward. "Charles?"

Just as she called his name, Charles Ragland shouted, "Halt!" He fired his revolver into the air.

Scarlett winced. "Charles Ragland, have you gone crazy?" she shouted. There was the crack of a second shot, drowning out her words, and Ragland seemed to jump into the air, then fall sprawling. Scarlett started to run. "Charles, Charles!" She heard more shots, heard shouting, ignored it all. "Charles!"

"Scarlett!" she heard, and "Scarlett!" from another direction, and "Scarlett," weakly, from Charles when she knelt by him. He was bleeding horribly from his neck, red blood spurting onto, staining his red tunic.

"Scarlett darling, get down, Scarlett *aroon.*" Colum was somewhere nearby, but she couldn't look at him now.

"Charles, oh, Charles, I'll get a doctor, I'll get Grainne, she can help you." Charles raised his hand, and she took it between hers. She felt the tears on her face, but she had no knowledge of crying. He mustn't die, not Charles, he was so dear and loving, he'd been so tender with her. He mustn't die. He was a good, gentle man.

There was terrible noise all around. Something whined past her head. Dear God, what was happening? Those were shots, people were shooting, the British were trying to kill her people. She would not allow it. But she had to get help for Charles, and there were boots running, and Colum was shouting, and oh, God, please help, what can I do to stop this, oh, God, Charles' hand is getting cold. "Charles! Charles, don't die!"

"There's the priest!" someone shouted. Shots fusilladed from the dark windows of the houses of Ballyhara. A soldier staggered and fell.

An arm closed around Scarlett from behind, she threw up her arms to defend herself from the unseen attack. "Later, my dear, no fighting now," said Rhett. "This is the best chance we'll ever have. I'll carry you, just go limp." He threw her across his shoulder, his arm behind her knees, and ran crouching into the shadows. "What's the back way out of here?" he demanded.

"Put me down and I'll show you," said Scarlett. Rhett lowered her to her feet. His big hands closed on her shoulders, and he pulled her to him impatiently, then kissed her, briefly, firmly, and let her go.

"I'd hate to be shot without getting what I came for," he said. She could hear the laughter in his voice. "Now, Scarlett, get us out of here."

She took his hand and ducked into a narrow dark passageway between two houses. "Follow me; this goes to a boreen. We can't be seen once we're in it."

"Lead on," Rhett said. He freed his hand and gave her a light push. Scarlett wanted to keep hold of his hand, never let go. But the firing was loud, and close, and she ran for the safety of the boreen.

The hedgerows were high and thick. As soon as Scarlett and Rhett ran four paces into the boreen, the sound of battle became muffled and indistinct. Scarlett stopped to catch her breath, to look at Rhett, to comprehend that at last they were together. Her heart was swelling with happiness.

But the seemingly distant sound of shooting demanded her attention, and she remembered. Charles Ragland was dead. She'd seen a soldier wounded, maybe killed. The militia was after Colum, was shooting at the people of her town, maybe killing them. She could have been shot—Rhett, too.

"We've got to get to the house," she said. "We'll be safe there. I've got to warn the servants to stay away from town until this is over. Hurry, Rhett, we've got to hurry."

He caught her by the arm as she started to move. "Wait, Scarlett. Maybe you shouldn't go to the house. I've just come from there. It's dark and empty, darling, with all the doors left open. The servants are gone."

Scarlett wrenched her arm from his clasp. She moaned with terror as she grabbed up her skirts and ran, faster than she had ever run in her life. Cat. Where was Cat? Rhett's voice was speaking, but she paid no attention. She had to get to Cat.

Behind the boreen, in the wide street of Ballyhara, there were five red-coated bodies and three wearing the rough clothing of farmers. The bookseller lay across the sill of his shattered window, blood-streaked bubbles falling from his lips with the whispered words of prayer. Colum O'Hara prayed with him, then traced a cross on his forehead as the man died. The broken glass refracted the thin light from the moon that was becoming visible in the rapidly darkening sky. The rain had stopped.

Colum crossed the small room in three long steps. He seized the twig broom on the hearth by its handle and thrust it into the bed of coals. It made a crackling sound for a moment, then burst into flame.

A shower of sparks flew from the torch onto Colum's dark cassock when he ran into the street. His white hair was brighter than the moon. "Follow me, you English butchers," he shouted as he plunged toward the deserted Anglo church, "and we'll die together for the freedom of Ireland."

Two bullets tore into his broad chest, and he fell to his knees. But he staggered to his feet and forward for seven uneven steps more until another three shots spun him right, then left, then right again and to the ground.

Scarlett raced up the wide front steps and into the dark great hall, Rhett one stride behind her. "Cat!" she screamed. "Cat!" The word echoed from the stone stairs and marble floor. "Cat!"

Rhett grabbed her upper arms. Only her white face and pale eyes were visible in the shadows. "Scarlett!" he said loudly, "Scarlett, get hold of yourself. Come with me. We've got to get away. The servants must have known something. The house isn't safe."

"Cat!"

Rhett shook her. "Stop that. The cat's not important. Where are the stables, Scarlett? We need horses."

"Oh, you fool," said Scarlett. Her strained voice was heavy with loving pity. "You don't know what you're saying. Let me go. I've got to find Cat—Katie O'Hara, called Cat. She's your daughter."

Rhett's hands closed painfully on Scarlett's arms. "What the devil are you talking about?" He looked down into her face, but he couldn't make out her expression in the darkness. "Answer me, Scarlett," he demanded, and he shook her.

"Let go of me, damn you! There's no time for explanations now. Cat must be here someplace, but it's dark, and she's all alone. Let go, Rhett, and ask your questions later. All that isn't important now." Scarlett tried to break free, but he was too strong.

"It's important to me." His voice was rough with urgency.

"All right, all right. It happened when we went sailing and the storm came. You remember. I found out I was pregnant in Savannah, but you hadn't come for me, and I was angry, so I didn't tell you right away. How was I to know you would be married to Anne before you could hear about the baby?"

"Oh, dear God," Rhett groaned, and he released Scarlett. "Where is she?" he said. "We've got to find her."

"We will, Rhett. There's a lamp on the table by the door. Strike a match so we can find it."

The yellow flame of the match lasted long

enough to locate a brass lamp and light it. Rhett held it up. "Where do we look first?"

"She could be anywhere. Let's start." She led him at a rapid pace through the dining room and morning room. "Cat," she called, "Kitty Cat, where are you?" Her voice was strong but no longer hysterical. It would not frighten a little girl. "Cat . . ."

"Colum!" screamed Rosaleen Fitzpatrick. She ran from Kennedy's bar into the middle of the British troops, pushing, shoving to get through, then down the center of the wide street toward Colum's sprawled body.

"Don't shoot," shouted an officer. "It's a woman."

Rosaleen threw herself on her knees and put her hands over Colum's wounds. *"Ochón,"* she wailed. She rocked from side to side, keening. The firing stopped; the intensity of her grief commanded respect, and men looked away.

She closed the lids over his dead eyes with gentle fingers stained with his blood and whispered goodbye in Gaelic. Then she caught up the smouldering torch and leapt to her feet, waving it to bring the flame back to life. Her face was terrible in its light. So quick was she that not a shot was fired until she reached the passageway that led to the church. "For Ireland and her martyr Colum O'Hara!" she cried triumphantly, and she ran into the arsenal, brandishing the torch. For a moment there was a silence. Then the stone wall of the church exploded into the wide street in a tower of flame and a deafening blast of sound.

The sky was lit brighter than day. "My God!" Scarlett gasped. The breath was knocked out of her body. She covered her ears with her hands and ran, calling to Cat, as one explosion followed another, then another and another, and the town of Ballyhara burst into flame.

She ran upstairs, with Rhett at her side, and along the corridor to Cat's rooms. "Cat," she called, again and again, trying to keep the fear from sounding in her voice. "Cat." The animals were orange-lit on the wall, the tea set on a freshly ironed cloth, the coverlet smooth on Cat's bed.

"Kitchen," said Scarlett, "she loves the kitchen. We can call down." She raced through the corridor again, Rhett at her heels. Through the sitting room with the menu books, account books, the list she'd been making of friends to invite to the wedding. Through the door onto the gallery to Mrs. Fitzpatrick's room. Scarlett stopped in the center. She leaned across the balustrade. "Kitty Cat," she called softly, "please answer Momma if you're down there. It's important, sweetheart." She kept her voice calm.

Orange light flickered in the copper pans on the wall beside the stove. Red coals glowed on the hearth. The enormous room was still, filled with shadows. Scarlett strained her ears and her eyes. She was just about to turn away when the very small voice spoke. "Cat's ears hurt." Oh, thank God! Scarlett rejoiced. Calm, now, and quiet.

"I know, baby, that was an awfully loud noise. You hold Cat's ears. I'll come around and down.

Will you wait for me?" She spoke as casually as if there was nothing to be afraid of. The balustrade vibrated under her clenched hands.

"Yes."

Scarlett gestured. Rhett followed her quietly along the gallery and through the door. She closed it carefully behind them. Then she began to shake. "I was so frightened. I was afraid they'd taken her away. Or hurt her."

"Scarlett, look," said Rhett. "We must hurry." The open windows above the drive framed a distant cluster of lights, torches, moving towards the house.

"Run!" said Scarlett. She saw Rhett's face in the orange light of the fire-filled sky, capable and strong. Now she could look at him, lean on him. Cat was safe. He put his hand beneath her arm, supporting her even as he hurried her.

Down the stairs they ran and through the ballroom. The firelit heroes of Tara were life-like above their heads. The colonnade to the kitchen wing was glaringly bright, and they could hear a blurred roaring of far-off angry shouts. Scarlett slammed the kitchen door behind them. "Help me bolt it," she gasped. Rhett took the iron bar from her, dropped it into its slots.

"What is your name?" said Cat. She walked out from the shadows near the hearth.

"Rhett." There was a frog in his throat.

"You two can make friends later," said Scarlett. "We've got to get to the stables. There's a door to the kitchen garden, it's got high walls, though, I don't know if there's another door out of it. Do you know, Cat?"

1167

"Are we running away?"

"Yes, Kitty Cat, the people who made the awful noise want to hurt us."

"Do they have stones?"

"Very big ones."

Rhett found the door to the kitchen garden, looked out. "I can lift you onto my shoulders, Scarlett, then you can reach the top of the wall. I'll hand Cat up to you."

"Fine, but maybe there's a door. Cat, we have to hurry now. Is there a door in the wall?"

"Yes."

"Good. Give Momma your hand, and let's go."

"To the stables?"

"Yes, come on, Cat."

"The tunnel would be faster."

"What tunnel?" There was an uneven quality to Scarlett's voice. Rhett came back across the kitchen, put his arm around her shoulders.

"The tunnel to the servants' wing. The footmen have to use it so they can't look in the window when we're having breakfast."

"That's horrible," said Scarlett, "if I'd known—"

"Cat, take your mother and me to the tunnel, please," Rhett said. "Would you mind if I carried you, or would you rather run?"

"If we have to hurry, you'd better carry me. I can't run as fast as you."

Rhett knelt, held out his arms, and his daughter walked trustingly into them. He was careful not to clasp her too tight in the brief embrace he could not withhold. "Onto my back, then, Cat, and hold around my neck. Tell me where to go."

"Past the fireplace. That door that's open. That's the scullery. The door to the tunnel is open, too. I opened it in case I had to run. Momma was in Dublin."

"Come on, Scarlett, you can bawl your eyes out later. Cat is going to save our unworthy necks."

The tunnel had high grated windows. There was barely enough light to see, but Rhett moved at a steady speed, never stumbling. His arms were bent, his hands under Cat's knees. He jounced her in a gallop, and she shrieked with delight.

My lord, our lives are in terrible danger, and the man's playing horsie! Scarlett didn't know whether to laugh or cry. Was there ever in the history of the world a man who was as crazy about babies as Rhett Butler?

From the servants' wing Cat directed them through a door into the stable yard. The horses were maddened with fright. Rearing, neighing, kicking at the gates to the stalls. "Hold Cat tight while I let them out," Scarlett said urgently. Bart Morland's story was vivid in her memory.

"You take her. I'll do it." Rhett put Cat in Scarlett's arms.

She moved to the safety of the tunnel. "Kitty Cat, can you stay here for a little while by yourself while Momma helps with the horses?"

"Yes. A little while. I don't want Ree to be hurt."

"I'll send him to the good pasture. You're a brave girl."

"Yes," said Cat.

Scarlett ran to Rhett's side, and together they

released all the horses except Comet and Half Moon. "Bareback will do," said Scarlett. "I'll get Cat." They could see torches moving inside the house now. Suddenly a ladder of flame raced up a curtain. Scarlett raced to the tunnel while Rhett calmed the horses. When she ran back with Cat in her arms, he was on Comet's back, holding Half Moon by the mane with one hand to keep him steady. "Give Cat to me," he said.

Scarlett handed his daughter up to him and climbed the mounting block then onto Half Moon.

"Cat, you show Rhett the way to the ford. We'll go to Pegeen's, the way we always do, remember? Then we can take the Adamstown road to Trim. It's not far. There'll be tea and cakes at the hotel. Just don't dawdle. You show Rhett the way. I'll keep up. Now go."

They stopped at the tower. "Cat says she'll invite us to her room," said Rhett evenly. Over his broad shoulder Scarlett could see flames licking into the sky beyond. Adamstown was on fire, too. Their escape was cut off. She jumped from the back of her horse.

"They're not far behind," she said. She was steady now. The danger was too close for nerves. "Hop down, Cat, and run up that ladder like a monkey." She and Rhett sent the horses running along the riverbank, then followed.

"Pull up the ladder. They can't get to us then," Scarlett told Rhett.

"But they'll know we're here," he said. "I can keep anyone from getting in; only one can come up at a time. Quiet, now, I hear them."

Scarlett crawled into Cat's cubbyhole and drew her little girl into her embrace.

"Cat's not afraid."

"Shhh, precious. Momma's scared silly."

Cat covered her giggling with her hand.

The voices and the torches came nearer. Scarlett recognized the boasting of Joe O'Neill, the blacksmith. "And didn't I say we'd kill the English to a man if they ever dared to march into Ballyhara? Did you see it, then, the face of him when I raised my arm? 'If you have a God,' says I, 'which I doubt, make your peace with him now,' and then I drove the pike into him, like spitting a grand fat pig." Scarlett held her hands over Cat's ears. How frightened she must be, my fearless little Cat. She's never nestled close to me this way in her life. Scarlett blew softly on Cat's neck, *aroon, aroon,* and rocked her baby in her lap from side to side as if her arms were the safe tall sides of a sturdy cradle.

Other voices overlapped O'Neill's. "The O'Hara'd gone over to the English, did I not say it long ago?" . . . "Aye, that you did Brendan, and fool I was to argue" . . . "Did you see her, now, down on her knees by the redcoat?". . . "Shooting's too good for her, I say we hang her with a choking rope" . . . "Burning's better, burning's what we want" . . . "The changeling's what we've to burn, the dark one that brought the afflictions, I say the changeling spelled The O'Hara" . . . "spelled the fields . . . spelled the rain from the clouds themselves" . . ." "changeling" . . . "changeling" . . . "changeling"

. . . Scarlett held her breath. The voices were so close, so inhuman, so like the yowling of wild beasts. She looked at the outline of Rhett's shadow in the darkness beside the opening to the ladder. She sensed his controlled alertness. He could kill any man who dared to climb the ladder, but what could stop a bullet if he showed himself? Rhett. Oh, Rhett, be careful. Scarlett felt a flooding, tingling happiness in every part of her. Rhett had come. He loved her.

The mob reached the tower and stopped. "The tower . . . they're in the tower." The shouts were like the baying of hounds at the death of the fob Scarlett's heart hammered in her ears. Then O'Neill's voice cut through the others.

". . . not there, see the rope still hanging down?" . . . "The O'Hara's clever, she'd be tricking us that way," another argued, and then all joined in. "You go up and see, Denny, you made the rope, you know its strength" . . . "Sure, go see for yourself, Dave Kennedy, since it's your idea" . . . "The changeling talks with the ghost up there, they do be saying" . . . "He's hanging still, his eyes open cutting right through you like a knife" . . . "Me old mother saw him walking on All Hallows', the rope was dragging behind blighting all it touched to shrivelled backness" . . . "I feel a cold wind down my back, I'm leaving this haunted place" . . . "But if they're up there, The O'Hara and the changeling? We need to kill them for the ill they've done us" . . . "Ach, isn't slow starving a death as good as burning? Put your torches to the ropes, then, lads. They'll not get down without breaking their necks!"

Scarlett smelled the rope burning, and she wanted to shout in jubilation. They were safe! No one could come up now. Tomorrow she could make a rope from strips of the quilts on the floor beneath her. It was over. They'd make their way to Trim somehow, when daylight came. They were safe! She bit her lips to stop herself from laughing, from crying, from calling Rhett's name so she could feel it in her throat, hear it in the air, hear his deep, sure, laughing response, hear his voice speak her name.

It was a long time before the voices and the sound of trampling boots faded completely away. Even then Rhett did not speak. He came to her, and to Cat, and held them both in his strong embrace. It was enough. Scarlett rested her head against him, and it was all she wanted.

Much later, when Cat's heavy looseness told of deep sleep, Scarlett laid her down and covered her with a quilt. Then she turned to Rhett. Her arms circled his neck, and his lips found hers.

"So that's what it means," she whispered shakily when the kiss ended. "Why, Mr. Butler, you fairly take my breath away."

Muted laughter rumbled in his chest. He unlocked her embrace and gently separated them. "Come away from the baby. We have to talk."

His low, quiet words did not make Cat stir. Rhett tucked the quilt closely around her. "Over here, Scarlett," he said. He backed out of the niche and walked to a window. His profile was like a hawk's against the fire-lit sky. Scarlett followed him. She felt as if she could follow him to the ends of the earth. He had only to call her name. No one had ever said her name quite the way Rhett did.

"We'll get away," she said confidently when she was beside him. "There's a hidden path from the witch's cottage."

"From what?"

"She's not really a witch, at least I don't think so, and it doesn't matter anyhow. She'll show us the path. Or Cat will know one, she's in the woods all the time."

"Is there anything Cat doesn't know?"

"She doesn't know you're her father." Scarlett saw the muscles tighten in his jaw.

"Some day I'll beat you black and blue for not telling me."

"I was going to, but you fixed it so I couldn't!" Scarlett said hotly. "You divorced me when it was supposed to be impossible, and then before I could turn around you had gone and gotten married. What was I supposed to do? Hang around your front door with my baby wrapped in my shawl like some kind of fallen woman? How could you do such a thing? That was rotten of you, Rhett."

"Rotten of me? After you went charging off to God knows where without a word to anybody? My mother was worried sick, literally ill, until your Aunt Eulalie told her you were in Savannah."

"But I left her a note. I wouldn't upset your mother for the world. I love Miss Eleanor."

Rhett caught her chin in his hand, turned and held her face in the uneven garish light from the window. Suddenly he kissed her, then he put his arms around her and held her to him. "It happened again," he said. "My darling, hot-tempered, pigheaded, wonderful, infuriating Scarlett, do you realize we've been through this before? Missed signals, missed chances, misunderstandings that need never have happened. We've got to stop it. I'm too old for all this drama."

He buried his lips and his laughter in her tangled hair. Scarlett closed her eyes and rested against his broad chest. Safe in the tower, safe in Rhett's embrace, she could afford her fatigue and relief. Luxurious weak tears of exhaustion ran down her cheeks, and her shoulders slumped. Rhett held her close and stroked her back.

After a long time, his arms tightened with demand, and Scarlett felt new, thrilling energy race through her veins. She lifted her face to his, and there was neither rest nor safety in the blinding ecstasy she felt when their lips met. Her fingers combed his thick hair, grabbed, held his head down and his mouth on hers until she felt faint and at the same time strong and fully alive. Only the fear of waking Cat kept the wild cry of joy from bursting out of her throat.

When their kisses grew too urgent, Rhett broke away. He gripped the stone sill of the window with corded, white-knuckled hands. His breathing was ragged. "There are limits to a man's control, my pet," he said, "and the one thing I can think of that's more uncomfortable than a wet beach is a stone floor."

"Tell me you love me," Scarlett demanded.

Rhett grinned. "What makes you think that?

I come to Ireland on those damned clanking chugging steamships so often because I like the climate here so much."

She laughed. Then she hit him on the shoulder with both fists. "Tell me you love me."

Rhett trapped her wrists in a circle of his fingers. "I love you, you abusive wench." His expression hardened. "And I'll kill that bastard Fenton if he tries to take you from me."

"Oh, Rhett, don't be silly. I don't even like Luke. He's a horrible, cold-blooded monster. I was only going to marry him because I couldn't have you." Rhett's skeptical raised eyebrows forced Scarlett to continue. "Well, I did sort of like the idea of London . . . and being a countess . . . and paying him back for insulting me by marrying him and getting all his money for Cat."

Rhett's black eyes glinted with amusement. He kissed Scarlett's imprisoned hands. "I've missed you," he said.

They talked through the night, sitting close together on the cold floor with their hands clasped. Rhett could not get enough of learning about Cat, and Scarlett delighted in telling him, delighted in his pride in what he learned. "I'll do my best to make her love me more than you," he warned.

"You don't stand a chance," Scarlett said confidently. "We understand each other, Cat and I, and she won't put up with babying and spoiling from you."

"How about adoring?"

"Oh, she's used to that. She's always had it from me."

"We'll see. I have a way with women, I've been told."

"And she has a way with men. She'll have you jumping through hoops before a week's out. There was a little boy named Billy Kelly—oh, Rhett, guess what? Ashley's married. I did the matchmaking. I sent Billy's mother to Atlanta . . ." The story of Harriet Kelly led to the news that India Wilkes had finally found a husband, which led to the news that Rosemary was still a spinster.

"And likely to stay one," Rhett said. "She is at Dunmore Landing, plowing money into restoring the rice fields and getting to be more like Julia Ashley every day."

"Is she happy?"

"She glows with it. She would have packed my things herself if it would have hurried my departure."

Scarlett's eyes questioned him. Yes, Rhett said, he had left Charleston. It had been a mistake to think that he could ever be content there. "I'll go back. Charleston never gets out of the blood of a Charlestonian, but I'll go to visit, not to stay." He had tried, he'd told himself that he wanted the stability of family and tradition. But in the end, he began to feel the nagging pain where his wings had been clipped. He couldn't fly. He was earthbound, ancestor-bound, Saint Cecilia-bound, Charleston-bound. He loved Charleston—God, how he loved it—its beauty and its grace and its soft-scented salt breezes and its courage in the face of loss and ruin. But it wasn't enough. He needed challenge, risk, some kind of blockade to be run.

Scarlett breathed a quiet sigh. She hated Charleston, and she was sure Cat would, too. Thank heaven Rhett wasn't going to take them back there.

In a quiet voice, she asked about Anne. Rhett was silent for what seemed to her a very long time. Then he spoke, and his voice was heavy with sorrow. "She deserved better than me, better than life granted her. Anne had a quiet bravery and strength that puts every so-called hero to shame . . . I was more than half crazy about that time. You'd gone, and no one knew where you were. I believed you were punishing me, so to punish you, and to prove that I didn't care about your leaving, I got the divorce. An amputation."

Rhett stared into space, unseeing. Scarlett waited. He prayed he hadn't hurt Anne, he said. He'd searched his memory and his soul, and he could find no willful hurt. She was too young, and she loved him too much, to suspect that tenderness and affection were only the shadows of a man's loving. He would never know what blame he should take for marrying her. She'd been happy. One of the injustices of the world was that it was so easy to make the innocent and caring ones happy with so little.

Scarlett put her head on his shoulder. "It's a lot, making somebody happy," she said. "I didn't understand that until Cat was born. I didn't understand a lot of things. Somehow, I learned from her."

Rhett rested his cheek on her head. "You've changed, Scarlett. You've grown up. I have to get to know you all over again."

"I have to get to know you, period. I never did, even when we were together. I'll do better this time, I promise."

"Don't try too hard, you'll wear me out." Rhett chuckled, then kissed her forehead.

"Stop laughing at me, Rhett Butler—no, don't. I like it, even when it makes me mad." She sniffed the air. "It's raining. That should finish off the fires. When the sun comes up, we'll be able to see if anything's left. We should try and get some sleep. We're going to be very busy in a few hours." She nestled her head into the hollow of his neck and yawned.

While she slept, Rhett moved her, lifted her into his arms and sat down again, holding her as she had held Cat. The gentle Irish rain made a curtain of soft silence around the old stone tower.

At sunrise, Scarlett stirred and woke. When she opened her eyes, the first thing she saw was Rhett's beard-shadowed, hollow-eyed face, and she smiled contentedly. Then she stretched, moaning softly. "I hurt all over," Scarlett complained. Her brow wrinkled. "And I'm starving to death."

"Consistency, thy name is woman," murmured Rhett. "Get up, my love, you're breaking my legs."

They walked carefully to Cat's hideaway. It was dark, but they could hear her soft snoring. "She sleeps with her mouth open if she turns over onto her back," Scarlett whispered.

"A child of many talents," Rhett said.

Scarlett stifled her laughter. She took Rhett's hand and drew him with her to a window. The sight that met their eyes was sobering. Dozens of dark fingers of smoke reached up from every direction, making dirty stains on the tender rose color of the sky. Scarlett's eyes filled with tears.

Rhett put his arm around her shoulders. "We can build it all back, darling."

Scarlett blinked away the tears. "No, Rhett, I don't want to. Cat's not safe in Ballyhara, and I guess I'm not either. I won't sell up, this is O'Hara land, and I won't let it go. But I don't want another Big House, or another town. My cousins can find some farmers to work the land. No matter how much shooting and burning, the Irish will always love the land. Pa used to tell me it was like his mother to an Irishman.

"But I don't belong here, not any more. Maybe I never did really, or I wouldn't have been so ready to go off to Dublin and house parties and hunts . . . I don't know where I belong, Rhett. I don't even feel at home any more when I go to Tara."

To Scarlett's surprise, Rhett laughed, and the laughter was rich with joy. "You belong with me, Scarlett, haven't you figured that out? And the world is where we belong, all of it. We're not home-and-hearth people. We're the adventurers, the buccaneers, the blockade runners. Without challenge, we're only half alive. We can go any-where, and as long as we're together, it will belong to us. But, my pet, we'll never belong to it. That's for other people, not for us."

He looked down at her, the corners of his mouth quivering with amusement. "Tell me the truth on this first morning of our new life together, Scarlett. Do you love me with your whole heart, or did you simply want me because you couldn't have me?"

"Why, Rhett, what a nasty thing to say! I love you with all my heart and I always will."

The pause before Scarlett answered his question was so infinitesimal that only Rhett could have heard it. He threw his head back and roared with laughter. "My beloved," he said, "I can see that our lives are never going to be dull. I can hardly wait to get started."

A small grimy hand tugged on his trousers. Rhett looked down.

"Cat will go with you," said his daughter.

He lifted her to his shoulder, his eyes glistening with emotion. "Are you ready, Mrs. Butler?" he asked Scarlett. "The blockades are waiting for us."

Cat laughed gleefully. She looked at Scarlett with eyes that were bright with shared secrets. "The old ladder is under my quilts, Momma. Grainne told me to save it."